"Deliciously real, modern, h...
—Katy Evans, *New York Times* bestselling author

"Relentless chemistry and sizzling romance make this book a must-read!"
—Laura Kaye, *New York Times* bestselling author

"This refreshing new series by James is a tender excursion into the lives of an uptight billionaire and a company employee."
—*RT Book Reviews*

"Fun, sweet and sexy. Lorelei James captures the angst and anticipation of a slow-burn family-run-office romance with engaging characters . . . Fans of Jaci Burton and Shiloh Walker will enjoy *What You Need*."
—Harlequin Junkie

"If you're looking for a quick, sexy read, this one is definitely for you. I can't wait for the next! Well-done, Lorelei James! Very well-done."
—The Reading Cafe

"The characters are perfect; the romance is perfect and takes things step-by-step. Not too rushed, not too slow . . . This is a series I'll be looking forward to seeing more of soon!"
—Under the Covers Book Blog

"[James] has blown me away with a beautiful romance that is sexy and sweet, and I loved every second of it!"
—Guilty Pleasures Book Reviews

continued . . .

When I Need You

THE NEED YOU SERIES

LORELEI JAMES

JOVE
New York

A JOVE BOOK
Published by Berkley
An imprint of Penguin Random House LLC
375 Hudson Street, New York, New York 10014

Copyright © 2017 by LJLA, LLC
Excerpt from *All You Need* by Lorelei James copyright © 2017 by LJLA, LLC
Penguin Random House supports copyright. Copyright fuels creativity, encourages
diverse voices, promotes free speech, and creates a vibrant culture. Thank you for buying
an authorized edition of this book and for complying with copyright laws by not
reproducing, scanning, or distributing any part of it in any form without permission.
You are supporting writers and allowing Penguin Random House to continue to
publish books for every reader.

A JOVE BOOK and BERKLEY are registered trademarks and the B colophon
is a trademark of Penguin Random House LLC.

ISBN: 9780451477583

First Edition: August 2017

Printed in the United States of America
1 3 5 7 9 10 8 6 4 2

Cover photo by Claudio Marinesco
Book design by Kelly Lipovich

This book is dedicated to my daughter Tessa, for getting up at the crack of dawn for cheerleading practice, for all the after-school practices, for all the school-night and weekend football and basketball games she cheered at for six years on the high school and collegiate level, for the strength and endurance she showed through injuries and during cheer drama, and for her upbeat graciousness when faced with the attitude that cheerleaders aren't "real" athletes. I'm proud that you're the fourth-generation cheerleader in our family, but mostly I'm proud that you are such an amazing young woman . . .

One

—

JENSEN

Getting a head-butt to the groin was the perfect capper to my crap day.

I stepped off the elevator on the second floor of my apartment building, pulling my roller bag behind me. When I turned the corner—*wham!*—a hard head connected with my crotch.

Grunting, I crumpled against the wall for a moment, thighs clamped together to try to block out the pain.

Motherfuck did that hurt.

When I didn't hear a "Gee, mister, I'm sorry," I glanced up to see my crotch smasher sailing down the hallway, long brown curls bobbing as if she didn't have a care in the world.

That pissed me off.

"Hey, little girl," I yelled.

The figure spun around and glared at me. "I'm *not* a girl."

"With that long hair I assumed—"

"You have long hair," he pointed out.

"I'm not wearing a dress," I shot back at him.

"It's not a dress. It's a *hakama*."

"Looks like a damn dress," I muttered. I closed my eyes and silently willed the throbbing pain in my groin to go away.

Stupid visualization exercises never worked.

Sighing, I pushed off the wall and opened my eyes. I said, "Look, kid, we . . ."

But he was gone.

Where the hell had he disappeared to so fast?

He'd probably slipped into an apartment. But I knew everyone who lived in my building, and no one had kids.

Maybe in the two weeks you've been gone someone new moved in.

That'd be an issue since Bob the building manager was supposed to restrict families with kids to the other building.

Did this kid's parents know he was running the halls unattended? Did they care?

If I ever ran into them, they'd get a piece of my mind about their son's behavior.

Why don't you shake your fist in the air too, you grumpy old man?

I'd cop to being grumpy, but I wasn't old. No matter what my body felt like some days.

I shambled down the hallway to my apartment. After unlocking the door, I dragged my suitcase inside.

The piney scent lingering throughout the space indicated the cleaning service had been here recently. When I snagged a sparkling water out of the refrigerator, I noticed my personal chef had delivered this week's meals. Now that I wasn't on vacation, I had to get back to healthy eating. Training started in roughly eleven weeks, and I already had enough to overcome without showing up looking like a lard ass.

My damn balls throbbed, so I grabbed an ice pack out of the freezer and hobbled into the living room. As soon as my butt connected with my square-shaped sofa, I breathed a huge sigh of relief. God I loved this couch. Sort of pathetic that I'd rather have it beneath me than a woman.

I heard my phone buzzing in the outside pocket of my suitcase, but I ignored it. I wasn't in the mood to talk to anyone. I needed time to chill. Yeah, I'd just returned from vacation, but only the last week had been flop-on-the-beach-with-a-beer time. I'd spent the previous week at the clinic in Florida with the doc who'd done my surgeries. He and his sadistic outpatient review team had performed every stress, mobility, agility and functionality test ever invented on my body to gauge the success of my surgeries last year.

They marveled at the progress I'd made since my last visit. They told me I'd surpassed their initial expectations for recovery. They listed all the medical milestones I'd passed. But they hadn't told me the one thing—the *only* thing—I wanted to know: Would I ever play football at the same level as I had before the injury?

An injury that had kept me off the football field all of last season.

Actually, it'd been a combination of injuries. A late hit had knocked me out. So in addition to getting a concussion, at some point during the play I'd dislocated my kneecap—not that I'd been aware of that injury at the time. When I'd finally come to in the *hospital*—that had been freaky as hell—I hadn't been able to feel *anything* from the waist down due to paralysis.

Paralysis.

Even now I can't wrap my head around that word.

When I think back, it seemed as if it'd happened to someone else. My neck in a cervical collar. My arm in a sling. As I lay in that hospital bed, I felt nothing. I'd wanted to scream but I couldn't get enough air into my lungs to even speak.

Then the drugs kicked in and I drifted back into the black void.

Upon awaking several hours later alone in my hospital room, I tried to wiggle my toes, roll my ankles, shift my thighs, force any kind of movement, but I just ended up sweaty and frustrated.

And scared. Holy shit I'd experienced fear in that hospital bed like I'd never known.

Sleep became my refuge. For twenty-four hours the doctors watched me for signs of improvement or decline. When I groggily complained about the throbbing pain in my right knee, the doctors did another full, thorough and painful examination. They determined the hematoma on my spine had caused the temporary paralysis. When the swelling decreased, so did the paralysis.

I'd never welcomed pain like I had that night. I refused pain meds. I wanted to feel every twinge and every burning, stabbing pain—it was better than never feeling anything again.

Two days after the paralysis scare, my family loaded me into the Lund Industries private Learjet. The medical professionals associated with the Minnesota Vikings organization recommended a surgeon in Florida, so I was off to Pensacola for diagnosis and surgery.

My shoulder injury required surgery, and the recovery time was four months. It was one of the most trying times in my life, despite the fact that the surgery had gone well and the prognosis for recovery was excellent. While I appreciated the unconditional support my family provided, they'd been extremely smothering.

During the second week of physical therapy, when I became frustrated with my lack of progress increasing my walking speed, I asked for another set of tests because I knew something else was wrong. The tests revealed I'd ruptured my Achilles tendon. The knee injury had masked that issue, and my knee turned out to be the least of my worries.

An Achilles rupture can be a kiss of death to a football player. I could name a dozen careers abruptly ended by that particular injury. After the surgery to repair the rupture—which I couldn't schedule until my knee was one hundred percent—the recovery time was a year. So sitting in the doctor's office in Florida, I knew I'd miss the entire *next* season.

Although I'd signed a three-year contract, this type of injury was a game changer. The team could pay me the remainder of my guaranteed salary and cut me from the team, turning me into a free agent. But if the Vikings released me due to their medical concerns, what other NFL team would want to take a chance on me?

None.

Thankfully I'd had the best year of my career prior to the injury, so I'd been placed on the injured reserve list. The big bosses assigned me a sports medicine therapist/trainer. Dante was a cool guy. He knew when to push me and when to back off. He and I spent a lot of hours together, yet I never forgot where his loyalties were. He'd accompanied me to Florida for my one-year postsurgical checkup—so he could accurately report the doctor's diagnosis back to the coaching staff. I guess they didn't trust that I'd be totally honest.

After the week in Florida, Dante tagged along with me to Mexico. While he sampled tequila and women at the exclusive resort, I spent hours walking on the beach and staring at the ocean, trying to figure out what to do with my life when playing football professionally was no longer an option. Because I could be facing that decision in as little as three months.

Right now I was exactly where I claimed I'd wanted to

be the past two weeks: sitting on my comfy couch in my apartment. So why was I so restless? Why was I lonely?

I tipped my head back on the cushion and stared at the ceiling.

You're lonely? Call your brothers. Or your sister. Or your parents. Or your cousins. They'd be here, or ask you to meet them someplace in a heartbeat.

But my feet didn't move. My will was as lazy as my body today. When I held out my hand toward my suitcase, my phone didn't magically fly into it like Harry Potter's broom did when he called out, *"Accio!"* That'd be a cool power. It'd be even cooler to have a magic wand that fixed everything.

I shifted the ice pack on my groin. I must've been sitting there longer than I'd been aware of because the gel had become gooey and warm.

Don't be a brooding asshole. Do something productive.

Maybe my neighbor Martin would be up for a video game marathon. If nothing else, the dude made me laugh, especially when he talked about the things he'd seen and heard around the apartment complex. I'd bet he knew who the nut-smashing kid belonged to.

Since Martin lived across from me, I didn't bother to put on a shirt before I stepped in the hallway. If he bitched about me being shirtless, I'd point out that my brother-in-law Axl—former tenant of my apartment—had strolled around buck-ass naked most of the time. At least I had my bottom half covered.

One other thing about my buddy Martin? He took mellow to a whole new level on account of he liked his weed. He never pressured me to smoke with him, not only because I had random drug testing through the team, but I suspected he preferred a higher-end product and wasn't inclined to share. But Martin was a great guy and a nonjudgmental friend. He wouldn't demand the details about my medical visit in Florida; he'd just be happy I was back.

I knocked. And waited.

And waited.

Sometimes forcefully pounding on the door was the only way to catch Martin's attention when he had his earbuds in. But if he didn't answer within a reasonable time frame, I figured he and his lady, Verily, were banging the headboard.

So I knocked louder.

No response after several long moments.

Rather than returning to my apartment, I used both hands, rapping my knuckles against the wood in staccato bursts—machine-gun style.

I heard the chain on the inside of the door rattling and couldn't stop my enormous grin, or from saying, "It's about fucking time, man," when the door started to open.

But my grin vanished when I realized the person framed in the doorjamb wasn't Martin, but a redheaded woman with fire in her eyes.

What the hell? Who was this chick answering Martin's door? I gave her a very thorough head-to-toe inspection—lush lips, killer rack, curvy hips molded by a tight black skirt and bare toes—before my gaze zoomed back up to meet her angry eyes.

I said the first thing that popped into my head. "Who the hell are you?"

Two

ROWAN

Jensen Lund didn't have the first freakin' clue who I was.

Not that I should've been surprised. He was exactly like every other high-achieving jock I'd dealt with: exuding an air of entitlement and ignoring the "little people" outside his sports stratosphere.

"Who are you?" Jensen demanded again.

I'd had a crap day and all I wanted was a few moments of peace while my son watched Netflix. I didn't owe this man anything. Especially given his rude behavior.

"I'm none of your damn business. Don't bother me again or I'll call the building manager and report you."

I slammed the door in his face.

It felt good. Maybe more dramatic than the situation called for, but good nonetheless.

Still . . . it did surprise me that The Rocket lived in this apartment complex.

Maybe he's slumming while construction on his mansion is under way.

That had to be it.

Besides, my brother would've told me that the lauded Vikings tight end was his neighbor. Then again, my rocky past with another football player might've convinced Martin not to even mention it to me.

No matter. We'd probably never see each other, and that suited me just fine.

As a single mother with two jobs, I needed a mental reset at the end of my workday to switch from dealing with college students to becoming Mommy to my six-year-old son. I felt zero guilt for letting Calder watch cartoons for fifteen or twenty minutes while my transformation took place.

After I slipped on my wireless headphones and hit play on my cell phone, I opened the sliding glass doors and stepped onto the balcony. Spring had definitely arrived in Minneapolis. Buds on the trees. Tulips, crocus, hyacinth and peonies poking up from the ground. Grass greening up. Birds twittering. I drew in several deep breaths. Music. Fresh air. I could feel the tension seeping out from my pores.

I'd already started dinner when Calder finished his TV show and scrambled onto the barstool, setting his elbows on the breakfast bar. "What's for supper?"

I finished chopping the onions and slid them into the pan. "Right now it's just cooked hamburger so the options are endless. Spanish rice, goulash, tacos, beef and rice or sloppy joes."

"Sloppy joes."

"Excellent choice, Chef Michaels."

He giggled.

That sound always made me smile. I glanced up, noticing for the first time what he had on. "Why are you wearing that?"

He shrugged. "I was playing ninja-samurai."

"With who? Alicia?" Alicia worked for me as a nanny during the week, picking Calder up from school and staying with him until I got home.

"Didja know these pants make a cool flapping noise when I run really fast?"

"I imagine so, but where were you running really fast?"

A beat of silence. Then he answered, "Uh, around."

"Around where?" This apartment was much smaller than our last one and there wasn't room to run.

When my son avoided my eyes, I knew something was up. "Calder Adam Michaels. Tell me where you were. Right now."

His words rushed out. "Alicia was on her phone *again* and I was bored so I went out into the hallway and ran the whole thing like three times. Then the last time this giant came around the corner and I ran into him with my head— *bam!*—right in his pee-shooter. He yelled a bunch of grown-up words and closed his eyes real tight. So I ran to the end of the hall and hid behind the door to the outside but he didn't find me so I musta hid real good, huh?"

There were so many, many, many things wrong with this scenario I didn't know where to start.

Stay calm. Do not yell.

"Did Alicia know you were gone?"

Calder shook his head.

All sorts of worst-case scenarios ran through my head, and I fought back my panic. How could I let it slide that she'd ignored Calder—he'd snuck out and she hadn't *noticed*?— when her *only* job was to watch him?

"Oh, and the guy called me a girl too," Calder added.

"What do you mean he called you a girl? I thought you ran and hid?"

"Umm, after I started to get away from him he said, 'Hey little girl' and I turned to tell him that I wasn't a girl."

"What did this guy look like?"

"A giant. With lots of muscles."

"Light hair? Dark hair?"

"Light hair. Long, kinda like mine."

No wonder Jensen Lund had knocked on my door looking so pissed off. "Did you apologize?"

Calder lowered his chin. "I forgot."

"Did you happen to see where he lives?"

"Right across the hall."

"First thing after supper you're going to apologize to him."

"Okay."

"Second thing: Is being bored an excuse to break my house rules?"

His head dipped again. "No."

"We've lived in this apartment building a week, Calder. Everyone is a stranger. You know better than to go anywhere by yourself."

He glanced up at me, his pale brown eyes full of remorse. "I'm sorry, Mommy."

"We'll figure out your consequences after we eat. The last question . . ." I paused. "Since when do you call your penis a pee-shooter?"

"Uncle Martin said to call it a pee-shooter when I'm a little dude because all it's good for is shooting pee. He said when I'm a big dude, I can call it a love gun."

Jesus, Martin, really? You had to break it down that much for your nephew? "In our house, it is *not* called a pee-shooter."

Calder's eyes took on a defiant glint. "Uncle Martin said you'd say that. He told me that since I have one—and you don't—I should get to call it whatever I want."

Seriously. Martin had to have been high during that conversation. But now wasn't the time to argue terminology with a hungry six-year-old. "We'll talk later." I pointed at the hallway. "Wash your hands."

Sagging against the counter, I considered my options with the Alicia situation. Did I call her now or wait until I'd calmed down? Would I be calmer before or after I marched my son across the hall to face Jensen Lund?

I wasn't looking forward to that.

C alder and I both dragged our feet until we reached Jensen's door. I knocked briskly four times.

A minute later the door swung open.

He seemed as shocked to see us as I was to see him. Half-naked. He'd answered the door bare-chested, in just a pair of athletic shorts.

Holy crap.

Every day I worked with athletes and their honed physiques, but this man's upper body was on a whole different level of perfection. Every inch smoothly sculpted from hours of repetition to get the maximum benefit of those massive muscles.

Thankfully he hadn't noticed me staring slack-jawed at his killer chest. He was too busy eyeing Calder and placing one knee over the other as protection from another groin shot.

Calder blurted out, "I'm sorry that I ran into your peeshooter and ran away."

Jensen's focus moved to me and his eyes narrowed. "Slamming shit without explanation or apology must be a family trait."

I raised my chin. "I tend to get annoyed when a stranger knocks on *my* door demanding to know who *I* am."

"Your door?" His gaze flicked to our apartment then back to me. "When I left a little over two weeks ago, Martin and Verily lived across from me."

"I'm subleasing their place."

"Does Bob know?"

"Bob the apartment complex manager? Yes, he knows."

He frowned. "Why didn't Martin tell me he planned to move out?"

"Martin hates saying good-bye. It's a thing with him. He's always been like that."

"How do you know Martin so well?"

"He's my brother."

"Seems there's a lot I didn't know about Martin." He took his hands off his hips and scrubbed them over his face before running a hand through his hair.

I watched the flex of his biceps and triceps. Talk about arm porn.

Knock it off, Rowan.

But my gaze dipped to that gorgeous eight-pack. I swallowed a sigh and a tiny puddle of drool that'd formed in my mouth.

"Can we come in?" my snoopy son asked.

Jensen absentmindedly stepped back to allow us access.

A small entryway funneled into the living area, which was completely filled with the biggest couch I'd ever seen.

"This is totally cool," Calder exclaimed. "Do you ever jump on it like a trampoline?"

I'd bet Jensen has tested the bounce factor of every piece of this couch multiple times, but not in the same way Calder was thinking, I thought snarkily.

When I glanced up and caught Jensen looking at me, I swore he'd just read my mind.

The damn man smirked at me. He snatched a wadded-up T-shirt off the back of the couch and slipped it on—shame, that—then spoke to Calder. "A tall guy like me would hit the ceiling on the first bounce, so no jumping. You can hop over, though."

"Cool!" Calder whooped and scaled over the back of the couch like the little monkey he was.

I'd have no problem getting a leg over . . . if I hadn't been wearing a dress.

Right after Calder had performed a couple of exuberant bounces, Jensen pulled the back section out, creating a crack wide enough that I could slip through.

"Thanks." As soon as my butt connected with the cushions, the couch sucked me in like I was being swallowed by a marshmallow.

Jensen flopped closer to me than I expected. He thrust out his hand. "Let's start over, okay? Jensen Lund."

Did I tell him I knew who he was because he'd walked past me every Sunday during football season for the past four years?

I shook his hand. "Rowan Michaels. That's my son, Calder Michaels."

Calder had already stretched out on his belly, facing away from the gigantic TV, set on a sports channel.

"So what's going on with Martin?" he asked. "He and Verily didn't break up, did they?"

"No. They had a chance to go backpacking through Europe with friends, so they took off."

"How long will they be gone?"

"Four months, maybe more. My lease was up on my apartment, so we're subletting. It gives them a place to come back to and me more time in the housing search."

"It's just you and Calder living over there?"

"Yes."

"Not to be a dick, but it sucks that Martin is gone. I'm gonna miss him. We hung out all the time."

I frowned. "You did?"

"Yeah. Why? He didn't mention me?"

I shook my head. "Did Martin ever talk about me?"

Jensen was quiet for a moment. "Actually, no. I wonder why that is?"

I knew exactly why—it was my little brother's (misguided) way of protecting me. "Martin keeps his life compartmentalized. Keeping his clients separate from his time spent snowboarding. Keeping his family separate from his friends. He hangs out with Calder at least every other week and we get together with our folks probably once a month—more if they're not in season."

"Wait." Jensen held up his hand. "This is going a little fast for me. First of all . . . Martin has a job? Besides snowboarding?"

"Of course he has a job. He's a freelance website designer." I paused. "See what I mean about him keeping things compartmentalized? You didn't even know what he does to earn a living."

"Makes me wonder what compartment he put me in."

"It depends on what you do when you're with him."

"We play video games, watch TV, play cards, drink beer." He looked at Calder and dropped his voice. "That's all I can get buzzed on because of . . . testing for my job."

Martin was a pothead. He never hid it from me or our parents. It didn't make me naive to call him a "responsible" stoner, but he'd finished college. He had a job and supported himself. He didn't cause problems. He lived his life the way he wanted. He was a good person, and that said more to me about who he was than what vice he chose to indulge in. "My life is so hectic that not even . . . herbs mellow me out."

Jensen laughed.

Damn. He had a great laugh.

I scooted to the edge of the couch. "Sorry your gaming buddy won't be around."

His gaze intently roamed my face. "You look really familiar to me. I thought you did earlier before you slammed the door in my face, but it's probably the family resemblance."

Or maybe I look familiar because we have met . . . oh, at least six times.

Yeah, my self-esteem took a knee. Not that I had the ego some of the cheerleaders on the squad did, but I knew I rocked this thirty-year-old body. I glanced over at my son, who was practicing his break dancing arm movements as he stared at the ceiling. I nudged his foot. "Time to go." I gave Jensen a totally fake smile. "It's a school night."

Calder crawled over the edge of the couch. I propelled myself upright and moved to stand behind him.

"Thanks for apologizing," Jensen said to Calder. "Takes guts to admit you were wrong."

I smoothed the static from Calder's long curls when he ducked his head.

Jensen looked at me. "I'm glad to hear Martin's off on an adventure and he'll be back at some point."

"Since someone *else* had an adventure today"—I playfully tugged on Calder's hair—"I still have to call my nanny and find out why she wasn't aware that Calder had left the apartment and was running unattended in the halls."

"I'd wondered about that."

"She's always been responsible and reliable even when I have to work late." Had I said that to convince him? Or myself?

He shrugged. "Everyone screws up sometimes. No harm, no foul. I'd give her another chance because I bet it won't happen again." He launched himself over the edge of the couch—one-handed like he was dismounting from a pommel horse.

God. Why did jocks always have to show off their athletic prowess? I looked at Jensen, expecting to see smugness on his face because he knew he'd executed a hot and sexy move and he also knew I'd watched him do it.

But he'd focused on Calder. "I have no problem tattling on you to your mom, ninja-boy, if I see you running amok in the hallway again."

Jensen was joking—and yet not—and he came across completely charming about it. "I'd appreciate it. My schedule is erratic so I'm not always home from work at decent hours."

"Where do you work?"

"At the U of M."

"Hey. I went to school there."

I know. So did I. I even cheered for you.

Calder yawned and nestled the side of his face against my stomach. "I'm tired."

Jensen sidestepped us and opened the door. "It was great meeting you, Rowan. And Calder."

I said, "Same. See you around, neighbor."

Three

JENSEN

I hauled my ass out of bed at four thirty the next morning.

Since I hadn't seen my older brothers for several weeks, they'd demanded workout time with me as soon as I returned. Mostly because they wanted to hear the doctor's prognosis.

As the youngest of four children I was used to being called the baby and treated like one. My siblings were high achievers: Brady—my oldest brother—was CFO of Lund Industries, the family business that grossed several billion dollars each year. My brother Walker had started his own construction company. My sister, Annika, was the VP of PR for Lund Industries. All of them, along with my parents and other assorted Lund family members, had supported me throughout my college football years and when I'd gotten drafted into the pros.

I'd lived my dream. I'd made a name for myself by hard

work and dedication to training and learning everything about the sport of football. But what other skills did I have?

Yeah, that was another question I still didn't have an answer to.

This early in the Twin Cities, traffic wasn't bad so I made it to Brady's place in decent time. My brother lived in an old warehouse he'd had renovated several years ago before the area had become super trendy. He'd installed a gym that boasted every amenity, so I loved working out here, but I'll admit since Brady had married Lennox, I didn't just show up as often as I used to.

I punched in the code at the gate and followed the driveway to the private parking lot. Walker's big rig pulled in beside my ZR1 and he waited for me as I finished my energy drink.

Walker grinned and yanked me into a back-slapping hug. "The prodigal son, home at last."

"Prodigal son, my ass." I topped my brother by three inches and fifty pounds and he still managed to make me feel little. "You're the son whose wife is carrying the first Lund grandchild. If anyone is golden, bro, it's you."

"It's a strange turn of events for me to be the first one to do something in this family."

"How's Trinity feeling?"

"Oddly calm. We're four months in and she hasn't freaked out once. Not even when she felt the baby move."

"Maybe she's saving the freak-out for the delivery room."

"Bite your tongue," Walker warned. "Any time women bring up delivery room horror stories, I bolt."

"No talking about babies," Brady said as we reached him, leaning against the steel door, a mug in his hand. He drained the contents and pulled me into a hug. "Glad you're here, Jens."

"You'd think since you're both the big bosses at your respective jobs we could've waited until six A.M. to meet up."

Brady ruffled my hair. Like I was five. "Need extra beauty sleep, pretty boy?"

"Piss off."

"Maybe he had a beauty in his bed and he didn't want to leave," Walker suggested slyly.

I snorted. "I spent all day yesterday in airports. Only thing I wanted to do in my bed last night was sleep."

Brady's was the only gym I'd been in that didn't smell like a gym. I crossed over to throw my can in the trash. Then I took a mat off the stack and unfolded it on the floor. I grabbed a thick foam roller and a couple of leg bands and sat on the mat with my right foot pressed against the wall.

Both Brady and Walker were silent, so I cranked my head around to look at them. "What?"

"We're not going to talk about it at all?" Brady said. "We're just getting straight to the workout?"

"That *is* why I'm here," I pointed out. "Besides, I have specific stretching exercises I have to do first and it takes a while."

"Does it help?"

"Yep."

I focused my weight training on my arms, chest and core. I'd been in therapy for a year and could perform the leg workout in my sleep. But I was superstitious enough not to get cocky and screw something up before my official meeting with the coaching staff later today.

Watching Walker and Brady sparring reminded me that Walker was no challenge for Brady, whereas Brady and I were evenly matched. But I also knew better than to get inside the ring. One wrong twist of my foot and I'd be back where I started.

After we finished, we took a breather on the benches by the water station and I studied my brothers.

Walker patted his beard with a towel and then wiped the

back of his neck below his man bun. Brady mopped his stubble, which would be gone by the time he donned his suit and tie and entered the Lund Industries corporate offices. He was the only kid who had inherited Dad's dark hair. Walker, Annika and I were all blond like Mom. So it cracked me up that Walker considered himself the black sheep of the family. That title should've gone to Brady just on looks alone.

"Why you studying us like you haven't seen us in months, bro?"

I met Brady's curious stare. "Just thinking about hair color and wondering what color Walker's kid will have. I'm hoping for a fiery-ass red with a temper to match."

"I don't care if he's bald as a cue ball or has orange-colored clown hair, just as long as he's healthy and my wife isn't at risk."

My bottle of water stopped halfway to my mouth. "He? You found out the sex?"

Walker grinned. "Just last week. We're having a boy."

"Congrats, man. That is awesome." I looked at Brady. "You and Lennox catch baby fever yet?"

"No." He picked at the label on his water bottle. "I mean, yes, we've discussed starting our family. I imagine we'll get closer to that when baby T-Dub makes his appearance."

"T-Dub? Dude. That's a lame mash-up name. Wal-Trin is totally better."

"Wal-Trin?" Brady said with a snort. "That sounds like a discount cold medicine."

Ignoring him, I said to Walker, "Please promise me Brady won't get in on the baby-naming pool."

"Maybe if you and Lennox wait too long, the newlyweds will beat you in the baby race," Walker teased Brady.

"First of all: Piss off."

Walker and I grinned at each other and bumped fists. Getting Brady riled up was always entertaining.

"Second, Annika said she's not ready to share her time with Axl yet." He cocked an eyebrow at me. "Now as the only singleton in our family, you should be worried that Mom's started her campaign to marry you off."

"It's already under way. Before I left for Florida she tried to set me up with this 'cute as a muffin' nurse."

Brady and Walker exchanged a look. Then Walker said, "Mom doesn't know about your three dating rules?"

"Seriously? Like I'd give Mom that kind of leverage? Hell no."

"So we're the only ones who know that the first thing to keep The Rocket from asking a woman out on a date is if her status is a single mother?" Walker said.

"Bite me," I ground out.

"The second thing is no cheerleaders," Brady added.

"And the third no-go . . . no health care professionals," Walker finished.

"Those rules have served me well," I argued. "So I'll stick with them."

"Until you meet a woman you want to nail who violates one of those rules and the Jensen Lund rule book will go right out the window."

"Wrong. I made those rules my sophomore year of college. I haven't broken a rule yet."

"Never?" Brady said.

"Never."

Walker raised both eyebrows. "No shit?"

"No shit."

"Props for sticking with it, but explain to me where these rules came from," Brady said.

"No single moms became rule number one after I saw what my buddy Bentley went through. He met this chick in class, asked her out, she kept turning him down because she had a kid. He had it bad for her and hounded her until she said yes. Once they got involved, he found out she had an asshole baby daddy and she worked two jobs to stay in school. Then Bentley started missing class to take care of the kid for her. He ended up dropping out. Then she dumped his ass six months later. He went through all that shit for nothing. So I'll pass."

"I get that seeing your buddy's life upended at age twenty would sour you," Walker said. "But this no-cheerleaders rule . . . What's that about?"

"In high school and college if I dated a cheerleader and we broke up—which we always did—I still had to see her at every game and team event. Then the rest of the cheerleaders on the squad hated me on her behalf. They were one collective mind in separate bodies. In the pros there are no-fraternization rules between the cheerleaders and the players."

"That's archaic," Walker said. "And probably illegal. I'd get my ass sued if I tried to tell my office manager Betsy who she could date outside working hours."

"It is what it is and it makes things easier for me."

"I agree with Dubbya, which is why Lund Industries doesn't have that kind of asinine rule in the employee handbook," Brady added. "It doesn't make sense. But your no-health-care-professionals edict doesn't really make sense either."

I scrubbed my hands over my face. "Look, I'm a football player. My body takes a beating on a regular basis. Nurses, massage therapists, fitness trainers, even yoga instructors, try to diagnose me if I mention an ache or pain. Like I should listen to *her* over what the team's medical staff is telling me? Then I take a blast of shit when I don't follow through with her advice. It leads to drama, and I don't do drama. And I definitely don't go against my professional trainers' recommendations. So I avoid the hassle by just saying no to that entire profession."

They both stared at me.

"For chrissake, what now?"

"That is actually a smart list, Jens."

I tried—and failed—not to take that as a backhanded compliment. "Surprised that I use my brain for more than memorizing plays and random chicks' phone numbers?"

Brady held up his hands. "Whoa. Defensive much?"

"Maybe I am." I squirted water in my mouth. "I'm sure the 'where do we hide Jensen in the family business' issue has come up if I'm released from the team. Unlike Jax, who's been assured there's always a place for him at LI when he's done with hockey, I've never gotten that same promise from you, or the uncles, or even Ash and Nolan."

Walker sucked in a breath. "That was harsh, Jens."

"It's true." I pointed my water bottle at him. "He's not denying it."

Brady leveled his CFO stare at me that sent his minions at LI running for the exit.

I managed to stay put.

"Shifting the responsibility of your future after football onto LI? Dick move, bro. Especially since you've refused to tell anyone what postfootball career options you're considering."

"It isn't like you haven't had time to think about it while you've been recuperating," Walker said. "There's no shame in admitting you don't have a fucking clue."

I closed my eyes and tamped down my temper. "Sorry. It's not your problem . . . I don't know what I'll do if the team cuts me. I've been superstitious that if I seriously consider postcareer options right now, the universe will see it as I've given up on my football career and it'll be over." I opened my eyes and looked at Walker first and then Brady. "I'm not ready to even think about moving on."

"Although that sounds like the cosmic-consequences stuff that Dallas believes in, I do understand where you're coming from." Brady kept his gaze on me. "My door is always open to you when you *are* ready to talk about a career change, okay?"

"Okay." I'd dreaded this conversation, taking the "it's all good" tack whenever anyone brought it up. So color me relieved it was over—for now.

Walker and I gathered our stuff and said good-bye to Brady. Outside, Walker paused by my ZR1 before he headed to his truck. "What's going on in your world this week?"

"Dante and I are meeting with the coaching staff today. He's giving them the full report from my week in checkup hell. I have rehab training every day. Besides that, not much. What about you?"

"We're slammed with renovations and we're turning down more work than ever. Jase and I discussed expanding, but we're clearing substantial profits as it is. For him, an increased workload would take time away from Tiffany and their baby girl Jewel. Given what he's been through to finally have a family, money isn't a driving force for him. For me either. I want to be with Trinity and baby T-Dub as much as possible." He grinned. "So I'm an old married dude content to spend my weekends puttering around and being at my pregnant wife's beck and call."

I clapped him on the shoulder. "It's what you've always wanted, so I'm happy for you."

"Thanks. Swing by and have a beer this week."

"I'll take you up on that."

I drove home and felt no guilt whatsoever crawling back in bed for a few hours. At least if I was sleeping I wasn't obsessing over what would happen during my lunch meeting with the guys who held my football future in their hands.

Four

ROWAN

Calder woke up in a grumpy mood. Normally he was a sweet, easygoing kid so I wasn't sure if he just didn't get enough sleep or if he dreaded something at school. When I asked him about it, he mumbled into his cereal so I let it go.

I dropped him off at school—thank heaven for all-day kindergarten—and then backtracked to the University of Minnesota campus. This weekend we had tryouts for next year's squads, and last year we'd had a thousand students try out for eighty spots. The dance routine was the same as last year's; we changed it every other year. That one small thing made the tryout process easier—the current cheerleaders were familiar with the routine so they could help teach it to newcomers.

I helped with the choreography of the dances and cheers, but mainly I served as an athletic trainer, advisor and coach to the stunt groups. In middle school, I'd spent three years as part of competitive club cheer group, four years in high school as part of a traveling competitive cheer squad, and four years on the U of M elite all-girl competitive cheer squad. After discovering my pregnancy the last semester of my senior year, I had to quit the squad.

I'd been lucky to get hired by the U of M athletic department as a trainer after my college graduation. The other benefit of my job was the onsite day care during the school year.

As challenging as training was, I missed the actual cheering at a sporting event. Dante, my former mentor, had scored a job working for the Vikings, and he suggested I try out for the Vikings cheerleaders.

Right. Those women weren't "real" cheerleaders. They were models. Probably empty-headed models, or dancers whose real job involved nightly pole work and lap dances. The supposed "pro" team didn't even do stunts! What kind of a cheer squad couldn't at least throw up a liberty a couple of times a game?

Dante checked my attitude. He reminded me of how hard cheerleaders had worked to overcome stereotypes and the dismissive attitude that we weren't considered "real" athletes. I'd needed to get knocked down a peg. My driving purpose with the collegiate athletic department was to ensure that all athletes—male and female—received equal training opportunities.

Spending eight or more hours in the gym every day demanded that I keep up with my students on a physical level. I'd stayed fit during my pregnancy, and within four months of Calder's birth I'd returned to my prepregnancy body. Even after Dante convinced me to attend an open practice session at the Vikings cheerleading camp, I doubted the organization wanted someone like me—a single mother with a one-year-old baby—to represent them.

Had I ever been happy to be proven wrong.

The cheerleader roster included women from age nineteen to thirty-four. From all walks of life—students, hairstylists, teachers, homemakers, nurses, personal trainers—all women who'd spent their lives cheering or dancing or both and hadn't been ready to give it up. Were the women beautiful? Absolutely. But that almost seemed to be a secondary concern; the cheerleaders' fitness mattered above all else.

I'd never been as nervous as I was the day I showed up for the first open practice. So many hopefuls had applied that they'd had to split it into five sessions of one hundred women in each session. I'd been sitting by myself, practically in the corner, when a brash blonde plopped herself down beside me and struck up a conversation. That turned out to be the best thing that had happened to me. Daisy and I became fast friends, and I wouldn't know what to do without her in my life.

We both made it past the preliminaries and the semifinals into the final round. We squeed appropriately when we both were selected as Vikings cheerleaders and celebrated by polishing off a hundred-dollar bottle of wine Daisy had been saving for a special occasion.

Although I was confident in my qualifications to cheer and dance, part of me couldn't help but wonder if I'd been chosen partially *because* I was a single mother and it created interesting PR. But I hadn't cared then—or now. I was proud to be a Vikings cheerleader.

Auditions were held every year, and being on the squad the previous year didn't guarantee a spot. I had a sense of accomplishment that I was about to start my fifth year on the team. Besides Marsai, who had an extra season on us, Daisy and I had been there the longest. I'd know in my gut when it was time to hang up my pompoms, but I felt I had a couple more seasons in me.

Today I had a meeting with Heather, the head of the cheerleading staff. I'd scheduled a longer lunch break so I could drive to the Vikings corporate offices and training center in Winter Park. While we were a few months away from the unveiling of the new U.S. Bank stadium, the excitement over the near completion of the billion-dollar facility was palpable everywhere.

With this expanded stadium, the cheerleaders were given a new set of expectations. To be honest, the pay to cheer for games is crap—none of us do it for the money and there's no such thing as a full-time cheerleader. The Vikings organization needed the cheerleaders to mingle in the skyboxes during the games, providing a more personal touch to those who could afford to shell out hundreds of thousands of dollars for the prized box seats. So in addition to the fifty cheerleaders on the field, they'd auditioned and hired fifty more women as "ambassadors" meaning they paraded around in uniforms similar to ours, chatting with fans and corporate sponsors while we sweated our asses off, dancing and cheering for all four quarters.

Heather hadn't decided whether these new ambassadors would have to learn all our dance routines and cheers, and she wanted feedback from the half dozen of us who'd been cheering the longest. Since the Vikings big bosses were also in the same offices, I'd had to change out of my usual athletic clothing into a business suit and heels. I rarely wore makeup to my day job, so I'd had to put on my game-day face and hairstyle.

My smart-ass students whistled at me as I tried to duck out of the gym undetected.

On the way to the offices I downed a protein shake and an apple. I never counted on a free lunch.

The meeting wasn't very productive. All six of the cheerleaders were opposed to bringing an additional fifty women into our practices. The corporate bosses wanted it to appear as if the ambassadors had just wandered off the field and were real cheerleaders. Even Heather had bristled at that. But she'd been prepared for it—she handed the CFO's assistant the revised costs for the ambassador program. Daisy and I exchanged a look, doubtful they were willing to fork out more money. But football coaches didn't work for free; why would they expect cheerleading coaches to work additional hours without additional pay?

The meeting ended shortly after that.

Daisy and I lingered in the main entrance. Unlike me, Daisy didn't have to change into business clothes for this meeting since she worked in the actuarial department of Wells Fargo Bank and lived in a suit and heels.

I said, "Well, that was a cluster."

"I suspected it might be."

"I overheard Rebecca say the ambassadors have to deliver food. I've done my time serving nachos and buffalo wings to half-drunk sports fans, thank you very much."

"I never served food. Cocktails for a while." Daisy lowered her voice. "Until I figured out stripping paid a helluva lot more."

I laughed. Daisy's stripper days were far behind her, but they had paid for her MBA—not something she freely shared.

"You mentioned something weird happening last night," she said.

Before I answered, loud male voices echoed to us. A voice I recognized. My face broke into a huge smile. I hadn't seen Dante in three weeks; he'd been off on official team business. My smile faded when I saw who accompanied him.

Jensen Lund.

Daisy said, "Dante's moving up if he's working with The Rocket."

I kept my cool even when Dante picked me up in a bear hug and spun me around.

"Heya, gorgeous! I was just thinking about you. I'd planned on popping in to the U of M training center and seeing what's what."

"Same old grind. We're down to two weeks before the seniors' graduation, so anyone in particular in that class you want to wish well, you'd better get in there next week."

"I'll do that." Dante's gaze winged between me and Daisy. He grinned at her. "Daisy, baby, when you gonna wise up and go out with me?"

"Never." She patted his smooth face. "But it *is* precious how you just keep trying."

"I will catch you in a weak moment." He remembered he wasn't alone. "Ladies, you know Jensen Lund."

I'd yet to meet Jensen's gaze—although I'd felt his boring into me, as he tried to figure out why I was here.

"Jensen, I'm sure you recognize two of the Vikings' finest cheerleaders."

That was when I looked at Mr. Oblivious.

His jaw tightened and he gritted out, "You're joking, right?"

Dante seemed confused. "Why would I joke about that?"

I locked my gaze on Jensen's as I spoke to Dante. "Because then The Rocket would have to admit that he doesn't pay attention to anything as trivial as cheerleaders when he takes the field, isn't that right?" I broke eye contact and looked at Dante. "He's run past me . . . a dozen times each season. We've attended the same corporate events every year since he was drafted. Oh and here's another irony . . . I also cheered for him at the U of M. So imagine how awkward it was for me last night when he introduced himself as if we'd never met."

Silence.

Daisy stepped between us and addressed Dante. "I'd suggest in addition to scheduling physical therapy you make an appointment to get The Rocket's eyes examined." She took my elbow and led me away.

She didn't release me even when we reached the parking lot. "Daisy—"

"Not a word until we're inside my car."

Great.

Daisy's "car" was an enormous Lincoln Navigator. I fought the tight fit of my pencil skirt as I clambered into the passenger seat.

"Buckle up. We're getting out of here so Dante doesn't get the bright idea of running interference between you two."

"It's not like Lund plans to chase me down."

She peeled out and pulled into a Caribou Coffee drive-thru. We were quiet until we had our drinks—iced coffee with a splash of cream and a shot of sugar-free caramel syrup—and she'd parked. Immediately she faced me. "Please tell me meeting Jensen Lund was the weird thing that happened to you."

"Of course it was."

"Spill the deets."

I told her all of it.

"Wait. I thought Axl Hammerquist lived across the hall from Martin."

"He did." I sucked down a big sip of coffee. "But I guess Axl moved out last year when he married Jensen Lund's sister."

"I remember reading about that wedding. It was like *the* social event of last summer."

For me, reading the paper took a backseat to reading books to Calder. "If you say so. At first I thought Martin hadn't mentioned it because of my aversion to football players. But now, I suspect he didn't say anything because Lund doesn't really live there. It's probably his place for hookups instead of at his bajillion-dollar mansion."

"Maybe. But his ego's really so huge he doesn't notice the people who've been on the sidelines his college and pro career?"

"Apparently."

Daisy tapped her icy-pink fingernails on the side of her drink cup. "So what are you going to do?"

"About what? If I happen to run into him in the hallway I'll be polite. I don't want Martin to have to deal with 'why is your sister such a bitch?' questions just because it stung my ego that Jensen Lund doesn't know me."

"It goes beyond ego, Rowan. At least yours anyway."

I shrugged.

"How tight is Dante with him?"

"No idea. Dante doesn't discuss any of the players he works with, which is smart. Some trainers are eager to make themselves look important by dropping names, then they're surprised when those clients fire them for being a blabbermouth. Although it is different with Dante—all the guys he works with on the team are somewhat famous."

"I can't imagine that Dante isn't ripping The Rocket a new one right now."

"Hopefully Dante won't chew out a franchise player and put his job in jeopardy. I really hope he doesn't stop by the training center today because I'm done talking about this."

Daisy raised her hand. "Say no more." She dropped me off at my car and I headed back to work.

Thankfully the rest of my afternoon was drama free—or as drama free as it can be when dealing with eighty members of the spirit squads.

My son was in a much better mood when I arrived home. Alicia provided a detailed breakdown of how they'd spent their after-school hours. I appreciated her promise that yesterday's events were a onetime error that wouldn't happen again.

After finishing supper, Calder and I watched *Dancing with the Stars* because my boy loved to dance. Although I'd attended dance classes from age four until I switched to club cheerleading at age twelve, when it came to choosing an activity for my son, I'd enrolled him in kendo—the Japanese sword discipline similar to fencing—instead of dancing. Maybe I had picked it because it was macho, but I remembered how cruel other boys at school could be when they discovered a male classmate studied dance.

Six months into his kendo classes, Calder had begged to join jujitsu. Since jujitsu had no formal katas, students were allowed to create their own. Seeing Calder performing a kata like a ballet made me realize I shouldn't force him onto a path he didn't want to take. So he quit both martial arts programs but kept the *gi* and the *hakama*. I enrolled him at a dance studio with a separate track for boys, and the kid had been in heaven ever since.

After his bath, we read the books he'd chosen during library day. I knew our nightly reading time would change next year in first grade when he could read by himself, so I cherished this time with my sweet boy.

"Mommy, what made you happy today?"

I kissed the top of his head, breathing in the scent of the baby shampoo I still used. "This. Snuggled up and seeing your excellent choices in books." I smoothed his hair from his eyes when he tilted his head back to look at me. "What made you happy today?"

"Chocolate milk at lunchtime."

I laughed. "You do love having a chocolate milk mustache. Was there something else?"

His forehead wrinkled so adorably I just had to kiss it.

"Well . . . we got to play with the big parachute in gym.

Don't you think it'd be awesome to jump out of an airplane with a parachute?"

"Not awesome at all. I'd never do anything like that."

"Someday I'm gonna do it. I'll spin and do backflips in the air over and over until I'm dizzy and float down through the clouds like a rainbow snowflake."

"Hmm. When you put it that way, I might consider it. When you're a grown man of thirty. All right, future daredevil parachutist, let's get you tucked in."

"Do I have to go to bed? Can't I stay up a little longer?"

"Nope. Tomorrow's your busy day. You've gotta be rested up because Grammy and Pop-pop are picking you up for the weekend, remember?"

I clicked on his nightlight and kissed his forehead. "Good night, sweetheart. I love you."

"Love you too, Mommy."

The one thing that I'd been blessed with was that Calder had been a good sleeper from the first day I'd brought him home from the hospital. Sure, he'd had his fussy times, but nothing like the horror stories I'd heard from other moms.

I cracked my laptop to double-check the tryout schedule. Working weekends was part of the gig in college athletics, but luckily, it wasn't every weekend. I'd just settled in when I heard three soft raps on my door.

Gee. I wonder who that could be.

He'd knocked softly enough that I could ignore it. He had no way of knowing that I hadn't already crawled in bed for the night—I glanced at the time on my computer—at nine o'clock.

That was almost worse, him believing I went to bed the same time as my six-year-old son. I crossed to the door to peer through the peephole. Even the fisheye view didn't distort his attractiveness.

Why was he here? I opened the door and held my finger to my lips. "Calder is asleep."

"That's why I waited. I thought it'd be better if we talked alone."

"Talked about what?"

For a moment, his confidence faltered. His gaze scoured my face as if he were trying to commit every feature to memory.

I bristled at his scrutiny. "What did you want to talk about, Lund?"

His sheepish smile brought out his dimples.

In addition to his slamming body and his stunning looks, he had darling dimples? So not freakin' fair.

"Maybe *talk* was a bad word choice. I want to apologize"— he reached behind his back and pulled out a stuffed animal— "for being the world's biggest jackass."

He held out a donkey with its head cranked around to stare balefully at the word EM-BARE-ASSED spelled out across its ample backside.

I laughed—I couldn't help it. This was so not what I'd expected from him.

Jensen took a step closer, dangling the donkey as a peace offering. "Rowan. I'm sorry."

A door slammed down the hallway. I preferred our conversation wasn't grist to fuel the Snow Village gossip mill, so I grabbed his wrist and said, "Come in, but keep your voice down."

"Thank you."

After shutting the door, I turned to see him settling on the couch.

That was presumptuous. Or was it a habit from when Martin lived here?

Jensen placed the donkey on the coffee table.

"Where did you find that?"

"There's an All Apologies store in Roseville. Anything you need to apologize for, or ask forgiveness for, they have something to fit the occasion."

"I've never heard of it."

"I hadn't either but it popped up on my Google search. So I checked it out."

"What else did you find besides a stuffed jackass?"

He leaned closer, resting his forearms on his knees. "All sorts of shit I couldn't believe. Like a box of chocolates with a card that said, 'Sorry I fucked your sister.'"

"Get. Out."

"Swear to god that's what it said." He paused. "As I was debating whether to take a picture of it, the clerk came over to warn me that was the last one and they had a hard time keeping that item in stock."

I laughed. Then I clapped my hand over my mouth because it shouldn't be funny.

Jensen smiled. "I know, right? The place was a freakin' trainwreck but I couldn't look away. But that wasn't even the worst thing they had that a guy needed to offer an apology for."

"Now you have to tell me what could possibly be worse— yet somehow a man believes is actually forgivable."

"A card that said, 'You lured me in from the moment we met . . .' on the front and then the inside read, 'and I'm sorry I missed the birth of our child while I was on my annual fishing trip with the guys.'"

"That is the worst. But given this is Minnesota, I imagine they have a hard time keeping that one in stock too."

"Yep. Anyway, the store had that one"—he pointed to the stuffed animal—"and another one that said 'I'm a jackass' every time you pulled the string. I actually liked that one better, since it was the same orange color as the Denver Donkeys uniforms, but I figured it wouldn't be cool if Calder got a hold of it."

That was surprisingly thoughtful. "I appreciate that."

"It *is* a totally off-the-hoof"—he grinned—"apology gift."

"You are punny, Lund. So riddle me this: Are you here only because Dante demanded you apologize to me?"

"He did tear into me—no less than I deserved—but I am here by my own choice to make things right." He paused and angled closer. "Look. I tend to be singularly focused. I've pissed off almost everyone I'm close to at one time or another because of that trait."

I studied his face—for what, I don't know. Sarcasm or smugness maybe. But he wore a look of resignation. "That's a lame excuse."

"It wasn't meant to be an excuse. And feel free to call bullshit on it, but it was more along the lines of an explanation."

I honestly wasn't sure how to respond to that.

"Without coming across as any more of a self-involved dick than you already believe me to be, it wasn't anything personal. I don't know the names or the faces of any of the cheerleaders." His eyes, such a deep blue, searched mine. "You are a stunningly beautiful woman, Rowan. In any other context besides football, I would've been all over you, demanding your name and number."

"Do I give myself a high five for receiving the mother of all compliments from The Rocket?"

Jensen scowled. "Don't call me that. It's a media nickname that has nothing to do with the guy sitting here before you now."

At least he didn't refer to himself in third person. "Understood. And I appreciate you coming all the way over here and clearing the air."

"All the way over here? Was that sarcastic since I live across the hall?"

Here was a moment of truth. "You really live in Snow Village full-time?"

"Yes. Why wouldn't I?"

"Because you're a professional football player and a Lund heir, and this place is way beneath your pay grade."

Another scowl.

Why did I find his mouth so interesting? I forced myself to focus on the words coming out of it.

"You thought I was using this place as my secret love nest or something?" He snorted. "Saw the gigantic couch and assumed?"

That annoyed me. "I don't have to assume anything when it comes to football players, Lund. At one time or another they're all players."

His eyes narrowed on me. "Odd that you don't have a high opinion of my colleagues when you're on the sidelines cheering for us."

"Maybe I don't have a high opinion for that exact reason. I know what goes on when that door to the luxury hotel suite closes after the game."

"That's not fair. How would you react if I said all cheerleaders are empty-headed mean girls?"

I opened my mouth to argue. But I realized he had a point. "Fine. Not all football players are that way."

"Thank you. And how did we end up arguing when my whole reason for coming over here was to apologize and make it easier for us to be neighbors?"

"Maybe because I'm a little argumentative."

"So you aren't anything like Martin."

"Funny. You needn't worry I'll egg your door for not recognizing me."

"It'd be worse punishment if you sent your son careening down the hallway to head-butt me in the nuts again," he teased.

I smiled at him. "I am sorry about that."

"He had no idea I was even there. With that intense focus the kid would be a great tackle."

"Calder is six. It's a little early to be fitting him with shoulder pads, a helmet and instilling that aggressive attitude. Besides, he's a dancer. That's what he loves."

Jensen studied me and I braced myself for the "dancing is for pussies" response. So he surprised me when he said, "You ever bring him to the games with you?"

"It's not like I could keep an eye on him. We're busy an hour before and after the game, not to mention we're in constant movement during the three hours we're on the field."

"Get someone to take him. Like Martin. Cheerleaders get guest passes for every game, right?"

"Uh, no. Not even one."

"Seriously? That's not fair."

I lifted a brow. "You really don't want me to go off on a tangent about the unfairness of that, do you?"

He held up his hands. "Nope. Let's change the subject." And he was scrutinizing me again. "What?"

"Are you sure you're not a gamer?"

"I've never had time to play. Martin has promised to show Calder the ropes when he's older so he isn't video game illiterate."

"Lucky for Calder. Martin constantly kicks my ass. The only game he can't beat me at is *Madden*."

"You weren't bullshitting me about hanging out with Martin all the time."

"When I took over Axl's place, I was in recovery mode from surgeries and had a shit ton of free time. Verily was gone a lot competing, so we ended up hanging out."

"Now it makes sense why he wasn't calling me three times a day complaining of boredom."

"You never visited him here?"

"He always had bongs sitting out, or his rolling station. I don't get the appeal, but this is—was—Martin's sanctuary.

Asking him to hide all that . . . not cool. It was easier for him to come to our place."

"What did they do with all of their stuff?"

"It's in storage." I didn't tell Jensen that Martin had opted for the six-month plan with the option to renew for a year. Part of me wondered if he planned on coming back. "I just realized that I told you why I was at the Vikings corporate offices today, but you didn't tell me why you were there. Training camp doesn't start for a while."

He reset the professional distance between us. "They wanted a status update on my injury since I spent a week in Florida with the doctor's team. Everything is still inconclusive and will continue to be until training camp." He stood. "Sorry. I didn't mean to take up so much of your time."

"It's okay. I was just going over last-minute schedule updates."

"For what?"

"Collegiate cheerleading tryouts are this weekend. I'm coordinating the stunt groups, which can be a challenge if we're out of balance on the number of bases and side bases to flyers, not to mention rotating guys in for the coed squad. It's two and a half days of cheer drama."

"That long?"

"It's super competitive and intense." I launched into an explanation of the different squads and the level of experience the athletes needed to have for intercollegiate competition.

He'd paused in the doorway during my spiel. "You bring Calder along?"

"I'm too busy to watch him. My mom and dad pick him up from school Friday and take him for the weekend. I don't see him until Sunday night, which sucks, but tryouts only happen once a year."

"Do your parents live in the Cities?"

"Two and a half hours northwest in Fergus Falls. They have apple orchards, so Calder gets to ride on the tractor and run wild." When he didn't respond, I realized I'd been babbling instead of letting him leave. "Sorry."

"For what?"

"Going on and on and boring you."

His eyes darkened and his gaze dipped to my mouth. "The last thing you are, Rowan Michaels, is boring."

When he loomed over me and I caught the scent of his skin—his cologne, or shaving cream, or even his laundry detergent, whatever it was I just wanted to find the source and breathe him in.

What is wrong with you?

I stepped back. "Thanks for the gift jackass."

That blue gaze turned sharp.

Dammit. "I meant, thanks for the jackass gift."

"My pleasure. Now that we're being neighborly, remember, if you need anything, a cup of sugar, or even eggs"—he grinned—"I'm right across the hall."

"Good night, Jensen."

"Sweet dreams, Rowan."

Five

—

JENSEN

Early Friday afternoon after Dante had tortured me and he was in a fine mood because of it, I said, "So the cheerleading team tryouts at U of M. You have access to that this weekend?"

"You mean am I helping out? No. If you mean do I have access to the training center? The answer is yes. Why?"

"I wanted to check it out. See Rowan Michaels in action, educate myself, given I was such a tool about who she is and what she does."

Dante leveled his death stare on me. "Really. That's how you're playing this, Rocket? Taking an 'academic'"—the asshole even made air quotes—"interest in what Rowan's job entails at the U of M?"

"Given the fact that she cheered for me my freshman and sophomore year, I think I owe it to her to see why I hadn't paid attention." That sounded plausible. Hopefully he bought

my ain't-no-big-thing attitude, when in truth, Rowan interested me far more than any woman I'd met since before my
injury last year.

"You owe it to her," Dante repeated. "That better not be
Jensen-speak for wanting a piece of her, because I have a
major problem with that."

For the first time I gauged him as competition. Good-
looking guy with dark hair and olive skin that indicated his
Italian ancestry. Dude was a total bro, built like a freight
train with the smarts to back up his ambition. But he was a
player, so it annoyed me that he thought he had the right to
warn *me* off. "Something going on between you and Rowan?"

He snorted. "I've known her since her senior year in
college. She's like my little sister so naturally I'm gonna
warn off a guy like you."

A guy like me who'd lived like a freakin' monk the past
year. After I returned home from the hospital, several of my
hookups vied for a chance to "help me out." But they started
to equate—confuse?—my need for a quick bout of sex with
a long-term commitment, so I put a halt to all of it. No dating.
No clubs. No team parties. While a small part of me missed
the rush of locking eyes with a woman, knowing I could have
her on her knees or on her back with just a sexy smile, the
truth was random sexual encounters weren't enough. In my
lonely self-reflection, I realized I wanted more.

"Got nothin' to say to that, Rocket?"

I shook off my melancholy. "Give me some credit. She
violates all three of my rules."

He tried—and failed—to intimidate me with silence.
Finally he sighed. "Fine. I'll get you in. But all you'd have
to do is give your name at the door and you'd be golden."

"Except I don't want anyone to know I'm there."

Dante's eyes widened. "Not cashing in on your celebrity?

You are serious about the educational-pursuit angle. I thought The Rocket loved being mobbed."

I used to. Now I avoided it whenever possible. "Just get me in and I'll blend."

He clapped me on the back. "Buddy, you're six foot five, built like the pro football player you are and your ugly mug has been in the news since you were sixteen years old—you don't know *how* to blend."

I flashed my teeth at him. "Watch me."

An older sister with a love of theater had served me well. Not only did I rock Halloween costumes, I'd learned that a couple of adjustments could change my appearance— or at least other people's perception. I left the dark blond scruff on my face, tucked my hair up in an old U of M ball cap and slipped on a pair of glasses with clear lenses that I kept around to go incognito.

I wore a stained pair of black sweatpants, the elastic bottoms pulled up below my knees, and a pair of white tube socks shoved down to the tops of my hiking boots. My teammate Devonte had left a size 6XXL quilted flannel shirt here a few weeks back. Defensive ends were massive so the shirt was oversized even for a guy my size. Shuffling with my shoulders hunched and my head down, I appeared a few inches shorter.

When I squinted in the foggy bathroom mirror, I felt confident no one—not even my own mother—would recognize me in this getup.

I climbed into my Hummer. Halfway to the campus MOM popped up on my digital screen. She'd keep calling if I didn't answer, so I accepted the call. "What did I do wrong that warrants a phone call from my beautiful mother on a Friday afternoon?"

"Why do you assume you are in error?"

"Because I've been home a few days and haven't seen you?" She'd ignored the flattery, which wasn't a good sign.

"I *suppose* I should be happy that you made time for your brothers."

"You and Dad are welcome to work out with us at five in the morning," I offered.

"When you are up with the hens, there is so *very* much of the day left to contact people, yah?"

That had backfired on me. I didn't even point out that she'd mixed up hens with roosters.

"You need a personal assistant to organize things. Then when my youngest son doesn't have time in his busy schedule for his mama, I can blame her and not feel like meddlesome botherer."

Once my mother got past slathering on the guilt, she was sweet, funny and thoughtful. "I'm sorry. What can I do to make it up to you?"

"Help me with two things. First, attend the Lund family brunch on Sunday. Bring a date if you wish."

I deflected on the date. "I'll be there."

"Second, you've considered my proposition for your Lund Cares Community Outreach project this year, yah?"

"Your suggestion is not a good fit for me. I told you that."

"Since when is football not a good fit for you, Jensen Bernard Lund, tight end for the Minnesota Vikings?" she demanded.

My hands tightened around the steering wheel. "Since I'm on the injured reserve list and if I damage myself in an activity that is *not* directly related to football practice or training with my coaches' approval, I'm in violation of my contract."

"Oh pigwash. Tiny boys in peewee football can't hurt big offensive player like you."

"You mean hogwash?"

"Yah. Whatever. You stand there to clap and yell encouragement. Maybe you wipe a few noses, clean off dirt, patch up scrapes—all just standing on the offside."

"Snot, blood and mud is supposed to sell me on this idea, Mom? Sorry, but no." I paused. "And offside is a penalty, not a place. You meant standing on the sideline." Which she well knew.

"See! You know all the important terms and rules. Naturally you are teacher."

I could not win with her. So I did what any desperate son does: I lied my ass off. "Helping with football camps, even through a charitable and respected organization like LCCO, is prohibited because it is in direct competition with the local and national athletic programs set up by the NFL. So I've done research on other options for my annual LCCO project. I'll let you know as soon as I have a solid idea, okay?"

"Do not delay or Priscilla will bring up that bachelor auction idea again since Ash hasn't committed to his annual LCCO project either."

"Bachelor auction." I snorted. "Wasn't that popular in like 2000? Isn't the idea of that laughable now?"

"Yes. I think Priscilla is in midlife crisis. She keeps bringing up the auction because she wants to stare at young, beautiful, built men and pretend it's for a good cause."

"Mom. That is way too much information."

She laughed. "With that . . . my work is done. Have fun with whatever you are doing that you do not wish to tell me about. Love you. See you Sunday."

Since I'd spent four years on the U of M campus, finding the training facility wasn't a problem. The football team hadn't trained in this building, and that was just another reminder of how segregated we'd been from the other student athletes.

The flannel shirt roasted me, but I had to keep it on. I shuffled up to the registration table and two college girls, one blonde, one brunette, stopped gossiping long enough to acknowledge me.

The blonde wrinkled her nose at me. The brunette kept a bland expression when she said, "You need a pass to get in here."

"There should be a pass left for me by Dante DeLillo."

The brunette sighed and pawed through the *D* section. "Are you Richard Head?"

Richard Head? Aka . . . Dick Head? Seriously? I'd expected something more creative. "That's me."

She all but threw the lanyard. "That pass is only good for the bleachers section."

"But I can sit anywhere I want in the bleachers?"

"Gee, do ya think?" the blonde retorted. "Just don't talk too loud or bother anyone or we'll ask you to leave."

"Okay." To further annoy them, I said, "Are you both cheerleaders?"

"Duh. Why else would we be here?"

In my experience that snotty attitude was a prerequisite to becoming a pompom waver. I walked away but still heard them snicker behind my back. But then all sound faded. The room darkened. All I could see was her, as if she'd been pinpointed in a spotlight.

Rowan moved with grace and style that set her apart from every other athlete on the mat. Smooth transitions with her body as she precisely executed arm motions and the smile on her beautiful face never faded. She'd pulled her red hair back into a stubby ponytail, and she wore maroon-colored yoga pants with a mustard-yellow athletic tank top, both pieces sporting the U of M logo.

Holy shit did the woman have a hot body—toned, muscled and yet curved in all the right places.

Clapping her hands, she stepped out, raising her arms above her head, mirroring her upper and lower body in a V shape. Then she did a hip-hop dance move, bringing her legs together for a moment before she threw herself back, executing a somersault in the air. Pivoting, she performed a cartwheel/back handspring combo, landing facing forward in the splits with her arms above her head, still smiling.

Amazing.

I started to applaud until I noticed no one else was clapping. Definitely didn't need to draw attention to myself. Turning away, I scaled the bleacher seats, choosing to sit in the center. I scanned the area. There weren't many people watching the tryouts—maybe thirty. But the sections where the competitors waited were completely full.

I'd just settled in when the music started—a mash-up of the peppiest parts of various songs—and once again Rowan was demonstrating, but she had a partner.

No. Way. Her partner was my cousin Dallas—who'd graduated from college last spring. In tandem they performed the same series of movements that Rowan had done solo.

I attempted to keep an objective eye. Dallas was a damn good cheerleader. She just wasn't as good as Rowan. Rowan had that extra . . . sparkle, for lack of a better description.

I wondered if she was still cheering because she craved the spotlight.

Maybe you should stop making assumptions. Isn't trying to change your preconceived ideas the reason you're here?

It was. But watching Rowan Michaels sauntering around in skintight clothes, bending her incredible body this way and that . . . total bonus.

Then a voice boomed over the sound system. "Listen up, competitors. Now you've seen the routine all the way to the end. This is the only group practice, so pay attention to what's going on in front of you and behind you. Know your own space. Flight one, take the floor. Cue the music from the beginning."

Two dozen girls spread out on the mat. Dallas stood at the front, leading the group, while Rowan and another woman walked along opposite sides of the competitors, holding clipboards.

The entire routine lasted a little over two minutes. It surprised me to see how well the competitors synced with each other, given their random number assignments. According to the signage I'd seen, they weren't allowed to try out with a predetermined group, for either the choreographed numbers or the stunting portion. When they performed a move I didn't know the official name for, I Googled it. I didn't want to come across like an idiot not knowing anything about cheerleading.

For the next hour, I watched twelve flights enact the same routine. A few competitors stood out, but I hadn't seen anyone on par with Dallas and especially not close to Rowan's performance level. I'd stuck around to see the stunt groups, but the people behind me said those tryouts weren't until tomorrow.

Before I could bail, a dark-haired sprite bounded up the bleacher steps.

"Fancy meeting you here, JB." She plopped down next to me. "And FFR? You can't pull off Walker's lumbersexual look."

"Nice to see you too, baby cuz. What the hell is FFR?"

"For future reference." She bumped me with her shoulder. "Dude, keep up with the current lingo. Totes ages you when you have to ask for an explanation."

"Gimme a break. You *totes* make up your own lingo," I pointed out. "Besides, I'm sure my aura registered confusion so you should've known. Or did you miss that reading, Miss Woo-Woo?"

She snorted. "Woo-woo. One of these days I'll take offense to that. But for now, I'm chalking it up to your unenlightened attitude. So what brings you here? In disguise, no less?"

"I'm here for enlightenment. I'm avoiding being recognized so not to detract from the competition Rowan is running." Not an egotistical statement, just fact. Pro football players were treated like celebrities—regardless of whether we deserved it.

"*Rowan?*" she repeated. "You mean Coach Michaels?"

"Yes."

"What's going on between you two?" Dallas demanded. "How do you even know her?"

"She and her son are subleasing Martin's apartment."

"Oh. Right. Now I remember that Axl's former neighbor was her brother. He stopped by practice a few times to pick up Calder."

I looked at her. "You know Calder?"

Dallas said, "Yep. I used to babysit him once in a while when Coach's regular sitters had a conflict. Sweet kid."

"I'm surprised to see you here on campus. You swore you were done with all of this after graduation."

"I was. I mean, I am." She started fiddling with the bracelets lining her forearm. "You probably don't remember, but I quit the cheer team for a while last year."

"Of course I remember. That was when you were involved with Iron Man."

Her gaze met mine. "Quitting the team had nothing to do with me doing a hot Russian hockey dude. Back then I'd had some other issues. Rather than create more problems for myself, I quit the team."

Why hadn't I heard of any of the other issues?

Maybe you had heard about it, you just chose to ignore it. Or you figured someone else in the family would take care of it.

"Coach Michaels let me sit out for the rest of the football season," she continued. "When I told her I still wanted to quit the squad when basketball season started, she refused to accept my resignation." She paused. "She understood I needed a focal point. And she was right. It was the only thing that got me through it. So when I heard she needed help with cheer camp, I volunteered."

I inhaled a deep breath. "Does anyone in the family know . . . ?"

"No. I'm already seen as the baby. Plus, everyone thinks I'm a freakazoid from being born with secondary perceptions. 'Oh, Dallas, honey, you're probably making things seem worse than they are.' Last year was mass chaos with the Lund Collective. Jax quit drinking. You were injured. Annika was in a secret relationship. Walker and Brady were trying to figure out how to balance their careers with being newly married. Nolan was picking up the slack at LI. Then my world collapsed when Ig—" She shook her head. "Then there's my brother."

"What's going on with Ash?" I said sharply. Of all my cousins, Ash always held it together.

"He's joyless. He has pulled so far into his shell that I can't even *see* his aura let alone read it." Dallas violated my space to warn, "Don't you dare tell anyone what I said about Ash, JB. I'm not kidding. You asked why I didn't confide in the Lund Collective, and there's your answer."

"Fine." I lightly flicked her nose, knowing she hated it. But we needed some levity.

"Don't do that, jerkwad." She harrumphed when she tried to shove me and I didn't budge.

"Maybe I didn't know any of this before, but I know it

now. If your aura starts closing in on you and you need to talk, call me, okay?"

"Dude. Your aura can't close in on you like a cloak of doom . . ." She frowned. "Although, when I think about it, that is kind of what it feels like. Suffocating darkness."

"See? I'm not totally clueless with the woo-woo stuff."

"But you are avoiding my question on what's going on between you and Coach Michaels."

"Nothing. We're neighbors. I'm here supporting her since her brother is on vacay."

"Uh-huh. It has nothing to do with her bein' totes adorbs, right?"

Jesus. *Totes adorbs?* Who seriously says that? And besides, *totes adorbs* didn't accurately describe the hot and sexy and so very, very . . . limber Coach Michaels.

Dallas bumped me with her shoulder. "It's okay to crush on her, JB."

"It's not like that."

That earned me an exaggerated wink. "Whatever you say." She leapt to her feet. "Gotta go. Coach is giving me the stink-eye."

I noticed Rowan staring at me.

So I gave her a double thumbs-up and a stupid, goofy grin. Not something Jensen Lund would do.

I decided to stick around a little longer and see what shook out. I snickered to myself . . . and wished I'd come up with that pompom pun in time to share it with Dallas.

Six

—

ROWAN

Seeing Jensen Lund at the U of M cheerleading tryouts should've been shock enough.

But knowing he'd gone to the trouble to disguise himself so his presence wouldn't disrupt the athletes had really shocked me. And driven home the point that there was more to the man than I'd given him credit for.

I wouldn't have known he was here if his cousin Dallas hadn't told me. Somewhere along the line I'd forgotten that he and Dallas were related.

After the last group session ended, I packed up my belongings and said good-bye to the staff who were leaving for the ice arena to work with the hockey cheerleaders.

I scaled the bleacher steps and sat next to Jensen on the bench seat. "Fancy meeting you here."

"Dallas spilled the beans."

"She was pretty nosy asking why you were here. I'm wondering too."

He folded his arms across his chest. "You spoke so passionately about what you do that I wanted a firsthand look."

"This isn't my normal day, thank goodness. The real culling process starts tomorrow. That's the worst part. The tears and tantrums. I'll pretty much want the whole bottle of wine tomorrow night rather than just a glass or two, even when I'm not the final judge."

"How much of your input is taken into consideration when the final decisions are made?"

"I'm called out if I put a huge *NO* on someone's paperwork."

"Does that happen often?"

I shrugged. And winced. That move aggravated the muscle in my shoulder that I'd pulled when I'd stepped in as a back spot for a stunt group. Before I could answer, Jensen leaned closer.

"I recognize that wince of pain, Coach Michaels. What did you do?"

Why did I like him calling me by my professional name? I faced him and we were so close that I noticed his glasses magnified the dark fringe of lashes surrounding those stunning blue eyes. "I pulled it during a demonstration. No big deal."

"When you did the cartwheel/back handspring/splits combo? Or the airborne somersault?

What was an airborne somersault? My thoughts scrolled to that section of the routine. "Oh, you mean a standing back tuck?"

"Yeah, that. Cool move."

I blinked at him. "Exactly how long have you been here, Lund?"

"Long enough. So . . . Which side? Left or right?"

"Left."

Then his big hand curled around the cup of my shoulder and his thumb just magically zeroed in on the sore spot. He lightly pressed. When I hissed in a breath, he dug his thumb in deeper.

"Sweet baby Jesus, yes, right there." I might've slumped forward in supplication and moaned without shame.

Briefly, the circling and swirling motion stopped, but then he resumed.

"Without seeming ungrateful, how the hell did you know exactly where to touch me?"

"I'm a man. I'd better know all the best spots a woman needs to be touched."

The way he'd said that? Pure sex.

"You know what I meant."

He paused. "I have the same issue on the left side after I've leapt to catch throws."

"Well, thank you. It's feeling better now."

"Bullshit. My hands on you makes you nervous. Deal with it. Turn to the left, reach across your upper body and wrap your left hand over your right hip."

I should've reminded him that *I* had the degree in sports medicine, but his tone didn't invite argument. As soon as I executed the movement the knot loosened and the pain vanished. Cranking my head around, I peered at him over my right shoulder. "That was incredible."

"I told you. I am very, very good with my hands."

The heat in his eyes was unmistakable.

Or maybe the lenses of his fake glasses were flashing a false reflection. "Thank you," I managed. "I'll have to remember that trick."

"Don't try it solo," he warned. "You tense up again, find me. I'm great in a tight spot."

I'll bet you are. I'd also bet you could loosen me up in no time at all.

He lowered his hand. Slowly. Almost reluctantly. "You didn't answer my question."

Question? What question?

"How much input you have on who makes the final cut on the various squads?"

"Honestly? A lot. If a candidate is difficult, and I mean a serious pain in the ass to other candidates, that's not someone we want to deal with several hours a day, five days a week, plus game times, for the next school year. We have an abundance of qualified candidates; why would we choose someone who doesn't understand teamwork?"

Jensen nodded. "Wish that attitude carried over to the pros. So freakin' many glory seekers. It's 'what can the team do for me?' rather than them being part of the team." He shot me a sideways glance and a wry grin. "And no way am I naming names."

"You don't have to, Lund. I'm on the inside, remember? I hear more team gossip than most."

"What do you hear about me?"

"Talented. Cocky as hell, but you've got the stats to back it up—or at least you did the last year you played."

"Any of your insider sources react with surprise that I'm still on the roster?"

"No more than anyone else who's been on the injured reserve list this long." I shook my head. "How'd we get off on this tangent? Anyway, thanks for coming today."

When I moved to stand, he clamped his hand on my thigh. "You're leaving?"

"It's been a long day and it'll be an even longer one tomorrow."

"But I still have a ton of questions."

I looked at him skeptically. "You do?"

"Yeah. So I could ask my questions over dinner. Either we could go out someplace or we could order in."

I leveled my best "you're up to something" evil eye at him

He laughed. "Man, you are hard-core with that suspicious mom glare. I swear, I have no nefarious plans. I just thought we could share a meal and conversation. If either sucks, you can bail and be home in two seconds."

Spending the night by myself wasn't appealing. Looking at Jensen Lund wouldn't be a hardship. "Fine. Want me to grab takeout?"

"How about you bring a bottle of wine and I'll deal with the food. Lebanese okay?"

"Sounds great." I stood. "So an hour?"

"See you then. Just knock."

I made my way to the bottom of the bleachers and back to the coaches' area.

Bree, one of the new student assistants for next year, said, "Is that weird-looking dude you were talking to your boyfriend?"

"No." I packed up my stuff. "Just a friend. Why?"

"It's creepy how he watched you. His eyes never left your butt the entire time you were walking away from him."

"He could hardly be looking at my face since I had my back to him, now could he?"

"Whatever. Old-people lust is gross."

I froze. Old people. Really? She thought I was . . . old? I whirled around to chew her ass about rude assumptions, but she'd already taken off. Probably a good thing.

But as I drove home, I had to wonder whether I had really been any different at age nineteen. Anyone out of college seemed old to me. And a thirty-year-old woman with a kid? Ancient.

Dealing with college students every day had made me grateful that part of my life was over.

I wondered if Jensen had many normal college days or if everything had revolved around his ability to catch a football. What degree had he earned before getting drafted into the pros?

Guess if we ran out of normal dinner conversation that was something I'd bring up.

*I*t's not a damn date, Rowan. Just pick something to wear.

I'd rummaged through my closet for the past ten minutes searching for an outfit that said friendly, but not sexy.

No dresses.

So . . . jeans and a T-shirt. But not like I tried too hard, wearing a hipster T-shirt with an emblem of an obscure band or brand of beer or clothing—which I had a drawer full of thanks to my hipster/stoner brother. I opted for a Justin Timberlake concert tee, black skinny jeans and no shoes. I'd just kick them off at the door anyway.

I'd called Calder before I left the apartment. But as usual, he'd been almost too busy to talk to me. I briefly spoke to my mom and she encouraged me to get some rest while I had the chance. I didn't tell her about having dinner with Jensen, because it was no big deal.

I knocked on his door, bringing a bottle of wine and two of the turtle brownies I'd baked earlier in the week.

Jensen answered the door wearing the same disguise he'd had on earlier.

I lifted a brow. "Incognito in your own apartment? Is there something I should know, Lund?"

He groaned. "The restaurant was way behind with orders and I just got home. Come in, and pour yourself a glass of wine while I get changed. I set everything up on the dining room table."

I'd never been farther into his apartment than his living room. As I turned the corner, I realized his apartment was laid out differently than ours. The dining room was a separate area instead of a part of the kitchen. Out the sliding glass door, a balcony ran the length of the kitchen and overlooked the pool. I opened the wine and noticed only one glass. Not that there was room for anything else on the table, as it appeared he'd ordered enough food from Emily's Lebanese Deli for ten people.

When he said, "All right," as he came up behind me, I jumped, sloshing wine all over my shirt and the floor.

"Shit. I'm sorry."

"Got paper towels right here." He tossed one on the floor and said, "See? No worries."

"Jensen. Maybe this was a bad idea."

Taking the glass of wine from my hand, he set it aside, moving in so close I couldn't see the tops of my feet, which I'd been staring at intently. Then he said, "Rowan. Look at me."

I tilted my head back and met his gaze. All I saw in his eyes was concern.

"What's going on? Why are you so jumpy?"

"I don't know. Maybe because this feels like a date, even when I know it's not."

His eyes searched mine and I couldn't look away. "Total honesty between us, okay?"

I nodded.

"I find you hot as fuck. You're smart, sexy and sassy and that pushes all the right buttons for me. But despite all that? There are a lot of things about you that make you exactly the type of woman I *don't* date. So go change shirts and get back here to have dinner with me—as friends. Okay?"

"Okay."

He grinned—that devastatingly wicked sexy grin that made female football fans' panties damp. "However, I will restrain myself from slapping you on the ass as I would my other *friends*."

"So noted."

"Hurry back. I'm starving."

In my bedroom I didn't even fret over which shirt to wear; I just grabbed one. I returned to Jensen's in under three minutes.

He'd already opened up all the containers and poured me another glass of wine. I noticed he'd gotten a beer for himself.

"Holy crap, Lund. Did you order the entire menu?"

He blushed. "I didn't know what you like. So yeah, I think I got one of everything." He pointed at the offerings. "Dolmathes—stuffed grape leaves—chicken kabob, kafta kabob, hummus, spinach pie, baba ghannuj, mistah bread, Lebanese chicken and rice, Lebanese green beans, lentils and rice, kibbi—kinda like meatloaf—and tabbouleh. I burn a lot of calories, so I need a lot of calories. Trust me. None of this will go to waste."

"This looks great. I haven't had Emily's in ages. I used to eat there all the time when I was in college. Sadly, Calder isn't a fan."

"I wasn't either at his age. Tastes change."

"I try to expose him to different foods. It's funny to watch parents who attempt to 'develop' their kids' palate by feeding them oddball foods at a young age. Those same kids skip the veggie trays and devour chicken nuggets and fries at birthday parties when their parents aren't around."

"My brother and his wife are having their first kid in a few months. It'll be interesting to see how they deal with stuff like that."

As we ate, he talked about his family. Made me happy to hear he was close with his siblings as well as his cousins. For as different as Martin and I were personality-wise, we'd made a point to stay close and I counted him as one of my best friends.

"So did you have the idyllic life growing up in a Minnesota apple orchard? Or were you one of those who couldn't wait to peel out as soon as you turned eighteen?"

I groaned. "Peel out? Seriously?"

He laughed. "I love puns and that was sort of a gimme."

"True. But no more," I warned.

"Damn. Next one lined up was to ask if you were the apple of your daddy's eye." He smirked. "Yeah, I know, I'm the guy who always reaches for the low-hanging fruit."

I held up my hand. "Lund. Stop."

"I'm done. Answer the question."

"I had a great childhood. My parents are awesome. They never pushed me to do anything except my best. Sounds clichéd but it's true. Dad inherited the farm from his grandfather and their orchards were certified organic—before it was cool to focus on organic farming methods. So we were raised left of center but we weren't ostracized for it. My folks never expected me to stick around, but I wouldn't be surprised if when Martin decides to settle down he goes back there and takes over for my dad."

"Really?"

"It's a perfect setup for him. He can grow his own and still take on web design clients because there's not a lot to do in the winter months." I shoved my plate aside and decided to start boxing up leftovers, when I noticed there weren't any. The man had put away a serious amount of food and he was staring longingly at the brownies. "You want yours now?"

"Yes. Man, I love homemade brownies." He brought the garbage can over, sweeping everything into the trash in one fell swoop.

Guess that was one way to clear a table.

Jensen returned with a gallon of whole milk and two glasses. "Want some?"

"Half a glass."

"Then you should only get half a brownie. It's sacrilegious not to enjoy them with milk."

"Who told you that?"

"My grandpa Jensen. He lives in Sweden and the man is serious about his sweets. No coffee or tea with his *fika* or dessert. Just cold milk."

I smiled and cut my brownie, giving him half. "Far be it from me to buck a family tradition."

"Rowan, I was kidding—"

"No, I'm stuffed and I've had more than my fair share of brownies this week, so you enjoy."

"Thanks."

After I took a small bite and a swig of milk, I said, "You're named after your grandpa?"

"Jensen is his last name. When he's around, my family usually calls me Jens 'cause Gramps tends to answer if someone yells *Jensen*."

"I imagine so."

"This brownie is freakin' fantastic."

I poured myself more wine. "Thanks for buying dinner."

"Happy to have your company tonight." He frowned. "You don't have to rush off?"

"No. I can stay a little longer."

"Good. The couch is comfier than these chairs."

I carried my glass and the wine bottle into the living room. Jensen pulled the back section apart so I didn't have to climb over. "What is with you and this enormous couch? One might think you were overcompensating." *You did not just say that.*

Jensen granted me a sexy smile as he vaulted over the edge one handed. "Bigger is always better, baby."

I wouldn't know about that.

"The last place I lived, the interior designer chose a dinky-ass couch and two spindly chairs for a living room four times the size of this entire apartment. Some 'modern concept' that I stupidly agreed to because what do I know about interior design?"

When he blushed and ducked his head after admitting his ineptitude . . . heaven help me. It was so sweet and charming and humble.

"The furniture was too small for a guy my size. I spent all my time in my bedroom because at least I could stretch out on my big bed and watch TV. I swore the next place I lived I'd pick out furniture I wanted. Comfortable stuff so I wouldn't give a damn if beer or pizza got spilled on it. Who wants to live in a fucking museum? Not me. Not ever again."

"I figured with your salary you could live anywhere you wanted, so that's why I thought this wouldn't be your main residence."

"I hadn't realized how much I hated where I was living until after my injury and it felt like the same sterile environment as a hospital. Then I started hanging out here with Axl and got to know Martin. I discovered I was much happier and more myself in this place, so I moved in when Axl shacked up with Annika." He sighed. "Still haven't gotten the dog I wanted."

"What kind of dog?"

"Probably a mutt from the pound. A big mutt."

Sipping my wine, I wondered if I could ask him what I wanted to know, if he'd meant his insistence of honesty between us.

"Don't go quiet on me now, Coach. If you ask a question I don't want to answer, I won't."

"You were born rich and grew up in a mansion. A lavish lifestyle has to be the norm for you. Is this an experiment in how the common people live?"

He laughed—it wasn't a nice sound. "Wow. Okay. When

I introduce you to my parents you'll kick your own ass for the assumptions."

That startled me. Why would he want me to meet his parents?

"My family is grateful I'm not in an assisted-living facility because I was permanently paralyzed."

"I wasn't trying to be a dick, Jensen."

"I know. But that question is also why I don't invite many of my teammates to hang out here. They'd all be like . . . 'Man, why you slumming? Why'd you give up that sweet crib with the million-dollar river view for this dump?' I also get asked why I even take a salary. I could just play football for free. It's not like I need the money."

My jaw dropped. "People say that shit to you?"

"All the time."

"And then I had to go and ask an equally boneheaded question." I groaned. "I'm sorry."

"Par for the course. There is one way you can make it up to me—and no, dirty-minded girl, it doesn't entail sexual favors—although I'd be a fool to say no if you offered me a couple."

I rolled my eyes at his hopeful look. "Don't go dragging me into your impure thoughts. So how can I make it up to you?"

"By answering an equally invasive question."

I refilled my wineglass in preparation and Jensen laughed. I found myself smiling back. This was so much easier with him than I imagined. "Hit me with the question."

His face took on an appealing earnestness when he asked, "What's the deal with Calder's dad?"

"Short version? He knocked me up senior year and acted like I'd gotten pregnant on purpose to trap him."

"Trap him how?"

Here was the moment of truth. "He was a football player.

Big Ten All-Conference trophy winner as defensive player of the year. Defensive tackle predicted to go high in the NFL draft. We'd been dating since sophomore year and he broke up with me at the start of our last semester of college. A month later I found out I was pregnant."

"What did he do?"

"Said the baby wasn't his. Accused me of wanting a free ride and warned I'd need a court-ordered paternity test to ever get a nickel out of him."

"Jesus."

I closed my eyes and forced out the words that still left a bitter taste in my mouth. "I was on the pill, I never missed a dose. But the free clinic I'd gotten the pills from had received a bad batch that had been recalled by the drug manufacturer. Only the clinic hadn't gotten the memo about the recall. Big blowup in the national media because it happened at ten other clinics across the country. Anyway, I ended up with free prenatal medical care, free postnatal medical care, and pretty much free medical care for Calder and me at the clinic for as long as we live here."

"While that's the least they could've done for you, get back to the part of the story where the baby daddy justified abandoning you and his child."

The wine loosened my tongue. Normally I wasn't an oversharer, but here I was, spilling my guts to a guy who'd played on the same team as my ex.

"Rowan."

I met his gaze.

"I promise anything you tell me doesn't go beyond us."

"I appreciate that. It's just you . . ."

His eyes narrowed. "I know him, don't I? Or at least I know who he is."

I nodded.

"Does Calder know him?"

"No." I ran my finger over the rim of the wineglass. "Martin has always been a big part of Calder's life. So has my dad. Calder has healthy, loving, dependable relationships with them, so he's not missing male role models." I glanced up when Jensen remained quiet a beat too long. "What?"

His gaze searched my face. "I'm trying to come up with the least obnoxious way to phrase this question."

"Just ask it."

"Does the asswipe baby daddy pay child support?"

I shook my head.

"You know that's total bullshit. Even if he isn't involved in Calder's life, his damn checkbook should be. You shouldn't have to shoulder the entire financial burden of raising a child, Rowan. Not to mention everything else you have to do without help."

Why did I like that he'd gotten so fired up on my behalf?

Because there is a pull toward this man you can't deny.

When Jensen opened his mouth, I held up my hand. "Let me explain the timeline. I was five months pregnant during the NFL draft in April. We graduated in May and he moved to the city that'd drafted him. Calder was born in August during training camp. We had a standing order for a paternity test. When the results confirmed he'd fathered my baby, his lawyer offered me a onetime lump sum . . . with a stipulation."

Jensen snorted.

"Accepting the money cleared him of all future parental responsibilities, with the exception if Calder was diagnosed with some heinous disease. Then he'd pay for half of the medical treatments."

"How generous."

"It is what it is. My stipulation was that he has zero contact with Calder."

"He's abided by that?"

"Completely. If down the road he grows a conscience and wants to establish a relationship with Calder, all contact goes through a mediator. He'll never have unsupervised or random interactions with my son. It hasn't been an issue so far."

"Does he still have an NFL contract?"

"Yes. The two times his team played in Minnesota? I requested a bye week from the cheer squad and took Calder out of town."

"Good for you." Jensen gave me a soft smile. "I admire the fact that you don't take shit from anyone."

"Thanks."

"So I remember you saying you were living at Martin's temporarily while you looked for a house. Have you had any luck?"

Although grateful that he'd changed the subject—and hadn't asked for my ex's name—I couldn't help but tease him for the question. I lightly tapped my foot against his. "You're already sick of being my neighbor, Lund?"

His lean cheeks went red. "No! I just—"

"Jensen. I was kidding."

He knocked his foot into mine. "See if I borrow a cup of sugar from you. I'll head down and ask Lenka first."

"Lenka," I repeated. "The woman who lives in the last apartment before the exit to the stairs? Long black hair, pale skin and is rocking the vampire vibe?"

"You've met her?"

"Briefly. Why?"

"Did she offer you her oral expertise as a 'Welcome to Snow Village' gift?"

I choked on my wine. Then I studied him for a moment. "You're not joking."

"I wish I were."

"I imagine you're no stranger to offers like that."

Jensen shrugged. "I imagine a smokin'-hot professional cheerleader isn't a stranger to propositions either."

"You'd be wrong. No guy is interested in landing fifth on my list of life priorities."

"You have a list of 'life priorities'?"

"Yes. Don't you?" *Doesn't everyone?* hung in the air unspoken.

He laughed. Hard. Then he said, "My life motto is 'just wing it.'"

"Well, I'm not the type to wing it. My life revolves around lists."

"So let me see if I can put your life list in order. Obviously Calder is first. Work is second. Training—cheer, et cetera is third. Dating is . . . fifth? What happened to slot four?"

"That's for friends. It's a short list so it deserves its own slot. Besides, I can't even remember the last date I had." It didn't matter if Jensen knew this about me; we'd already established a friendship line.

"None of the meathead college guys who train at the athletic center have hit on you?" he said skeptically.

"Sure they have. I ignore them. If they get persistent, I impart my dating rule and they back off because they realize the futility of even trying."

"What rule is that?"

"I don't date athletes."

"Seriously?"

"Seriously. It's ironclad. No exceptions."

He cocked his head. "Meaning . . . you don't date college athletes. To avoid the potential conflict of teacher/student involvement?"

"No, I mean no athletes. Doesn't matter if he's an ama-

teur, a pro, a competitor in the senior games or in the Para-
lympics. No athletes. Period."

"Harsh stance, Ro."

Ro. I liked his use of my family nickname as much as
I'd liked him calling me Coach Michaels. I shrugged. "Once
burned . . . one thousand times smarter."

"While I understand your logic, and the egotistical part
of me wants to demand a chance to change your mind about
athletes—football players in particular—I'm not the guy to
take up the challenge." Jensen smiled and held out his beer
bottle for a toast. "It's a good thing we're sticking to being
friends, Coach."

I touched my wineglass to his bottle. "Very good thing,
Lund."

"So . . . *friend*. Wanna watch a movie with me?"

"Only if it has lots of gratuitous violence and sex, an
abundance of dirty words and explosions . . . and not a
single animated character."

Jensen snatched the remote. "*Deadpool* it is."

S omehow, I ended up spending Saturday night hanging
out with Jensen too.

Friday night after I learned he had excellent taste in movies, we swapped cell numbers. On Saturday afternoon when
I'd gotten a break to check my phone, I saw two text messages from him.

**JL: Movie nite part 2. Have you seen the latest Judd
Apatow flick?**

JL: Or *Transformers*?

I texted him back.

Me: You can find something better than those! I'll be
done around 8.

He responded immediately.

JL: Picky woman. Fine. Nothing cool. Just knock.

I didn't show up until nine.

He asked me how tryouts went, as if he was genuinely
interested.

This friendly neighbor thing with him . . . I liked it. A
lot. He wasn't an egomaniac—we didn't discuss his football
career. I didn't talk incessantly about my son. We just jok-
ingly bickered and had normal, adult conversation. I couldn't
even compare it to hanging out with Daisy. With Daisy I
wasn't distracted by things like massive flexing muscles, a
deep, masculine laugh and dimples bracketing a perfect pair
of full, smiling lips.

Yes, Jensen Lund was one hundred percent prime alpha
male and one hundred thousand percent off-limits.

Although he'd slip in sexual innuendo given the chance,
it caused me to roll my eyes, not feel creeped out like with
some guys. He had no problem voicing his opinions or questioning mine. I liked his oddball sense of humor. Every once
in a while I'd get a glimpse of his cockiness, but not as much
as I'd expected from a man like him who literally had it
all—and what he didn't have he could buy.

My level of comfort with him was such that I conked out
during the movie.

Rough-skinned fingers caressing my cheek roused me. I
awoke to see Jensen stretched out a mere foot away—not on
the opposite side of the couch where he'd started the evening.

His lips curved into a sinful smile. "I hated to wake you,
but woman, you snore like a bulldog. There's no way I could

catch up on my beauty sleep with that racket, so I hafta toss your cute butt outta my crib."

I snickered. "Catch up on your beauty sleep? I oughta do womankind a favor and keep you up all damn night, because the last thing you need is to look better than you do right now." As soon as the words fell from my mouth, I chastised myself. I started to blame my lapse in judgment on sleep brain, but he reached out and gently placed his finger across my lips.

"Don't." His eyes had lost their teasing sparkle and burned with intensity. "Don't take it back or explain it away. Let me have that one thing from you tonight."

Not what I'd been expecting at all.

But Jensen didn't back away. Instead he feathered his thumb across my lips. "You'd better go before I give you a reason to stay."

He moved his hand when I started to speak. "Cocky much?"

"Only when it's warranted. I'm very good at two things that begin with the letter *F*, Ro. The first is football. The second . . . doesn't have a damn thing to do with being friends." He bestowed that dimpled grin on me. "I'll leave that one to your imagination." He rolled across the couch and did the one-armed dismount thing. Then he offered me his hand.

"Pass."

"Don't be suspicious of my motives, *friend*."

"You flatter yourself. My leg fell asleep and if I tried to stand right now I'd fall at your feet, and dude, I'd never live *that* one down."

Jensen laughed. "I never know what the hell is gonna come out of that sassy, sexy mouth of yours. That's why I had a great time hanging out with you this weekend, Coach."

The pins-and-needles feeling had subsided, allowing me to scramble over the edge of the couch. "Back atcha, Lund."

"So we'll do it again sometime?"

"Sure." I didn't know what else to say so I left it at that.

Jensen stood in the doorway and watched as I unlocked the door to my apartment.

I turned and said, "Good night, Jens."

"Sweet dreams, sweetheart. See you soon."

Seven

JENSEN

After spending two nights hanging out with Rowan Michaels, I knew exactly why Martin hadn't mentioned his sister.

She wasn't my type.

She was nothing like the easy chicks that vied for my attention.

Nothing.

I liked blondes.

She had fiery red hair.

I avoided confrontational women.

Rowan slamming the door in my face the very first time we met should've irritated the piss out of me. Her dressing me down in front of my trainer—the very next day—should've reinforced the not-your-type mantra.

Instead of going with my usual response of blowing the whole thing off, I'd bought her an apology gift.

The next afternoon I'd shown up at her place of employment—in disguise, nothing stalkerish about that.

I'd given her a mini backrub. In public no less.

Then I'd demanded she have dinner with me. And stay to watch a movie.

The following night, I insisted we watch another movie together. She showed up late, bitched about my movie choice, complained about my microwave-popcorn-making skills. Which led to more arguing, more teasing, more laughing and a popcorn fight.

Then we both rather innocently fell asleep on my couch.

Not an innocent thing on my mind when I woke up and saw her lying next to me, softer, more beautiful than ever relaxed in slumber. She looked as if she belonged there.

I had no idea what was happening to me.

I liked—no, I loved—my solitude.

In the year I'd lived in the apartment, I'd had my sister over twice, my mom over three times and my sisters-in-law over once. Other women? Never.

In the four days I'd known Rowan? She'd been over to my house every single day.

Four times in four days.

I'd known her four days and I couldn't get her out of my mind. That curvy little body, that brusque attitude, that sneaky, sexy smile.

It was perfectly normal to think about shoving my hands into that flaming red hair, staring into those expressive hazel eyes as I took those lush lips in a deep soul kiss, right?

Yes.

Jesus, Jensen. Justify much?

Logically I wanted her because I couldn't have her.

Rowan Michaels broke every single one of my dating rules.

Every.

Single.

One.

So it was a good thing we'd come to an agreement. Just friends. Nothing more.

And yet it made zero sense that I'd Googled Rowan's asshole baby daddy within five minutes of her leaving my place that first night. Somehow I'd convinced myself I needed this information about her and Calder since we were neighbors.

It wasn't that hard to figure out the douchebag's name, since only five guys had gotten drafted from U of M into the NFL during my undergrad years.

Me.

Ryan Rickhert. Center for the Browns.

LaShawn King. Running back for the Titans.

They were both offensive players—and African American—which put them out of contention.

Bart Kuehn. Safety for the Buccaneers. Not exactly the big-ass defensive guy Rowan had described.

That left one guy.

Hardy Morell—nicknamed "Hardly Moral"—the asswipe defensive tackle who had a rep for playing dirty on and off the field.

I couldn't imagine beautiful, smart, feisty Rowan putting up with blowhard Hardy, or the stuff he'd bragged about doing with coeds. Some of which I'd seen him doing firsthand, much to my complete disgust—then and now.

But even I could admit that things that happened in college didn't necessarily define a person for the long term. So I might've given him the benefit of the doubt . . . had I not known Hardy was the same dirtbag cheater in the NFL that he'd been in college.

He led the league the past six years in penalties. Last

year he'd gotten suspended the last two games of the regular season thanks to an illegal late hit that sent a Ravens running back to the hospital.

So what kind of man had he become off the gridiron after he'd abandoned his pregnant college girlfriend?

A DUI his rookie year.

Fines for nearly every pro game he'd played.

Ejected from the neighborhood where he lived in Jacksonville for repeatedly breaking the morality clause in his homeowner's association by throwing ABC (anything but clothes) parties at the community pool house.

He'd been romantically linked with a female sportscaster from ESPN. Then with a *Sports Illustrated* swimsuit model. Then with Miss Florida. It appeared that he was the same partying frat boy.

No doubt Rowan and Calder were better off without him.

But ultimately, I understood the real reason that Martin hadn't mentioned his sister: He'd put me in the same category as Hardy Morell.

But the only thing I cared about was that Rowan didn't put me in the same category.

Because we were friends.

Keep telling yourself that, buddy.

Sunday morning I was tempted to blow off my workout. But I figured there'd be great brunch food at Uncle Archer and Aunt Edie's house and I'd rather feast guilt-free.

No surprise I wasn't the only player at the training facility. Throughout my injury season I'd kept up my training— as much as my condition allowed. The roster changed every year with the exception of the guys considered franchise players. That term had been applied loosely to me, not because I was an irreplaceable key player, but because if my injury was deemed career ending, I would have spent my NFL career with the Vikings franchise.

Not exactly the type of franchise player I'd hoped to be.

"Hey, Rocket, whatcha doin' here, man?" Devonte asked, pulling me out of my brooding.

"Hoping to learn from you the secrets about becoming a two-time Pro Bowler—despite your rep for being a slacker."

He grunted. "Just for that, I'm gonna deadlift you, smart-ass."

A chorus of *oohs* rang out.

Mitchell, the third-string tight end, moved in beside me and placed his hand on my shoulder. "Think that's his way of calling you dead weight, Rocket?"

"Probably. I can't outlift you, D, but I sure can outrun you."

"You sure?" Devonte switched the toothpick in his mouth from the left to the right side. "You ain't been runnin' *any* sprints as far as I've seen or heard."

"Maybe I'm waiting for the right time to show off my improved technique."

"Or maybe you lost your mojo," Richards, the cocky cornerback, yelled from the end of the bench.

I flipped him off despite the uncomfortable tightening in my stomach.

"What areas were you planning to work today, Lund?"

"Chest and arms. Abs. Balance ball. Why?"

Devonte's composure remained cool. "Because there's a change in plans."

"Yeah? Says who?"

"Says me." He flashed those pretty pearly whites. "Soon as you're warmed up with cardio? You're runnin' a dash check."

I started to say, "Try and make me," but as I inventoried the room—eight of us in all—I realized I had no choice.

Jesus. My protein shake threatened to come back up. It

was one thing to worry about failing on my own; it was another thing to fail in front of a damn crowd.

"Ain't no one here gonna blab the results to the front office," Devonte assured me.

Wrong. Either way what happened on the track wouldn't stay on the track.

Reckoning day had arrived.

"Whatever. Give me twenty to warm up."

"I'll warm up with you," Mitchell offered.

Yeah, they were making sure I couldn't sneak out. "Sure."

Most guys tuned out the world during cardio. I didn't listen to music or podcasts or audiobooks. Instead I focused on the cadence of my steps on the treadmill as I started out slowly and gradually picked up the pace. When I hit the full-run stage, I focused on my breath and keeping my body loose.

Mitchell turned everything into a competition with me— or at least he tried to. Whenever I sped up, so would he. If I wasn't concentrating on form I'd fuck with him just because he'd expect me to.

Ten minutes into the warm-up, I did a quick mental inventory. Heart rate good. Respiration rate good. Pace . . . faster than normal. Just a twinge of pain in my knee. No pain or strain in my Achilles. No tension in my shoulder— either the right or the left. Jaw relaxed. Abs tight; hands loose. Today my body felt more in tune physically than I had in several weeks since before my checkup. I took that as a positive sign that I was up to the task of pushing myself just a little further.

I kept up the full-out running pace for six more minutes and used the last four minutes to cool down. When the machine shut off, I snagged a towel, mopped my face and headed to the track.

Several guys were parked on the turf "stretching"—aka

sitting on their asses pretending to work out as they waited for the show to start. They eyed me with speculation and I literally had to shake off the fear pulling my guts into knots. I rolled to the balls of my feet and bounced a couple of times. First, arms above my head as if I were trying to launch myself into the sky. Then I jumped and pulled my knees into my chest.

"Do the running-man dance move next," Richards called out behind me.

A spinning back kick to his jaw would shut him up, but I knew better than to take a chance with a twisting maneuver—even in jest.

I wandered over to the stretch of the track where three lanes were marked off for the forty-yard dash. Thoughtful that Devonte had supplied me with a starting block. If I saw him holding a starter pistol, going "thug life" on me, I'd be laughing too damn hard to run. The massive African American defensive end might act like he'd just wandered out of an urban housing project, but the man's family owned a multimillion-dollar shipping company that stretched along the East Coast from South Carolina to Maine.

"You ready, White Bread?"

I snorted. That wasn't a racist comment. My wise-ass friend called me White Bread because the Lund family had gotten its business start in the grain and flour milling industry. I grinned at him. "Just watch the damn timer, Black Sails."

Devonte leaned closer. "Getcha head in the game, brother. We got us a few gate crashers."

"My head is there, D. Let's hope my body is."

He nodded. "Hit the block. Leon is timing you."

Good. That way there'd be no accusations that Devonte had rigged the timer.

I addressed my teammates standing around. "Do I get one shot at this? Or you gonna let me run it more than once?"

Bob "Bebo" Johnson, one of the special teams' trainers I hadn't noticed, stepped forward. "You gotta run it three times, Rocket. A ninety-second break between heats. There's a block at the other end and Ray-Ray is timing you from down there. He'll cue you when your break is over and when to line up."

"Cool." I took a swig from the bottle of water Mitchell held out to me. "You gonna announce my official time after each run?"

"Up to you," Bebo said.

Giving him my trademark cocky grin, I sang, "Shout it, shout it, shout it out loud," complete with air guitar.

Laughter echoed around me.

"Hit the block, smart-ass."

As soon as I got into position, my focus became absolute. I willed my body to work, to do the job I'd spent years training it for. This time it wasn't about anything but speed.

I heard the crack of the starter pistol and I was up and gone. Arms pumping, legs churning, heart racing, eyes homed in on the finish line. I blew past Ray-Ray and kept going another ten feet. I rested my hands on my knees to catch my breath for a moment, waiting to hear my time. The run had felt fast. But at this point *felt* didn't mean squat.

Ray-Ray shouted, "Four point nine seven, Rocket."

Fuck. That was too damn slow. My team record was 4.59 my rookie year—which was the same forty-yard dash time as our star running back.

What did I need to change?

React no differently than when you've got the ball in your hand. Burst of speed at the beginning to deflect the defense; additional burst at the end to score.

"Fifteen seconds, Rocket," Ray-Ray said.

I dropped into the starting block.

You got this. Nothing hurts, hit it hard.

The pistol went off and so did I. My existence boiled down to the air billowing in and out of my lungs, my steps eating up the blacktop and the fast thud of my heartbeat in my ears.

Whoosh, right past Devonte and Leon.

Leon yelled, "Four point seven four seconds!"

Okay. Better. That'd been my preinjury speed average for all four seasons.

I cranked my neck side to side. Swung my arms around. Did a couple of vertical jumps.

"Fifteen seconds," Leon warned me.

One more. That's it. I blew out a long exhale as I set my feet in the block. Head up, eyes on the prize, body pumped with adrenaline.

Same drill. Put those motherfucking doubts to rest for the last time today.

It seemed my feet barely touched the ground after the pistol popped and I was racing past Ray-Ray.

I spun around.

Ray-Ray whooped. "The Rocket is back! That last run was four point six two, my man!"

I quickly did the math in my head. That averaged out to 4.77—which was an excellent percentage for a guy my size with my recovery history. Chances were good with more sprint training I could lower it by a tenth of a second.

Almost before I could catch my breath I had teammates surrounding me, clapping me on the back, slapping my ass.

Bebo gave me a chin dip and returned to texting on his phone.

One guess that he wasn't in contact with his wife at this time on a Sunday morning.

But I couldn't be unhappy about it.

"Word's gonna get out about this, White Bread," Devonte said.

"If it had gone the other way?"

He shrugged. "Word still would've gotten out. The front office knows how to spin. Let's just be glad this is one thing they ain't gotta put a shine on. The shine is all you, Rocket."

And it'd keep the media's interest off some of the other stories we'd managed to keep on the down-low.

"Now that you've proven you still got prime jet fuel in those legs, let's hit the weight room."

I must've mixed up the times for the brunch because the servers were tearing down the buffet when I arrived. I managed to heap two plates with food and considered my mother's point about me needing an assistant to keep track of this kind of stuff because apparently I sucked at it.

My sister and her husband, Axl, joined me.

"What's your excuse this time?" Annika asked.

"Work."

"Work?"

"My job as a football player, remember? I got cornered to run the forty-yard dash. Nothing I could do but do it."

"And?" Axl said.

"Three runs averaged four point seven seven, so not bad."

"Jens, that's great and you know it," Annika said.

I gave her a fist bump. "Training has paid off. So what'd I miss here?"

Annika started listing family members. "Let's see . . . Lucy dropped Mimi off and things were tense between her and Jax. Nolan showed up with flavor of the week and I swear she's barely legal."

I glanced over at the pink-haired chick wearing a leopard print bodysuit, clinging to Nolan like he was catnip.

"Ash," Annika continued, "I don't know why he's not here. Walker and Trinity left right after we ate because

Walker is psycho about Trinity getting enough rest. Brady and Lennox are playing lord and lady of the manor up at the cabin. And Dallas . . ." Annika exchanged a look with Axl. "She was here briefly but she bailed because she's having a rough go of it."

"Why? I saw her Friday and she seemed fine."

"She is fine when no one brings up Iron Man." Annika's gaze narrowed. "Which I assume you didn't do since you were too busy ogling cheerleader boobs and butts during team tryouts at the U of M."

Naturally Dallas had blabbed about that to my sister. "Did she tell you I was there strictly in an educational capacity?"

"She mentioned it—not that I believed her. Anyway, today as soon as she saw Axl, she started grilling him on whether he'd heard anything from Igor."

"How long has it been since anyone has mentioned him by name?" Iron Man was our lame code for Igor, the Russian hockey player.

"Months. So I want to know . . ."

My mind drifted as Annika kept chattering. Igor had been a teammate of Axl's with the Minnesota Wild. Right after the start of last year's season, a death in Igor's family sent him back to Russia for the funeral. But while he was there, an issue arose with his work visa. No one in the government could explain why his visa had been revoked. No one in the United States had heard from him, and no one could get in touch with his family; it was as if he'd disappeared. Not even the NHL legal department had the power to cut through the bureaucracy. The government agencies they'd reached out to didn't have answers or plain hadn't answered.

In the third month with no word about his whereabouts, our normally upbeat cousin had become inconsolable because she could no longer "feel" Igor's presence on this earthly realm. My aunt and uncle freaked out when Dallas went off the rails, ranting about gypsy curses, conspiracy theories and the power of the Russian mob. Then she crawled into bed and refused to eat, refused to shower, refused to leave her room. After two weeks of feeling helpless, her older brother Ash had run interference, tasking Annika to track down a specialized spiritual spa. Then she, Axl and Ash had convinced Dallas to check in to realign her chakras, reset her aura, or immerse herself in whatever woo-woo type of healing she needed to return to being our sweet, kooky, loving cousin.

It'd worked. It'd taken two months, but she'd returned to the Lund Collective back to normal—well, normal for Dallas. Although she'd graduated from college almost a year ago, she'd yet to choose a career path—even when a job waited for her at Lund Industries. But given the big mess with Igor's disappearance, no one had pushed her to make any decisions about her future.

"Jens," Annika said sharply.

My gaze snapped to hers. "Sorry. What did you say?"

"I asked why you're so interested in Rowan Michaels."

I looked over my shoulder. "Keep it down. You want Mom hauling ass over here?"

"Why? Do you have something to hide?" she shot back.

"No, but apparently Martin did. I had no idea that he even had a sister." My focus moved to Axl. "Did you?"

"Yah. But I didn't know she cheered for the Vikings."

"She's the hot redhead with the killer body and the huge"—Annika grinned—"smile."

I met her gaze. "Even you know who she is?"

"Only because you had zero playing time last year. Watching the cheerleaders was more entertaining than watching the game." She swigged her beer. "Is she giving you a hard time?"

"For not remembering that we'd met before under other circumstances? Yeah, you could say that."

Axl laughed. "Poor footballer. Pretty woman moves in *right* across from you and you cannot do anything but . . . drool all over that rule book you're so proud of."

"Piss off, puck-tard."

"Rowan is totally hot in that 'I'm super limber and can crack your head like a walnut between my muscular thighs' kind of way that all dudes totally dig."

I leaned in closer to my sister. "Are you drunk?"

"Don't tell me you weren't secretly watching her perform the Rockette kick line at the home games last season and fantasizing about having her ankle by your head as you—"

Axl put his mouth on her ear, cutting off her stream-of-consciousness rambling.

I didn't even want to know what he'd whispered that'd made her blush that hard. I left the table but I doubted they noticed.

The afternoon had been low-key for a Lund gathering.

I spent time talking cars with my dad and we made plans to meet at our usual private racetrack. His vintage 1967 Corvette was no match for my ZR1, but that didn't keep him from trying to whip my ass several times over the summer.

By the time I returned to my apartment complex it was almost dinnertime.

Exhausted, I took the elevator to the second floor, rather than the stairs.

In the hallway, Calder's voice gave him away before he turned the corner. Out of instinct I twisted my pelvis to protect my balls.

Calder wasn't alone. He held the hand of a man with long silver hair pulled into a ponytail. The dark red flannel worn over a pair of overalls provided a better hint of his identity.

Just then Calder noticed me. "Hey!"

"Hey yourself. Whatcha been up to?"

"I was at Grammy and Pop-pop's farm."

I walked toward them. "I figured you were gone, it was far too quiet around here. No one running in the hallway playing ninja-samurai."

"Know what? I met some kids in the other building."

"Yeah? That's cool you'll have kids to play with this summer."

"If Mommy lets me."

Calder leaned his head against the man's side, as if he had a sudden bout of shyness.

The man stared at me hard and kept a protective hand on Calder's shoulder.

I offered my hand. "Jensen Lund. I'm betting you're Rowan's father."

He harrumphed but he shook my hand—more like he crushed it. "Michael Michaels."

"It's good to meet you, sir. I've lived here for over a year so I'm friends with Martin too."

He continued to size me up. "I know who you are, son. I've been a Vikings fan since I was Calder's age."

"It's good to hear that kind of team loyalty. It's a rarity."

"Loyalty and integrity are the two most important attributes a man can possess."

Calder tugged on his shirt and peered up at him. "What's in-teg-rity, Pop-pop?"

Integrity was not kissing the hell out of your sexy-as-sin mother last night.

Or maybe that was willpower.

I must've made a derisive noise because the next thing I knew, Michael Michaels aimed his piercing gaze at me. "Maybe The Rocket can explain integrity."

No pressure.

I crouched down in front of Calder. "Let's say you're goofing around outside throwing rocks and you accidentally throw one too hard. It breaks a window and the person who lives in the apartment isn't home. No one saw you do it, so no one would ever know that *you* broke the window so you'd be tempted to keep it a secret."

He blinked those big brown eyes at me.

"But if you tell your mom you did it—"

"She'll make me apologize and accept the consequences," he blurted out.

"Exactly. Integrity means telling the truth even if you're afraid of the consequences. It means doing the right thing, even if it's the hardest thing."

Calder glanced at his grandpa as if he didn't believe me.

Michael Michaels made an affirmative grunt. "Happy to see you have a brain and aren't just jock-stock."

"Ask me about incidents leading up to the Civil War and I can impress you with specific dates. Only time my history degree comes in handy."

"I'm a history buff too."

"Yeah? Any particular time period?"

"Lately? The Roman Empire."

Then we were just two history geeks going on about books and maps and all the details I hadn't paid attention to until college. A history degree—not a teaching history degree—was pretty worthless. But once I'd discovered history wasn't only found in dry, dusty tomes in a library, I couldn't be dissuaded from making it my major.

Calder became bored during the conversation and raced up and down the hallway. Or he danced and twirled. Or he attempted cartwheels and handstands. He wasn't loud, just energetic. I remembered having unlimited energy as a boy. Why walk someplace when you could run? Or skip?

Calder only shouted, "Pop-pop! Watch this!" one time when he performed a full-out run that ended in him leaping into the air and landing soft as a cat in front of us.

"You nailed that landing. Good job."

The door to Rowan's apartment opened and a tall woman stepped out. She stopped and looked at me curiously. A smattering of freckles spread across her high cheekbones and regal nose, laugh lines creased the corners of her mouth and her eyes—the exact same color as Rowan's and Martin's. But her most arresting feature besides her smile? The shoulder-length dreads that looked like thick black ropes wrapped with silver.

Without thinking, I said to Michael, "Holy hell, man, now I see who Rowan inherited her stunning looks from."

Luckily, he didn't take offense. He chuckled. "Her mama's still something, ain't she?"

"Yes, sir, she is."

Then she sauntered forward and offered a slender, callused hand. "I heard that flattery, Jensen Lund. You are every bit as handsome as I've been warned about. I'm Rochelle Michaels."

I grinned at her. Then at Rowan, scowling at me behind her mother's back. "Very pleased to meet you. Sorry for staring, but I imagine a woman who looks like you is used to it."

"Oh my. And you're just as charming to boot."

Calder jumped in front of me. "Guess where we're going?"

"To play glow-in-the-dark mini golf?"

He giggled. "No. Guess again!"

"To an all-you-can-eat ice cream shop?"

Another giggle. I shot a quick look to Rowan. The soft,

sweet, loving smile when she looked at her son gave me a funny feeling, which made no sense.

"Nope!" Calder said, grabbing my attention again. "We're going to Chuck E. Cheese!"

"Fun. Sometimes your uncle Martin and I went to Dave and Buster's."

"Where they don't limit you to two beers all night," Michael said under his breath.

Rochelle elbowed him. "If you don't have plans, Jensen, you're welcome to come along."

"Thanks for the invite, but I spent all afternoon with my family. This morning I hit it hard at the training center, so I'll be parked on my couch the rest of the night recuperating."

"The team is already training?" Michael said. "Thought that wasn't until the end of July."

I recognized he was a true football fan. "Special circumstances for me, as you can guess, given my injury. Had to run the forty today. Three times."

"How'd you do? If you don't mind me askin'?"

"You'll probably see it in the paper tomorrow, but my average was four point seven seven."

"Damn, son. That's great."

"It felt good."

"Pop-pop, come *on*. I'm starved," Calder complained. "You said we were going like *two* hours ago."

He ruffled his grandson's hair. "We're goin'. Nice meeting you, Lund."

"You too." I looked at Rowan, to see her looking at me. Same odd tickle—but this time it wasn't only in my belly.

"Dad, you and Mom go ahead," Rowan said. "You have to take Calder's car seat out anyway. I'll be right there."

I rested against my apartment door, waiting for us to be alone. After I heard the elevator ding, I said, "So you think I'm charming?"

Rowan crossed her arms over her chest. "My *mom* thinks you're charming."

"But I bet she heard it from you, ergo, *you* think I'm charming, Coach."

"Full of yourself much, Lund?"

You'd like to be full of me, sweetheart. And I'd enjoy every hot second filling you up.

I didn't say that out loud; I didn't have to. The blush spreading across Rowan's cheeks hinted that she'd been sidelined by the same thought.

"Without further feeding your ego . . . I have something for you."

"You talked to your mom about me. My ego can take the rest of the night off."

Rowan laughed. "You are unbelievable. Stay there. I'll grab it before I go."

She wasn't gone long. She handed me a plate wrapped in foil. "I baked brownies for Calder's lunches this week. I had extra. I know you liked the other ones I brought over. So . . . enjoy."

"Seriously?" That was really sweet. "This is awesome. Thanks."

"You're welcome."

I didn't say anything flip. I was genuinely touched by her thoughtfulness.

"I've gotta go." She walked backward down the hallway—so I wouldn't ogle her ass?

Dammit. I had to be more discreet about that.

"I'll want my plate back, Lund."

And that was how the five-day streak of seeing Rowan Michaels stretched into ten days.

Monday night, I "borrowed" a cup of milk for my brownies. Which I then ate at Rowan's table with her and Calder.

Tuesday the window in Calder's bedroom had gotten

stuck. Rowan asked if I could use my ridiculous amount of muscles for something useful and get it unstuck. I probably would've taken my shirt off—I'd seen the woman eyeballing my chest the first time we'd met—if her son hadn't been around.

Wednesday I returned the plate. After I knew Calder had gone to bed. That garnered me an invitation to come in for coffee. Then Rowan and I ended up talking for an hour, not really noticing that both of our cups had gone cold.

Thursday Rowan and Calder stuck around and asked questions about my Corvette as I polished it after I'd spent the afternoon at the racetrack with my dad.

Even though Friday morning dawned gray, cold and chilly I looked forward to how the weekend would play out. And how much Rowan Michaels would play a part in it.

Eight

***

ROWAN

M y head pounded.

I was soaked to the skin from the late-afternoon cloudburst.

My arms felt encased in concrete as I overloaded myself with grocery bags so I didn't have to make two trips from the car to my apartment. The elevator doors opened and I managed to poke the number two with my elbow.

As the car ascended, I closed my eyes to block out the elevator's reflection of the bedraggled woman staring back at me.

I needed wine. As soon as I changed into dry clothes and put the groceries away, I'd pour a glass or three to chase away the wet chill sinking into my bones.

I'd made it half the length of the hallway when Jensen stepped out of his apartment. The rustling of grocery bags alerted him to my presence and he glanced up.

"Hold on a second and let me help you." Jensen started toward me.

"It'd be a huge help if you could just open the door to my apartment, please."

He darted across the hall and knocked twice on my door before opening it. Then he said, "Stand back, incoming with supplies," through the open doorway.

Calder and Alicia gaped at me as I hustled into the kitchen, near collapse from the weight of all the bags. Or maybe my straggly appearance caused their alarm. My clothes were dripping. Even my shoes were squishing, courtesy of the ankle-deep water I'd stepped into in the grocery store parking lot.

When I straightened up, I noticed Jensen frowning at me. Before I could snap off "What?" he loomed over me.

"Are you all right?"

"I'm fine."

He said, "You should've let me carry the bags."

"I had it under control."

His gaze did a head-to-toe sweep before he cocked an eyebrow at me as if to say *Oh really?*

I knew that I resembled a wet cat—not a look Mr. Tall, Blond and Muscled ever suffered from. I bet Jensen would look magnificent wet. Water zigzagging down the muscles in his chest until the droplets funneled into the grooves of his eight-pack abs. Or the stream of water diverted to that deeply cut V starting at his pelvis.

"Uh, Rowan?"

Evidently my brain had gotten waterlogged; a naked and wet Jensen Lund should not have been foremost on my mind.

I glanced over at Alicia. "Sorry I'm late. I know you have to go. I hope you brought an umbrella."

She flashed a sympathetic smile. "This time of year I stash one in my car and one in my backpack."

"Smart girl."

Her gaze flicked to Jensen, then back to me. "Do you need me to stay until you get settled?"

"Thanks, but no. I'll be fine once I get out of these wet clothes. Have a good weekend and I'll see you Monday."

As soon as she was out the door, Jensen said, "Calder, buddy, could you grab a couple of towels for your mom?"

"Sure!" He raced off.

I tried to peel my trench coat off but it was plastered to my arms. I tugged on one sleeve and the sodden fabric didn't budge an inch. Plus, it didn't help that my hands were freezing and I couldn't get a decent grip.

"Let me do it," Jensen said.

"I'm f-fine—"

"Stop." Warm hands framed my face, and then Jensen tilted my head back. His fiery blue eyes bored into mine. "Suck it up and accept that I *am* helping you."

His big, rough-skinned hands slipped down my throat to the base of my neck. Grabbing the lapels of my coat, he jerked with enough force to get it off on the first try.

Of course he's practiced at getting a woman out of her clothes, my pride remarked snarkily.

Then Calder bumped into me and thrust two towels at him. "Here."

"How about you help her dry off while I hang up her coat." Jensen disappeared around the corner.

After handing me a towel, Calder dropped to the floor and mopped up puddles with the other one.

Tears sparked in my eyes. He was six years old. He shouldn't be cleaning up after me. When he looked up and saw my tears, he said, "Mommy, why are you crying?"

"Because I'm lucky to have such a sweet, helpful boy."

"And because she's cold," Jensen inserted. "So I think your mom needs to take a hot bath. While she's doing that, we can put away the groceries. If there's time left over, we could hang out and watch TV." He waited until I looked at him. "How's that sound, Mom?"

Like heaven.

"I know where everything goes," Calder announced. "But I'm not supposed to climb on the counters."

"Luckily I'm tall enough to reach the top of all the cupboards in here."

"Don't worry about it. I can do it after—"

"Mommy, your shoes are leaking," Calder blurted out.

"Shoot. I'll just—"

"Hang on to me while Calder takes off your shoes." I started to protest, but Jensen was right there, his mouth on my ear. "Let him help."

Grudgingly I leaned against Jensen, trying not to get him wet and lifted my right foot. Calder tugged hard on my slip-on athletic flat.

Water squished out.

After the left shoe was off, Jensen said, "Can you sneak those wet shoes in the closet, ninja-boy?"

"Yeah. They kinda smell bad."

I glanced over to see Calder wrinkling his nose and holding my shoes at arm's length as if they were coated in skunk oil.

Then Jensen leaned in to speak softly to me once more. "Do you trust me with your son?"

Jensen had been friendly to Calder this week—not in a pandering way, which I appreciated. I nodded.

Relief crossed his face. "Go take care of yourself. Warm up, relax. I'll be out here if you need anything."

"You don't have plans tonight?"

"Nope."

My eyes narrowed on him. "Then where were you going when you left your apartment and saw me in the hallway?"

A sheepish grin tipped his lips. "To knock on your door to see if you and Calder were up for ordering in pizza."

That sweet smile and sweeter words just did me in.

"But now that I see you have all these groceries, you probably had something planned—"

"Nothing planned. I'd love pizza."

"Me too," Calder said. "And cheesy breadsticks."

Jensen smiled at him. "A little dude after my own heart. I love cheesy breadsticks."

"Hey! Uncle Martin calls me little dude."

"So I shouldn't call you that?" Jensen asked carefully.

Calder considered him. "It's okay. You can call me that too."

"Cool." Jensen set his hands on my shoulders and gave me a little shove. "Hit the tub. We've got this handled."

"You're sure?"

"Yep."

I shuffled forward, grabbed the bottle of Zinfandel I'd opened last night and a coffee mug instead of a wineglass. With the day I'd had I wouldn't be surprised if I dropped the glass on the bathroom tile and injured myself.

I went directly into the bathroom and started the water, dumping in my favorite jasmine-scented bubble bath. I poured a mug of wine before I undressed.

Two big gulps of wine and fragrant steaming water worked their magic on me. I closed my eyes and relaxed.

My mug became empty far too quickly, but rather than leave my cocoon of warmth for a refill, I remained in my tub of tranquility.

The next time I opened my eyes, the bubbles had dissipated and the water had turned tepid. My languid feeling faded as I stood on the bathmat and realized I hadn't brought any clothes in with me. Nor had I remembered to grab the big bath towel Calder had brought into the kitchen. All that was left were the regular-sized towels that barely covered my son, let alone me.

I'd have to make a break for my bedroom. I doubted Calder or Jensen was lounging outside the bathroom door waiting for me to emerge. In fact, I hadn't heard any boisterous boy noises—I'd take that as the all clear.

No stealth or tiptoeing around; I opened the door and strode out, my hand strategically holding the towel between my breasts . . . and I ran square into a brick wall.

A brick wall with warm, callused hands.

Jensen said, "Not watching where you're going is a habit for both you and your son."

I glanced up but Jensen's eyes weren't on my face.

At all.

And he didn't seem inclined to let go of me either.

"Ah, I really need to get dressed."

He retreated. "Sorry."

I sidestepped him because the man took up a lot of space. "I'll be right out."

He said nothing.

But when I turned around after I'd opened my bedroom door, I saw that his focus had been on my ass.

Then he closed his eyes and muttered something like "Off-limits, off-limits, totally off-limits."

Couldn't be. I had to be hearing things. I closed the door.

I dressed in black yoga pants, a gray long-sleeved T-shirt and fuzzy socks. I did manage to towel-dry and comb my hair, but I skipped putting on makeup.

When I entered the living room, Calder and Jensen sat side by side on the couch. My son had selected the first season of *Dancing with the Stars* as their entertainment. I got that heavy feeling in my gut and my mama bear instincts came out full force. Jensen, the super jock, had better not utter any snide comments to make Calder self-conscious in his own home.

"That was a really fancy move," Jensen said to Calder. "You think she knew how to do that before she got picked to be on TV?"

"Huh-uh. They show her practicing it like a billion times," Calder said.

"Getting good at anything requires lots of practice. Rewind it. I wanna see her do that again."

I stood behind them and watched some TV actress extend her leg up in the air and place her hand on the floor, then drop her extending leg back down and kick the other leg up in the air—all while smiling at the camera.

"Do they teach you how to do that in dance class?" Jensen asked Calder.

"Not yet. Maybe they'll teach us at camp. Wouldn't that be cool?"

"Totally. The camp sounds amazing. So if you learn how to do it, you gotta teach me."

Calder tipped his head back to peer into Jensen's face. "You'd want to learn to do that?"

"If I knew how to do that? I'd be doing that move all the time. Then my teammates would be jealous that I'm also secretly a ninja dancer."

My son giggled.

Jensen ruffled Calder's hair. "You laughing at me, little dude?"

"Uh-huh." Calder's giggles were a balm to my soul.

I didn't have the heart to tell my son that I'd received word today the dance camp he'd looked forward to had been canceled.

Calder saw me. "Hey, Mommy, know what?"

"What?" I cut around the end of the couch and perched on the edge of the recliner.

"He has never *ever* watched *Dancing with the Stars*!"

I raised my brow at Jensen. "No. Really?"

"During the season I watch game tapes, so I don't have time to check out TV shows until the season is over," Jensen explained.

"So what *is* your favorite show?" I asked him.

Leaning forward, he rested his forearms on his knees and said, "Guess."

"*Inside the NFL*," I offered.

"Nope." He flashed that charming, dimpled grin. "Try again."

"*Ballers.*"

"Woman, give me credit for having interests off the grid-iron. It'd be like me assuming your favorite is *Making the Team* or whatever that show is called about becoming a Dallas Cowboys cheerleader."

"Point taken. Okay. Your favorite show is . . . *America's Next Top Model.*"

Jensen rolled his eyes.

"I know, I know!" Calder piped up. "It's *Chopped*!"

I didn't mask my surprise. "The cooking show? Seriously?"

"Yep. I can't cook at all, so I'm obsessed with it. Those contestants are badass making a dish out of stuff like fish heads, cotton candy and broccoli and having limited time to do it."

"You're not s'posed to say that bad A-word," Calder said.

"Oh. Right. Sorry."

"But Mommy says bad words sometimes," Calder continued. "Sometimes a *lot* of bad words. Like when—"

"I'm sure Jensen isn't interested in those very *rare* times," I said, to head off Calder's examples, of which there were more than I cared to hear about.

"So Mommy can be bad? Good to know," Jensen murmured.

Before I could regain control of the conversation, Calder said, "Guess Mommy's favorite show," to Jensen.

"*Parenthood*," Jensen said with a smirk.

"Ha ha."

"No? Damn—I mean darn. I thought I had it. How about . . . *Bring It On*?"

"That's a movie."

"My bad. Is it . . ." He shot Calder a sideways look. "*Dancing with the Stars*?"

"Yes!" Calder clapped. "Me and Mommy have the same favorite show."

"She's definitely got good taste."

Three raps sounded on the door, followed by, "Delivery from Papa John's."

Jensen vaulted over the back of the couch—in that sexy one-handed maneuver—before I even moved to grab my purse.

"Wait—"

He said, "Nope," over his shoulder. "I got this."

While he paid, I set out paper plates, napkins, cups and a jug of milk on the dining room table.

When Jensen returned with the pizzas, he pulled out the chair next to Calder.

"That's where Mommy sits." Calder pointed to the chair across from him. "You can sit over there."

I mouthed "Sorry" at him. Calder was set in his ways about a few things.

"No worries."

We helped ourselves to pizza. I said, "Thanks for buying us dinner. My turn next time."

Wait. Would he think that was presumptive?

"Sounds fair." He looked at Calder. "So that's your spot at the table."

He nodded.

"Since I live by myself, I can sit anywhere I want at my table. So I never sit in the same place two days in a row."

"How come?"

"From the time I was in a high chair until I graduated from high school, I had no choice but to sit at the same place at our family table. And since I'm the youngest, it seemed like I was the last one to get food."

"Do you sit in the same place at home now?" Calder asked.

"Nope. But I am bigger than both of my brothers so now I get the food first."

Calder took a huge bite of his cheese pizza and said, "You are a giant."

"Calder. Do not talk with your mouth full."

He mumbled, "Sorry."

"And when you're done chewing, apologize to Mr. Lund. You are aware of the no-name-calling rule in our house." I glanced at Jensen, wondering if he'd jump in and assure me that Calder didn't have to apologize. My biggest pet peeve when attempting to teach my son to mind his manners was when people—even my brother—tried to let it slide. Might be a small thing to them, but as a single parent, I needed Calder to listen to me and obey the rules I set for him.

Jensen said nothing as he helped himself to two more slices of pizza.

Calder took a big swig of milk before he said, "Sorry, Mr. Lund."

"I'm cool with you calling me Jensen, or Jens."

"Pop-pop said they call you The Rocket 'cause you run so fast."

From the corner of my eye, I saw Jensen tense up.

But Calder, being a six-year-old in his own little world, didn't notice. He continued on. "I could call you that."

"Nah. Jensen is my grandpa's last name and I was named after him, so stick with that, 'kay?"

"Okay."

Calder didn't chatter like he usually did. He kept sneaking looks at Jensen, as if trying to figure out why Jensen was here.

We were on the same page there.

After helping clean up, Jensen said, "I'll leave you guys to enjoy the rest of your night." He smirked at me. "If you decide to go out again, maybe carry an umbrella."

"Hilarious." I handed him a box with the leftovers. "Here."

"Did you keep some?"

I shook my head. Evidently he hadn't noticed that only three slices remained from two large pizzas. "You paid. I've got plenty of food. I forgot to say thank you for putting the groceries away."

"No problem." He studied me. "You sure you're okay?"

Apparently I hadn't hidden my mood very well. I forced a smile. "I'm good."

"All right." He said, "Later, little dude."

Calder stood on the couch and said, "Later, Rocketman."

Jensen laughed. "He's determined to call me that."

I poked Jensen in the chest. "You have the word *rocket* as a nickname. That is the coolest thing to a little boy. You would've done the same thing at his age."

"True."

"Good night, Lund."

"Later, sunshine."

Sunshine? When I'd been moody from the moment I saw him?

He'd probably meant that sarcastically.

After I'd tucked Calder in bed, I was half-tempted to call it a day and crawl between the sheets myself. But I knew I'd just stare at the ceiling and fret.

I poured another mug of wine and crossed to the patio door, watching rain slide down the glass like tears and pool on the concrete balcony. The dreary weather perfectly fit my mood.

Not only would the cancellation of the camp be devastating to my son, I'd already arranged my summer work schedule around the day camp hours. Finding a replacement camp at this late date would be nearly impossible. But I'd have to start looking right away.

Four soft knocks on the door pulled me out of my brooding.

I had no idea how long I'd been staring aimlessly into the night, but I knew who I'd find standing in the hallway.

And I was really glad he'd come back.

Nine

JENSEN

Maybe I was an idiot, but I knocked on Rowan's door two and a half hours after I'd left.

I wasn't sure if she'd answer. Part of me wasn't sure why I was even there.

Except another part of me recognized I found it too hard to stay away from her.

Rowan opened the door and blocked it, her arms crossed over her chest. "Did you forget something?"

I stared at her lips. The cocky side of me almost responded, *Yeah, baby, I forgot to kiss the hell out of you before I left.* I tamped that idea down. "I thought you might want to talk about whatever is bothering you tonight."

"What makes you think anything is wrong?"

My eyes searched hers but I didn't say anything.

"Maybe I'm just tired. Maybe I was about to go to bed when you came a-knocking."

Such a little liar you are. But I'd learned that if I didn't respond, she'd find the silence uncomfortable and tell me everything I wanted to know.

Three . . . two . . . one . . .

"Fine. Come in. But I finished off the wine."

"Good thing I'm not looking for a drinking buddy."

She harrumphed behind me after I walked past her into the living room.

I took the chair opposite the couch.

Rowan plopped in the middle of the sofa and eyed me suspiciously. "What's really going on?"

"You tell me. I've hung out with you every night this week. That means, like it or not, I can tell when something is wrong." I leaned forward, resting my forearms on my knees. "So talk to me. Maybe it'll help."

She sighed. Blinked. Fidgeted. Sighed again.

I lifted an eyebrow. "That bad, huh?"

Then she bit her lip as she focused on my mouth.

"Damn. Now I get it. You can't talk to me because your issues are *about* me, aren't they?"

"What?"

"Admit it: You want me." I grinned at her. "You aren't the first woman who finds me irresistible after agreeing to the just-friends parameters. As much as I'd love to take you for an all-night ride on the magic rocket—"

"Omigod. You are unbelievable!"

"That's what I've heard—firsthand with the screams, moans and praising my name as a sex god—so there's no use denying it or you pretending—"

"For your information, egomaniac, my mood has nothing to do with you and your big rocket and supposed ability to induce screaming orgasms. I'm upset and distracted because the dance camp that I signed Calder up for months ago, the camp he loved so much last year, got canceled today. I have no idea what I'm going to do, or how I'm going to break it to him because it will break his little heart."

I paused for a moment. "See? That wasn't so hard."

Rowan gave me a sheepish smile. "You're a sneaky one, Lund."

I shrugged. "I'm also pushy. So tell me the rest of it."

The edge of authority in my voice didn't cause her to bristle up; she let everything pour out and it broke my heart.

Her worry that every camp would be full or financially out of reach. Her confusion as to why the camp organizers waited until almost the last minute to spring the bad news on the parents. That led her to a rambling stream of consciousness about their organization's finances—not that she'd seen their profit-and-loss statements—but wouldn't they have realized sooner than today that they'd have funding issues? Their responses to her questions had been vague, and the director had indicated there'd be no refunds on the deposit.

I saw her relief after she'd let off steam. I understood her reluctance to share her worries—we had that in common. My brain could only take so much silent ranting before I wound up with a brutal headache.

In one breath Rowan told me she hated that I'd pushed her to talk because she didn't want to be that annoying person who does nothing but complain about everything. In the next breath she thanked me because her usual confidant—Martin—wasn't around.

I said, "That's some shitty day you've had, sunshine."

"What sucks is there's nothing I can do about it, but I can't stop obsessing over it."

I leaned back in the chair. "So this camp . . . Is it strictly for dancers?"

"Two hours out of the six are dedicated to dancing. Then there's theater and art stuff."

"Did they hire different instructors for each activity? Or did the dance instructor wear more than one hat?"

"Each creative area had a separate staff member."

I paused for a moment. "Was there an issue with staffing?"

"Serena—she was the director—didn't give specifics. Part of me thinks there were too many issues to blame the cancellation on just one thing."

"Can you give me a basic breakdown on why the classes were unique and the appeal to you as a parent?"

Rowan looked at me oddly, as if she'd expected me to say "The situation sucks for you, dude" and move on to a topic that interested me. But for whatever reason, she gave me a detailed breakdown of activities, fees, camp goals and the camp's attempt at ethnic and economic diversity.

Those words started the wheels churning in my head. "Where'd they hold the camp?"

She listed the address and I whistled. "What?"

"No wonder. That area is turning into a prime location for reurbanization."

Miss Skeptical frowned at me. "No offense, but how do *you* know that?"

"I've been dabbling in buying real estate. My brother Walker co-owns a construction business that specializes in restoration. Last year they were looking at investing in a couple of buildings. But some out-of-state conglomerate bought up all that property in a two-block area. They raised the rent across the board."

"Isn't that illegal in rent-control situations?" she asked.

"Not with the right lawyer. Not as long as they're claiming that the extra income is earmarked for major upgrades they have planned. Now, three quarters of those buildings are empty. According to my brother, there's been no renovation. He and his business partner are keeping a close eye on things because they suspect the company will just bulldoze that whole neighborhood. Although nothing in that area is considered historical."

"No wonder it's such a cluster. The facility they rented is right in the middle of that two-block stretch you're talking about." She sighed. "Which means it's not a 'we spent all the camp profits on booze and blow' type situation."

I laughed. This woman and her random responses cracked me up.

"This is serious stuff, Lund."

"I know. So how long has this group been in business? Are they a nonprofit?"

That startled her. "I'm not sure. Why?"

"Just curious. Not that it matters since they're defunct."

"Exactly. So I'm no better off now than before you bullied me into ripping open my bleeding mother's heart."

"You'll be a hundred times better off for your honesty, especially with me." I stood. A brilliant potential solution to her problem had occurred to me. I needed a moment to pace and sort it out. "Gotta use the can. Be right back."

My palms were actually sweating when I returned to the living room.

I was afraid she'd instinctively bat away the helping hand I offered. Rowan Michaels had more pride—and the stubborn streak to go with it—than anyone I'd ever met. I wasn't sure I could fake an air of nonchalance if she shot my idea down without really listening to it.

She eyed me as I sat down. "Everything okay?"

Guess I'd taken longer in the bathroom than I'd thought. I glanced at the coffee table and noticed she'd discreetly placed a roll of antacids next to the glass of ice water she'd gotten for me. That was Rowan in a nutshell: seeing to the needs of the people around her. My normal reaction—I didn't need her mothering me—was replaced by a warm feeling in my chest that wasn't from indigestion.

"Jensen?" she prompted.

"I'm fine. But I do want to talk to you about something that occurred to me. And I need your word that you'll listen without judgment or a knee-jerk reaction until I've finished."

Rowan cocked her head. "You have my attention."

"Have you heard of LCCO? Lund Cares Community Outreach?"

"Only because Dallas talked about it. Sounds like the organization does great things in the Twin Cities."

"We do. Every member of the Lund family is involved in some way. Each year we choose a project. It can be anything from organizing a coat drive like my sister, Annika, does, to building sets for a community theater like my brother Walker, to working with at-risk youth like my brother Brady." It sucked admitting this next part. "As the youngest in my family, I've let my mom and my aunts decide what charitable needs I should meet, and I go where they tell me. So I've never been a self-starter when it comes to my yearly LCCO project."

Rowan frowned. "I'd think your project would be a no-brainer, Jens. You're a sports celebrity. You could host youth football clinics and get thousands of kids to apply."

"But that's not really doing something worthwhile to anyone outside the sports community. Besides, I have team obligations for kids' football clinics. Just last week my mom harassed me about getting my shit together and committing to a project or she'd find one for me." I couldn't repress a shudder at the very idea of baring myself for a bachelor auction. "So tonight, after hearing about the loss of Calder's favorite summer camp, and knowing he isn't the only kid who'll be affected by the loss, I'll make creating a new camp my LCCO project."

She didn't say anything; she just gaped at me in disbelief. I found myself trying to sell her on it. I'll admit a lot of it was me talking out of my ass because I hadn't paid attention to the particulars when I'd been involved in other LCCO projects. I'd never started one at ground zero.

When I paused to take a drink, Rowan seized the chance to speak. "Okay, I'm throwing this out there and please don't bite my head off. But you can't take an arts camp—which I assume you know nothing about—and turn it into a sports camp, and expect the parents who had committed to the arts camp to be happy about the change because *any* camp is better than no camp."

And I thought I'd been making progress with her. That she'd finally seen me beyond being a meathead football player with a one-track mind on sports. It was tempting to say, *Screw it, and good luck; sorry you can't see that I have a functioning brain outside my helmet and I'm only trying to help you.*

I started to do just that: get up, toss off a terse "Whatever" and let her figure out a better way. But then I realized that was *exactly* what she expected I'd do—maybe even what she *wanted* me to do. Take offense, storm off and prove I have a football player's temper by throwing a tantrum. Then she could keep her pride by not admitting that I could help her.

Screw that.

Raising my head, I met her defiant gaze with one of my own. "At what point during my explanation of how LCCO could possibly help fix this situation did I specifically say that I planned to turn the dance and art camp into a football camp?"

Rowan stared at me. Scowled at me. Scowled at her empty mug.

"You can't answer that because I *never* indicated that in order for LCCO to become interested, I'd pitch it as a sports camp."

"Isn't that expected? Given who you are?"

I leaned forward. "I get off on defying people's expectations, Rowan."

"So you seriously expect me to believe that all you have to do is tell LCCO about the situation, and they'll ride in like a bunch of white knights and save the summer camp?"

"Yes."

"Why?"

"Because my last name is Lund." I flashed my teeth at her. "Nepotism: It's a good thing."

"Cocky much?"

"Only when it's warranted."

"How can you be so sure?"

"How can you be so stubborn?" I shot out of my chair and loomed over her before she got it in her head to flee. "Oh, sweetheart, I'm on to you. You want to say no. You want to tell me to take my nepotism and shove it on my way out the door."

Another glare.

"So are you going to let your pride put Calder's happiness as well as the other campgoers' at risk because you don't want to admit you need some help? Or because you don't want to accept that help from *me*?"

"I hate this."

Being this close to her I noticed the pulse beating in her throat. I noticed the way she'd arched up slightly toward me, instead of away from me. I noticed she'd parted her lips as if she wanted me to kiss her.

Or maybe . . . that's how she looks when she's pissed off, cornered and about to strike.

Either way? It was sexy as hell.

I denied my driving need to taste her, touch her, feel her body moving beneath mine. If I wanted her to see me as more than a player, I had to prove it to her.

"Stop crowding me," she finally said.

"I will as soon as you answer the question."

Rowan closed her eyes. "All right. The truth? I hate that you can swoop in like some superhero and save the day." When she opened her eyes it shocked me to see them shimmering with tears. "While I hate it because I know it's *my* stupid pride making me resistant, I am thankful that you *can* possibly save the day."

I sat beside her. Without thinking, I curled my hand around the side of her face. Seeing this strong, feisty woman cry cut me deep, and I wanted to soothe her. "Rowan. What else is going on?"

She whispered, "I wanted to be the hero, okay? I know it sounds petty and ungrateful, but I wanted to be the one to find a way."

"You are the hero in Calder's life every single day. Never forget that." I brushed away a tear and brought her closer to me. "I'm not doing this because I have a white-knight complex. I just want to help. Let me." I paused. "That said, if it makes it easier for you to accept my help, imagine this whole thing is a giant stroke to my . . . ego."

"Seriously, Jensen Lund. How can you be cocky *and* humble?"

"It's hard, let me tell you. But I've managed to pull it off and I know you're impressed with a capital *I*."

She laughed softly.

"Besides, on my continuing journey of extreme selflessness, you *did* find a way to make the camp happen. You told *me* about it."

"Dude. You never quit."

"You'd be disappointed if I did, Coach."

"True." She paused. "I expected you'd try to cop a feel since we're in each other's faces."

"A, I'm totally insulted that you think I'd take advantage of you in your fragile emotional state."

She snorted.

"And B . . . do you equate *expected* with *disappointed*? Because if that's the case, I'll latch onto that luscious ass of yours with both hands, right now."

No surprise that was what had her squirming out of my arms.

I should've quit while I was ahead.

"In all seriousness. I'll meet with my aunt Priscilla—aka the big boss at LCCO—Monday and discuss the situation. I don't know that she'll have options or suggestions immediately, but if you could be available by phone so I can pass along any of her questions or concerns, that would speed up the process."

"I'll be in the office and not out in the training center next week, so that won't be a problem."

"Cool." I pushed to my feet. "It's late." I did have the fear of overstaying my welcome. But my fear that I'd get used to spending time with her and want more of it was equally strong.

I'd reached the door when she said, "I don't even know where to start thanking you."

"I haven't done anything yet."

"Yes, you have. You've given me hope."

When she said sweet and sappy things like that? My insides went mushy.

Ten

JENSEN

One thing I knew was that I'd have a better chance of convincing Aunt Priscilla to fund my project if I presented my case in person at the LCCO offices. Plus, my mother's presence would help sway my aunt if she seemed hesitant. An official business call meant I couldn't show up in athletic gear. After my three-hour workout, I returned to my place to slip on a suit.

As I stood in front of the mirror tying my tie, I went over my game plan—which admittedly wasn't much. Luckily I excelled at spur-of-the-moment ideas and could adapt my suggestions on the fly.

At the Lund Industries corporate headquarters, I parked in the underground garage reserved for family members. We even had a private elevator so the executives could arrive and leave undetected. Recently the elevator had been put on weekend lockdown in an attempt to curb the Lund workaholic tendencies—or so I'd heard; I hadn't been in this building on a weekend since my childhood. My weekends had been devoted to football since I'd joined my first peewee league at age ten.

Astrid, the prissy college intern who took her receptionist job very seriously, looked up at my approach. No smile from Astrid—no surprise. That might add an extra two seconds to her workload. "Mr. Lund. I wasn't aware Lund Industries had a board meeting."

I smiled at her. "As usual, Astrid, you're right. I'm here to see—"

"Jensen?" A familiar voice echoed behind me.

I turned and faced my mother. "Hey, Mom."

She hugged me, enveloping me in warmth, silk and the scent of Joy perfume. "You are solid, not wispy dream fragment." Stepping back, she flicked her gaze over me. "Was there press conference today?"

"No."

"You coming from funeral?"

"No."

Her eyes widened. "You dressed for a date! Yes, I approve of the suit." She squinted at my tie and tsk-tsked. "Come closer so I fix that ugly knot. Looks like noose, not a four-hundred-dollar tie."

"There is no date. Unless I can convince my beautiful mother to *fika* after my meeting with Aunt Priscilla."

"Honey-sweet words dripping from your lips just like your father," she scoffed with a smile . . . as she attempted to straighten my tie.

Astrid cleared her throat. "I don't see you on Priscilla's calendar today, Mr. Lund."

"I'm hoping my aunt could squeeze me in."

"Her schedule is full today. Perhaps—"

"Of course Cilla has time for her nephew," my mother

said to Astrid sweetly. "We appreciate that you keep us on right trail but sometimes . . . we must freewheel."

"You mean *track*," I corrected Mom before Astrid did.

"Yah. Whatever." Mom grabbed hold of my arm as if I were a ten-year-old in trouble. Over her shoulder she said to Astrid, "Hold the phone, please."

I had the mental image of Astrid literally holding the phone until we finished the meeting.

Mom squeezed my arm. "When you were little boy, I could wrap whole hand around scrawny chicken arm. Now? My fingertips don't touch from you having athlete's arm."

"Athletes' *foot* is a thing—not a good thing—but there's no such thing as athlete's arm, Mom."

"I say it is so, it is so." She opened Aunt Priscilla's door and made the after-you gesture.

My aunt smiled at me. "Jensen. What a lovely surprise."

I chose the floral visitor's chair on the left across from the desk, leaving the chair on the right for my mom.

After we were settled, my aunt said, "We can skip the usual chitchat and get to the point, since I doubt this is a social visit?"

I appreciated Aunt Priscilla's directness. She'd always been the aunt who organized formal outings for the Lund kids, forcing us to wear matching T-shirts if we were going to a populated place. She defined *organized*, so it wasn't nepotism when her son, Ash, the COO of Lund Industries, named her head of Lund Cares Community Outreach. Both my mother and my other aunt, Edie, devoted time to LCCO, but it was Priscilla Lund's baby.

LCCO had expanded in recent years. Given the staggering amount of money at her disposal and her husband's status as a billionaire heir to the Lund family fortune, Aunt Priscilla could've been a snotty, snooty socialite. But she used her powers for good, not evil, and she always put family above everything else.

"Astrid indicated you were swamped today, so I'll give you a brief rundown. My neighbor is a single mother and she'd set her summer schedule around a dance camp that her son attended last year. My understanding is the program strives for economic and ethnic diversity. But the program either lost funding or lost their venue and it's displaced thirty kids whose parents had counted on this camp. So I thought I'd ask if LCCO could step in."

"This is late notice, Jensen."

"I know. It's late notice for the families since school gets out in three weeks."

My aunt's gaze turned shrewd. "Is everything else in place? The staffing, et cetera, and you're asking LCCO to provide the facility?"

I shook my head. "My neighbor suspects this organization knew at least a month ago they wouldn't be able to host the camp this year."

"So no facility and no staff?"

"No, ma'am."

She removed her neon-pink reading glasses and rubbed her temples with her fingertips. "It's a tight spot, Jens. If the administrators for the company needed a physical location to hold the camp, I'd have no problem issuing a check today."

"But . . . ?"

"But while LCCO supports the local arts community, we don't fund anything at one hundred percent. The organization is considered a partner, even if the financial split isn't fifty-fifty. They have to be invested some way, and it sounds to me as if there is no organization any longer."

I scratched my cheek. "I hadn't considered that."

"Did the defunct organization require deposits to hold the kids' place for the camp?"

"Yes. I wanna say it was a hundred bucks. Nonrefundable."

"So thirty kids at a hundred bucks a pop . . ." She shook her head. "The organization should've charged double that. If they didn't have a financial cushion, there's no alternative but to pack it in. I've seen this happen too many times recently."

Not what I wanted to hear.

My mother sighed. "My heart hurts for the children. It is not their fault."

I remembered Calder's glum body language yesterday.

Dammit. There had to be a solution.

Aunt Priscilla asked, "How many hours a week were the kids scheduled to be at camp?"

"Eighteen hours. Monday, Wednesday and Friday from nine A.M. until three in the afternoon."

"Not full-time."

"That's the issue with the parents trying to find an alternative. Most places require the kid to be enrolled full-time."

"Do you know the weekly camp fees per child?" my mother asked. "That income could cover some of the program, so it wouldn't be fully funded by LCCO."

I took my cell out of my jacket pocket. "Give me two seconds to fire off a quick text to Rowan."

Me: Financial breakdown questions ahead.

RM: Hit me.

I typed in the questions and read Rowan's text responses out loud. This went on for ten minutes.

My aunt said, "Last questions. Staffing, food service and medical."

All of which I dutifully texted.

Me: How many staff members for thirty campers?

RM: Six. All six were there every day.

Me: Did campers bring their own lunches?

RM: Yes. The camp supplied the snacks.

Me: Thanks for all the info. That's it for now. I think.

**RM: Rocketman, I'll give you whatever you want if
you can actually help us with an alternative solution
to this ☺**

I grinned. No mistaking that; the woman was flirting
with me.

Me: Whatever I want? Don't you think that's a little . . .
reckless?

**RM: I'm due for reckless behavior ☺ and I'd owe you
BIG TIME**

Me: I'm holding you to that.

"Jensen," my mother said sharply.

The little sneak had been reading over my shoulder.

"So, here's what I found out," I said quickly shoving my
phone in my pocket and filling them in.

After I finished, Aunt Priscilla looked thoughtful. "That
does change a few things. The staffing issues aren't nearly
as impossible when the attendees are expecting intense master classes. But we'd still have to find someone to oversee
the camp and coordinate—"

"I'll do it."

My mother actually gasped after I said that.

I faced her. "What? You don't think I'm capable of doing this?"

"If you are capably overseeing it, when will you train?"

"Whenever I want. Just like now. Official training camp doesn't start until July. If I get the right people to help with this camp, someone can take over for me."

"Sounds like you've already thought about who you're hiring," my aunt said.

"The only staff that gets paid are the dance and music instructors. Everyone else will be strictly volunteer. I plan to put the Lunds back in LCCO." I smirked. "Lots of talent in this family."

My aunt smirked back at me. "You're finally getting even with my daughter for making you play dress-up with her when you were kids?"

"Yep. Dallas will say yes without question when I tell her Rowan is in a bind."

"Rowan," she repeated. "That name didn't register until just now. This Rowan is—was—Dallas's cheer coach at U of M?"

"Yes. She and her son, Calder, live across the hall from me. Rowan's brother is Martin Michaels . . . remember Axl's groomsman with the dreads?"

"Of course," my aunt said. "He was certainly the life of the party."

I grinned. "That's Martin. He and his girlfriend are traveling through Europe, and Rowan is subletting the apartment this summer."

"How old is her son?"

I felt my mother's gaze boring into me, but I ignored it. "Calder is six."

"Almost the same age as Mimi. This kind of camp would be good for her."

I kept it to myself that I'd planned to ask Lucy, Mimi's mother, to help out. "So what's the next step? Do I get my volunteers lined up while you secure the venue?"

"That'd be best. Swing by at the end of the week and we'll see where we've gotten to."

I stood and skirted the corner of the desk, leaning in to kiss her cheek. "Thanks, Aunt Priscilla. You put the *awe* in *awesome*."

She smiled. "You're welcome. Now shoo, you charmer. I'm behind schedule."

Out in the hallway, Mom had me by the arm again and towed me into the conference room. She planted herself right in front of me. "You tell me everything about this Roman, Jensen Bernard Lund."

"Rowan. Not Ro-man or Ro-nin. Her name is Row-an."

"Fine, yah, whatever. This *Row-an*. Did she demand you help with this camp?"

My tiny bit of amusement vanished. "No. I offered to help her."

"Why?"

"Because that's the way you raised me."

"Do not." She paused and exhaled, but her laser-focused Mom gaze never left mine. "Do not treat my concern for you as a joke."

"I'm not. But don't assume that I'm a sucker for every beautiful woman with a hard-luck story either."

She blinked as if that hadn't occurred to her. "I'm sorry." She placed her hand on my chest. "Ever since you were little boy you have a soft heart. Now grown man, hard body, but still soft heart."

"Softhearted doesn't mean I'm soft in the head," I said gently. "Trust me, okay? Rowan and I are friends. She's raised Calder on her own and done a great job because her son is a sweet boy. I saw how much he looked forward to the camp and knew I could help them and the other families who were affected."

"So you spend time with them?"

I'd opened myself up for that one. "Occasionally."

"Because you are . . . friendly with her."

"Yes. And she's a Vikings cheerleader."

"Which one?" she demanded as if she knew them all.

"She has red—"

"The redhead high kicker is *your* Rowan?"

I really had to watch the stadium tapes and see Rowan in action if my *mother* was aware of her cheerleading skills. "She's not *my* Rowan."

"But you want more than friends with her?"

"She breaks all my rules."

"Rules," she scoffed, "are made to be beaten."

"You mean broken."

"Yah. Whatever." She smirked at me. "You didn't deny the desire to be more than friends because you cannot lie to your mother."

I had lied to her more times than I would ever admit, but that wasn't the point. "It doesn't matter what I want. Rowan doesn't date athletes."

Her eyes narrowed. "Why not?"

"Calder's dad was a football player. He's not in his son's life at all. So Rowan has rules too. Can we please drop this?"

"For now." She offered me a dazzling smile.

My gut clenched. That smile meant she was up to something. "What else?"

"I wish to meet this Rowan the redhead and her sweet son."

If she thought I'd argue about that . . . she'd be wrong. What better way to prove Rowan and I were just friends than to act like introducing her to my family was no big deal?

You are kidding yourself. It is a huge deal.

Shoving that thought aside, I said, "Sure. Next time you come over we'll wander across the hallway for introductions."

Another suspicious Mom laser-eye probe.

I smiled at her. "So we're good?"

"Yah."

"I'm off to start recruiting volunteers. But don't warn any of the Lund Collective I'll be hitting them up for this favor, okay?"

"Surprise them like Jack-in-box—popping up at worst time?"

"Something like that." I kissed her forehead. "Later, gator."

"Bison."

I laughed because my sweet, slyly funny, meddling mother also put the *awe* in *awesome*.

As I approached the receptionist's desk, I realized Astrid wasn't scowling at me for a change. "Hey, Astrid. I need to make an appointment with Aunt Priscilla on Friday."

"Already done."

"Thank you. Sorry if I messed up the schedule today."

"I shifted a few things around. Not a big deal." Then she smiled at me.

What the hell? I'd never seen that before.

"But if you're truly feeling bad, I'll let you make it up to me."

Not this. Before I pulled out the standard "I'm one hundred percent focused on getting my career back on track with zero time for dating," she spoke—but it wasn't to hit me up for dinner.

"I overheard what you've got cooking with this camp thing, and I want in."

"Excuse me?"

"The camp. I want in. I want to help."

"What about your job here?"

The annoyance returned to her face. "It's an internship, so I'm done in two weeks. I start training my replacement next week. And if I don't have anything lined up regarding my major? My parents will expect me to come home for the summer."

"You don't get along with them?"

"I get along with them fine, it's the rest of the people in my small hometown that I don't want to be stuck with." She peered down the hallway and then refocused on me. "It could be an extension of my internship. Hands-on experience in addition to administrative experience with a nonprofit like LCCO will look great on my résumé."

I crossed my arms over my chest. "I'm listening."

"I'm an organizer. I could be there during all of the camp hours. I'd be good at herding little people to where they needed to be in a timely fashion. I could handle the weekly payments from the parents and make sure the money hits the right LCCO account. I could order supplies. I could fill out the reports for the number of volunteer hours."

My head? Spinning. This wasn't a "Hey, kids, let's put on a camp!" kind of project if I had to fill out reports.

Astrid paused and gave me a challenging look. "You had no idea about the required LCCO reports, did you?"

"No, but I bet I know who ordered those reports." I paused. "My brother the CFO."

"In triplicate, no less."

Jesus. "Now I have a question. How old are you?"

"I turned twenty-one last month. Why is that relevant?"

I shrugged. "Just wondering if the reason you want to stay in the Cities instead of going home is to party like it's 1999."

Astrid rolled her eyes. "Props for the Prince reference, but I've never seen the fun in getting drunk and acting stupid. Besides, since this would be an unpaid internship, I'd have to keep my other job waiting tables at Brit's Pub."

I offered her my hand. "I'd be happy for your expertise. But—"

"But keep in mind, as a Lund, you're large and in charge, running the show, yada yada. Got it."

"Has a smart-ass always lurked beneath the brusque receptionist?"

"Yes, but a respectful smart-ass, Mr. Lund, sir."

"You and me are gonna get along just fine, Astrid. Text me your number and I'll be in touch."

I wasn't sure, but I might've seen her saluting in the reflection of the elevator doors.

Since I was already in the building, I figured I might as well clear the next hurdle. I took the elevator to the PR department—my sister Annika's domain.

I bypassed her assistant and knocked on her door before walking into her office. "Hey, sis," I said as I strolled toward her.

"Why, yes, Jensen, please just barge in any time you feel like it. It's not like I'm doing real work here."

Her snappish tone had me pausing midstride. "What the hell is that about?"

She sighed and spun her chair to face me. "Just sharing the loathing, bro. Mondays suck. I'm stuck doing the worst part of this job because I'm the boss."

Annika's mentor and former boss had decided to stay home full-time after her last baby. Since Annika had been second-in-command, she was the logical choice to take over. "What are you doing?"

"Running cost analysis for our two biggest campaigns last quarter." She pointed at me. "Don't think I didn't see your eyes glaze over the instant I uttered 'cost analysis.'"

I grinned at her. "Busted. But seriously, is this a bad time to talk?"

That was when Annika gave me a quick once-over. "Not

that you don't look great all GQ'd up, but what's with wearing the suit in the off-season? Did someone die?"

"Mom said the same thing to me."

"Obviously we're both concerned someone has been drinking Polyjuice Potion and is impersonating you."

"Hilarious."

"Let's sit in the lounge area."

"Look who's all fancy with her 'lounge' area in her fancy-ass office."

"Shut it or I won't share my almond pastries with you," Annika warned.

"Who made them?"

"I did. I made a shit ton because Axl loves them." She stopped in front of her space-age coffeemaker. "Coffee?"

"You know how to work that thing?"

"Yeah, it's real hard poking the buttons."

After we were settled in with our coffee and pastries, she said, "What's going on?"

So I told the story for what felt like the bazillionth time. Then I followed it up with the camp situation and how I'd come up with a solution.

"It sounds like you've got everything under control after your meeting with Aunt P."

We never called her Aunt P to her face for obvious reasons. "I'm lining up volunteers. Which is where you come in."

Annika said, "Hit me with it."

"Can I talk to Lucy about her summer plans for Mimi and if she would be interested in sending Mimi to camp and teaching craft classes?"

"Every day for the entire summer?"

I shook my head. "Three days a week, six hours a day."

"Why are you asking me?"

"Because you're her boss. If you can't spare her I'd understand."

"I'm sure she'd be all over it. Especially since she won't lose income by helping out."

I hadn't thought of that. "What do you mean?"

"Any LI employee who volunteers for an LCCO event is paid their regular salary." Her eyes searched mine. "You're on the LI board of directors, Jens. How did you not know that?"

I shrugged. "Some of that shit bores me to tears, so I tune out during the meetings."

"You and Walker." She smirked. "And I suspect Dad is right there with you guys. Anyway, things are projected to slow down in our department during the next couple of months, so the timing is good."

"So I can ask her?"

"Yes. But if she says no . . . I won't get involved, okay?"

"Deal." I started to get up.

"Ah ah ah, not so fast." She pointed at me. "Park it. Tell me more about Rowan. Because you've got it bad for her."

"She and I are friends. That's it."

"Right. That's why you're going to all this trouble for her kid."

I kept my cool demeanor. "First off, I had to come up with a project for LCCO anyway. This one fits the parameters. Second, she's my friend's sister. Martin wouldn't want me messing with her. Third, Rowan breaks every one of my rules. I could look the other way if it was just one, but it's all three. Fourth, she doesn't date athletes."

Annika laughed.

"What's funny about that?"

"You. Trying to convince me that any of that matters. The fact that she breaks all your rules is a cosmic clue and a celestial sign that you should just toss out the rule book."

I scowled at her. "You've been hanging out with Dallas too much if you're talking about cosmic clues and celestial signs."

She leaned forward. "Nope. Still haven't convinced me."

Screw it. I drained my coffee like it was a tequila shot. "You're right. Rowan is amazing. She's smart. She's so damn devoted to her son and for some reason I find that incredibly hot. She's funny. And sweet. But she's not a pushover. That red hair fits her fiery personality perfectly. She doesn't act fake nice to me because I'm famous and rich and then she's a raging bitch to everyone else. She's genuinely nice." I blew out a long breath and ran my hand through my hair. "Calder's dad, a pro football player, screwed her over, so she's all 'pass' when it comes to athletes—especially pro athletes. And worst of all, at least from my side, is that I didn't have a clue that she's been a Vikings cheerleader the entire time I've been part of the team. Oh, and she cheered for the U of M football team too." I felt my cheeks heat. "So yeah. I'm the stereotypical egotistical football player who doesn't see anything in the stadium beyond my teammates standing on the sidelines and the damn end zone. How would I ever make up for that dickhead behavior?"

"You can't. But I think it's great you're trying to redeem yourself even when there's no chance the two of you will ever have a romantic relationship."

I bristled. Even my sister didn't have faith I could overcome Rowan's perception of me.

Annika pointed at me. "Oh, wipe the mulish look off your face, Jens. If you showed her the sweet, charming Jensen I know and love, she'd be all over you. I'm just saying it's too bad the NFL has that stupid rule about cheerleaders and players not getting involved."

As I'd gotten to know Rowan, I'd conveniently forgotten that rule. Which, now that I thought about it, bordered on infringing on personal freedom. Why did the national organization believe they had the right to tell me who I couldn't date?

"Although technically," she said slyly, "with you being on the injured reserve list, you're not an 'active' player until the coaching staff officially deems you eligible."

I stared at her. "You scare me sometimes."

"Why?"

"Because you are unparalleled in finding sneaky-ass justification to get what you want."

"Dude. I'm in PR. It's all about the spin."

No lie there.

"What am I contributing to camp?"

"Cookies. Or whatever Swedish treats you're baking for Axl."

"Done."

I glanced at the clock across the room. "Thanks for making time to talk to me given your busy executive schedule."

She waved me off. "I always have time for you. Here's one bit of sisterly advice."

"Shoot."

"While this friendship is new and exciting to you, she has to do the day-to-day parenting stuff. Be her friend, but don't insert yourself into their daily lives without a clear invitation that's what she wants. Keep it cool and casual, okay?"

I hated to hear it because she was probably right. I needed to back off. "I get it." I stood.

Annika followed me to the door. "Who else are you recruiting besides Lucy?"

"Dallas. Trinity. "

"My advice? Ask Trinity when the big, bad daddy-to-be isn't huffing and puffing around, demanding she stay off her feet."

"On it. I'll keep you updated."

I couldn't remember the last time I'd had such a productive day besides having a great workout or making progress on my physical therapy.

Everyone I'd contacted about volunteering for camp had

stepped up—that was one of the reasons we, Astrid mostly, had chosen Camp Step-Up as the new camp name.

I'd been texting with Rowan sporadically. I hadn't asked her plans for the night—even when we needed to discuss camp specifics.

Tonight, I needed something besides flirting and conversation.

I needed action. Real action that I hadn't had for over a month.

I made the call.

"'Bout time you came crawling back to me. The beer is cold, the joystick is hot and I am ready to kick your ass at *Assassin's Creed*, baller."

"In your dreams is the only place I'll ever lose to you, puck-head." I paused when Axl told me in Swedish to do something obscene to myself with a cruller. "Do you have food or should I pick some up?"

Axl snorted. "It's sacrilegious not to eat pizza when we're playing. We'll order in. Bring more beer. And none of that cheap shit you billionaire Minnesotans insist on serving. The good stuff."

Snobby Swede. There wasn't a damn thing wrong with Grain Belt beer. So that was what he was getting. "Be there in thirty."

Eleven

ROWAN

I half expected Jensen to be lounging outside my door, bursting with news about the meeting with LCCO.

But I'd been home forty-five minutes and hadn't heard from him. How much of an idiot did it make me that I missed him? I'd gotten used to him showing up.

The flurry of text messages from him surprised me. I hadn't expected him to be quite so gung-ho about setting up an alternative camp, even when we were under a time crunch. But his follow-through gave me a bigger peek into what made him tick. So I added tenacity to the other fascinating facts I'd learned about Jensen Lund.

His personal space was meticulous. The times I'd been in his apartment I hadn't seen a single thing out of place.

He lived in athletic clothes, which was awesome for getting a glimpse of his world-class body. But he didn't flaunt his physique—even when he should have because it defined powerful. In fact, if I did happen to catch him without a shirt on, he immediately excused himself and covered up. Damn shame, really, but his body shyness? Completely unexpected.

He always wore a ball cap outside the apartment complex. He had such glorious hair that I hated his near-constant state of hat-head, but I understood that a cap gave him some camouflage.

He had few visitors. Because he came from a large family and was part of a football brotherhood, I imagined he'd have people over 24/7. Yet it appeared he preferred solitude. I snickered at that thought. Maybe he actually had a chance at solitude now with Martin away for a few months, because my brother could be a total pest when he was bored and alone.

Yeah, you haven't done such a hot job leaving Jensen alone either. You find some reason—excuse—to see him every day.

Not that Jensen is any better, my conscience argued. He always had some kind of a reason for knocking on my door—even if that reason was lame like he "heard a weird noise in the hallway" and needed to check and see if we were okay.

But we were friends, right? Friends made time for each other.

Friends don't make eyes at each other. Friends don't send each other flirty texts. Friends don't notice things like the difference between the scent of his body wash and his shampoo. Friends don't waste time wondering if the scruff on his face would be downy soft or bristly against your cheek when he kissed you. Or how it'd feel on your neck, your chest, your belly as he kissed progressively lower.

I shook my head to clear it. Dammit. How had I veered into that territory?

Right. Listing all the things I knew about Jensen that few others did.

Like he didn't have many books in his living room, but the ones he displayed looked well worn. He had three complete sets of Harry Potter books—hardcover, paperback and a leather-bound edition. He also had a wand in a box from Ollivanders and a PROPERTY OF HOGWARTS beer stein on the shelf next to the books, which I found sweet.

He'd hung up his family pictures in his kitchen. There weren't many, and the only people I recognized were Dallas and her brother, Ash, and his sister, Annika—because of her being tight with Dallas—and Axl Hammerquist, who I'd met once. There wasn't a single picture of him in his football uniform anywhere, which I found very telling.

His kitchen sorely lacked the most basic cooking utensils. He'd confessed to Calder that he couldn't cook, so I found it . . . endearing that *Chopped* was his favorite TV show. But Jensen liked to eat. He ate quickly, as if he'd win a prize for finishing first. But even as he shoveled food in, his manners were impeccable. I'd been tempted to ask if as a kid he'd been required to take etiquette lessons, given the Lunds' social standing.

Surprisingly, it'd been easy to forget that the man was one of the heirs to a billion-dollar corporation. At times I'd even forgotten he was The Rocket, the beloved football star, the man with national endorsement deals, a hundred thousand followers on social media and the good guy—a dude's dude—with the charming smile and the bad-boy reputation for rotating women into his bed like they were auditioning for the play of the week.

Whenever he'd shared a meal with us and I'd watched him across the table, laughing and talking with my son, I saw none of those things. Granted, Jensen Lund remained the hottest man I'd ever seen up close and personal, but he was funny, honestly engaging and so unbelievably sweet.

But the intense way he studies you indicates there's

*something deeper there than friendship—for both of you.
You're drawn to his cocky self-assurance that when he strips
you naked, he'll show you—very thoroughly—how hot and
fast The Rocket can make you burn.*

When? What had happened to *if?*

Calder jumped in front of me, startling me, bringing
immediate guilt for the lewd direction my thoughts had
taken.

"I'm hungry."

"Any requests?"

He leaned forward and placed his hands on my knees,
giving himself stability as he bounced. "Sometime can we
do *Chopped?*"

"I don't know what you mean by doing *Chopped.*"

"Like we write down some stuff we have in the kitchen
on pieces of paper, and then pick three things and cook
something with them?"

As if coming up with healthy meals for a six-year-old
wasn't challenging enough. "I suppose we could try it one
of these days. But what if we ended up with something like
fish sticks, peanut butter and mustard?"

Bounce, bounce, bounce. "Well . . . we *could* mix the
peanut butter and mustard together and use it to dip the fish
sticks in."

I laughed and latched onto his skinny arms to stop the
bouncing so I could kiss his forehead. "You are such a clever
boy. Maybe I should put you in charge of dinner every night."

"Then I want fish sticks!"

"Fish sticks it is. It'll take a little while for them to cook,
so grab your backpack and let's go over what you did in
school today."

After I had the food under way, I sat next to Calder at the
table. I picked up a picture he'd drawn of a stick figure, the
legs, torso and arms colored black. "What's this?"

"Me in my dance clothes."

Ah. That explained the color choice. Boys wore black leotards to class. "And what are you doing?" There was a brown half circle beneath his feet, which were the same flesh color as his face, and that amused me, but I kept my poker face.

"Standing in a mud puddle." He pointed above the image. "That's a rain cloud and it's raining all around me."

I didn't see the usual happy additions that he always added to his drawings. Flowers, rainbows and butterflies. "Why does the picture seem sad?"

"Miss Gray asked us to draw how we felt on the weekend. I was sad about no dance camp, so I drew the sky crying."

My stomach twisted. "The sky was crying about it but you weren't?"

Calder leaned into me. "I was in the rain because I was crying too."

Talk about making me teary. I pressed my lips to the top of his head. "I'm sorry you were sad. I'm sad about it too." I hadn't mentioned the possibility of a new dance camp in case it didn't pan out. Even when I had hope LCCO would come through, I wasn't leaving anything to chance. I had the names of three other camps to contact tomorrow.

"Tell me what else you did at school today."

Then Calder returned to being my animated boy. "And then when Alicia and I went for a walk? Guess what? Two kids from the other building asked if I wanted to play!"

"That is pretty cool. Did you catch their names?" Their parents' names? What apartment they lived in? If their parents were paying attention to them or if they were just letting them run free?

"Nicolai. He's in second grade. And Andrew is in first grade." He paused. "So can I play with them?"

"We'll see."

"That always means no," he said, defeated.

Then the timer dinged, I headed to the kitchen and he followed me. "I want to help make the sauce."

"You're serious about mixing peanut butter and mustard together?" Sounded unbelievably gross.

"Yeah. But on *Chopped* you can add other stuff to make it taste better."

I handed him the dinner plates and had a sudden brainstorm. "At my favorite Thai restaurant there's a dish called sesame noodles and it tastes like peanut butter and soy sauce mixed together. So we could add soy sauce to it."

That set him to bouncing again.

"Careful with the plates, boy-o." I took out all the ingredients.

Calder dragged the step stool into the kitchen and we whisked everything together—with the least bit of mustard I could get away with, lots of soy sauce and a pinch of sugar.

"Okay, Chef Michaels, give it a taste."

He dipped the spoon in and didn't immediately make the *yuck* face. "Hey, it's good!"

"So I don't need to get out the ranch or the ketchup for the fish sticks?"

"Huh-uh. I'm gonna dip my chips in it too."

The sauce had turned out better than I'd expected. And Calder ate every last bit on his plate for a change. Go figure.

After that we drifted into our nighttime routine, readying his backpack and his bag for dance class. Preparing everything the night before saved us from butting heads first thing in the morning.

Calder took a long bath with his toys, allowing me to clean up the kitchen before I scrubbed his hair. Then it was jammies and reading time.

I was about to shut the door when Calder sat up in bed. "Mommy. Wait. You didn't tell me your favorite part of the day."

The quieter, settle-down time of day with him, where all the chaos and disappointment of the day vanished, filled me with peace and joy like nothing else. But he'd deemed that answer boring since I said it every time, so I said, "You first."

"Making the *Chopped* sauce. That was awesome . . . sauce." He giggled.

Hearing him giggle was a close second to the best part of every day. "That was my favorite part too."

"Can we do it again sometime?"

"Absolutely. Sweet dreams, my sweet boy. I love you."

"Love you too, Mommy."

Right after I sat down, my mom called. I spent half an hour filling her in on the camp situation. Then I brought up the random e-mail I'd gotten earlier today from the owner of a private cheer club about setting up a meeting with me. The oddest part? The club had been the biggest rival to the club I'd competed with, the next town over from where I'd grown up. Even from the preliminary e-mails, it sounded as if they wanted to offer me a job. Which excited my mom because Calder and I would have to move out of the Cities and closer to them. Then Mom got Dad on the phone and he promised if I made the move, he'd give me land of my own to build a house on. My parents tended to take a whispered suggestion or even a germ of an idea and blow it completely out of proportion.

That was all way, way too much for me to think about in one day. After I ended the call, I cursed my tendency to overshare with my parents—but they were the only people in my life I trusted and could talk to.

Jensen's voice echoed in my head. *"Who do you talk to*

*when things are weighing on your mind? I hate the thought
of you dealing with everything alone."*

It wasn't like I had a choice.

Maybe I'd talk to him about the cheer club thing.

So I held out hope that Jensen would drop by. But when
I hadn't heard his distinctive knock by eleven o'clock, I went
to bed.

hadn't heard from Jensen all week.

Which I considered a bad sign. He hadn't gotten the
funding or the space from LCCO to revive the camp and
he was too embarrassed to face me with the truth. So he
avoided me.

I found myself more annoyed with him than disappointed. Maybe I'd congratulated myself a little too much
on my ability not to fall for a player's promises.

I'd refrained from giving Calder the bad news. The last
week of regular dance classes for the school year had already put him in a melancholy mood. I'd found part-time
summer day care that had a hip-hop class once a week as
well as an art class. I planned on putting down the hefty
deposit on Monday after I got paid.

Since it was Friday night, Calder stayed up later. We
listened to music—a reggae, blues and jazz station on Pan-
dora my brother had recommended—as we worked on the
500-piece puzzle that Grammy and Pop-pop had sent home
with Calder. A puzzle comprised of kittens wearing birthday
hats I'd remembered from my childhood.

So that's what I continued to do for two hours after
Calder had gone to bed. I drank wine, listened to stoner
music and assembled a cat puzzle for ages six and up.

Crazy wild night for me.

Four familiar raps sounded on my door.

My heart beat a little faster, and that ticked me off.

It was nearly midnight—not an acceptable time for him to drop by.

So I ignored him.

But you don't really want to. You want to fling open the door and chew his very fine ass.

Mr. Persistent knocked again.

This time I answered, only opening the door as far as the chain allowed. "What."

"Hey. Can I come in?"

"No."

That startled him. "Why not?"

"Because it's late." *And I'm mad at you, dickhead.*

Even through the slight crack in the doorway I saw those blue eyes narrow. "Did you just call me a dickhead?"

Dammit. "I don't know what I said. It's late and I'm tired. Good night."

"Wait. Don't you want to hear about camp?"

"I waited to hear something on Monday. And Tuesday. And Wednesday. And Thursday. It's Friday—"

"I'm in love," he sang out.

My jaw dropped. "You did *not* just sing The Cure."

Jensen grinned. "I did. And damn, Coach, I am impressed that you know them."

"The original emo band? Of course I know them. But *you* listen to The Cure?"

"Nope. My parents did. We grew up listening to totally 'rad' '80s music. Plus '70s soul, rock, folk, funk and disco."

His gaze fell to my mouth and I felt it as keenly as if he'd softly placed his lips there.

"Rowan. Please let me in."

Shut the door. Send him away.

"You can't stay long." *You are a sucker, Rowan Michaels.*

I closed the door, unhooked the chain and reopened it. "I mean it, Lund. Two minutes."

He paused just inside the doorway. "Look. I'm sorry. I didn't have any new news about camp until this afternoon."

"And it's bad news."

"Why would you assume that?"

"Because I didn't hear from you all week and when I do the first thing you say is *sorry*."

"The apology was because you hadn't heard from me. Besides, I'm sure you're familiar with the saying 'no news is good news'?"

"I'm sure you're familiar with the saying 'don't leave me hanging'?"

"God, woman, you are such a pain in the ass . . . but I missed you this week."

That gave me pause. "You did?"

"Yeah." He jammed his hands in the front pockets of his jeans. As if he was nervous.

A sweet, unsure Jensen Lund. *Two helpings of that, please.* "Okay, I sort of missed your smug mug too, Lund. Where were you keeping yourself?"

"Occupied here and there. I figured you needed a break from me hanging around, interrupting your family time with Calder."

I stepped closer. The fact that I felt compelled to reassure him surprised me, but I set my hand on his chest briefly anyway. "If you'd become a pest, I'd tell you." I smiled. "Or I'd swat at you. I—we—liked having you here."

"Good to know." He relaxed. "How was your week?"

"Long and weird. Yours?"

"Painfully slow. Emphasis on painful."

"Why? Did you pull something in training?"

"Some weeks just feel physically more challenging. Even

when it's the same routine. This was that week for me." He flashed me his dimpled smile. "My two minutes are up. Are you really kicking me out when I haven't told you anything about the camp?" His gaze darted to the hallway leading to the bedrooms. "I'll be quiet."

"Fine. Come in." After I relocked the door, I turned around to see him right there. "What?"

"When I first moved here Axl told me no one locked their doors unless they were out of town. Evidently I'm not as friendly, because I've always locked mine. That annoyed Martin especially since he had free access when Axl lived there."

"I bet Axl's apartment was the only one Martin had free access to. I don't believe people in this building—or this city—are that trusting. Can you imagine coming home and finding Lenka digging through your cupboards?"

"Or worse. Pawing through my dresser drawers." Jensen gave a mock shudder.

I nudged him with my shoulder. "Got something in there that'd cause embarrassment?"

His blue, blue eyes locked onto mine with such confidence, with such male heat that I became dizzy. "I've got nothing to hide. I'd let you take a peek in my drawers any time."

My brain failed to call up a clever retort.

His nearness reminded me how fantastic he smelled. And when he said, "Move that cute ass into the living room so we can talk," he reminded me of his mastery of the bossy compliment.

I settled at the card table where Calder and I were putting together the puzzle. Jensen perched on the edge of the recliner as if he had to be ready to spring into action at any time.

"So tell me, Lund . . . the camp. Go? Or no-go?"

"It's a go."

Then he went into such detail that my eyes started to glaze over.

But it sounded like a miracle. When I said as much, Jensen became flustered. "Everyone I needed to come through did. I got lucky with Astrid."

"Excuse me?"

He groaned. "Not like that. Astrid, an LCCO intern, will be the project manager. She pushed to be part of it and if not for her, I'd probably still be trying to fill out the mountains of paperwork."

Ridiculous to be jealous of Astrid, but I was. "Calder will be thrilled. And I'm relieved. So is my bank account. The other camp I found was three times as much money."

Jensen frowned at me. "You had so little faith in me, Coach?"

"I hadn't heard from you. School is over two weeks from today. I had to have a plan." I glanced down at the piles I'd sorted. We'd built the outer frame and I'd finished the Persian cat in the orange hat that looked like a dunce cap with tassels.

"What are you doing?"

"Playing the guitar," I mumbled, because it was pretty damn obvious what I was doing.

"You're extra punchy tonight." He popped to his feet and moved in behind me.

"Because it's late."

He said, "Mmm-hmm," and parked himself right beside me. "A cat puzzle, huh?"

"Not that I need to defend it, but this came from my folks' house. Martin gave it to me for my eighth birthday."

"How do you remember that?"

I tried a white piece but it didn't fit, so I set it in the discard pile. "My parents didn't make a huge deal about birthdays.

I got one present from them and one from my brother. 'Less is more' made the gift memorable, so I could probably tell you every present I received until I turned fourteen."

"Try this one there." He handed me a white-and-gray piece. "Are you raising Calder the same way?"

"Trying to. But he has an uncle who likes to buy him stuff, and he's an only grandchild. High-dollar toys aren't a possibility since I'm on a budget, so the one-gift thing works for now." I snapped the piece he'd handed me into place. "Did the Lund kids have a Ringling Brothers–type birthday party circus every year?"

"Nope. My mom kept birthdays low-key. It's a Swedish thing. My parents also limited the number of our classmates' parties we could go to."

I looked at him. "Because . . . ?"

"Our classmates and their parents assumed the rich kids would bring expensive presents. So we got invited to a lot of birthday parties. Mom and Dad had to draw the line somewhere."

"Setting limits for your kid isn't fun."

"Setting limits for anything isn't fun." Jensen's eyes met mine. Then his gaze roamed over my face.

"What? It's been five days and you're looking at me like you don't recognize me."

"I look at you, but I don't always see you, Rowan."

I found it hard to breathe.

"Hanging out together . . . You're just Coach Bossy Pants, a contrary redhead, a fierce mother to your son, a friend who makes me laugh, makes me think, makes me mad, bakes for me . . . and I forget you're a stunningly beautiful woman. Then I get this close to you and I'm reminded in vivid detail that you are mega-hot, with those fuck-me bedroom eyes and kiss-me-now lips. Christ, you smell like cookies and flowers and sex and I just want to devour you."

"Jensen."

"*Devour* you," he repeated as if I hadn't heard him the first time. He crouched down until we were eye to eye. "Ask me why I stayed away this week."

"Why did you stay away this week?"

"Because I'm a shitty friend."

"Why are you a shitty friend?"

"Because I don't want to be friends with you." He invaded my space until I felt his breath on my lips. "I want to devour you."

Pretty sure my lungs stopped functioning at that point.

Twelve

JENSEN

Rowan blinked at me. A sexy slow blink, and my heart started to pound.

When she sank her teeth into her lower lip, I experienced that incredible rush of anticipation.

Finally.

I would finally get to kiss her.

She'd tilt her head and it'd be on.

It'd be one of those slo-mo, soft-focus, romantic movie kisses. Lips sliding together. Parting only to suck in a fast breath before the intense I-wanna-fuck-you sex kisses overwhelmed us both.

Then Rowan reached out . . . and playfully patted me on the cheek. "Dude. If you're that hungry I could fix you something to eat."

What?

She wasn't serious . . . was she?

My gaze narrowed on her lips. Her mouth moved. But I couldn't hear anything over the *rat-a-tat-tat-tat* sound of machine gun fire as she thoroughly shot me down.

Thoroughly.

Man. I needed a traffic cop to sort out the number of mixed signals this woman was sending me.

So I did what any self-respecting guy with a *Titanic*-sized hole in his ego would do . . . I said *fuck it* and kissed her anyway.

Not the tasteful, soft-porn type of kiss I'd envisioned. Not even the teeth-clacking soul kiss I craved. I gave her a hard, swift kiss, right on her surprised mouth, followed by a light head butt, because apparently I was still a twelve-year-old boy and that was how I let her know I liked her even after she'd torpedoed my ego.

"You *are* tired if you thought I was talking about food," I said offhandedly as I stood.

"Jensen . . ."

"It's late. I just wanted to share the good news about camp. Astrid is creating registration documents, release forms, medical forms and all that necessary stuff that's out of my wheelhouse. So it'll probably be Monday before I can get that to you."

"Jensen."

"She mentioned that she'd like to have a phone conference with you early next week to discuss the best way to get in contact with the other parents whose kids were displaced. Oh, and during the cost analysis, we determined we need to add another ten kids to the camp for a better balance in the classroom. So if you have other kids in mind, talk to Astrid about adding them to the list."

"Jensen."

"We're opening up the building next week and I'll be there as much as my training schedule allows, getting it ready for opening day so you probably won't see me much—"

"Hey, dickhead. Stop babbling."

I turned around and faced her. "That's twice with the name-calling tonight, Coach."

"You brought it on yourself by talking over me."

"By all means. You've got the floor."

"Thank you. I . . ." She inhaled and slowly let it out. "I'm a shitty friend too, all right?"

Do not say anything even remotely smart-ass-y, Lund.

"This is new to me. It wasn't supposed to happen—"

"But it did. And ignoring it won't make it go away."

"As if I ever had a chance of ignoring you," she retorted.

My body language said, "Is that a bad thing?" even when I remained quiet.

"And I don't know what to do with it, okay?"

"I could give you a hint."

"I'm serious."

"So am I."

She sighed. "Fine. What is your hint?"

"The next time I want to kiss you? Let me."

"Oh for fuck's sake."

I laughed.

"Stop joking around." She blinked at me. "You are joking, right?"

I didn't answer. Let her come to her own conclusions. Or . . . let her stew. I smiled and said, "Good night, Rowan."

I t'd been a long week.

Things weren't completely ready, but I'd called a staff meeting for Friday morning anyway.

A staff meeting. Me. Mr. Tune-Out during any meeting

longer than five minutes where I wasn't watching guys get pummeled.

I had a feeling karma was about to bite me in the ass.

Every other camp-type situation I'd been involved in had been with other football players. So the work was split up between at least half a dozen of us. The camps never lasted long: three hours at the most. Then we'd have an autograph session.

This summer camp sent me into unknown territory and I'd dragged poor Astrid along for the ride. She'd been great this past week, but I needed her to be on top of everything the next three months because I'd be hit-and-miss. Realizing I preferred being a worker bee to being the big boss when it came to my LCCO responsibilities meant I had no ego about putting Astrid on the payroll and upping her responsibilities. But the truth was, my main responsibility was to train and prepare for football season.

I rolled out of bed and headed to the fitness center in the apartment complex. I wouldn't have time for a full workout before I met with the staff, but I could at least get cardio out of the way.

After four hard miles on the treadmill, I showered. I threw on some clean clothes and heated up one of my prepared breakfasts that didn't suck—steel-cut oats with almonds, blueberries and honey. I filled out the form online for the following week's meals as I ate and hit send when I finished.

My family gave me crap for employing a personal chef. Before Brady had met Lennox, he ate whatever meals his secretary brought him—usually at his desk. Walker was marginally better cooking for himself. But his company provided lunch for their employees, so I failed to see how having healthy meals delivered to my door was any different.

Besides, because I was a professional athlete my caloric intake needs fluctuated. Hiring an expert to keep my protein-to-carb ratio balanced for optimum performance was no different than hiring any other professional. I could probably roof a house myself, but why would I want to when I could hire a roofer?

I didn't understand why my mom took it so personally that Chef J prepared my meals when she'd had a full-time cook and several other domestic workers when I was growing up.

She's concerned because she wants a woman in your life to share meal prep responsibilities, not a random guy in a restaurant across town.

But even if I was in a serious relationship? I wouldn't expect my partner to adhere to the same diet I did during the season or learn how to prepare it.

"Dude. If you're that hungry I could fix you something to eat."

Rowan. I still couldn't believe she'd said that to me when I'd wanted to kiss her.

I hadn't seen her much this week. Once in the elevator as I returned home and she was leaving to run Calder someplace. Once in the hallway between our apartments. Calder had started a long story about . . . I honestly couldn't remember. I'd spent the entire time watching Rowan. Wondering if I'd taken spinning my wheels to a whole new level. Wondering why I'd ditch my three nonnegotiable rules in a hot minute if she gave me a sign she wanted more than this bogus attempt at being friends.

But the stubborn woman hadn't made the effort. I'd wait her out. I could be damn stubborn too.

At the site of Camp Step-Up, a former elementary school, I parked my Land Cruiser next to an older-model Saturn.

Astrid climbed out of it as I walked past. She fell into step with me, holding the biggest insulated coffee mug I'd ever seen. "Morning," she said brightly. "I'm glad you're here early."

"Better early than late."

"I've already been here for forty-five minutes," she confessed.

"Why didn't you go in?"

"We haven't discussed specifics on arrival times and if I'm allowed to open the building early. Or if I fall behind on my work"—she made a sarcastic little snort, as if *that'd* ever happen—"and I have to stay late, if you're all right with me locking down the building."

"Since you have the code I'd think it'd be a given that you can come and go as you please."

She stopped, forcing me to stop. "*This* is what I'm talking about. I don't assume anything. We have to make these types of decisions as a team. I'd think it was a given that *you'd* know all about teamwork."

"You're right. We need to be on the same page of the playbook."

Astrid rolled her eyes. "Seriously? You couldn't have said 'the ball is in your court' or anything that doesn't use the clichéd word *playbook*?"

"Hey, it's no joke that a playbook is the bible in my world. And get used to the sports analogies, because that's how I roll. Since we're both early we'll have time to go over whatever list you've got—I'm assuming there's more than one." I pointed to her enormous coffee cup. "You have enough to share?"

"Nope."

"Stingy with the caffeine. I'll remember that. Let's see if you know how to work the new security system."

Astrid struggled to juggle her coffee as she punched in the code, but she got it right on the first try.

We wandered into the area that'd served as the office and dumped our stuff. LCCO had done few updates, but the entire facility would be cleaned next week.

This was one of the smallest elementary schools I'd ever been in. No wonder the school district had sold this property. The building had sat empty for the past fifteen years prior to LCCO purchasing the property three years ago. They'd used it for storage and as a place to organize items for various charity events. After talking with Aunt Priscilla, I'd learned that LCCO remained unsure on future plans for the space. Renovating was economically unfeasible—according to Brady, the Lund Industries CFO, as well as Walker, the Lund family construction expert.

The gymnasium had a stage that stretched along the back wall. In the corner was a line of portable lunch tables. In the opposite corner a door led to a small kitchen.

"Was this a working kitchen when this school was in use?"

"It's hard to believe they had enough room in here to prepare meals for over a hundred kids every day." I opened the first big refrigerator and cold air poured out.

"Are we letting the kids put their lunches in the fridge? Or is it just for snacks?"

I scratched the back of my neck. "I don't know. That's one we'll play by ear." I tipped my head toward the door. "Grab the clipboard and let's start checking things off. We'll start by making sure the art supplies were delivered to the right room."

As we cut out of the gym and into the hallway, unencumbered by rows of lockers, I remembered that we hadn't had lockers until junior high. We'd kept all of our school supplies in our desks and hung our coats in the closet in the classroom.

"This place is totally retro," Astrid said. "I feel like we stepped back in time."

"Can you believe there were only eight classrooms in this entire school?"

She shook her head. "One *wing* of my elementary school had eight classrooms."

"Makes you realize just how super-sized everything has become." I opened the door to the first room.

The individual desks had been cleared out. A stack of pallets marked ART SUPPLIES took up one corner.

After giving the wall of windows a cursory glance, I said, "I hope this room doesn't get too hot." Walker would lose his mind if he saw a single bead of sweat on his wife's brow. And then he'd probably install central air.

I'd been here before, but Astrid hadn't. She rocked at multitasking; we cleared half of her list as we wandered from room to room.

The last doors on the far end opened into what used to be a library.

"Oh wow. This is depressing, seeing all these empty shelves." Astrid ran her hand along the weathered oak. "At every school I spent vast amounts of time in the library. I'll bet this place was cozy when it was filled with books."

When I was growing up, spending time in the library was torture. I was an outdoor kid. I wanted to be on the playground or in gym class. I wasn't a bad student as much as a distracted one. The only series that kept my attention longer than fifteen minutes was Harry Potter, and only if I could read it outside in my tree fort.

"What activity is going on in here?" Astrid asked me.

"I'll let the instructors hash it out, but I'm betting this room won't be used at all."

She smirked. "So if you can't find me, you'll know the first place to look."

"Hello?" A voice echoed down the hallway.

When I saw my sister-in-law Trinity, I couldn't help but hug her; she looked so damn cute with that baby bump. "Hey, mama. Where's your ugly half?"

Trinity whapped me on the arm. "Walker is carrying in my bags because you know I'm not allowed to do a damn thing."

"As it should be." My eyes narrowed. "He *is* gonna let you be here unattended, right?"

"Fortunately they're in the busy time of year and he's all over town. But I suspect you'll see him at lunch break since it's his mission to ensure I eat all my veggies." Trinity smiled at Astrid. "Hey. Good to see you stretching your wings outside the LCCO office."

Astrid turned and pointed. "Closest bathroom is right there."

I stared at her hard. "Why would you feel the need to tell her that first thing?"

"Because I'm pregnant," Trinity said. "I'm in the bathroom only slightly more often than I'm in the kitchen foraging for food."

Astrid gave me a smug smile. "My sister had a baby last year. I got used to scouting out the bathroom for her everywhere we went."

Walker strolled in, his arms overloaded with bags. "Dallas is looking for you."

"Come on, Astrid, we've been summoned."

We found Dallas in the gym, conversing with a woman in a leotard and tights and a hipster-looking guy, complete with beanie.

Dallas saw me first, and in her normal fashion she came at me in a dead run.

I braced myself and caught her.

She laughed. "Am I ever going to knock you down, you big oaf?"

"Are you ever going to stop acting like an eight-year-old and trying to knock me over?"

"Probably not." She dropped to her feet.

"Then right back atcha."

"So is everyone here?" she asked.

"Not yet."

"This is going to be a rockin' camp, Jens. These kids are so lucky." She hugged me. "Thanks for making me part of this. I won't let you down."

I offered my hand to the woman. "You're Vanessa? I'm Jensen. Thanks for sticking with the program."

"I'm happy to be here. I love these kids and I should be thanking you for finding a way to make the camp happen."

Before I could credit LCCO, the hipster offered me his hand. "I'm Todd, the music teacher. I'll echo what Vanessa said. It's awesome that you were able to keep—and expand—the camp."

Astrid stepped forward. "Hey, everyone. I'm Astrid. I've talked to you all on the phone. I'm here for whatever you need."

"To add to that . . . I won't be here for all six hours of camp, but Astrid will. I'm the idea guy and she's the program administrator who makes it happen, so always talk to her first."

Astrid's eyes grew huge behind her glasses. But even from the short amount of time I'd spent with her, she'd proven herself more than capable of running this thing.

"Who're we missing?" Dallas said.

"Lucy." The door opened and we all turned. "And there she is right now."

Walker and Trinity joined us.

For the next hour as we went over every minute detail, my feelings of panic only increased. Talk about cocky, thinking I could just run a freakin' day camp. These people all had dedicated roles in this. What was mine?

I saw Walker and Todd separating conference tables. "Astrid. What am I supposed to be doing?"

"Just stand there and look pretty."

"It'll get real ugly real fast if you keep saying shit like that."

"Relax," she warned, holding up her hand. "I was trying to be funny, but obviously I didn't succeed, which is nothing new in my world." She stepped in closer to confide, "Look, Jensen, you *are* a celebrity. On registration morning, these kids' parents will want to meet you since you're sponsoring the camp—"

"Let's clear this up once and for all. LCCO is sponsoring the camp, not me personally. I'll be involved, but I'm not the key player. If not for Dallas, we'd be short two instructors. If anyone deserves credit, she does. Plus, she convinced her mom to loosen the purse strings on this project."

"She really came through, didn't she?" Astrid said as she focused on my petite cousin, holding court with Vanessa and Trinity. "She is absolutely amazing."

"Careful, that sounds like a girl crush," I teased.

Astrid tipped her head back and met my gaze. "Uh, yeah, about that. I pretty much crush on all women. *Only* on women."

I let that sink in. "Get out. So you weren't flirting with me in the office that day you begged to be part of the project."

She laughed. "'Fraid not. Bet that was refreshing for you, huh?"

"Very."

We walked back to the office. After we'd settled in, Astrid at her desk behind her laptop and me at the table beside her with a clipboard full of notes, she said, "As much as I'd love to flirt with Dallas now that I don't work for her mother, I'm aware that she's not even a little bi-curious. 'Hopelessly hetero,' she assured me."

"You came on to her?"

"Geez, no. She read my aura, and apparently my attraction to her was as obvious as a big ol' neon sign."

I gave Astrid the side-eye. "You believe in that stuff?"

She shrugged. "I believe that more things in life happen because of serendipity than people are willing to admit."

That made me think of Rowan.

What doesn't make you think of Rowan?

What was my role in her life? Did I even have one?

Focus on the here and now. "Anything else I should know about you, Astrid?"

"Personally? I'm vegan."

"So I won't send you to pick us up lunch."

She laughed. "I'm a Taurus."

"Better to *be* one than to drive one," I said dryly.

"You are every bit as funny as Rowan assured me you were."

I stopped doodling in the margins of my notes. "Rowan said I was funny?"

"Yep." Astrid had refocused on her laptop.

Don't ask, man. Just . . . don't.

"What else did she say about me?"

"I don't remember specifics. But you've definitely found an admirer in her."

I should have told Astrid that Rowan and I were strictly friends.

But Rowan admitting *I'm a shitty friend too* . . . I couldn't seem to get that out of my head. Even when I shouldn't hold out hope things would veer off the "friends" path and we'd blaze a trail right into my bedroom.

Bedroom? Wishful thinking, man. The woman wouldn't even let you kiss her.

I sighed.

Astrid's fingers stopped clicking on the computer keys. "Why the heavy sigh, boss?"

I've lost my mojo.

What the fuck was wrong with me? Since when did I use the word *mojo*? No wonder I wasn't getting laid.

"I do remember something else Rowan said about you."

My gaze connected with hers. "What's that?"

"That you have a lot of patience."

There was another cock-deflating compliment. "Do I even want to know how that came up in conversation?"

Astrid blushed. "Look, I don't know you very well. And I spent time talking and Skyping with her, getting other parents' contact information. She said you'd be great with the kids. That not many guys would show the same patience with a thirty-year-old woman that you did with her six-year-old son."

That jarred me. Patience was a good thing?

She hadn't asked me to be patient with her.

But you have been.

"She doesn't look like she's thirty," Astrid said off-handedly.

"What's that have to do with anything?"

"Some guys have a problem dating older women."

"A, I'm twenty-eight so she's a whopping two years older than me. B, we're not dating. We're neighbors." Even if we were dating, her age wouldn't matter to me. That got me to thinking . . . our age difference didn't bother Rowan, did it?

"How does she take her coffee?"

"Black."

"What does she drink to relax?"

"Wine. Mostly Zin." It wasn't like there was twenty years' difference between us.

"What's her favorite TV show?"

"Dancing with the Stars."

"What kind of music does she listen to?"

"Country. Some hip-hop. Reggae. Weird old stuff." She and I would be a killer team for music trivia.

"Her favorite color?"

"Blue."

"Her favorite sports team?"

"It'd better be the damn Vikings since she cheers for us."

I glanced up at Astrid and scowled. "What's with the twenty questions?"

"It was only six questions. And you didn't hesitate to answer any of them. So you're more than neighbors, boss."

We're more than friends too.

Although I hadn't even kissed Rowan, we had a connection I'd never felt with any of the women I'd fucked. Crude way to think of it, but I could accept that that was all it'd ever been.

"As her neighbor . . . do you water her plants?"

"She doesn't have any plants."

"Do you pet sit for her? Take care of her cat?"

My mind veered off the track and straight onto the smut town express. *Oh hell yeah, I'd like to pet her pu—*

"Do you borrow stuff from each other all the time?" Astrid asked.

"Like what? A cup of sugar?"

She belted out Maroon 5's "Sugar" in a truly impressive falsetto.

I laughed. "When the kids are here for camp? No more drinking on the job."

"Don't you have training to go to right now?" She held up her phone so I could see the time, and then she pointed to the door. "Go tackle practice dummies or something equally violent and let me do my job in peace."

I stood and said, "Peace out, yo," and left for the training complex.

D ante tortured me.

After our workout, I hurt in places I'd forgotten had muscles. Then he forced me into the cold-hot-cold-hot muscle therapy. I swam slow laps in the pool. Then I hit a hot shower. After that I lowered my aching body into an ice bath. Finally I ended up in the sauna. As I lumbered down the hallway to my apartment, I contemplated crawling in bed and calling it a week.

My phone rang and the caller ID read: ROWAN. I glanced at her apartment door. "Hey. I'm in the hallway about to walk into my apartment."

"Thank god. Look, I hate to ask you this—"

"Just ask."

"Coach T called an emergency meeting for the cheer team tonight, and neither Daisy nor Marsai is in town so I'm acting team captain. It starts in an hour. Alicia has to leave to go to her other job, so could you watch Calder until I get done?"

"Sure."

"Thank you! I'll call Alicia right now and tell her you'll be over—"

"Calder can come to my place. It's been a long day and I wanna veg on my own couch. Send a key with him so if he needs anything we can go over and grab it. I need about ten minutes."

"I'll let her know. Thank you!"

I changed clothes and checked out my fridge. My weekly meals weren't delivered until Monday so I had two entrées left. Crispy fried tofu with sugar snap peas, served with a side of kale, quinoa and beet salad. Tomorrow's dinner was shredded teriyaki turkey with cauliflower and broccoli, and a plain baked sweet potato. Neither of those meals would appeal to a six-year-old boy. Maybe it'd be better if we stayed at Rowan's place. She had a fully stocked pantry.

But her couch had the texture of a concrete block. Her TV? Half the size of mine. Not that I required luxurious accommodations, but I loved the comfort of my own home. It was the first place I'd lived since I'd left my childhood home that felt like mine.

Knock knock.

I opened the door to Alicia and Calder.

"Hey, little dude, I'm happy we're going to hang out for a bit."

Calder clung to Alicia. Usually he raced in and started bouncing on my couch.

I looked at his babysitter.

"Calder had a rough day at school, didn't you, bud?" Alicia squeezed his shoulder. "He was looking forward to his mom coming home."

Great. He didn't want to be here. How did I handle that? *Figure it out. You'll be facing this at camp a time or two.*

Alicia handed me the key. Then she hugged Calder. "See you Monday." She mouthed "Good luck" to me before she disappeared down the hallway.

I shut the door.

Before I could ask where he wanted to stash his backpack, he said, "I'm hungry."

"I don't have much for food. So unless you can come up with a delicious dish using garbanzo beans, eggs and cheese, we'd better grab food from your kitchen and cook it here."

"Why don't you have more food?"

"I have a chef who makes my meals, and I'm almost out." His eyes got big. "You have your own *chef*?"

"He's not just my chef. He cooks for other people too."

"Can I come over and watch him cook?"

"Absolutely I'd let you if he prepared my meals here. But he cooks in his restaurant kitchen, packages up the food, and then it's delivered to me. So all I have to do is take it out of the refrigerator or freezer and heat it up."

Silence.

Calder stared at me. "Like a frozen dinner?"

"Exactly like that."

"There's a chicken nugget one in my freezer. I could have that."

"Let's go grab it. I'll put mine in the micro here first."

We ended up cooking Calder's meal in his microwave and carrying it over so he could eat it right away. I poured us each a glass of milk.

Dinner was a silent affair.

Calder kept looking at the front of his frozen package, then at me. Finally he said, "You're not really a giant."

"I wish I were a giant like Hagrid in Harry Potter."

He blinked at me.

"You don't know Harry Potter?"

"Mommy says I can't watch those movies until I'm eight."

"You've never seen them? Uh. Okay. But I'd wait until after you've read all the books. Because the books are way better than the movies."

Calder burst into tears.

Shit. That was totally freakin' random.

I crouched down by his chair. "What's going on?"

"I'll probably never get to read them because I'm the worst reader in my class!"

"What? Who told you that?"

"Today Tiara said I was gonna flunk kindergarten!" Calder flung himself at me and sobbed as if his soul had been ripped from his chest.

Without knowing what to say, I picked him up and carried him to the couch. He continued to cry, great big racking sobs. Poor kid. I wanted to fix this for him ASAP. Call up one of those expensive private learning centers and demand they send over their best kindergarten tutor right freakin' now.

After he'd stopped hiccupping, I said, "That's why you had a rough day at school?"

He nodded.

"Did you tell Alicia what happened?"

"I told her someone was mean to me."

"She might've been able to make you feel better." Better than this lousy job I was doing.

"I didn't want her to think I'm dumb. That's what Tiara called me. A dum-dum."

"Well, as my babysitter Maria used to say, 'Consider the source.'" Maybe that was too far over his head. "Did you tell the teacher?"

"I don't wanna be called a tattletale either."

"How can I help you?"

Calder shifted and looked up at me. "Can you help me read?"

What could I say to that? *No. Sorry, kid, you're on your own with this whole reading thing. Just because I read doesn't mean I'm qualified to teach you.*

Instead, I said, "Sure. Whatcha got?"

He bounded over the edge of the couch, grabbed his backpack and bounded back. From his backpack he pulled out *Go, Dog. Go!*

"I remember this book." The cover indicated it was for early readers. "Have you read it?"

"Mommy reads something to me every night."

"Lucky you. My mom read to me every night too. So how about if we make a deal? If you read this book to me? I'll read Harry Potter to you."

His eyes widened. "For real?"

"For real. I never joke about Harry Potter."

He bit his lip. "I don't wanna get in trouble for breaking the house rules."

"Your mom said you couldn't watch the movies. But she didn't say anything about someone reading the books to you, did she?"

"Nope."

"Then we're in the clear." I smiled. "Start that tale—*tail*, get it?—of *Go, Dog. Go!*"

"You're funny." Calder read slowly, not that I had any idea what constituted speed reading for a six-year-old.

After he stashed his book, I grabbed the hardback edition of *Harry Potter and the Sorcerer's Stone*. We snuggled into the corner of the couch and I started to read.

We were so engrossed in the story that neither of us noticed someone knocking at the door until it turned into pounding.

I vaulted over the edge of the couch and opened the door.

Rowan tried—and failed—not to seem annoyed. "I've been texting you for almost forty-five minutes."

"I think I left my phone on your kitchen counter when we went over to get food. Anyway, Calder and I are fine. We've been reading and lost track of time."

She walked past me and stopped in the living room. "What are you reading?"

"Harry Potter!" Calder yelled, and bounced over the edge of the couch to run at his mother. "Isn't that so cool, Mommy?"

"Yes, it is." She smiled and tousled his hair. "I missed you today."

"Did you know that Harry Potter had to live under the stairs?" he demanded.

"I remember that." She glanced over at the dark TV. "You guys aren't watching *Chopped*?"

Calder looked at me. "Uh-oh. We forgot."

I sent Rowan a challenging look.

"You'll never hear me complain about him choosing to read a book over watching TV, Jensen."

"Good to know."

"Grab your backpack, boy-o," she said to him. "Bath time, then bedtime, because you have to be up early tomorrow."

"Why?" Calder complained.

"Because I have to work in the morning and Talia is

coming over to watch you. She hasn't been here before, so you'll have to show her around."

"Who's Talia?" I asked her.

"She's a former student of mine. Since she's enrolled in summer classes and only wants part-time work, she agreed to babysit Calder."

"But I thought Alicia was your nanny?"

"Just during the school year. Alicia's still in high school and her family travels a lot in the summer. I need a babysitter that'll be around."

"Rocketman could be my babysitter," Calder declared. "Then we could read Harry Potter *every day!*"

I grinned at him and then locked eyes with Rowan. "While that sounds great, I'm sure your mother would get tired of seeing me every day. That happens sometimes with *friends.*"

Her cheeks turned bright red.

"I'd play with my friends every day if I could," Calder said.

"I'm with you there, Calder. It's fun to play with your friends until you realize maybe one of them is toying with you."

"That's not true—"

"I'd share *my* toys if you'd let my friends come over," Calder said, oblivious to the underlying conversation.

"How about you, Coach? Got any *friends* you want to invite over to play?"

Rowan seemed anxious to get away from me as she herded her son toward the door.

Hmm. Too bad, sweetheart. Patience is a virtue but persistence has a better chance of payoff.

"I'll tag along," I said. "Last place I remember having my phone was over there."

"You could bring the book and read more after my bath,"

Calder suggested. He walked backward, facing me. His mother had him by the backpack as she practically dragged him away.

"We'll save it for another time, okay?"

"Promise?"

"I promise."

Inside their apartment, Rowan disappeared with Calder into the bathroom and I heard their voices—but not what they were saying—until the water kicked on in the tub.

I found my phone by her stove. Then I parked myself at the end of the hallway, waiting for her to emerge.

Her cheeks were flushed. Red wisps of hair stuck to her face. She looked so damn cute and frazzled. She squinted at me. "You're still here?"

"Yep. Waiting for payment for my babysitting services."

"Okay. Let me grab my purse—"

"Rowan. I was kidding."

"Oh." She slumped against the wall, leaving about a foot of space between us. "Thank you so much for watching Calder tonight. Seriously, Jensen, you were a lifesaver."

"My pleasure."

A beat passed. Then two.

I said, "You all right?"

"No. You fluster the hell out of me, Lund."

There it was. Finally. "Are you expecting an apology, Coach?"

"Would you give me one?"

"Hell no."

She laughed. "You are the very definition of cocky."

"And you are the very definition of stubborn."

"I don't know that it's being stubborn as much as it's a habit."

"What's a habit?"

"My default reaction when a man hits on me."

I fought a grin and lost. "You're willing to admit you know that's what it was?"

"Yes. And the end result of my default reaction is to put it—him—in a box. It's the same box I've been using for years."

"It's probably pretty crowded in there by now."

She snickered. "Of course *you* wouldn't know that because you refuse to be labeled and neatly compartmentalized into my box."

"While I'm happy you recognize I don't fit, it sounds as if you're pissed off about it."

"I am."

I shrugged. "Guess that sucks for you."

"See? That's what I'm talking about. It'd be easier if you didn't have such a sly and charming sense of humor. If you acted like an entitled billionaire. If you were rude and impatient. If you weren't so awesome with my son."

I cocked my head to look at her, but she avoided my gaze.

"It's hard to be friends with a guy like you."

"Explain 'a guy like me.'"

"A guy with that body and that face who is so genuinely thoughtful. A guy with that body and that face who makes me laugh and feel good every time we hang out. A guy with that body and that face who hasn't ever given a woman like me a first look, let alone a second glance. So when I realized that yes, a guy like you with that body and that face is interested in me, in *that* way, I had no idea how to handle it. Besides embarrassing the hell out of myself by pretending *you* misunderstood because I didn't want you to know how lame I actually am when it comes to recognizing this attraction stuff. Then going out of my way to ignore you this past week as I obsessed about it and tried to figure out what to do."

My lips curled up slightly. "Have you come to any new conclusions?"

"That I'm horrible at this and a shitty friend."

"That's not news, Rowan."

She sighed. "I know. So I'll . . . try harder, okay?"

"Try harder to be a better friend?" I said with an edge to my voice.

"Mom!" Calder yelled. "Come here."

"Just a second, honey."

"Mommy, I got soap in my eye and it stings!"

Rowan spared me a quick look. "Can we—"

"Go. It'll keep."

As soon as she disappeared, I did too.

Neither patience nor persistence seemed to make a bit of difference when dealing with Rowan. She hadn't decided whether to take that next step over the friendship line with me. Didn't matter how I felt about it, or her, or what I wanted, and that sucked. This was a clear reminder that I was better off keeping my focus trained on things in my life that I could control.

In my apartment, I grabbed a sparkling water and my keys before I headed out.

Best option for distracting myself from the oh-so-tempting Rowan Michaels was to keep myself busy and out of the building this week.

Thankfully, I had friends and family members to help me out.

Thirteen

ROWAN

"I hate Saturday practices," Daisy said under her breath.

I sat on her feet as we did partner sit-ups and I silently counted each rep.

"Hate"—she said as her chin touched her knees and rolled back down, only to repeat the motion—"hate" as she pulled herself up again.

Hate rhymes with *eight* . . . and dammit, I lost track of her reps. Because she was close to done, I said, "Time."

Daisy flopped on the mat and groaned.

I nudged her hip with my knee as I lowered myself to the mat beside her. "Rest while you're spotting me. Coach's bad mood means I don't want her yelling at us or adding more reps."

"Fine."

Tightening my stomach muscles, I began the exercise. I

focused on breathing, trying to ignore my friend's probing stare. "You are keeping track of these?"

"I'm supposed to keep track? Shit. I was daydreaming about polishing my silver," she said dryly.

"Good thing I'm keeping track." That was the truth. Call it OCD, but I'd been partnered with others who didn't bother to count, so it'd become a habit. When I still felt Daisy staring at me, I closed my eyes.

"Time," she said, but I'd already stopped.

"Ladies," Coach said into her megaphone. "Push-up rotation starts now. Get into position and we'll do this on my count."

Another muttered "Hate" sounded beside me.

I kept my focus on form as Coach barked out numbers to twenty-four. Then we did gator crawls for two dozen reps, followed by clapping push-ups for a dozen more reps. We did five sets of holding plank for a minute and half plank for another minute. By the time she told us to take a break, the muscles in my arms were nearly spasming. I flopped face-first on the mat next to Daisy.

"My mom used to be a cheerleader. She claims they only had practice so they could ogle the players without getting into trouble. She swears they never ran a single lap—not that any of them could've made it around the track even once, since she and her fellow cheerleaders smoked." Daisy sighed. "Where do I sign up to be that kind of cheerleader?"

I snickered.

"Do you think we're done?" Daisy continued. "Coach has inflicted all the usual torture and then some."

The woman was such a talker. I'd learned early on in our friendship that her chatty style of communication didn't always require a response.

The first coaching assistant blew the horn that officially ended practice.

Daisy popped to her feet like she'd gotten a second wind and offered her hand to help me up. "Let's go to Sebastian Joe's and gorge on ice cream."

"That defeats the purpose of the past two hours, doncha think?"

"You are a real Debbie Downer, Michaels."

I had child care covered for another hour and a half, which gave me a little wiggle room. "Ice cream on the condition that we don't shower."

"A whore's bath it is."

Raina, the first alternate, overheard that and wrinkled her nose. She'd been a pain about every little thing because of her resentment for not making the cut. As first alternate she had to attend every practice, but that didn't guarantee she'd get to cheer at any games this season. Daisy and I joked that if any "accidents" befell other squad members, we'd suspect Raina had pulled a Tonya Harding, since she'd do anything to be on that field.

I felt a sharp sting on the back of my thigh and turned to see Marsai gripping a twisted towel. "Dammit, Marsai, that's gonna leave a mark!"

"Aw, poor baby. I'll kiss it and make it better," she cooed and blew me a kiss.

"Hey ho," Daisy said to her. "If you're puckering up to kiss anyone's backside, it'd better be mine."

Marsai propped her hands on her hips. "I'll tag-team you, sound fair?"

"As long as you do me first," Daisy answered.

Raina pushed between us. "Coach T would write you up if she heard this conversation. It's not appropriate. She'd expect better from her team captain."

"Gonna tattle, little girl?" Marsai taunted.

"It'd be no less than you deserve," she retorted, and flounced off.

"Piece of work, that one."

"Eh. She's all bluster and no balls," Marsai said.

Daisy and I reached the open door to the locker room, only to have everyone going past us because apparently Coach T had called us all back.

I'd die if she forced us to do another circuit. My arms were wobbling as it was.

We stood on the field, waiting for Coach T to pull out the megaphone—she loved that damn thing—to let us know what was going on.

Just then the outer door banged open and the football team barged in.

What the hell?

I scoured the group—not because I was searching for one blond hottie in particular—but more than half of the guys were missing. A full roster of players ate up a lot of space. Training camp didn't start for weeks and that happened in Mankato, not at the Winter Park complex.

"Why do they all look as if they were frog-marched here at gunpoint?" Daisy said.

"Same reason we do. Brutal practice." That was when I noticed the athletic staff accompanying them wasn't the second-tier trainers, but the ones who worked directly with the offensive coordinators and specific players.

I hadn't seen Jensen all week. Even Calder had asked about him.

It would've been funny, cheerleaders on one side of the field, squaring off against players on the other side, if it hadn't been for the waves of hostility emanating from the players' side. The derision on a few faces didn't help. As if we had no right to be here.

My back snapped straight. I loved the sport of cheerleading. I wasn't a football fanatic. I'd loved cheering for basketball just as much and considered trying out for the

Timberwolves team, even when it was more dance-focused than cheer. So I hated the reminder from some of the players themselves that they saw us as nothing more than a nuisance that detracted from their athletic prowess on the field.

Daisy said, "Sometimes I want to dick punch these guys when they look down their noses at us like that."

"I'm right behind you, Daze. Go for it."

Feedback from the speaker system had us all cringing. Then one of the managers from the corporate office—I never could keep them all straight since there were so many—stepped onto the field wearing a headset.

"Good morning. I'll start off with the reason for this meeting. As you know, the Vikings organization purchased land in Eagan last year to build a new corporate headquarters and training center. There's been much speculation and erroneous information in the press about the status of our plans. We're making a major press announcement next week." He addressed the players. "So if you're approached by any member of any local or national news outlet for the inside scoop, you are required to answer 'no comment.' This is a deal that's been sixteen months in the making, and the organization does not need one of you giving the press so much as a sound bite. Is that understood?"

Male grumbles rumbled down the sideline.

"There will be serious repercussions if anything is leaked. And trust me, we can—and will—track down the perpetrator. We have rules for a reason, rules we expect everyone to follow."

For the briefest moment, I wondered if he'd shown up and called the team and the cheer squad together to remind us of the no-fraternization rule. My gaze immediately shot to Jensen, who appeared to be studying his cleats.

Don't be paranoid. Clearly with the way Mr. Big Shot is

*addressing the players, it's about other rule violations you
aren't aware of.*

Then Mr. Corporate went all *Rah! Rah! Team!* as if *we*
needed a pep talk.

Daisy exhaled a soft snoring noise, and it was hard not
to laugh.

Coach T interrupted the speaker's monologue, using the
megaphone. "Respectfully, Brian, as none of the breach of
protocol seems to be directed at my athletes, I'm excusing
them from the remainder of this discussion."

Brian seemed taken aback by Coach's boldness. Evidently he didn't know her very well. "Of course. And as I've
hit the major talking points, I'll turn it back over to the
coaches."

The big, burly coach yelled, "Everyone is dismissed."

Thank god.

Access to the players' locker rooms was on our side of
the field, and as soon as they were released, they started in
our direction at a dead run.

Since Daisy and I were the first in line to the tunnel—
we'd been the last ones out—we waited to let them pass. But
not all of them did.

Hugo, the backup center, nearly plowed us over.

Daisy mumbled about him being a big, dumb ox.

Jensen, near the front of the line of players, smiled when
he saw me. Then he jogged over.

Oh no. No, no, no, no, no. What are you doing?

"Hey, Rowan, do you have a minute?"

I felt every pair of eyes zoom in on us. With surprise,
curiosity and a few burning looks of hostility.

What the hell was wrong with him? We'd just suffered
through a fifteen-minute lecture on the importance of rules,
and he'd decided to ignore that and blatantly break them?
In front of my coach as well as his?

He can ignore it because the rules don't apply to him.

When he got close enough that only he and Daisy could overhear me, I said, "What are you doing?"

"Talking to you."

"Don't."

Jensen froze. "What's wrong?"

"We are not supposed to interact according to—"

"That's a bullshit rule and you know it."

"But it *is* a rule. Everyone is staring at us."

He glared at anyone who met his gaze before he directed it back to me. "So?"

"So trot your smarmy little rule-breaking self to the locker room."

Instead of backing away, Mr. Contrary moved closer. "What has gotten into you?"

"Stop it, Lund. I'm not kidding."

"You're serious about me not even talking to you?"

"Yes. Just go."

"Like hell."

Frustrated, I turned and walked away.

A scuffle broke out behind me as Daisy tried to stop him. But much bigger men in the NFL had tried to stop him without success. The next thing I knew, The Rocket had landed in front of me.

"Are you embarrassed to be seen with me?" he demanded.

"I'm pissed off that you don't understand I *can't* be seen with you."

That sent him back a step.

"You don't give a damn that you are creating issues for me by insisting that we talk right here in front of everyone. We can't. Go back to pretending you don't know who I am, especially when we're here."

I sidestepped him and this time he didn't follow.

Daisy literally had my back until we got into the locker room. Then she said, "I don't see you for three weeks and suddenly now you're chummy with The Rocket?"

Chummy. Who even used that word anymore?

"I expect to be filled in over ice cream . . . unless the story is so hot that it'll melt the cone right out of your hand?"

I rolled my eyes. "Not. Even. Close."

Since several of the girls were new, the locker room was more subdued than usual. I appreciated the silence while I could because when the season officially started, it'd be a zoo. After I washed my face and neck and redid my ponytail, I fired off a quick text to Talia to check on Calder, and she immediately responded that everything was fine.

Daisy sauntered toward me, her hair falling loose around her shoulders, looking as if she'd just stepped out of a salon. She'd skipped the high heels in favor of flip-flops, but her body still swayed as if she'd stepped onto a runway. It'd be easy to be jealous, but after years in the world of dance and competitive cheer, I accepted that some women were born with the ability to look fantastic with little to no effort.

She glanced at my phone in my hand. "All clear with your sitter?"

"Yep."

"I feel like we should be hitting the bar for an adult beverage."

"Ice cream sounds better."

"Roger that." She shoved her Jackie O–styled sunglasses back in place. "Follow me. I know a shortcut."

I refrained from pointing out that the last time she said that we ended up jumping a curb and driving the wrong way—on a one-way—for a block.

Sebastian Joe's was always busy, even in the winter when the temps dipped below zero, so when the weather warmed up, the line was long.

Daisy did a quick sweep of the crowd before leaning in closer to murmur, "You and The Rocket. Every detail. Now."

I told her about how he'd basically taken over the night I'd come home sopping wet, in a lousy mood about the camp cancellation. "He hung out with Calder and watched *Dancing with the Stars* with us because he'd never seen an episode."

"I'm sure Calder rectified that immediately," she said with amusement.

"Yes, he did, with absolute glee. Boggled my mind that Jensen enjoyed it."

"Get the eff out." Daisy tipped her head and peered at me over the tops of her sunglasses. "He was cool with Calder . . . the way he is?"

Daisy was the only person I didn't bristle up at when asked that question. My boy was sweet, kind, loving, funny, smart, adventurous, athletic and artistic. He was also effeminate. But that was part of who he was. I loved everything about my son. I accepted everything about him, as did the people in our lives who mattered to us. I'd never understood why some people felt it was their right to pass judgment on him. Or to make rude, nosy or just plain nasty comments about a little boy who'd never dream of uttering something so cutting to a stranger. It wasn't possible to shield him from everything, but I'd be damned if I'd let anyone into our lives who didn't treat my kid with the acceptance he deserved.

"Ro?" Daisy prompted.

I looked up at her. "Jens has never been anything but wonderful to Calder. Even when Calder head-butted him in the groin. He listens to him with the patience that's needed to deal with any six-year-old. They watch *Chopped* sometimes and he's even read Harry Potter to him."

"So it's *Jens* now, huh?" she teased.

I blushed. "He told us he doesn't want to be called The Rocket off the field. Calder sometimes calls him Rocketman but Jensen seems amused by it, not annoyed. His behavior doesn't jibe at all with the reputation he has. Then after Calder was in bed, he came back over because he said he could 'tell' something was bothering me."

"Did he make a move on you?"

"No. We talked. I told him about the camp problems and he came up with a solution on the fly. Being cynical, I sort of said, yeah whatever. Then he proved me wrong. You know he's one of *the* Lunds. They have their own organization— Lund Cares Community Outreach—that provides services for community groups. LCCO stepped in and stepped it up, keeping our same dance instructor from the previous camp, but also adding in theater, art and vocal music to the curriculum. No football or sports of any kind."

"I'm impressed," Daisy said. "Unless you're freaked out because you think he's got an ulterior motive for being Mr. Helpful and that's why you were a little psycho with him today."

Immediately I bristled up. "What? I wasn't psycho. Protecting myself isn't psycho! He was completely out of line by singling me out in front of everyone. We're not supposed to be—"

"That no-fraternization rule is total bullshit," Daisy argued. "It was outdated in the '70s. Hello, we're two decades into the new millennium and we're all well past the age of consent. Let us make up our own minds about who we want to fraternize with."

I didn't disagree with her. I hated to admit that when I was with Jensen I didn't think about that stupid rule at all. I was too busy trying to figure out what to do about the magnetic pull between us, which was why I was so upset with him for bringing it to everyone's attention today.

"But, honey, admit it, your reaction to him merely talking to you was . . . slightly psycho."

"Fine. I overreacted." I sighed. "I'll try to explain it to him later."

"Good luck with that. He was pissed off."

Yet another thing everyone noticed.

An ear-piercing shriek echoed in front of us.

Daisy said, "Someone is taking the 'you scream, I scream' portion of the ice cream rhyme literally."

I laughed.

After we chose our flavors—Red Papaya sorbet for her and Caramel Coffee Oreo for me—we wandered back to the parking lot.

Daisy said, "I have an idea. Let's show off these fine bodies that we've slaved to maintain. Grab your kid, pack swimsuits and an overnight bag and come to my place. We'll spend the afternoon lazing by the pool admiring all the manflesh that populates ye old *ce*-ment pond. Then we'll kick back, color and play games with Calder, eat a disgustingly healthy dinner and after your boy is tucked in, we can share a bottle of wine and watch *Thor* or anything starring hot, half-naked men."

"That sounds like heaven." Usually I reserved my weekends for time with Calder, but I'd gotten used to Martin whisking his nephew off on an adventure. Hopefully a sleepover at Daisy's would count. "Calder's dance class ends at three. I'll pick up food on my way over."

"See you then."

I got in my car and headed back to Snow Village.

Avoiding Jensen Lund wasn't possible when you lived across the hallway from him.

Or if he didn't want to be avoided.

I packed everything for our overnight trip. Rather than try to juggle all our stuff and a heavy bag of garbage, I left

Calder in the apartment and dragged the bag down to the Dumpster.

After I'd tossed the bag in and closed the lid, I spun around to see Jensen leaning against the side of the building.

My heart jumped. So did my pulse at the glint in his eyes.

I glanced at the outer set of stairs. If I could get around that metal pole fast enough . . .

"You're not seriously thinking about trying to outrun me, are you, sweetheart? I didn't earn the name The Rocket for nothing."

"Why did you follow me?" I stared at his empty hands. "You aren't out here dumping garbage."

He shrugged. "I heard your door close, saw Calder wasn't with you and figured it'd be a good time to talk about what happened this morning."

I held up my hand. "You were out of line."

"For merely talking to you?"

"Yes. According to the rules, we aren't supposed to—"

"I do not give a good goddamn about that rule."

"That is apparent," I retorted. "How many of your teammates asked you why you approached me?"

"About half."

"And the trainers?"

He shifted, almost nervously.

"They *all* did, didn't they? And you want to know why? Because you didn't see any other players even acknowledging the cheerleaders as they blew past them. You don't have a reputation for breaking team rules, so you brought everyone's attention to the fact that we know each other."

"So you *wanted* me to ignore you?"

"Yes!"

"Un. Fucking. Real. The first time we had this discussion you were pissed off that I didn't know who you were. Now that we're friends, you're pissed because I do know you? That makes no sense, Ro, and you know it."

"*You* don't have to worry about being shit-canned for breaking the rules. I do. Getting fired from the cheer team because of rumors we're sneaking around will have a lasting impact on my future employment as a cheer coach. We both know those types of rumors—whether substantiated or not—can destroy a career. What I don't need is my résumé to say 'fired and disgraced Vikings cheerleader' instead of 'retired Vikings cheerleader.' No private cheer school will hire me, say nothing of any colleges."

His jaw tightened. "That'd never happen. I wouldn't *let* it happen."

I stomped up to him. "Don't you see how that's worse? You coming forward and insisting we're *just friends*? The only way to avoid any whisper of impropriety is if you don't act like we're best pals when we're in a situation like we were in today." My chest was heaving and I was practically yelling at him. I took a step back and tried to level this uncharacteristic burst of anger.

Those beautiful blue eyes of his turned hard and cold. "So I'm good enough to watch movies and share meals with in private, but in public you'd prefer I acted like a dismissive asshole."

"I'd prefer you didn't pay any attention to me at all," I retorted.

"There are two problems with that argument, Coach. First, we live in the same damn building across the hallway from each other. We see each other every day, so it's pretty fucking obvious that we would know each other. Second, why are you worrying about future job problems when you already have a job with U of M? They wouldn't fire you over rumors."

I threw up my hands in total exasperation. "You don't know that. And I never intended to stay at the U my entire career. Right now I am a valuable commodity to any cheer program with my years of experience on the pro side and the collegiate side as well as the athletic training side."

He stared at me.

"What?"

"You're not a commodity," he said softly. "I've spent my life believing that's all I am. That's all I'd ever be."

I hated having this conversation with him. I knew it hurt him. It hurt me too. "I'm sorry you feel that way, Lund, but you are privileged. Nothing will ever affect you the same way it does me."

"You're right." He pushed away from the brick building. "Evidently the time we've spent together hasn't affected you at all if you're so quick to dismiss it as *nothing*."

That stung.

"That's not what I meant, Jensen. And that's not fair."

I thought he'd move in and loom over me, but he kept his distance.

"You want to talk about unfair? I've never let myself get close to a woman like you. A woman of substance, of principles and responsibility and loyalty. You scare the hell out of me, Rowan. You're smart and funny and thoughtful and beautiful and I knew after that first night we had dinner that it'd be hard just being friends with you. But if friendship was all I could have of you? I was willing to take it because I liked being around you. I liked being around your son. I really liked that you seemed happy to hang out with me. The real me. Not the football player or the rich guy everyone else sees. I hoped if I was patient that you could see that our interest in one another and the attraction we both feel could lead to more than friendship."

I truly didn't know what to say.

"But the 'principles' part of who you are that I admired came back to bite me in the ass. I get that you are a list maker and a rule follower. What I don't get? That you're willing to blindly follow someone else's rule even if it causes you to lose out on something that could have a positive impact on your life.

"I'd never do anything to jeopardize your livelihood. But I don't think your extreme overreaction today was about how our friendship will affect your career. You're just as scared about what's been building between us as I am. The difference is? I want to embrace it, not run from it."

"I'm not running from it," I said hotly.

"Yeah, sweetheart, you are. You're latching onto any excuse to keep things as they are."

"It's not an excuse, Jensen."

"So if the no-fraternization rule didn't apply? Things would be different? You would've talked to me today instead of shutting me out? You would've let me kiss you last week instead of shutting me down?"

I said, "Yes," without hesitation.

"Two words: injured reserve. You know what that means?"

"I know what injured reserve means," I said crossly.

"Do you know that technically when I'm on injured reserve . . . I'm not officially on the roster? If I'm not officially on the roster, then the rule isn't in effect for us. Think about that."

My jaw might've hit the concrete.

Jensen walked away without another word.

Fourteen

JENSEN

I believed I'd prepared for every contingency for the official opening of Camp Step-Up.

But I hadn't expected projectile vomiting from the oldest kid in attendance.

Nor had I anticipated getting challenged to a "touchdown celebration dance-off" by a seven-year-old girl.

Neither did I understand why a kid brought a snake in a bucket for show-and-tell, because we didn't have show-and-tell. Also, how had the kid's parents *not* noticed their son carrying a bucket with a snake into the school?

Luckily Astrid was a snake charmer or possibly she spoke Parseltongue because she dealt with the snake and with the kid. And probably his parents.

The next issue involved my cousin Jaxson. He was supposed to drop off his daughter, Mimi, except as soon as Jax realized Lucy's mother was teaching arts and crafts, my in-your-face hockey-playing cousin demanded that I find a volunteer position for him. Right. The guy beat the shit out of people with a stick for a living—not a lot of need for that skill in the real world, to say nothing of at a day camp for kids under age ten.

Jax was determined to "do his part as a Lund." Rather than upsetting Mimi—who was thrilled her father wanted to be around longer than ten minutes—I planned to put him off until registration ended. I flat-out refused Jax's demand to be assigned to Lucy as her classroom aide. I happened to like Lucy and I was fond of my balls being attached to my body.

This wasn't a decision I could delegate to Astrid. I gave Jax one option: He could be the janitor. He didn't balk. He said yes and "welcomed" the chance to prove he'd changed.

But I didn't have time to dwell on that because I had another unexpected crazy Lund family member to deal with—Brady. He demanded to know why the camp wasn't offering academic tutoring.

There was some fun. Conjugating verbs and solving story problems. *Not.*

I reminded Brady that Camp Step-Up focused on the arts. It wasn't petty that if I, a pro athlete, wasn't allowed to teach these kids how to catch a ball, then similarly Mr. CEO Finance Whiz couldn't try to make math fun.

Okay, maybe it was a little petty.

Speaking of petty . . . Rowan and Calder were the last to arrive for registration. I hadn't seen either of them for a week.

A week in which only my pride kept me from asking Bob, the apartment complex manager, if Rowan had moved out.

A week in which I'd convinced myself the only reason I'd wanted Rowan to begin with was because I couldn't have her. That "out of sight, out of mind" would cure my obsession with her.

But as I looked at her, I realized my feelings hadn't changed. At all.

Immediately Rowan focused on Astrid, but Calder was all about me.

"Hey, Jensen! I can't believe I didn't see you all week."

"Did you miss me?"

"Yeah. I didn't even watch *Chopped*."

I couldn't mask how much I needed to hear that. "I missed you too, ninja-boy."

"Didja know I graduated from kindergarten last week?"

"I never doubted for a second that you'd pass." I leaned closer to whisper, "Did you say, 'In your face!' to Tiara the troublemaker?"

"Huh-uh," he whispered back. "I'm not mean like her."

"Good for you for having in-teg-rity." I held my fist out for a bump. "Congrats on officially being a first-grader."

He bounced a couple of times and pointed at the paperwork in front of me. "Does it say that I'm a first-grader?"

"Of course it does."

"That's why I got up really, really early today because I was so excited to come to camp!"

Do not look at his mother and ask her if her son was so eager, then why are they arriving late?

"During camp you should be respectful and call him Mr. Lund," Rowan said to him.

Calder blinked those big brown eyes at me. "Really?"

"Nope. Doesn't matter where we are, you call me Jensen, because we're friends."

He looked relieved. "Okay." Then he was back to bouncing with excitement. "Know what else?"

"What?"

"I made my own lunch today! Guess what it is."

"A PB and J, baby carrots and a root beer."

"Huh-uh." He leaned in and whispered. "It's fancy."

I tried to keep a straight face, but his earnestness just got to me and I grinned. "I'm not a fancy-food guy. You know I can't cook worth sh—beans, so hit me with this fancy-schmancy sandwich that Chef Calder created this morning."

"Deviled ham on toast!"

"Wow. That is right uptown."

"And I have a hard-boiled egg, pepper sticks and hummus too."

"Pepper sticks?"

"Sliced red and green peppers to dip into the hummus," Rowan said.

"Thanks, Coach Michaels, for the clarification."

"What's in your lunch?" Calder asked.

I groaned. "Shoot. That's the one thing I forgot this morning."

"Oh. Well . . . you can have some of mine."

This boy's sweetness slayed me. I reached out and tugged on his hair. "Thanks for the offer, little dude, but you'll be starved after dance class."

"Maybe you could call your mommy and she'll bring you something."

"Come on," Rowan said to Calder, "let's put away your lunch and find your dance class."

She left without making eye contact with me.

As soon as Rowan was out of sight, Astrid said, "Brrr . . . it's cold in here." *Clap clap.* "There must be a mad coach in the atmosphere." *Clap clap.* "I said . . . Brrr—"

"Yeah, yeah, I get it. Hilarious."

"So, what did you do to the ravishing Rowan to make her act like that to you?"

I pinned Astrid with a hard look. "Don't you have shit to file? Calls to make? Clerical duties to perform?"

Astrid saluted. "Yes, sir, boss man. Sir. I'll keep my questions to myself." She pushed away from the table. Then she stopped in front of me. "But that doesn't mean I'll keep my opinions to myself."

Of course not.

"Even when Rowan acted cold to you, when she watched you interacting with her son . . . she thawed out a lot. She even smiled. Twice."

"So you're a voyeur too?"

She laughed. "I couldn't help but watch her because she is one hot mama. But she couldn't keep her eyes off you, even if those eyes were shooting daggers. Watching you two *neighbors* dance around each other is gonna be entertaining. I might even bring popcorn."

I pointed at the office.

She laughed again . . . and did the cheer from *Bring It On* until she vanished from my sight.

Surrounded by meddling smart-asses appeared to be my lot in life.

The morning went smoothly, but with the kids' excessive amount of energy, I opted to give them a fifteen-minute break between activities and before lunch. With Jax at my disposal, I had him supervise the kids inside while I took on the role of playground monitor.

My ever-efficient program director, Astrid, even brought me a whistle.

The old playground equipment hadn't been removed after LCCO's purchase of the property, so I had to ban the kids from sliding down the metal slide, which sat directly in the sun. Most of them wanted to hang from the monkey bars or swing on the swings. Alex, the ace projectile vomiter, asked me if we'd brought any balls.

"What kind of balls?" I asked him and the group of six kids with him.

"A basketball," he said.

I did a quick check of the playground equipment. "I don't see any hoops."

"I could teach them how to play foursquare."

"I'll bring one as long as *everyone* who wants to play gets a turn. This is a fun camp, not a place where anyone needs to be competitive either in art or dance or music or recess."

Alex gave me a disbelieving look. "But someone is always better than someone else."

Astute kid. "True. But I know from experience that working together as a team raises the level of everyone's abilities. That means including everyone. That means taking turns. If you all can promise me that—in writing—then I'll bring one ball on Wednesday and we'll see how it goes."

"In writing?" Eloise, a freckled, pigtailed, scrawny girl of about eight repeated.

"Yeah. You know. Like when we sign that no-bullying contract at school," Alex said.

A collective *ah* of understanding arose from the rest of the kids.

"You know what would be really cool?" a nine-year-old named LaShawn said. "If we got a really big piece of paper and everyone could sign it. Then we could tape it by the door so we'd all see it every time we went outside as a reminder."

"Excellent idea. I'll talk to Astrid and track down a piece of paper so we can do it before everyone leaves for the day."

The kids were so pumped up and talking a mile a minute, we missed the first call to lunch.

Evidently Astrid had gotten herself a whistle too. She blew that sucker hard enough that we all stopped and faced her like a pack of trained dogs.

"Lunchtime. Find your lunch on the tables. Where you sit today won't be where you sit every day, because we want everyone to get to know each other."

I narrowed my eyes at her. Who came up with assigned seating? I hated that in elementary school. I was the shy kid and a slow eater, so no one talked to me and I was always the last one to leave the table. That was probably why I learned to shovel food in so fast I barely tasted it.

After I did a quick check of the playground to make sure no one was out here hiding, I headed toward the door. I froze when I heard her shout, "Lund, wait up."

I stepped into the shadow of the building, away from the street side, and watched Rowan amble toward me.

She thrust a plastic grocery bag at me. "Here. I brought you lunch."

Just like that, my resentment over her silence the last week vanished.

You're an easy mark, Lund. You're too soft when it comes to women.

No, I just had it bad for this one sweet woman, who took time out of her busy day to do something thoughtful for me.

"Is this a piece of humble pie?" I joked.

Rowan snorted. "Funny. I'm not making you eat crow either."

"Good. While I appreciate you bringing me lunch, if it comes with the expectation of an apology, I'll pass." I paused and slipped my sunglasses on top of my head. "I'm not sorry for what I said. I meant every word."

"I . . ." She turned her head away. "I overreacted, okay? I do that a lot. I hate that about myself."

"Why would you hate anything about yourself?"

Her gaze finally met mine. "I miss signs, I misread signals and then I immediately become defensive because I realize too late that I screwed up." She exhaled. "I'm sorry. My dismissal of you—of us—being whatever we are, hurt you. That wasn't fair when you've been nothing short of amazing since we moved in. So I brought you lunch, hoping I could get a brief moment of your time to apologize."

"Apology accepted."

A beautiful smile lit up her face. "That fast?"

"Yep. It's over, done with and we can move on." I allowed a quick grin. "As the youngest kid in the family, I learned to forgive and forget in record time. Or I found myself ostracized by my siblings and cousins and there was nothing I hated worse than playing with myself."

A devious look danced in her eyes. "I've heard guys *like* to do that all the time."

I blushed. Damn Nordic skin. "I meant playing *by* myself."

"Sure you did, Lund."

Just like that, we were back to normal.

"Anyway, I can't stay. I have to get back to work."

I moved in until we were toe to toe, forcing her head back to meet my gaze. "Thank you for the food. Thank you for the apology. I was depressed I'd have to watch *Chopped* by myself again this week."

"Right. You wouldn't want to disappoint Calder. That's become his favorite show because he gets to spend time with you."

"I like hanging out with him. But this is one of those big signs you're misreading, so let me help you out by taking the damn blinders off."

She watched me warily.

"Admit we're more than friends, Rowan."

"We're more than friends, Jensen."

"Tell me you missed me, sweetheart."

"I missed you, *sweetheart*."

She wouldn't be Rowan without some sarcasm. "Assure me that if we're in a team meeting situation, you won't be dismissive and act like you don't know me."

"If we're in a team meeting situation, I won't be dismissive and act like I don't know you. *However,* for your part after a team meeting, there will be no hugs, no kiss-kiss on the cheek, no whispering in my ear, no patting my ass, no *staring* at my ass and no 'Hey, babe, you left your shirt on my couch' type of comments."

"Fine. After a team meeting no hugs, no kiss-kiss on the cheek, no whispering in your ear, no patting your ass, but I'll stare at your ass if I want to—ain't nothin' gonna change that—and no 'Hey, babe, you left your shirt on my couch' type of comments." I smiled. "See? We can compromise and work this out."

She drilled me in the chest with her index finger. "Also, when I'm trying to be serious you have to stop looking at me like you're imagining me naked in your bed."

"Not happening. And give me some credit, woman, I don't only think of you naked in my bed. Sometimes I imagine you naked against the wall. Or naked in my shower. But my favorite is you naked on my kitchen table, all spread out in a lickable, fuckable feast."

"Jensen Lund. You can't tell me stuff like that."

I lifted a brow. "You'd rather I acted on it?"

"Yes. I mean no. I mean yes." She closed her eyes. "I suck at this."

"Then I have one question for you. Do you want this?" *Do you want me?*

"Yes. But I need to ask you to do something for me."

Yes, as soon as we're alone I'll pull down your shorts, spread your thighs wide open and drop to my knees so I can feast on you until you scream my name.

Somehow I forced that sexy image from my head and managed to say, "Hit me with it."

"Give me a reason not to second-guess myself—and this—again."

My heart beat as if I'd just sprinted a mile when I reached for her, curling my left hand below her jaw.

Those hazel-green eyes blinked at me with uncertainty.

I slanted my mouth over hers and kissed her.

Keeping my lips soft and the kiss gentle . . . not what I wanted. Rowan didn't need sweet; she needed heat and passion. She needed to see me as the man with a voracious sexual appetite who had been denying his hunger for her for far too long.

I traced the seam of her lips with the tip of my tongue and she opened her mouth on a soft gasp. Then I used both hands to hold her in place as I kissed the hell out of her. I dove into her mouth, again and again, changing the angle of her head so I could kiss her deeper. Harder. Longer.

She fisted her hands into my shirt and pulled me closer.

My head buzzed like I'd downed a dozen shots of tequila. My dick was hard as a goalpost. I couldn't remember the last time I'd gotten an erection from just a kiss.

In public. In broad daylight.

Not smart.

I slowed the kiss. Then I nibbled on her swollen lips, kissing each corner of her mouth. But even though our lips were no longer touching, I couldn't let go of her. My thumb stroked the edge of her jaw. My fingers were tangled in her hair.

When I opened my eyes, she was already looking at me.

She whispered, "Holy fuck."

I didn't release her. I didn't smile or make a smart-ass comment. I just let my eyes drink in every nuance of her face as I tried to level my breathing and unscramble my brain.

Rowan maintained the iron grip on my shirt as she studied me in the same way.

"Jensen—"

I pressed my thumb over her lips. "I talk first. You listen."

She parted her lips as if she intended to argue, but she remained silent.

"Now that I've had a taste of you?" I dragged my thumb along the inside rim of her bottom lip. "I want more. I want it all."

She nipped at my thumb and I moved it, allowing my hands to slide free from her hair to rest at the base of her neck.

Her eyes turned serious. "This is uncharted territory for me."

"It is for me too." I kissed her lips and her forehead before I dropped my hands.

"I didn't want this to happen."

"Liar."

A flash of guilt shone in her eyes. "Okay, I never thought it would happen with you."

"Because I'm an athlete? Or because you think I'm a player?"

"Both."

"Football is a game for me. I'd never play around with your feelings. What's between us? Not a game. That's another thing I want you to remember when you're dissecting the fact I finally fucking kissed you."

Her eyes searched mine. "How did you know I'd be dissecting it? God, Lund, how do you know me so well?"

"I pay attention when it's important. And make no mistake . . . you are important to me."

The way she kept running her hands over my chest with purposeful but unintentional sensuality kicked my desire to the next level. She'd be a thorough lover—of that I was certain. She gave her all to everything she did; sex wouldn't be any different.

She pressed her palms against my pectorals. "Why did you just growl at me?"

I leaned in and put my lips to her ear. "Because I was thinking about you being naked in my bed and touching me like that."

Rowan shivered. "I worry that I'll be a disappointment."

"Why?"

"Because it's been a while for me." She groaned into my neck. "And I can't believe I just told you that."

"You think telling me that you haven't been screwing around the past six years you've been raising your son alone is gonna deter me?" I softly blew in her ear until she shivered again. "Fuck. No." I kissed the side of her neck and forced myself to push her away. "Go back to work, Coach."

She blew out a deep breath. She turned to leave—man, I loved to watch that ass of hers in motion—but then she stopped and whirled back around.

This time I had no idea what she'd say. But it turned out she didn't say anything at all—at least not with words.

My sexy spitfire cheerleader trapped my face in her hands and kissed me. Her tongue pushing past my lips, searching for mine. Her fingernails digging into my scalp, knocking my sunglasses to the ground. Her quiet hum of desire vibrating between us like a promise.

She teased: a nibble of her teeth on the fleshy inside of my bottom lip. She seduced: a rhythmic sucking on my tongue. The dizzy sensation swamped me, forcing me to curl my fingers into the brick behind me to keep from touching her.

Then she used the damp slide of her lips across mine to gently break the connection.

Rowan had just made it clear that I might've made the first move, but *she* was making the second.

After a lingering sweep of her hands through my hair, she stepped back and walked away without saying another word.

Best. Lunch. Ever.

———

Later in the afternoon, I wandered through the school. Trinity had young artists spread out in a circle on the floor as she demonstrated how to draw a flower with colored pencils.

In the café-torium, Dallas directed the thespians in an improv scene about working in a busy restaurant.

In the music room, Todd strummed a guitar as the kids shared the names of their favorite songs.

In Lucy's craft room, the students were choosing supplies off the long table while Lucy explained the options for the day's jewelry. An angry Jax lurked in the back of the classroom, so I beckoned him out.

"What?"

"Don't do this, man."

"Do what?"

"Make this about you. If you're volunteering to spend extra time with Mimi, then you shouldn't be in Lucy's room glaring at her. Whatever issues you two have, they don't get addressed or dealt with here."

Jax squared off against me. "Mimi *is* in that class right now. So I was in there because of her. When I tried to help her, Mimi said she wasn't a baby and didn't need my help."

"So you stuck around to glare at Lucy because it's somehow her fault that Mimi didn't need your help?"

"Yes. No." He sighed. "Fuck. I had no idea that Lucy was an expert at this artsy-fartsy stuff to the point of it being her business for a while."

After seeing firsthand what Rowan went through every day being a single parent, I had no sympathy for my whiny-ass, overprivileged cousin. "You didn't know because you didn't bother to ask. It's no secret that making jewelry went from being Lucy's hobby to her livelihood because you refused to support her and your daughter." I got right in his face. "It pisses me off that Lucy was struggling, right under our noses, raising *your* child alone while you were off hitting the bottle and nailing every chick who so much as breathed on you. And you had the balls to lie to all of us about it. So now that you're finally on the right path, don't put your frustration with yourself and your parental shortcomings on Lucy. Don't turn into that bitter guy who blames everyone else for his crappy decisions."

"I see she's recruited another member of my family to Team Lucy," he said testily.

"Wrong. I am on Team Jax-steps-up-and-proves-he's-changed. Wishing things were different doesn't make them so. Mimi loves her mom. Being an ass to the person your daughter loves the most . . . think about that. It's not a smart move."

Jax blinked at me and I swear I saw a lightbulb go off. After a moment he said, "When did you get all smart and philosophical, little cuz?"

I lightly punched him in the shoulder. "You oughta try using your brain to think rather than just to stop hockey pucks."

"Piss off, baller."

"Speaking of piss . . . the boys' bathroom is gross."

He sighed. "I'm on it."

Once I finished checking on all the classes and staff, I returned to the office.

Astrid glanced up. "I assumed you'd already left for training."

"I'm going." I shouldered my duffel bag. "You'll make sure—"

"Yes. I have a checklist. I'll text it to you when I'm done."

"Great. Thanks."

"Will you be in tomorrow?"

I stopped halfway to the door. "No. Why? Did you need me to be here?"

"Not that I know of. But can we plan on a quick staff meeting early Wednesday morning before the campers get here?"

"Sure."

"Cool. I'll bring donuts."

Vegan donuts. There was something to look forward to . . . said no one ever.

Fifteen

ROWAN

Asking Talia to stay with Calder an extra hour gave me a moment of mother's guilt, but I needed to talk to my BFF about what was going on with Jensen. Or more accurately—what I wanted to go on with him.

Daisy sailed through the door of the coffee shop. Upon seeing that I'd ordered her favorite cold brew, she said, "I could seriously kiss you right now, Ro."

"Some days I wonder if all of this would be easier if I swung that way."

"So this is an emergency. You never say things like that."

"It's not like I've been secretly having girl-on-girl fantasies. I imagine it'd be easier dating a woman since I know how a woman's mind works."

Daisy considered me. "What am I thinking about right now?"

"Are you seriously giving me a lesbian aptitude test?"

"Stop stalling. Prove you're an Indigo Girls super fan and wow me with your intuition."

"All right." I tapped my fingers on the table as I contemplated. "You're deliberating if it'd be worth it to return to the office to finish the two projects you left undone when you had to rush to my rescue and talk me off the ledge."

Her husky laugh turned heads. "You couldn't be more wrong. See that hot guy in a suit sitting by the windows? We've been eye-fucking since Monday. Tuesday he dropped off a note on a napkin asking if I was single. It was cute and flirty and quirky enough that I've been here after work every day this week. We'll see if he takes the lead or if I have to make the first move. Because either way? Win-win." She snagged the last packet of Splenda. "So the fact you and I both have vaginas doesn't provide you with an innate understanding of how my brain—or my vagina—works."

"Point made." I debated asking her about Markus, a guy she'd clicked with on one of those dating sites. Last I'd heard they were setting up a face-to-face meeting.

Daisy said, "So what happened to send you teetering on the ledge?"

"Jensen kissed me. Kissed me like I haven't been kissed in . . . well . . . ever."

"When? Where? And why is this the first I'm hearing of it?"

"It happened Monday at camp."

"Jensen kissed you like you've never been kissed . . . four days ago, and instead of grabbing onto him by those massive biceps to see what else he could do with that sexy mouth, you . . . ?"

"Backed off so I could process it."

Daisy smacked her own forehead.

"What?" I said testily.

"And did you come to a different conclusion after you've

had time to 'process' it than you did right after he kissed you?"

I stared at her. Hard. As if I could make her rethink her (absolutely accurate) assumption about me.

"That's what I thought."

"So I should've . . . what? Just jumped him right there on the street?"

"You tell me. Because that's what this is about, right? You need to talk it out and let go of some of your issues—hang-ups, preconceived notions—whatever you want to call it that's keeping you from acting on your impulses."

Now that I was sitting across from her, I didn't remember why I insisted on meeting face-to-face. I'd rather crawl in a hole than admit the truth. Even when Daisy was my closest friend, this wasn't something we'd ever seriously discussed.

A soft hand landed on my forearm. "In all seriousness. This is a no-judgment zone. Talk to me."

"Where do I even start?"

"With the hardest thing first."

I blurted out, "I hardly ever think about sex. I haven't since before Calder was born. I spent the first year of his life exhausted. I spent the second year trying to find my balance between being a mother and a trainer and all the cheer stuff. The last time I had sex was three years ago at my friend Marissa's wedding and it was so hurried I don't think it counts." My face flamed from the rapid-fire admissions and I couldn't even look Daisy in the eye. "I haven't been on a date since Rand."

"Rand was a freakin' tool," Daisy retorted.

"It still stung that he never called me again."

"But it's not like guys aren't hitting on you all the time, Rowan. Why do you always say no when you get asked out?"

I met her gaze. "Because I haven't met any man that I've wanted to say yes to."

"Until Jensen."

"Until him."

"Why him?"

"Don't you think I've asked myself that a hundred times? Yes, he's so good-looking it borders on obscene. Yes, he's worked his butt off for that jaw-dropping physique. Yes, he's got more charms than a jewelry store. Yes, he's cocky. He's the very last type of man I should be fantasizing about locking in my bedroom for days." I tilted my face away from her probing gaze. "I've never experienced such an over-whelming physical reaction to a guy. He gets close to me and all I want to do is climb him like a tree. So instead of sex being the last thing on my mind? I'm thinking about sex all the damn time." I paused. "Even that's not the whole truth. I was thinking about saying 'screw it' to the no-fraternization rules and begging him to screw my brains out before he brought up the IR list exemption."

Silence.

I glanced up.

Daisy's mouth hung open. Not only because I'd honestly voiced my inner turmoil, but her gaze winged between me and whoever stood behind me.

A shadow fell over me as Daisy's crush stepped up to the table.

Floor, please open up an escape portal for me right freakin' now.

"Sorry to eavesdrop, ladies, but I needed to grab Daisy's attention." He crouched down in his fancy-ass suit and kept his focus fully on my flustered friend. "You and I are having dinner at Ike's immediately after you set your lovely, but conflicted friend, on the right path."

"You'll wait for me? Even if this conversation takes an-other two hours?" she said skeptically.

"I'll wait. But let's see if I can't speed things up." Mr.

Crushworthy-in-a-Suit smiled at me. "I overheard more than I should have. You don't know me, but I am a man who knows exactly what I'd want from a woman who has an intense physical attraction to me." His gaze didn't waver from Daisy's when he said, "She should act on it. Trust me: A man likes it when a woman takes it to the next level." He pushed to his feet and walked away.

Daisy's eyes tracked his every movement and she allowed a cocky grin before refocusing on me. "See? Even Markus agrees you should take that leap of faith."

"Omigod, that's Markus?"

"Yep. He's a hottie, isn't he? He's a guy, take his advice."

"I'll bet *Markus* would tell me to bang my TA if he thought it'd convince you to bang him."

"I'm a sure thing for him tonight, so I am not letting you deflect this convo back to me." Daisy leaned in. "It's about damn time you found a man who trips your trigger. I hate that you've equated *selfless* with *sexless*. It's always made me sad that you put your physical needs at the bottom of your 'life priority' list. Just once I'd love to see you flip that list on its head and do something out of the norm, maybe a little out of control, maybe even something with the potential for regret." She pointed at me. "Don't give in to the panic like it's third and long. Go for it like it's a guaranteed first down."

I rolled my eyes. "As long as we're using football euphemisms, the truth is I'm afraid I'll fumble in the end zone. God knows Jensen doesn't have that issue, since he's used to scoring."

Daisy laughed. "You'll be fine, Ro. Very greedy, I suspect, when you're faced with him completely out of that uniform. So my advice? Make certain when you blow the whistle and it's game on, that you've allowed yourself enough time to get to the goal and you're not rushing the play."

I snickered.

"You are one sexy mother—literally. You deserve to score with one of the finest men to ever grace the gridiron."

"I shouldn't worry about either of us getting . . . disen-franchised?"

"Girl, if anyone can burn the rule book, it's The Rocket. He is on the A team. But it's still best only to be reckless when you're alone behind closed doors."

My phone buzzed and the caller ID read: TALIA. "Hey, T. What's up?"

"We're at the pool and Calder's friend Nicolai showed up with his dad. They want to know if Calder can spend the night."

Nicolai and his family lived in the other building in Snow Village. Although Nicolai was two years older, he and Calder had a great time when they played together at the pool or the playground with the other kids. "I'll be there in twenty minutes and we'll talk about it then."

I ended the call and glanced up to see Daisy making eyes at Markus across the room. "I'm out. Thanks for listening. Sorry I'm such a newb at this scoring stuff."

Her gaze met mine. "You won't be for long. I hope you're on your way to earning a spot at the Pro Bowl."

At the community pool in the apartment complex, Talia sat on the edge at the shallow end, watching Calder diving for a toy. She didn't look at me until after Calder surfaced. "Time's up, mer-boy. Your mom is here."

Calder waved at me and took his time swimming, splash-ing and bouncing his way to the steps.

"Everything went okay today?" I asked her.

"He was a little tired after camp and fell asleep in the

car. But he perked up when we came down here for his swimming lesson."

"Thanks for staying late. I appreciate it."

"No problem. Nicolai's dad said for you and Calder just to come over to their place with Calder's stuff whenever. He said he'll feed Calder supper too."

That gave me pause. "They're assuming I'm letting Calder stay over?"

"Why wouldn't you?"

"You don't think Calder is too young to spend the night at a friend's?"

Talia leveled a look on me that indicated maturity beyond her twenty years. Then again, she was majoring in early-childhood development. "From what I've seen, Nicolai's parents are just as involved in their son's life as you are in yours. I've never seen Nicolai running around here unattended. It's not like Calder would be in Roseville. He'd be in the next building over."

"True."

"Can I ask you something?" Talia said.

"Sure."

"There are half a dozen kids around Calder's age in this apartment complex. It's a gated community. This pool is rockin'. So is the playground. But I don't hear from Calder that you let him play with those kids very often. Only if you're with him. Do you think that's best? Given he's got a built-in social network so close by? It'd be good for him, as an only child, to develop some interpersonal skills."

"It's hard to just say 'go out and play' in this day and age. But I'm working on it."

"Good. Because I think some separation would be good for you too."

I sighed because I knew she was right. "Camp is great,

but it's only three days a week and I know he misses being around other kids. I want to find a balance between his needs and us spending time together . . ." *And my own needs.*

I held out a towel for my shivering son and wrapped it around him before I kissed the top of his wet head. "How's my guppy today?"

"I'm not a guppy. I passed to the next level. Right, Talia?"

"Absolutely. You are in the flounder-level class now."

He craned his neck to look up at me. "Didja hear that Nicolai asked if I could have a sleepover?"

"Yes, I heard."

"Is it okay? Please? *Please?* I promise I'll—"

"How about if we talk about it at home?"

His smile fell. "That means no. You always say no."

Hello, guilt.

Talia slipped a maxidress over her swimsuit and crouched down to talk to Calder. "Hey, Gloomy Gus, your mom didn't say no. She probably wants to talk about the rules for staying overnight at a friend's house before she says yes. So promise me you'll listen to her, okay?"

"Okay. I promise."

"Now give me a hug, mer-boy."

Calder squirmed out of the towel and launched himself at her.

We were so lucky to have Talia. I hugged her too before sending her on her way.

After Calder changed from his swimming trunks into his clothes, we talked about the rules. The kid was beyond excited to go to Nicolai's as he packed his backpack and a duffel bag of toys. I didn't have time to change out of my work clothes before we were out the door and on our way to building two.

While the boys raced off, I spent ten minutes talking with Nicolai's parents and exchanging phone numbers. I'd met

them several times, but hadn't known that Gabriel had retired from hockey and now coached a club hockey team,
and Nicolai's mother, Gejel, was a curling instructor. They
were both friendly with Martin and Verily—seemed everyone in the Snow Village complex knew my brother. I de-
clined their offer of joining them for dinner, which I decided
was a dumb move as I walked back to the apartment by
myself. Why did I turn down adult conversation?

*Because the type of adult conversation you want to have
is inappropriate in front of your son.*

I stopped in the middle of the hallway because I
realized . . . I had an entire night to do whatever I wanted.
And what I wanted to *do* most in the world? Jensen Lund.

Sixteen

JENSEN

I'd just finished my Schell beer when my doorbell rang.

Couldn't be Coach Buzzkill since she always knocked.

Maybe she wants to apologize for all but hiding out after that kiss . . . four days ago.

Right. I might as well imagine she's offering that apology on her knees.

"It's open."

My cousins Ash and Nolan strolled in.

"Hey, cuz," Nolan said. "Surprise."

"Hope you don't mind us dropping by," Ash said. Placing one hand on the edge of the couch, he vaulted over the side, landing ass first on the cushion directly across from mine.

"By all means, make yourself at home," I said.

Ash gestured to my bottle of beer. "See if Jens has any more of those before you join us in the 1970s pit couch."

Nolan said, "On it," and disappeared into my kitchen.

I looked at Ash. "So you were what? In the neighborhood?"

"I doubt either of us would venture into this neighborhood without a specific reason." He smirked. "Or a loaded firearm."

"Ha ha. Asshole."

"We haven't hung out in a while. So thanks for keeping us on the permanent visitors list so we can just 'drop by' your humble abode whenever we want."

"I knew that gesture of goodwill and family solidarity after I bought this property would come back to bite me in the ass," I muttered.

Nolan returned with three bottles of Schell. After he handed us each one, he threw himself into the corner of the couch. "Seriously, Jens, you could have an orgy in this thing."

"You say that every time you're over here."

He shrugged. "My mind gets stuck on one track."

"Never have him house-sit," Ash deadpanned.

"No kidding. So you showed up to drink beer? Get your sorry asses kicked at *Grand Theft Auto*?"

Ash and Nolan exchanged a shocked look.

"What?"

"He doesn't know?" Nolan said.

"Apparently not," Ash replied.

"Know what?" I demanded.

"That when you turn thirty, your right to play video games is revoked," Ash said.

"It's the universe's way of telling you it's time to move on and do something productive with your free time," Nolan added. "Since both Ash and I have passed the three-oh mark, we're banned for life."

I sipped my fresh beer. "There's nothing wrong with gaming."

"Name one person who spends his leisure time with his ass glued to the couch and a joystick in his hand that maintains a successful, fulfilling life."

"Axl."

"Is under thirty."

Shit. "The guys on *The Big Bang Theory* are all rocket scientists, astrophysicists and engineers, and they're big-time gamers," I pointed out smugly.

"Dude. Those are fictional characters. I guarantee if you ran across a guy like Sheldon Cooper in real life you'd beat the fuck out of him," Nolan said.

Yeah, I could see that.

"Besides, we're pregaming here with one beer," Ash said. He spared my sweaty workout shorts and tank top a quick look. "Then we're going out."

Don't groan and whine that you just got home.

"Hit the shower and dress casual—in anything besides athletic clothes with a Vikings logo," Nolan advised.

Nolan had a hard-on for fashion in a totally hetero way. He was a Lund Industries executive and his daily uniform was a suit, so his idea of "dress casual" differed from mine. Even slouched on my sofa he maintained an aura of cool sophistication. He wore dark denim and a slim-cut, pale blue shirt with a subtle stripe; the cuffs had a contrasting checked pattern in red. His loafers were funky-unique without being eye-rollingly weird. His style was on trend but not like he was trying too hard to be hip. Or worse, dressing like a hipster, attempting to convince others a stupid fashion statement looked cool.

My feeling of fashion inferiority arose. I'd never developed a sense of style, mostly because I hadn't needed to. I spent eighty percent of my time in workout gear or in uniform. I'd hired Brady's tailor to craft custom suits for me—a guy my size couldn't just buy off the rack—but my closet sorely lacked clothing for casual social occasions such as this.

"Stop staring at him," Ash said to me. "Nolan is already full of himself."

My gaze moved to Ash. As COO at Lund Industries, Ash also lived the suit-and-tie existence. His off-the-clock style was preppy outdoorsman. In terms of cars, I thought of Nolan as sleek and showy like a Ferrari. And Ash—understated power, a workhorse in stealth mode like a Viper.

"It takes less effort than you think to look this good. One session with my personal shopper will change your life, Jens. Trust me on this."

Maybe the time had come. It wouldn't kill me to care about my appearance. Since Nolan had repeatedly offered to help me create a polished—more grown-up—look, I'd be an idiot to say no.

I toasted him with my beer bottle. "You know what? I'm in. Set up something this week."

Nolan's jaw might've hit his knee.

Ash laughed. "I didn't see that one coming. Apparently, neither did Nolan."

"Fuck off, Ash. Give me a moment to bask." Nolan leaned in. "You're not screwing with me?"

"No. I look like a bum most of the time. I don't know what kind of clothes I like because I've never thought about it. Annika's always helped me, but it's weird to ask her now that she's married." I shrugged. "Hiring a professional to help me is the smartest option. Especially if you trust him."

A moment of silence passed. Both my older cousins assessed me.

Finally Ash said, "Who's the woman?"

I blinked at him. "What?"

"Gotta be a woman you're trying to impress if you're willing to deal with Jacques, the personal shopper from hell."

"Sorry to disappoint, but it's not for a woman." Not entirely.

"Why now?"

"I'll be in the spotlight for the first time in over a year during training camp with interviews. I should take that part of the job seriously and look professional."

"Speaking of jobs . . . why didn't you ask either one of *us* for help at this LCCO summer camp?" Ash said.

"You even asked my jock brother—who's never progressed from drawing hockey stick figures—to lend a hand," Nolan said.

"Whoa. I didn't *ask* Jax. When he registered Mimi on Monday and saw Lucy, he informed me that he was sticking around. Last thing I need is him harassing her, so I told him the only way he could be on the premises was if he joined the staff as the janitor."

Nolan laughed. "Bet that went over well." He paused. "But I don't see you sporting a black eye for the suggestion."

"That's because Jaxson 'Stonewall' Lund is the custodial engineer and number-one gopher—a little U of M humor there—for Camp Step-Up."

"Get out."

"It was his only option. I won't roll over for a fucking *hockey* player," I sneered, "even if he is my cousin. My LCCO project, my rules."

Silence.

Then Nolan pointed at the sliding glass door. "Is everyone hiding out there getting this on video?"

I looked at Ash and he shrugged. "What are you talking about, Nolan?"

"I'm being pranked, right? That's the only explanation for the bizarre things that have transpired in the last ten minutes."

"No prank. After I meet with your shopper I'll give you competition for the most stylishly dressed Lund. As far as Jax . . . fun fact. He wields a mop as well as a hockey stick." I smirked. "I dropped a urinal cake on the floor just to see if he'd take the shot."

Ash burst out laughing in a way I hadn't heard in a long time. "This is gonna be some fun tonight."

"You guys haven't told me where we're going." Nolan and Ash exchanged another look. I hated that secretive shit. "No strip clubs."

"It's not a strip club. It's a pub."

"No, it's a sports bar," Nolan said.

"Name a sports bar that has karaoke," Ash demanded.

"Guys. No offense, but no matter what you call it, it doesn't sound like a place I wanna go."

"Tough shit. We're going there because we own it."

After a beat of silence, I laughed. "Am *I* being pranked now?"

Nolan shook his head. "Short version. During Jax's drinking days, he invested in a bar with one of his puck bunnies. After he sobered up, he realized running a bar was no longer a retirement option. The partnership contract is a mess. But the bottom line is he can't sell his half. His partner can't sell hers. They're stuck, so Ash and I are acting partners on Jax's behalf. We're trying to establish a decent working relationship with Simone, the partner. There is potential to turn the bar into something unique and profitable; we just don't know what that is yet."

"This puck bunny . . . ?"

"Is no dumb bunny," Nolan said. "She's been running the bar as is, and it's her sole source of income. She sank all of her retirement funds into it. We've had the Lund legal team look into the contract and it's nothing like they've ever seen. She was just as much a victim as Jax."

"What's this Simone chick like?"

"A ball-buster who carries a grudge against athletes."

Great.

"Get moving, we wanna show off our soon-to-be hippest bar in the Cities."

"Do we drink free since you own it?"

Ash snorted. "It doesn't work that way."

"While you're showering, I'm going through your closet," Nolan said. "You *will* wear the clothing I lay out for you."

I stood. Best not to argue. But I sure as hell was scoring at least one free drink for my trouble tonight.

emerged from my bedroom fifteen minutes later.

Both Ash and Nolan stared at me.

Then Ash peeled a fifty from his money clip and handed it over to Nolan.

"What was that about?"

"Ash is pissy because I nailed your style—*Men's Health* meets Abercrombie—on the first try. He said you'd ignore my suggestion and wear a hoodie and jeans."

"Like The Rocket needed more fuel. Jesus, Nolan, he looks a million times better. You've created a monster."

I'd been skeptical of the "look" Nolan had put together for me. My navy suit pants with the subtle gray stripe, which had a slimmer cut—but nowhere near skinny jean territory because I'd never found a pair that'd fit over my thighs. Without the matching suit jacket, the pants could pass for jeans. Nolan had picked one of my shiny, skintight sleeveless workout shirts in electric blue. The bottom hung long enough to cover the waistband so I could skip the belt. I hated having my arms exposed, so I'd been relieved to slip on a collarless warm-up jacket in light gray cotton—more fashion than function since it didn't have pockets or a hood—but it looked dressier than it was paired with the pants. I'd ditched the tasseled loafers Nolan had chosen in favor of my Sperry Top-Sider boots.

The result of all this fussing? I did look damn good. Most importantly, I looked like me, not like I was trying to fit into someone else's skin—and clothes.

"Thanks for rearranging the packaging," I said to Nolan. "I'll grab a hat and we can go."

"No hat, Jens."

I faced him. "I have to wear a hat."

"It's a habit," Nolan argued. "A hat doesn't mask you as well as you think it does, especially if it's sporting a football team's logo."

"Since my injury I only wear team gear when I'm required to. But I always wear a hat in public. Always."

"When was the last time you were recognized?"

"Wednesday. I ran to the convenience store by the school to grab a package of Oreos for snack time and some chick snapped a pic of me. Later the Twitter caption said, 'The Rocket can put his hand—or his whole face—in my cookie jar anytime he wants.'" I paused. "Oh, and I was recognized . . . because I wasn't wearing a hat."

"Give it up, Nolan," Ash said. "We've been out with him enough times to know when he gets recognized, he gets mobbed and it's not fun."

Three knocks sounded on my door. My gaze winged from Ash to Nolan. "Did you invite Brady and Walker?"

"Uh. No."

I opened the door.

Rowan stood on the other side.

Not the Rowan I saw every day. This Rowan wore a dress that exposed her long neck, smooth shoulders and a great deal of great cleavage. This Rowan was taller in the leopard-print stilettos. This Rowan had softly curled hair, bright red lips and some smoky-colored stuff on her eyelids that hinted those hazel eyes held all kinds of dirty secrets.

I'd been so busy eyeballing her that I hadn't noticed she'd been doing the same thing to me.

At the time I said, "What the hell, Coach?" Rowan said, "Damn, Lund."

Nolan said, "Who's at the door?" before he barged in next to me.

I watched him leer at her—the fucking pervert. Starting at the tips of her red toenails in those sexy-ass shoes, up her shins, pausing to gawk at her muscular thighs where the hem of the black dress ended. Then up over her curvy hips, briefly taking in the nipped-in shape of her waist, lingering way-too-fucking-long on those sweet tits, to finally rest on the breathtaking beauty of her face.

"Hello, gorgeous," he murmured in that seductive tone. "Hey. I know you. You cheer for the Vikings."

Jesus, really? Even Nolan had noticed Rowan?

Not everyone is as blind as you, dude.

Well, the blinders had come off and it was *on*.

"Actually, you're the best cheerleader they've got," he continued. Then he elbowed me out of the way—seriously, he elbowed me *out of my own damn doorway* to get to her— and offered his hand and a charming smile. "Nolan Lund."

"My much older cousin," I inserted, and gave him a little shove out of the way. Okay, maybe not such a little shove because he had to catch himself on the wall.

But I only had eyes for her.

With my hands gripping the inside of the doorframe so I wouldn't get all grabby-handed with her, I said, "You."

"Uh. What about me?"

"You're so smokin' hot you've shorted out the logic center of my brain." Letting my arms bear my forward weight, I leaned close enough to her to take a bite out of that full lower lip. "That pretty, perfect red mouth of yours. Christ. It's like a beacon luring me in."

She cocked her head. "How many shots of tequila have you had?"

"None." I grinned at her. "Seeing you is a shot of pure sexual adrenaline, baby."

"Jens, man, give it a rest." Nolan yanked me backward—the dude was way stronger than he looked. "Forgive my cousin's manners, he plays with his balls for a living." Nolan stepped into the hallway. "I didn't catch your name, Red Hot."

"It's Rowan Michaels."

Just then Ash sidestepped me. "Rowan!" He whistled. "Been a long time, but, doll face, you look as spectacular as ever."

Of course freakin' *Ash* knew Rowan too.

"Thanks, Ash. Good to see you again." Her gaze zipped between the three of us. "Lotta Lunds in one place."

"We're on our way out." Ash smiled at her. "But there's always room for a gorgeous lady." He accorded her hot, sexy body an appreciative once-over. "Come out with us. Unless you already had plans."

Rowan regarded me for a moment. "Actually, it appears my plans fell through. My son is having an overnight at a friend's house and I'm—"

"In luck because you're coming out with us," Nolan said. "Where are you going?"

"A bar downtown," I said. "So if it's not your thing—"

"Maybe it *is* my thing," she retorted. "Give me a minute to grab my phone and my purse and I'll be right back."

As soon as her apartment door closed, I had Nolan crowded against the wall. "Rowan is off-fucking-limits. You touch her? You'll need your tailor to sew pieces of your *body* back together, not just your suit. Feel me?"

"*Et tu*, Jensen?" Nolan sighed. "Fine. I get it."

"Mr. *Men's-Health*-meets-Abercrombie off the radar leaves more ladies for us, Nolan."

"True." To me, he said, "Go grab the hat you insist on wearing. And your keys. Rowan can ride with me. Ash can copilot for you."

I didn't want Rowan riding with Nolan.

Nolan got in my face. "I'd never poach."

"I know that. It's just . . . this is new, all right? I don't know what I'm doing with her."

"It appears whatever you're doing is working. Red Hot couldn't keep her eyes off you." He sighed. "And it pains me to say this, but I don't think it has a damn thing to do with how much better you're dressed tonight."

J ust to be a smart-ass I grabbed an Abercrombie ball cap I'd never worn.

The bar was located in the Mill District in a cool three-story brick building, sandwiched between two other brick buildings. The sign above the door to the bar read BORDER-LINE in vintage pink neon. Before we went in, I snagged Ash by the arm. "If you decide to renovate, call Walker. This is his dream project."

"Already on our radar," he said.

On the way to the bar, Ash hadn't tried to give me advice about Rowan, which I appreciated. If my siblings had seen the interaction between Rowan and me, I'd get an earful.

My thoughts scrolled back to the conversation with Dallas when she'd mentioned her concern about Ash. Maybe he put up a great front, but he didn't act miserable. In fact, he seemed more relaxed than usual.

He caught me staring at him. His eyes narrowed. "What'd she say to you?"

Maybe he'd inherited the same sensory perception as Dallas. "She indicated you'd been living a 'joyless existence,' which seemed a harsh assessment, but I didn't push her for details. I figured if you wanted us to know, you'd tell us." I pinned him with a hard look. "Right? No one has to be an island in this family. Thought we established that after everything went down with Jaxson."

Ash scrubbed his hands over his face. "We did. And I appreciate the reminder. It's why Nolan and I showed up at your place tonight. Not to sound like whiny pussies, but we felt out of the loop with this camp thing. Everyone else was involved. That's also when Nolan and I realized we'd been secretive about this bar to protect Jax. Turns out, Jax doesn't care. So you're the first Lund we've brought in, so to speak."

"Cool. I may need a job if this football thing doesn't pan out this year."

"If it doesn't work out, not to go all woo-woo and shit, but it wasn't meant to be."

"Speaking of woo-woo . . . don't think I didn't catch—football pun for ya—you deflecting the conversation from your sister's concerns about *your* mental well-being."

"*She's* a master at deflection. The girl's got secrets. Ugly ones." His jaw tightened. "Ones she should've come to me about. Instead, I had to get an earful from a pissed-off Russian. So what Dallas thinks she 'saw' in me the past year? Partially true. But she confused unhappiness with controlled rage."

What the holy hell was going on?

"I can't get into the details. It's better that you don't know"—he flashed his teeth—"from a legal standpoint. The good news? Dallas is . . . well, Dallas again. I don't have to keep my distance from her now that some time has passed."

"This has to do with Igor?"

"Igor did what needed to be done. I owe him. I've no doubt he'll be back at some point to collect." Ash clapped me on the back. "Ain't ya glad ya asked?"

"Hell no. But I'm not obsessed with digging out secrets like some female Lund family members. I'll probably forget this entire conversation by tomorrow." Total lie there. "I figured if I got around to asking about your woe-is-me attitude after we'd knocked back a few beers, that you'd tearfully confess you were still busted up over what's-her-face."

"Tearfully. Right." He snorted. "You mean Olivia?"

I frowned. "Olivia? I thought the ball-buster's name was . . . Victoria or something?"

Ash laughed. "You're really in the dark. *Veronica*—ancient news. Olivia . . ." His humor faded. "Long story and there's been way too much drama tonight already for me to subject you to more. Let's get our drink on."

He opened the door and I followed him in.

The bar carried that musty smell I associated with century-old buildings. We walked up a short ramp, pausing at the top.

I should've been checking out the space, but my eyes scanned the bar patrons until I saw Rowan.

The cheeky woman let her eyes scroll over me. From my boots up to the brim of my ball cap, then back down to linger on my mouth before her gaze reconnected with mine. Her smile? Sexy, secretive and a little naughty.

My body reacted instantly. Dick hard. Mind set on the one track of getting her alone and making her mine.

Ash and I snagged the two empty seats at the high-topped bar table. Immediately I scooted mine closer to Rowan's, leaning in to whisper, "Enjoy it while you can, sweetheart, because we won't be here long."

Amusement glinted in her eyes. "I never get to kick back in a dive bar with a table of hot guys. So cool the fire in your jockstrap, Lund. We'll get there."

I grinned at her. "I think Nolan got it right in calling you Red Hot."

"What can I get you to drink?"

My focus moved to the waitress standing between Nolan and Ash. "What's on tap?"

The woman addressed Nolan. "This is why table signage is a waste of money. Guys like him?" She indicated me with a jerk of her head. "Expect the server to recite the beer list. It doesn't matter if the beer menu is written in colored chalk in *gigantic* letters across the enormous blackboard above the bar"—another jerk of her head toward the blackboard she'd described, directly behind her—"they're in a bar for personal service. That means spending the money properly training the servers to be friendly and knowledgeable."

Nolan let a smile slowly bloom on his face—the one I called you're-about-to-get-schooled. "Then we'll leave the 'friendly' aspect of training to someone more qualified than you. Careful about using that black Irish temper on me, Simone."

Ash made the time-out sign between them. "Don't start, you two. We'll take a pitcher of Leinie's."

"And a glass of your finest Zinfandel for my lady," I said, not caring that it had sounded cheesy.

Simone addressed Nolan again. "Balls-for-brains over there *does* realize that no one at this table is drinking free tonight?"

Balls-for-brains? Yeah, she did have a hate-on for athletes.

Rowan tapped Simone on the arm to get her attention. "Just so we're clear . . . while I applaud your creativity, to-night it's *my* right to level any insults at him about his balls, not yours."

Silence.

Then Nolan pantomimed a mike drop.

Simone tilted her head at Rowan. "You? I like. Your glass of Zin is on me." Her gaze encompassed the table. "I'll start a bar tab for the rest of you assholes." She sauntered off.

"So . . . now you've met Simone," Ash said dryly.

I said, "Too bad she's not a silent partner."

"Good one, JB."

Rowan frowned. "Do I want to know why you called him JB?"

"Habit when we're in public and he doesn't want to be recognized by his distinctive name." Nolan winked at her. "I'll let you ask him what the B stands for."

After Simone dropped off our drinks, the four of us fell into an easy conversation for the next hour.

I took a moment when Rowan was discussing cheerleading athletic scholarships with Ash to soak up the atmosphere. Everything in here was vintage. The long carved bar, the wood floors, the smoke-stained tin ceiling. The two stories of windows and the curved staircase leading to the second floor. There wasn't a single TV in the joint. Music played in the background, but not at a noticeable level. A great vibe filled the space and I could see why Jax had invested.

Rowan's hand slid up my thigh, startling me so I nearly spilled my beer.

"Sorry. I just—"

I held her hand in place when she attempted to pull it away. "Never apologize for touching me."

"I haven't had a chance to say that you look great tonight."

"Nolan's doing. But I am going to make an effort to look less like a college frat boy from here on out."

"You're mistaken that any woman would look at you and see a 'boy.'"

This was what I'd been waiting for. For Rowan to be comfortable enough to show me that the physical aspect of us didn't scare her. I understood her skittishness. She'd been so loaded down with responsibilities at such a young age that she never had a chance to explore the sexual side of herself. Oh, it was there. I saw it. I wanted it. I couldn't wait to bear the brunt of all that pent-up sexual energy because I knew how to handle it.

Seeing Nolan and Ash deep in conversation, I set my elbow on the table to give us some privacy. "What were your plans for tonight that fell through?"

"Seducing you."

I would've choked on my tongue if my mouth hadn't gone dry.

"After I left Calder at Nicolai's, I stood outside your apartment. I almost knocked to tell you I had a free night. But showing up looking like I normally do didn't seem special enough." She glanced away for a moment. "My hesitation with you hasn't been about you."

Special enough. Christ, she didn't have the first clue about how special she was. I angled my head to softly kiss her shoulder. "I get that."

"So I got dressed up and gave myself a pep talk." She released a nervous laugh. "I even practiced saying sexy things out loud because I worried I'd go speechless when I saw you naked."

"You're killin' me here."

"It took three tries before I had the guts to completely cross the hallway."

I had a sudden panic about how long it would have taken her to find that courage again if I hadn't been home tonight.

Question now is: Why the hell are you here *and not at home, naked with her, proving that her trust in you isn't misplaced?*

I slowly pulled her hand up my thigh until it reached the hardness between my legs. "See what just *thinking* about you in my bed does to me?"

"Kissing you has the same effect on me." She dragged an openmouthed kiss from the edge of my jaw to my ear. "So hot it feels like fire dancing across my skin."

"Rowan—"

"Hey, guys. Chill on the PDA."

I eased back but didn't take my eyes off hers. "Fine. We were leaving anyway."

"Nope. Karaoke starts in ten."

"Well, have fun with that."

"JB, I'm holding you to your promise."

I finally glared at my annoying cousin. "What promise?"

"You skipped karaoke at Axl's bachelor party. You skipped it at Mimi's birthday party. You swore—pinky-swore with Dallas and Annika as your witnesses—that the next time we were in a karaoke situation, you'd sing. It's time."

"And if I say fuck no?"

Ash dangled my keys over the table—when in the hell had he snagged those from me?—and smirked. "Then you forfeit. I call Uber to haul your loser ass home and I will make sure everyone in the family knows you're a chickenshit pinky-promise breaker."

Why was Ash pushing me on this? He didn't give a damn about karaoke. Was he purposely trying to keep me—

"Got eyes on the prize," he said casually.

Then it made sense. That was code for we were being watched.

I hated this part of being a public figure. I didn't bother to ask where the person spying on us was sitting. Ash never lied about this. And he'd never been wrong.

Nolan had bailed to watch the situation, even pulling taps as if he were just tending bar. Both my cousins were recognizable—though like me, not so much in the spotlight the last year—so splitting us up was a good idea.

"Stop glaring at each other," Rowan said. "If Je—JB doesn't want to do karaoke, that's his decision."

"Karaoke setup is on the second floor," Ash said. "Private. Simone will see to it."

"Fine. I'll do it." I took out my phone. "Give me time to find a song."

"Good luck. But you ain't allowed to sing 'Twinkle, Twinkle, Little Star' or 'Row, Row, Row Your Boat.'"

"Dick."

Ash laughed, left the table and walked out the front door.

Rowan tapped me on the arm. "You want to tell me what's going on?"

"It's a stupid family thing."

"That's why you're ignoring me and scrolling through your Twitter feed, as if that's where you'll find the perfect song?"

"I'm taking requests." I hadn't seen any tweets about me in the past two hours. Good.

After another minute of no conversation, Rowan said, "How about 'All by Myself' because that's the way your night is looking, *JB*," and excused herself to storm off toward the bathroom.

About two minutes after Rowan left, the lone guy I'd spotted up by the window started toward me.

Putting my phone to my ear, I kicked my feet up on Rowan's chair and stretched out. Then I launched into a conversation in a thick southern accent. So when the guy slunk past me, he heard a bunch of *y'all*s and me yakking about hiring a livestock transport truck to haul pigs from Kansas City to Tulsa.

Nope, buddy; I'm not a football player trying to be a normal guy out for a few beers with my family and my woman. I'm a good ol' boy from Texas dreaming of being a pig farmer.

The guy bought it. He left through the front door.

Simone wandered over to the table. "I'm supposed to tell you to head upstairs after your date returns. Your cousins will meet you up there. Then we'll shut the door like we're closed for a private party."

"Thanks, Simone."

She leveled an evil smile on me. "I already named the price for my cooperation."

Great. "And that's what?"

"Warm up those vocal cords because you really are singing a round of karaoke."

"Humiliating the player is your price?" I said tightly.

She shrugged. "I'd think you'd love the chance to prove you've got balls." Then she sashayed away.

Behind me I heard, "I don't know if I should be jealous or annoyed about that woman's obsession with your balls."

Seventeen

ROWAN

"I only care that you're talking about my balls, baby," Jensen said to me. He stood and grabbed my hand. "Come on. Karaoke is upstairs."

"Is this a long-running 'family' thing where you have to humiliate yourself on a regular basis?" I demanded.

"Nope. It's a matter of honor. I said I'd do it, and I'm doing it."

Up on the second floor, I scanned the empty, dark space. "At least there's no one up here."

Just then, Simone yelled, "I locked the front door, JB. But prepare yourself because we're all coming up there."

He muttered, "Awesome."

I slapped my hands on his chest. "What is going on? For real."

"A guy downstairs recognized me. Or thought he did. With some fast thinking, we avoided a situation." His eyes clouded. "Celebrity . . . it's part of my life. I get it. But it's not part of yours. It's not part of Simone's. Ash and Nolan are used to it, but this bar is a new venture for them. Doesn't appear I'll be able to make this place my new secret hangout."

"I hate this for you."

"It is what it is, Ro. And what it is tonight, is me doing my penance and shutting my cousins up." He grinned. "There's like eight people down there. Plus the four of us? I'm getting off easy if there are only a dozen witnesses. The rest of my family would video me for blackmail material."

"Why do you trust that none of these strangers will secretly tape you and this performance will hit social media tomorrow?"

He scratched his neck. "Faith, maybe? Nolan said Simone guaranteed privacy and she personally vouched for all the regulars."

"Too bad Ash bailed on you."

"Ash is here. He just left to move my car." Jensen sighed. "That part of public life sucks ass. Some reporter told people what I drive. Fans see my Corvette and it's game over for me. Which means I don't drive it as much as I want to."

"Poor baby." I patted his chest. "Then maybe you shouldn't have plunked down so much cash for a screaming-ass-yellow ZR1."

"It's gold, not yellow," he corrected. "Vikings gold, to be accurate. And the interior is Vikings purple. But I didn't go for the personalized license plate . . . so there is that."

"My bad. That *totally* renders you—and the car—incognito."

Jensen hooked his arm around my waist, hauled me close and pressed a quick kiss on my lips.

Or maybe he'd meant it to be a quick kiss. But neither of us moved away.

His hand slid down to cup my ass and he brushed his lips

across my ear. "You look beautiful tonight. Have I said that?"

"Yes." I nuzzled my cheek against his. "But I'll never get tired of hearing it."

"You're beautiful every night, Rowan." Jensen's lips found mine. There was nothing sweet and fast about this kiss. Nothing tentative about it, but he took his time exploring my mouth and my reactions. His fingers stroked the curve of my ass with such deliberate sensuality that my knees went a little weak. When I didn't bat his hand away, the next thing I knew, both hands were caressing my butt. Squeezing and teasing and rocking my pelvis against his so I could feel how I affected him.

The heat generated between us sent my nerve endings into overdrive. I tingled from head to toe. My heart raced and I'd never experienced such a sense of urgency. The only thing that would calm the growing wildness inside me was more of his confident caresses, more mouth to skin contact, more . . . everything.

The stairs creaked, and voices echoed up to us.

Keeping me sheltered by his body, he spun me around and walked us backward. His eyes held such intensity my belly swooped. "Can we get out of here as soon as I'm done with this?"

"Please."

He parked me at a table and dropped a firm kiss on my lips.

Ash and Nolan joined us. They trash-talked him until Jensen walked up to the DJ station.

Simone's regular customers sat on the far side of the bar.

Jensen returned after he made his song selection.

Nolan handed him a bottle of water. "Thought you might need to clear the frog out of your throat, Kermit."

"I'd skip trying out for open mike night at the comedy club, Nolan."

Ash snickered.

Jensen held out his hand. "Gimme my damn keys."

Simone had the microphone and she said, "JB, come on up. You're the next contestant on *Name That Karaoke Tune*. And please, no help from the audience."

My stomach knotted when Jensen lumbered up to the front like his feet were encased in concrete. He fussed with the microphone, keeping his head down. I was tempted to race up, snatch the mike from his hands and tell him he had nothing to prove to his cousins.

As Jensen adjusted his ball cap and waited for the DJ to cue the music, I'd regretted every comment I'd cracked about his lack of experience in the arts.

There were four beats and the song kicked in.

At first, I thought the DJ had forgotten to mute the vocals because the sound coming out of the speakers . . . sounded exactly like the recording.

Exactly.

My jaw dropped when I realized that *was* Jensen belting out "Rich Girl" like he was auditioning for Hall and Oates.

Holy shit.

Jensen Lund could sing. Really sing. Like a musical-theater-major kind of sing.

Totally unexpected song choice, but he had the range for it.

Immediately I jumped to my feet and started whistling and clapping.

Behind me, Nolan said my name, but I couldn't tear my eyes off Jensen for a second to turn around to see what he wanted.

"Red Hot!"

I spun around. "What?"

"We know you're a cheerleader. Park it. And no herkeys,

for god's sake. I can't see my cousin making an idiot out of me."

"Sorry." I scooted my chair off to the side.

In my peripheral vision, I saw Nolan peeling bills from his money clip and muttering as he stacked them on the table in front of a smug-looking Ash. I raised an eyebrow at him.

Ash grinned. "Nolan bet me a lot of money that Jensen wouldn't take the karaoke challenge, but he did. Then he bet me a lot more money Jens would suck at it. Obviously, Jens doesn't suck."

"Did you know he could sing like this?"

"No comment."

"Come on. You knew. How?"

"In high school Dallas was having issues with some mean girls calling her a 'rich bitch.' Jens got wind of it through Annika and he set up a karaoke machine at my parents' house. He took Dallas to task, told her to own it and be proud of all our family had done. Then he challenged her to sing 'Rich Girl' at the school talent show. So I heard him sing it a few times as he helped her get ready for it."

"Then you default, fucker, if you knew he could sing," Nolan said, trying to take the money back.

I let them bicker and refocused on Jensen. He was completely into the music, not paying attention to us at all. So when he finished and saw me on my feet cheering for him, he smiled shyly. His face turned a little red when others in the bar started to chant "Encore, encore!"

Even Simone wolf-whistled.

He nodded at the DJ, who had the next tune already lined up. I didn't recognize "Rock Me Gently" but it had a very 1970s, Neil Diamond vibe to it. I wondered how Jens knew the song and remembered him talking about his parents' eclectic musical tastes. But at that point how he knew it didn't matter; I was fully under the spell of Jensen Lund's voice. The smooth style with a rock edge just . . . fit him.

I cheered louder for the second song than I had the first. So did the crowd.

As awkward as he initially appeared, now the man looked as if he owned that stage.

He'd suckered me and his cousins big-time.

I could hardly believe he picked "Gettin' You Home" by Chris Young as his next song. How had he known it was my favorite?

Of course. Calder.

As I watched him moving side to side, giving his performance his all, the words he sang to me hit me hard. The longing in that sexy growl promising the ultimate sexual satisfaction. I nearly had a mini-O right there, with Jensen's mesmerizing eyes staring into mine as if I were the only woman in the room. Heck, as if I were the only woman in the world.

After he finished the song, he took a half-assed bow and started toward the table. Slowly. Never taking his eyes off mine.

I couldn't wait for him to act on that wicked, sexy, dirty aura vibrating off him.

When Jensen reached us, Ash said, "Quite a performance there, cuz."

"Thanks." Still keeping his gaze locked onto me, he dug his hand into his front pocket, pulled out some folded bills and tossed them on the table. "Great hanging out with you guys, but we've gotta go."

I didn't question him—neither did his cousins. He held out his hand to me and I took it.

Then we were booking it out of the bar at breakneck speed.

Once we reached his car, Jensen slowed down. He turned and gifted me with a sweet kiss. A brush of lips, a soft flick of his tongue. Not the openmouthed hunger he'd shown me in the bar.

"Rowan," he murmured against the corner of my mouth. "Need you naked in my bed. All night."

"You can have me naked on the couch, against the wall and in the kitchen too."

He devoured me.

Hands on my ass. The lower half of his body grinding against mine in the way that broadcast he'd rock my world when we were finally skin to skin.

When we paused to catch our breath, he said, "Let's go before I lose what little willpower I have left and get even more reckless."

I'd forgotten I was playing grab-ass in public with The Rocket and it'd be newsworthy if the press caught us lip-locked and dry-humping in the parking lot of a dive bar. He'd already dodged one bullet tonight. "Sorry."

He tipped my head back to stare into my eyes. "What?"

"I forgot." I ran my fingers down that infamous chiseled jawline. "In the weeks we've spent together I've forgotten you're this super athlete with celebrity status and a major media presence. Now I think of you as just a normal guy who lives across the hall from me." *I think of you as mine.*

"Saying sweet shit like that will get you fucked right where you stand."

I blinked at him. "You're not mad?"

"I'm relieved." He moved his lips to my ear and whispered, "Get. In."

On the car ride home, Jensen's hand rested on my thigh when it wasn't on the stick shift. Every time I took a breath inside the tightly enclosed space, the scent of his cologne filled my lungs. At every stoplight he curled his hand around the side of my face, bringing my mouth to his for another hot and hungry kiss.

At every stoplight.

Jensen didn't talk. In another circumstance I might've been worried I'd said or done something wrong. But his silence indicated he was as focused on what came next as I was.

The complex gate came into view. Jensen paused long enough for the digital reader to register the bar code in his window, and the gate opened.

Immediately after he helped me out of the car, he framed my face in his hands. He wore the oddest look.

"What?"

"Have you changed your mind about tonight?"

"No. Why? Have you?"

"No." He traced my bottom lip with his thumb. "We've lost some momentum."

"How do you plan to get it back?"

"I'm more of a 'show' guy than a 'tell' guy."

"So show me."

Jensen probably would've forced me to sprint if I hadn't been wearing heels. The man was too damn impatient to wait for the elevator, so we raced up the stairs.

I experienced a surreal moment as we started down the hallway . . . as if the length had expanded, like looking into an infinity mirror until you couldn't see the end. So it seemed to take an eternity before we reached Jensen's apartment.

Guilt pricked my conscience when I glanced at my apartment door. I hadn't thought about Calder much at all in the past few hours. What kind of mother did that make me?

"Stop," Jensen said directly into my ear. "You're allowed a night of fun. You're a great mom, but that's not all you are. You are crazy, sexy hot, baby."

He crowded me against the door. As he kissed the side of my neck, his left hand followed the contour of my body from the outside of my thigh, to my hip, up to my ribs and over to my breast.

"I need you," he growled in my ear, sending goose bumps cascading across every inch of my skin. His keys jangled as he opened the door and we nearly fell inside.

Then we were all over each other.

We kissed crazily as he walked us backward out of the entryway.

He didn't even release my mouth when I kicked off my high heels.

Still kissing as my back met the wall in the living room and my purse hit the floor.

I'd never known what it was like to be wanted—or to want—this desperately.

His kisses sizzled on my skin like drops of water on a woodstove.

I hissed, "Yes," as if I were literally letting off steam from the heat building between us.

His foray into licking, sucking and nibbling on my neck didn't last long. He returned to my mouth, teasing me with a feathery brush of his damp lips over every line, divot and curve of my lips. He systematically destroyed everything I've ever known about kissing.

There were kisses.

And there was the way Jensen Lund kissed.

I reached for him blindly, desperate to touch any part of him.

Next thing I knew, he held both my wrists together in one hand, behind my back.

His mouth was on my ear. "Am I doing something you don't like?"

"No!"

"Then keep your hands out of my way."

"But—"

He shut me up with another brain-scrambling kiss as he unhooked the halter straps of my dress, letting the silky material brush over every inch of my skin. His callused fingers followed the satin edges of my strapless bra to the back and he undid the clasp.

My bra fell away.

Big, hot hard palms covered my chest. His rough skin stroked the softness of mine as he cupped one breast in each hand, letting his thumbs sweep across my nipples as lightly as a whisper. Over and over until I moaned with frustration and broke the kiss.

His masculine, slightly mean chuckle vibrated against my throat.

I whispered his name and a soft *please*.

Jensen's thin thread of control wavered. Groaning, he hoisted me higher against the wall, kissing my breasts as thoroughly as he had my mouth. Muttering unintelligible things into my cleavage.

I squirmed and arched and went a little wild.

That turned him wild.

He quickly yanked the bottom of my dress up to my waist. When his fingers connected with my bare backside, he froze. Another growling groan. His breath came hard and fast against my swollen nipples. "If I'd known you were wearing a thong under this dress we never would've gone to that damn bar."

"Then I wouldn't know how well you can sing."

I felt him smile against my breast and then his mouth meandered back up, zigzagging sideways to scatter hot, wet kisses from the ball of my shoulder up to the hollow of my ear. "I wanna make you sing." He traced the outer shell of my ear with the very tip of his tongue. "Actually, I want to make you scream."

Oh god. I'd never survive this. Jensen Lund was way too much man for me to handle. I was already quaking like a damn leaf in a windstorm and we weren't even fully naked yet.

"Rowan," he said sharply.

"You give me chills when you say my name all growly like that."

He curled his left hand around my hip and trailed the tips of his fingers up the inside of my thigh as he continued to kiss and nuzzle my neck.

My knees literally started to knock.

Jensen chuckled. "You know what'll stop that?"

"I don't want anything to stop it, Jensen. I want more."

"Spread. Your. Legs."

I had no idea that a steely command delivered in a whisper could be so sexy.

I had no idea I'd just . . . obey.

I had no idea he'd lose his cool when he felt how hot and wet I was between my legs.

Jensen took my mouth in a fierce kiss. As ruthless as his mouth was, his fingers were gentle as he started to stroke me, right over the lace of my thong.

With his determination and skill it'd take very little to finish me off. But no way was I stopping this crazy rocket ride and asking him to slow down. I'd enjoy every blasted second of it.

When the fuse inside me finally blew, I had to rip my mouth away from his so I could breathe through the pulsating vibrations that had me shuddering in his arms.

Jensen kissed my neck, maintaining the perfect rhythm until I recovered.

I swallowed hard—evidently gasping from an incredible

climax left your mouth dry. Who knew? Not me, as I'd never experienced that before.

I shook my head to clear the fuzz and buzz.

Then Jensen's cocky smile landed on my lips. He was back to rebuilding the momentum and that buzz of awareness between us.

I felt the power of him all the way to the soles of my feet. A persistent vibration.

Wait a second. That buzzing wasn't just my body's reaction to him. My phone was in my purse. Buzzing on the floor by my feet.

I had to tear my mouth away from his again. "Jensen."

"Bring those lips back here. I'm not even close to done with them," he said on a husky whisper.

"Hold on for a second. My phone is buzzing."

Jensen immediately released me to the floor.

I pulled my cell out and my heart jumped into my throat. The caller ID said GABRIEL. Nicolai's dad. "Gabriel? Is everything all right?"

"I hate to call you, Rowan, but Calder says his tummy hurts. He said he feels like he could throw up."

"Has he?"

"No, but I wasn't sure what he could take for it, so I thought I'd better see what you want to do."

I stood. "I'll just come and get him. I'll be there in like five."

"I think that's for the best. He looks pretty pale."

My stomach roiled. "Thanks, Gabriel." I hung up and started toward the door, my mind focused on getting to my son as fast as possible.

"Whoa." Jensen stepped in front of me. "What's going on with Calder?"

"He's sick, so I have to go get him."

"Of course you do, sweetheart, but not looking like that."

I glanced down. The upper half of my dress was bunched around my waist. My bra—no idea where the hell that had gone. But the fact of the matter was, my boobs were hanging out as was my ass. "Omigod."

"Here. Let me." Jensen was as adept at getting me back into my clothes as he'd been getting me out of them. Then he tilted my head back and smoothed his hands over my hair. "Better."

"Thank you." I looked down to hide my face in the guise of searching for my shoes. "I'm sorry. This isn't how I wanted . . ." I swallowed the tears that clogged my throat from worry for my child and frustration that I had to leave it like this with Jensen. "I'm sorry. You're probably mad—"

"Stop." He invaded my space, his hands cradling my face as he forced me to look at him. "I know we have to go, so we can talk about it later, but don't think for one second I'm pissed off at you because your son got sick." He kissed me quickly, but tenderly. "You need to grab other shoes, or will you be all right walking barefoot?"

My brain had gotten stuck on *we*. "Jens, you don't have to—"

"Help you? Wrong. I'm here, so suck it up and let's go." After another quick kiss he held the door open for me and as soon as we were in the hallway, he reached for my hand.

In that moment I knew I was on dangerous ground with him.

But I couldn't think about that now.

He squeezed my fingers and said, "Breathe, mama. You won't do him any good if you pass out before we get there."

I inhaled deeply and let it out slowly. Some of my light-headedness disappeared.

The sidewalk was cool beneath my feet as we crossed to the next building. Our key card only worked for our building, so I had to use the buzzer. By the time we reached the apartment on the second floor, Gabriel waited for us in the doorway. "Sorry about this. Gejel is sitting with him on the couch. I don't think it's anything he ate, since we all had the same thing and none of us are sick."

"I'm sure it's not food-related. He just gets overly excited sometimes and this happens."

Gabriel finally looked at the big man standing behind me with his hands on my shoulders. "Hey, Jensen. Good to see you. Wish it was under better circumstances."

"Me too."

I'd barely made it through the door when Calder launched himself at me. "Mommy, my tummy hurts."

"I know, baby." I tried not to squeeze him too tightly. "We'll get you home."

"But I don't wanna go! Nicolai probably won't ever want me to have a sleepover again," he said between hiccupping sobs.

Nicolai's mom said, "That's not true. Nico had a blast with you tonight. He's sad you're sick. But we want you to get better so you can come over again soon, okay?"

Calder nodded. Then he noticed Jensen.

Jensen crouched down. "Hey, little dude. You ready to go?"

He walked over and set his head on Jensen's shoulder. "I don't feel too good."

"I heard. Hang on." Then Jensen picked my son up as if he carted him around all the time.

Calder snuggled into him.

"Here's his stuff," Gejel said.

I grabbed the backpack and the duffel bag. Good thing I had Jensen's help; I couldn't have carried all of this and Calder and opened all the doors. "Thanks for having him over," I said to Nicolai's parents.

In the hallway, I said, "Do you want me to carry him?"

He pierced me with that "Are you serious?" dark look as his answer.

I had walked ahead with the key card to open the door to our building when I heard retching. I whirled around to see vomit splattering on the pavement behind Jensen. My gaze moved from my son's back as he heaved over Jensen's shoulder, to Jensen's face—or rather his profile, as his focus was on Calder.

"Set him down."

"In a second." Jensen rubbed Calder's back. He murmured, "You okay?"

Calder threw up again.

I stomped closer. "Give him to me."

Very calmly, Jensen said, "I've got him. I think it'd be best if one of us wasn't covered in it."

Oh no. "He . . . it . . . got you?"

"Down the back of my shirt and my legs."

Now I felt ill.

Calder heaved again.

Jensen kept running his hand up and down Calder's back, murmuring to him.

And Calder didn't fight to get down.

I stood by, feeling helpless.

Several long minutes passed with no additional heaving.

Jensen looked at me and said, "We're good to go."

I unlocked the building door and held it open. Jensen chose the stairs and I followed behind him, wanting to see how covered he was.

Oh yeah. His back and his pants were a mess.

When we reached my apartment, Jensen said, "Where do you want him?"

"Bathroom."

He lowered him to the floor, by the toilet. Then he

stepped back. "I'm going to my place for a quick shower and change of clothes. Leave your door unlocked, so I can come back."

I'd crouched next to Calder, who'd closed his eyes and rested his cheek against the bathtub. "That's okay. You've already gone above and beyond—"

"I'm coming back," he repeated. "Don't shut me out. Please."

This man. I couldn't wrap my head around this side of him. He continually surprised me. "Okay."

He sent me a relieved look, and then he left the bathroom.

Calder stirred and blinked at me groggily. "Mommy?"

"I'm here. How's your tummy?"

"It hurts. It's all jumpy inside."

Poor baby. I pressed my hand to his forehead. Clammy, but not overly hot. I pushed his bangs out of his eyes. "What can I get for you?"

"Gonna be—"

I had him over the toilet before he finished the sentence.

He'd hit the dry-heave stage. Hopefully that meant his stomach was about to settle down. I managed to get him undressed. Then I wet a washcloth and sat him on the edge of the tub and gently wiped him down.

The floor creaked and I glanced over my shoulder to see a freshly showered Jensen leaning against the doorjamb. "What do you need?"

Calder blinked at him with confusion.

I said, "Clean pajamas would be good. There's some on top of Calder's dresser."

"I don't wanna wear pajamas. I'm hot," Calder said crossly, and shivered.

"How about just a T-shirt?" Jensen said diplomatically.

"SpongeBob," Calder insisted.

"On it."

The T-shirt lasted only a few moments before Calder started throwing up again.

This episode had gone beyond excitement to some kind of stomach bug. I rummaged in the medicine chest but didn't see any of my usual over-the-counter fixes. Pepto-Bismol always worked and Calder willingly took it, which was half the battle.

"Mommy, I want to lay down. The light is bright and it's hurting my eyes."

"I can cover your eyes with a washcloth, but until I'm sure you won't get sick in your bed, we'll have to stay in the bathroom."

Calder dropped to the floor and curled himself around me. His body was hot and it hadn't felt that way twenty minutes ago. Dammit. I should've grabbed the thermometer.

Jensen said, "What do you need?"

"There's a thermometer on the bottom shelf of the medicine cabinet."

"This?"

"No. Other side. That's it." He handed it to me. "Thank you." I ran the thermometer across Calder's forehead. Twice. Both readings said one hundred and one degrees.

Shoot. I knew I was out of children's pain reliever too because it was on my list of things to pick up. And of course, Calder needed it right now.

"Ro. Sweetheart. Talk to me. Tell me what I can do."

"I need . . ." I hated asking for help. *Hated* it.

Jensen lowered to his haunches next to me until I had no choice but to look at him. "Ask me."

"Could you go to a twenty-four-hour drugstore and pick up Pepto-Bismol and kids' Tylenol? I'm out of both."

"No problem. Anything else?"

"Maybe some crackers and ginger ale?"

"On it." He stood. He paused for a moment and pointed

to my purse on the floor next to me. "Keep your phone close. I'll text you options so I don't get the wrong things."

I almost told him whatever he got would be fine, but that wasn't true. I had specific products in mind and he was astute to know I wouldn't be satisfied with whatever. "Let me give you some cash."

"Worry about that later. It'll probably take at least half an hour."

"Thank you." I shifted Calder on my lap—he'd fallen asleep—and opted to close my eyes for a moment.

Ten minutes later my phone buzzed with images of the massive amounts of choices for kids' pain relievers. I zoomed in on the one I wanted, screen-captured it and texted it back to him. Repeat with the Pepto-Bismol.

Calder had crashed completely and his body was hot, even though he wore only his underpants. He wasn't a heavy kid, but he was solid. Both my leg and my arm had fallen asleep. But he'd finally settled and I'd have to wake him up soon enough when Jensen returned.

It'd probably be the last time he'd be here. Yanked up short on the promise of hot sexy times and then barfed on by a six-year-old and turned into a middle-of-the-night errand boy. I was surprised The Rocket hadn't sprinted away.

Yeah, it was some fun getting mixed up with me.

I pressed my lips to the crown of Calder's head, taking comfort in the fact that I was doing the right thing, the best thing, the most important thing in the world—raising a well-adjusted, healthy, kind, loving, thoughtful human being. I'd always been happy—content even—with it being just me and my son growing together, going through the day-to-day ups and downs of life.

I knew all this in my heart, in my gut, in my mother's soul, so why did I have a hollow feeling I couldn't shake? I worried I'd started to attach myself to the wrong person, in the wrong place. Wasn't Jensen more shifting sand than stable ground?

You've always been an island. You've felt the seismic shift of the plates beneath the surface of your life that are loosening the moorings since the moment you met him. Things change. You can fight against nature or you can accept that some things are out of your control.

The door to my apartment clicked, startling me from the odd direction my thoughts had taken.

Jensen set the meds on the bathroom counter. "Has he been sick again?"

"No. He fell asleep right after you left."

He rubbed the back of his neck. "Sorry it took longer than expected."

"It was probably good for him to sleep."

"Do you have to wake him up? Or can you just put him in bed?"

I brushed my hand over Calder's head. "He's got a fever, so he has to take the Tylenol."

"Will he be able to keep that down?"

"Time to find out." I shifted, dislodging him from his comfy spot curled into me.

He grumbled and tried to burrow back in.

"Hey, sweetie. I need you to take some medicine. It's the grape kind."

Jensen handed it to me.

Calder blinked a few times and sat up. I held the cup to him and he downed the purple liquid in two drinks. "I'll give you a sip of water. But just a sip until I know you can keep the medicine down, okay?"

He nodded.

So we waited for his stomach to react. Jensen leaning on the doorjamb, Calder and me on the floor.

My son half dozed again. It'd been an hour since he'd

thrown up, so I thought maybe we could skip the pink stuff and go straight to bed.

"Calder. Baby, you have to move so Mommy can get up."

"I've got him," Jensen said. He reached down and plucked him up.

I stood, but my leg buckled from being asleep and I caught myself on the edge of the counter.

Jensen turned around. "You all right?"

"I'm fine. Just pins and needles."

Calder's big eyes stayed on me as if he was confused about what was going on. So I shuffled along behind them.

I didn't bother with the light in Calder's room. As soon as Jensen set him on the bed, I sat on the edge. Mostly to fuss with him: pull the sheet up, press my cool hands to his overheated face. "How's your tummy?"

He struggled to sit up and I wished I'd grabbed a bucket. "Mommy. Mr. Fuzzles. I forgot him at Nicolai's. You have to go get him! I can't sleep without him and he's probably scared that I don't want him anymore because I just left him there!"

"Ssh. Honey. Mr. Fuzzles is in your backpack. I'll grab him as soon as you lie back."

"I'll get Mr. Fuzzles," Jensen said behind me. "It's a stuffed . . . ?"

"Orangutan. The backpack is on the dining room table."

Even in his panicked state, Calder could barely keep his eyes open.

"You want crackers? Or ginger ale for your tummy?"

He shook his head. His entire body sagged with relief when he had Mr. Fuzzles. Crushing him to his chest, he turned and closed his eyes.

I remained there until I knew he'd fallen asleep. I left the door open and headed into the living room. Jensen had been so quiet I suspected he'd left. But there he was, brooding out the sliding glass door. He turned to face me, his expression unreadable.

"He's asleep?"

"Finally." I ran my hand through my hair and didn't know what else to say. I could feel Jensen staring at me.

The least you can do is thank the man.

"So, uh, thanks for sticking around and helping tonight. Especially after Calder got sick on you. If your clothes are ruined I'll replace them, just let me know how much they cost. And how much do I owe you for the—"

"Would you stop?"

I didn't meet his gaze until his shadow fell across me.

"Come here," he said gruffly.

"Jensen, you don't—"

"Shut up and let me hold you. You're shaking." He wrapped me in his arms.

That felt good. He felt good. Solid. Comforting. I closed my eyes and sank into him.

After a bit, I said, "I'm sorry. I doubt you saw the night ending this way."

"I don't assume anything, Rowan."

"Oh." Not what I'd expected.

Maybe you should change your expectations when it comes to this man, since he's exceeded all of them.

"You settled enough to listen to me?"

That caused me to bristle.

His mouth brushed my ear. "Why did that simple question get your back up?"

"Because it's not a simple question. It sounded accusatory."

"Maybe it was. So I'll lay it out. You pissed me off tonight, Coach."

My back went even more rigid.

"I wasn't pissed because your son got sick. I'm pissed

that you think so little of me. You assumed because we were interrupted that I'd be mad. That I care about sex—or lack of it—more than your son's well-being and your peace of mind."

I didn't deny it; I *had* thought that.

"Why did you assume I'd kick you out of my apartment and leave you to deal with everything on your own?"

I tried to squirm away but his hold tightened.

"See? When push comes to shove . . . you shove. If I hadn't been around to help you tonight, I've no doubt you would've done it all yourself."

"How would that have been different than any other night in my life? It's no reflection on you, Jensen, that I'm resistant to accepting help. I've never been in this situation before. Where I'm . . . on a date or hookup or whatever it was and I get a call that my son is sick. I don't date. Because of exactly what happened tonight! Calder getting sick was the universe reminding me I am a single mother and I don't have the luxury of going out and acting as if I don't have a responsibility in the world." I managed to hold it together—just barely.

"So I'm just a hookup? You'd bang me, get it out of your system and assume things would go back to the way they were between us before?" he demanded softly.

"I don't know. I wasn't thinking clearly. It was a whirlwind. A night of fun at a funky bar. And afterward, the way you touched me . . . the way you wanted me. For a little while I got to have the fantasy. So thank you. But this is the reality of who I am."

"You think I don't know that about you?"

"Knowing it and experiencing it are two different things." I kept my gaze aimed at his chest. "Calder comes first for me. Every single time."

"As he should."

"But?"

Jensen nudged my chin up to look into my eyes. "No buts. Your dedication to being there for your son will never be an arguable point for me."

"Then what are we arguing about?"

"Nothing. I had to force you to take my help tonight. All I'm asking is, next time? Don't fight me on it. Save us both the time and wasted energy and accept it."

I blinked at him. "There'll be a next time?"

"Well, if I have any say in it . . . yes."

My eyes searched his. "Why aren't you running the other direction?"

He laughed. "I have no fucking idea."

I laughed too. At least he was honest.

"Do you want me to go?"

Did I? I wasn't naive. Things had changed between us tonight, but I wasn't ready to embrace all of it. Maybe that was the problem. I wanted to compartmentalize everything just like my brother did. I would've thrown myself into a wild night of sex with Jensen, but I balked at the idea of him falling asleep and waking up with me in my bed in front of my son. That wasn't fair. Maybe I had to send him away until I could accept all of what was growing between us and not just the easy, obvious parts.

"Rowan. Sweetheart, that wasn't a trick question."

"I know. I just . . ."

"I'll go. Do me a favor. Shut down that hamster wheel in your head. Whatever is spinning in there will keep." He pressed a lingering kiss to my forehead. "Try and get some rest. If you need anything, call me or text me. I'll have my phone right next to me." Then he gave me a little head-butt. "Don't be stubborn."

"I won't be. I promise."

Jensen turned toward the door. But then he turned back. "Oh. One more thing."

"What?"

"This." He slanted his mouth over mine and brought me flush against his body. He kissed me with all the fire and finesse he'd shown me earlier, but this kiss had a sharper edge to it. As if to remind me that he could be helpful, thoughtful Jensen, but he was also one hundred thousand percent a hot, hungry male who would bide his time, but in the end, he would have me.

"Lock the door behind me," he murmured against my mouth when we came up for air.

Then he was gone.

Eighteen

JENSEN

hadn't heard from Rowan, so I assumed Calder had settled down for the rest of the night.

Although I'd been up late, I rolled out of bed at my usual time and met with Dante at the training center. None of my teammates had shown up, so it was a quiet but intense workout. Especially since Dante seemed more preoccupied than usual.

Legs wobbly, arms aching, I parked myself in front of the industrial fan in the locker room, letting the sweat drip off my face and hair onto the towel between my feet.

"What's going on with you lately?" Dante said, startling me.

I didn't bother looking at him. I'd grown tired of defending myself at every turn. I'd proven myself to anyone in the organization who'd demanded it of me, whenever they'd demanded it. "I more than kept up today and you damn well know it. The amount of speed I've lost since the surgeries is nominal and will have zero effect on my ability to run the ball. I'm stronger, more agile, so I can block faster. I've never been in better shape so I seriously don't know what you want from me, Coach."

Silence.

Dante laughed. Not a nice laugh either. "Coach, huh? Guess you put me in my place. So much for my belief we're friends outside of me being your trainer."

I said nothing, because knowing Dante as I did, he wasn't finished.

"To clarify, Rocket, when I asked what was going on with you, I meant in your life outside of football training. In the past month, I don't hear from you aside from texts asking about the workout schedule. We used to hang out. We used to go out. Now, it feels like you've *cut* me out." He paused. "I'm not the only one who's noticed. When was the last time you spent time with your teammates? You used to make an effort. Hell, Jensen, you used to be fun. Clubs, parties, women, you were up for anything, anytime. What happened to that guy?"

"That guy doesn't exist anymore." I finally met Dante's gaze. "And good fucking riddance to him. What I find interesting is that you noticed *after* our Florida and Mexico trip that I'd changed. Know why? Because you kept your distance from me after my injury. You and everyone else on the team. There's no reason to invest time in a *former* player and teammate, right?"

"Not true, bro."

"Totally true, bro, because I lived it. There's no need for a 'feel sorry for me' conversation, and I've never brought it up for that reason. My family hired the best doctors to fix me. My family aided in my recovery. My family rallied around me. My family reminded me that I was more to them than a football player. Somehow along the way, I'd forgotten that.

"Ever since I was drafted, I get the superstar treatment. While it's great, it's not real. And my teammates, as you pointed out, always counted on *me* to be part of the posse. Booze, women, elite clubs. These players have multimillion-dollar contracts. So why did I end up footing the bill for most of those wild nights? You know why? Because I'm a nice guy. I'd rather just pull out my credit card than bicker about who had how many shots of Hennessy. Not a single one of them noticed . . . until I stopped going. It wasn't me they missed as much as my wallet. Like I said, I'm not whining. I'm not bitter. What I am? Is wiser. That doesn't change the fact that I will go to the dirt for these guys when we're on the field. But as soon as that uniform comes off, I'm not The Rocket. I'm finally grasping the fact I have a lot more to offer the world than my celebrity—as fleeting as that may be."

I didn't wait for his response. Instead I returned to my locker, stripped and hit the shower. The hot water loosened my muscles. The steam cleared my head. As a shy kid, I'd had a hard time speaking up for myself. Growing up as the fourth kid in my family, I found it easier to let my siblings speak for me. Around age sixteen, after Annika had gone to college, and Walker had moved to Sweden, and Brady was killing himself in grad school, I had no choice but to learn to assert myself.

I hated it. It took me a few years to be comfortable with it and not apologetic. The only place I had no problem asserting myself was on the football field. The women who hang around athletes are the aggressors, and I happily let them be. To say I didn't have to work hard to get laid? Massive understatement. I hated when I had to become an asshole to get them to leave me alone. I'd learned my lesson there, but much later than I probably should have.

After I dressed and was on my way out, I noticed Dante waiting by the exit for me.

Great. Now I'd have to listen to his rebuttal. With my twenty-minute shower I'd given him plenty of time to come up with one.

Maybe if I just walked past him without making eye contact . . .

"I wondered if you had drowned in there."

No such luck on ducking further conversation. "Nope. I'll see you Monday, D."

"Hold up."

I kept walking.

He followed me. "Who is she?"

"Who is who?"

"The woman you're seeing."

"What makes you think I'm seeing anyone?"

"Come on, Jens. This is *me*. There's a woman you're trying to impress by staying on the straight and narrow. Fine. Whatever. But who is she?"

So, nothing I'd said in the locker room had resonated with him.

That's because if it had, he'd have to shoulder some of the blame for your attitude. It's easier to blame his short-comings on someone else. You've known this about him. That's why you've kept your professional distance, even when he has no idea you don't consider him anything more than just your trainer.

It still made me sad, though, that my honesty counted for nothing.

Good thing I had my sunglasses on; that way he couldn't see the total bullshit in my eyes. I faced him. "You busted me."

He grinned. "I knew it. So who is she?"

"Her name is Astrid. You don't know her."

"She sounds hot. I'll bet she's as fiery as an asteroid between the sheets, amirite?"

I said nothing. But I didn't need to.

Dante clapped me on the back. "Anyway, I'm happy to hear that. Part of me worried that you were hooking up with Rowan Michaels."

"Why would you give a shit about that?"

"Because she is one hundred percent off-limits, man. She and I are friends, and I'd hate to see her fired because you can't keep your hands off her pompoms."

Took all my willpower not to take a swing at him. "You're full of shit, D. Why would she be fired?"

"Because they can't fire you. They'd fine the hell out of you for breaking the no-frat rule, but her? Gone. It's not like anyone would notice." He snickered. "You wouldn't notice. There are a dozen women ready to slip on those tiny white booty shorts and go-go boots and shake their T and A for the crowd. But there's only one Rocket."

In my mind's eye, I'd cracked him a good one in the jaw and as he lay sputtering and bleeding on the blacktop, my tires spit gravel on him as I drove off.

Dante proved how much of a tool he was when he said, "Call me. I wanna meet this Astrid chick you're filling with rocket fuel."

Unwanted thoughts created a logjam in my head. For the first time in a long time, I didn't want to go home. I needed some distance from Rowan. Maybe for her own good.

I drove to Brady's place. I had the code for his private gym and an open invitation to use it whenever I wanted. Shooting hoops would be a great waste of time.

Once I was inside the cavernous space, I grabbed a basketball. Sitting on the bench, I messed around, dribbling and bouncing the ball. Then I headed toward the hoop.

I'd shot maybe four times from the free throw line when I heard the door open that separated Brady's living space from the ultimate man cave/garage.

"So the Vikes cut you and you're brushing up on your basketball skills to try out for the Timberwolves?" Brady said as he descended the metal staircase.

"What little faith you have in my recovery, bro." Four bounces. Shoot. *Swish*.

"Jens. You know I was yanking your chain."

He stopped beside the line and I gave him a once-over. "Nice suit. You wear one even on a Saturday? Dude."

"FYI: I had a business breakfast meeting, so of course I wore a suit. I've only been home an hour and I hadn't changed yet. Dick."

I laughed. "Speaking of dick . . . your fly is undone. You're not wearing a belt and your tie looks like one of my day campers put it on you. I won't even get into what a mess your hair is, Mr. Perfectly Coiffed."

Brady flashed me a cocky grin. "What can I say? My wife can't resist me when I'm wearing Tom Ford. Especially on the weekend."

"That explains why you guys are late to brunch most Sundays."

"Yep."

"I didn't show up looking for company. I sure didn't mean to interrupt."

"You didn't. Lennox went back to sleep after I wore her out." Brady snatched the ball from my hands.

"You're not dressed to take me on, one on one, GQ."

He snorted. "It's against the rules for you to play basketball, bro. You might twist something important. But the suit won't stop me from kicking your ass in a game of horse."

"Whatever. I'll even let you go first."

"How gracious of you." He shrugged out of his suit jacket and zipped his fly. Then he shot a three-pointer from the side. *Swish*. He aimed that cocky grin at me. "Nothin' but net."

"Lucky shot."

He chased the ball and pitched it to me. "You're up."

I dribbled. I shot. *Swish*. "See? Easy pickin's from right there."

Brady shot and missed.

Then I shot and missed.

"Not that I'm not happy to see you, Jens, but you do tend to show up when there's something on your mind."

"Yeah. Well. Maybe I need advice. But I also need to tell you about it in my own way."

He bounced one off the backboard into the hoop from the free throw line.

I moved in and sank the same shot.

"The way it's going with this game, you'll have all afternoon to get it out."

While he was choosing his spot to shoot from, I said, "It's about Rowan."

"Rowan," he repeated. "The single-mother cheerleading medical professional who breaks every one of your dating rules?"

Smart-ass. "That's her."

"What's going on?"

"I think I might be kinda sorta halfway in love with her."

Brady stopped dribbling. "You think, you might . . . kinda, sorta . . . halfway? Nope. Nothing wrong with that vague-ass statement."

"Excuse the hell out of me. I've never been in love, so I don't know how it's supposed to feel. I should—*it* should— feel more solid, right? I mean, I should *know* if it's the real deal?"

He sighed. "I'd hoped maybe you were here for financial advice, because I can dole that shit out in my sleep. But this?" Brady shook his head. "Until I met Lennox, I had zero experience with that kind of love."

"Which is why you are the perfect person for me to talk to about this. Walker's been in and out of love with a dozen women. Triple that number for Nolan. Jax . . . he's been in an altered frame of mind so I doubt he even remembers if he was in love. And Ash is hung up on that Olivia chick. So it's your lucky day. I'd sound like an idiot if I admitted this to anyone else."

"Admitted what?"

"That maybe I'm mistaking friendship and fondness and responsibility for something deeper with Rowan because I don't know what is normal." My face was on fire—not from overexertion. I hung my head and set my hands on my hips. "Do you know what a totally self-involved asshole I feel like admitting that out loud? Even to you?"

"Yeah, Jens, I do know."

I met his gaze. "Help me sort this out. Please."

Brady pointed to the bench. "This conversation requires beer. And yeah, I stocked that low-cal, low-carb kind so it doesn't mess with your training diet."

"Been expecting me, have you?" I joked.

"More like I hoped you'd come around more often." He handed me a beer and sat on the opposite end of the bench with his. "I'm a list guy. That won't work in this case, so just go with the stream-of-consciousness thing you do and I'll try and keep up."

My brother wasn't being flip. Our brains worked in different ways and we'd known since we were kids that in order to understand each other, we had to adjust our listening skills. It was one of the best things our parents had taught us, since they'd dealt with it because of our mother's background as a non-native English speaker.

So I laid it all out for him. From my list of dating rules to Rowan's list making anything between us a nonstarter. From the perspective that she had something to lose if anyone discovered our involvement, to my stubbornness that no one should get to dictate that for us. I liked her kid; I hated the responsibilities of single parenthood resting solely on her shoulders. I could see myself being around her and Calder every day and liking it more each day. I listed every single thing I liked about her. Every single thing that drove me crazy. I didn't keep track in my head because I knew Brady was compiling a mental list. When I finished speaking, I took a long pull of beer and allowed my brother some time to process it.

After a few moments, he said, "There's one thing you didn't mention at all." He paused. "Sex."

"Because we haven't had sex yet."

Brady raised both of his eyebrows. "You're serious."

"Last night we were like . . . this close, but Calder got sick and that was that."

"Then to be honest, I don't think you'll know if this is the real 'love' deal until the sexing happens."

"Seriously? That's the last thing I expected you to list as criteria."

"Oh yeah? I'm shocked as hell that you haven't slept with her and yet you think you're falling for her. That is not you, Jensen."

"Maybe it's how I am now. I'm not the freakin' needy manwhore I used to be."

He faced me. "Hear me out before you get pissy and defensive. One thing I can tell you about being in love? Sex is a huge part of it. *Huge.* Because the sex is different. It's the ultimate manifestation of all the things you love about that person. It is a physical expression of more than just affection. It's important to a long-term relationship. And if you and Rowan reached that stage last night and her responsibilities to her son put a halt to everything, you have to ask yourself if it'll always be an issue. If her son's needs will always come before yours, no matter what."

After he said that, I felt a sense of relief. I'd been thinking the same thing, but Brady spelling it out for me so matter-of-factly made me feel less like my concern was coming from a pair of blue balls and resentment I hadn't wanted to admit. I hadn't been telling her what I thought she wanted to hear last night when I said I wasn't upset about us not doing the deed. Her kid was sick. The mood had been shattered. But that was last night. What if we were in the mood tonight? Could she let go with me if her son was in the next room?

"From a strictly logical point of view," Brady continued, "a spontaneous sexual relationship will be damn difficult with a kid around all the time. Especially when Calder's father isn't in the picture and he isn't away every other weekend for visitation, giving you and Rowan at least *some* alone time. You won't get that lust-filled stage, where you cannot keep your hands off each other and you go at it wherever the mood strikes you. No sex in the kitchen, or on the dining room table, or on the couch during the late news, or against the wall by the front door as the groceries are scattered at your feet, or on the floor in front of the fireplace. The only place you'll be safe having sex away from the kid is in the bedroom and maybe if you're lucky, the bathroom. Is that something you can live with? Not just for the short term, but for years?"

Whoa. While Brady had made several points I needed to think about without man-sex-guilt, his rather specific list of all the taboo places sex couldn't happen sounded like he'd been thinking about this long before I'd brought it up. I took another swig of beer. "As usual you're spot-on. But, dude, you asked me that like you were asking yourself. So what's the deal?"

Brady laughed. "Can't pull one over on you." He fiddled with his beer bottle. "Lennox wants to have a baby."

That explained it. "And?"

"And I love the life I have with her. I love that we can just go wherever the hell we want. I love that if I want to bang her in the breakfast nook because she looks so damn beautiful with the sun streaming through her hair, I can, and not have to worry that there's a baby in the high chair watching us across the table. Lennox is everything I ever wanted in a life partner. And I can't help but feel that I'm not enough for her, if she wants to have a baby."

"Have you told her any of this?"

He shook his head. "We've been married a couple of years, but it doesn't seem like I've had enough time with her. She had a super shitty childhood, her mom is a piece of work and Lennox never expressed a burning desire to have a baby. So I don't know if she wants this because Trinity is pregnant. So is her BFF Kiley. I have this . . . fear—probably an irrational one—that if we had a baby, we'd gain a family but I'd lose my wife. The way she is now. The way I love her now and I don't know if I'll *ever* be ready for that."

I whistled. "This is some heavy stuff."

"For both of us."

"Have you thought about talking to Dad?"

Brady looked at me oddly. "Dad? Seriously? You think he'll be honest about whether a kid ruins your sexual relationship with your wife while he's looking into the eyes of his oldest son?"

"Yeah, I think Dad will be honest with you. Even if it stings a little. Even if the 'sex with Mom' portion of it makes you uncomfortable. Face it. He's an expert at being a great father, maintaining his place in the family business and sustaining a marriage for years—to a woman he's still crazy about—beyond the years they raised kids. I know we all assume Mom and Dad tell each other everything, but I know firsthand that's not true."

"Dad, huh?" Brady took another drink of beer. "Didn't see that one coming. I figured you'd tell me to talk to a counselor."

I shrugged. "It's an option. But it's better to go with someone you trust first. A guy who understands where you're coming from." I finished my beer and stood. "Which is why I showed up today. Thanks, by the way."

"I don't know that I helped you, without dragging my own shit into it."

"You did. After my injury I quit being the guy that let my ego and my dick make my decisions about how I spent my time off the field. But I needed the reminder that I'm not the guy who'll settle for a sexless existence either."

"Good." He walked me to the door. "You'll be at brunch tomorrow?"

"It depends on where I end up tonight. And no, I'm not assuming that I'll be rolling out of Rowan's bed in the morning. I need some distance. I thought I'd go up to the cabin."

Nineteen

ROWAN

Calder remained sick all day Saturday.

By Sunday at noon he'd bounced back as if the past thirty-six hours hadn't happened.

I'd enforced quiet time, which was almost harder for him than being sick . . . until he discovered the brand-new puppies puzzle Jensen had left on the table with the crackers and ginger ale. He'd settled in to work on the puzzle, asking me only every other hour when Jensen was coming over.

I wish I knew.

I'd sent Jensen a text this morning giving him an update on Calder.

His response?

Thnx.

That'd been it.

Since then I'd been restless.

And it hadn't helped it'd been so quiet in the apartment

complex that I could hear the elevator ding down the hallway.

I listened to the comings and goings of our neighbors in the eight apartments in our wing of the building.

I heard Lenka and Bob the building manager talking about the sticky sections of asphalt in front of the mailboxes.

I heard Inga and her sister Isla, both professional ice skaters from the Ukraine who spoke limited English, giggling and teasing each other in their native language.

I heard Joseph and Dieter, a married couple from Germany, both figure skating teachers, arguing about whose turn it was to clean out the cat box.

I heard Isabel, the cyclist from Switzerland, holding a conversation in French on her phone as she walked past toward her apartment—the last one on this floor.

Mischa and Pavel's apartment across from Isabel's sat empty while they visited family in Hungary.

Beatrice, a former biathlete, now a flight attendant for Icelandic Air, was in Iceland for a month visiting her kids, so her place was empty too.

I heard nothing from Jensen's apartment. No music or TV. I'd become so attuned to him that I knew how his keys sounded when he shoved them in the lock. A sound I hadn't heard since Friday night.

Because I obsessed about . . . everything really, I replayed Friday's events over and over.

Trying to figure out if I'd misread our post-Calder-vomiting conversation.

Calder comes first for me. Every single time.

As he should.

But?

No buts. Your dedication to being there for your son will never be an arguable point for me.

Then what are we arguing about?

Nothing. I had to force you to take my help tonight. All I'm asking is, next time? Don't fight me on it. Save us both the time and wasted energy and accept it.

There'll be a next time?

Well, if I have any say in it . . . yes.

Had he meant it?

Maybe the better question was . . . had I? Why would a man want to get involved with me if he knew he'd never be my priority?

Ding ding.

Maybe Jensen had realized that. Maybe his silence indicated he'd decided we were better off just being friends, casual friends, before things became too complicated.

You're making things complicated. You're making excuses. When all you need to do is make a few changes.

I heard Daisy telling me: *I hate that you've equated self-less with sexless. It's always made me sad that you put your physical needs at the bottom of your "life priority" list.*

Even Talia had given me advice: *But I don't hear from Calder that you let him play with those kids very often. Only if you're with him. Do you think that's best? Given he's got a built-in social network so close by? It'd be good for him, as an only child, to develop some interpersonal skills . . . Because I think some separation would be good for you too.*

I loved my son. I was a good mother, but I was more than just a mother.

As Jensen had pointed out: *You're allowed a night of fun. You're a great mom, but that's not all you are. You are crazy, sexy hot, baby.*

The only way I could believe that was to enforce it. Take a few steps back. Reassess. Give Calder room to grow and develop friendships. Pursue friendships myself with other parents. I'd feel more comfortable loosening the reins with Calder if I knew how quickly the other kids' parents jerked back their reins on their kids if they stepped out of line. That meant taking the time to get to know them.

I wasn't the only single parent in this apartment complex. Andrew's mom was widowed. Noelle's mom was divorced. I wasn't sure on Benji and Emily's family situations. But it occurred to me that all the kids who lived in the other building were onlys. No wonder they ran together in a pack.

So what did Andrew's mom do when Andrew got sick and she needed medicine? Or Noelle's mom when she had to work late? Did they have someone in their lives to rely on? Or were they like me, slogging away, day to day, acting as if they could do it all?

Maybe we all needed a little help.

Gabriel and Gejel had reached out to me and I'd been embarrassingly self-assured that I didn't need help. I was used to dealing with whatever life threw at us; it was me and Calder against the world.

But it didn't have to be that way.

My child and I would both be better off if it wasn't that way.

Things change. People change. It's time for you to change, Rowan.

I grabbed my cell and called Nicolai's parents before I talked myself out of it.

"Hey, Gejel, it's Rowan Michaels. Yes. He's much better." I laughed. "Like he'd never even been sick. I know, right? Anyway, thank you for having him over Friday night. I've been thinking about a couple of things I'd like to run past you and Gabriel." I glanced at the clock. "Twenty minutes is perfect. Calder will be thrilled to get some fresh air. Okay. See you in a bit."

After I ended the call, I said, "Get your suit on," to Calder. "We're meeting Nicolai and his family at the pool."

His face lit up. "For real?"

"For real."

He whooped and danced around.

Yep. The kid was definitely feeling better.

Sunday evening, after I'd fortified myself with a glass of wine, I texted Jensen.

Me: I hope your weekend got better. We missed you.

Me: I missed you.

Me: I wondered if we could talk? Early tomorrow night? Over dinner?

Me: I'll cook. Send me your dietary restrictions if there are any.

Me: I really missed you.

He didn't respond for nearly fifteen minutes.

JL: Dinner sounds good. No restrictions. What should I bring?

I started to type *condoms*, but backspaced over it.

Me: Just bring yourself ☺

JL: Should I bring Harry Potter so C and I can catch up? We've missed a few nights.

Me: No Calder. Just us tomorrow night.

I watched the typing text message icon start and stop. Start and stop. Start and stop. Then I received:

JL: Okay. Be there at 6

Of course I was running late on a Monday.

I hadn't gotten home until five fifteen. I loaded up Calder's overnight bag—this time including Pepto-Bismol for if his stomach got wonky—and we walked over to Nicolai's.

I'd worked out a swap with Gabriel and Gejel. Calder stayed with them tonight and Nicolai would stay over with us Friday night, allowing his parents to celebrate their anniversary at a B&B up north.

This babysitting co-op thing might end up being a sanity saver for everyone.

I didn't get back to my floor until five fifty-five. Too late to throw the lasagna in the oven, so I'd have to go to plan B.

It'd become a habit as I moved about the training center to spin my keys on my finger until the metal hit my palm, then spin them back out. An annoying habit, I'd been told, but one that I couldn't break even when I wasn't at the gym. I spun my keys in the elevator.

Smack. Jingle. Smack. Jingle.

I continued to spin them as I exited the elevator and turned the corner on the second floor.

The *smack, jingle, smack, jingle* caught Jensen's attention, and he turned to face me.

My heart zoomed from zero to two hundred in those four long seconds we stared at each other.

With the way he'd slung his equipment bag over his shoulder, the strap pulled his shirt taut so the fabric clung to every muscle in his back and his arm.

Oh, how I've missed you, you sexy beast.

Of course, I didn't say that. I waited for him to say something first.

But why? Doesn't he always make the first move?

Not always. You're usually the first one to retreat.

I internally cringed because that was true.

Jensen's eyes remained on me as I closed the distance between us. I tried not to fidget even when I knew I looked like a trainwreck. No makeup, my hair pulled back in a stubby ponytail, wearing my usual work uniform: maroon athletic pants sporting the U of M logo, and a too-tight gold workout top with a compression bra that squished my boobs flat. Not exactly the date-night attire I'd prepared to wow him with.

"Hey. I'm running behind."

"That's fine. Practice ended late anyway." Then he took two steps toward his door.

Two hitching steps that put a grimace on his face.

"What did you do to your leg?" I demanded.

"Nothing. Don't worry about it."

"Too late. Tell me what happened."

"Really, Coach. It's fine."

"Then you won't mind if I take a look." I dropped to my knees on his left side and ran my hand down the back of his calf. "Is it a burning or a snapping pain?"

"Neither. Shooting."

"Worse when it bears forward weight?"

"Forward weight sends the shooting pain up my shin, not my calf."

"Turn your knee in, please." He complied. "Worse? Better? No change?"

"Better."

Damn, he had muscular calves. Perfectly sculpted and veiny. But who had that type of muscle definition by their shin bone?

"Rowan?"

Awesome. I'd just felt him up. Actually, it was pretty freakin' awesome because I'd never had my hands on this part of his body before. I pushed on the outside of his calf from his ankle, slowly up to his knee. "Have you added more cardio this week?"

"No."

"Running on a different surface? Asphalt, concrete or turf instead of treadmill?"

"Nope."

"New shoes?" When he didn't respond, I looked up at him.

"Yeah, I got new shoes. But they're the exact same brand I've been wearing. Same style, same size, same laces, same everything."

"Except they're new. With different soles. Could be a little harder. Or softer. Wider. Narrower. Without measuring, I'd say the flare by the heel is narrower than your previous pair. You're running on the outside of your foot to try to compensate. It's putting pressure on the tibialis anterior."

He crossed his arms over his chest. "If it's the shoes, then why aren't I having any issues with the right foot?"

"Because you've been favoring your right side for a year and a half since your injury. You automatically compensate for it."

"So, Coach, what's your recommendation?"

I blinked at him. "To talk to your trainers about it."

"That's it? *You're* a trainer."

"I'm not *your* trainer. Big difference. A massage would help."

"You offering?" he said huskily. "Because if you're on your knees I can think of another part of me that's in worse need of a rubdown."

My heart just . . . caught fire.

Or maybe that was my panties.

"What is it about you that has me all tied up in knots?" Jensen reached down and pulled the tie out of my hair. "You break all three of my rules." Then he slid his hand down to cup my jaw. "And for as much shit as I gave you about being a rule follower? I am too. I've never broken any of them before. Never wanted to. Until I met you." He let his hand fall to his side. "Sweetheart, get up. I've only got so much control."

I had a front-row seat to seeing how being on my knees affected him. I scrambled to my feet and took a few steps back. "I'll just go get ready."

Jensen bestowed a thorough sweep of those molten blue eyes over me. "Get ready for what?"

"Our dinner date."

"It can wait. Where's Calder?"

"Staying overnight at a friend's."

"Did you plan that?"

"Yes. After our plans fell through Friday night, I decided to make some contingency plans. Not just for one night. For the long term." I kept my eyes on his. "Spending time alone with you . . . I'm making it a priority. This isn't a onetime thing for me."

He tipped his head back to the ceiling and said, "Thank you, Jesus." Then he pinned me with his laser-sharp gaze. "Now what?"

Despite my worries that my sexual inexperience would frustrate or disappoint him, I seized the moment. "Now . . . you put your bold talk into action."

Twenty

JENSEN

Rowan conveyed exactly what I needed to hear.

Not just the promise of hot sex, but proof that she'd dealt with her doubts about us.

What a goddamned relief.

She sauntered closer with a sensuous sway of her hips.

Once we were toe to toe, I flattened my palm on the base of her throat and gently curled my fingers around her neck, feeling her pulse jump beneath my stroking thumb.

She glanced down at my hand, and then those mesmerizing hazel eyes met mine with complete trust.

Without a word, I reached behind me and opened the door.

As soon as we were locked in my apartment, I had my mouth on her. My hands on her. Greedy to touch and taste every part of her.

Rowan kissed me, her passion equally all-consuming.

"Bedroom," I growled after I broke the kiss.

"Couch."

That gave me pause. "Why?"

"You ever fucked a woman on that enormous puffy couch that you adore so much, Lund?"

I smiled against her neck. "No."

"Then I want to be the first at something for you too."

"Too?"

She stood on her tiptoes and placed her mouth on my ear. "You're the first man I've let into my heart and into my life since before Calder was born."

Might be kinda, sorta halfway in love . . . Nope. Totally in love with this woman.

I forced her to look at me. "The *only* man," I corrected fiercely.

"Then I want to be the *only* woman you fuck on that couch."

"How about if you're the only woman I ever fuck . . . period."

Her eyes gleamed. "Deal."

Elated, I picked her up and tossed her over the back of the couch.

She squealed.

I planned on hearing that a lot tonight.

"Strip naked. Striptease another time."

"Anxious?" she said in a sexy coo as she pitched her athletic shoes toward the entryway.

"You have no fucking idea."

"I do actually." Her damp workout shirt landed on my head. Immediately the scent of her—a mix of laundry detergent, her perfume and the light musk of her sweat—hit me like a damn drug. I managed to say, "You have lousy aim, Coach."

"My aim is true. That was a prompt for you to hurry up. I'm already half-naked."

My shoes flew off. My shirt gone in an instant. I paused before I ditched my workout shorts. "Hang on." I opened my duffel bag, rooting around until I found the box of un-opened condoms. I lobbed the box into the corner of the couch before I vaulted over the edge.

Like me, she still wore her bottoms, but her upper half was bare. I crawled toward her and she waited, resting on her elbows, those gorgeous full breasts on display, her eyes dark with heat, her lips parted. "What's first on the menu of sexual delights, since we're skipping dinner?"

"Let's start with this." I kissed her as if that were all I wanted from her: one kiss. Then another. And another. While feeding her more fleeting, flirty kisses, I settled next to her, lying on our sides, facing each other. I traced the edge of her jaw with the back of my knuckles. "What?"

"I want to touch you."

"You can do that as much as you want, beautiful." Seeing her hesitation, I placed her hand on my chest. "Start here."

Her tentative touch lasted about fifteen seconds. Then her greed took over. She outlined the thick slabs of muscle that were my pectorals. First with her fingers, then with her tongue. Emboldened by the groans she'd wrought from me, she circled my nipple with the pad of her thumb as her other hand coasted down my arm. She paid particular attention to mapping the tendons, cords and veins on my forearms until every hair on my body prickled with awareness as the electricity between us began to build.

From the moment she'd bared her breasts I'd been biding my time, trying not to act obsessed about getting my hands and mouth all over them. But watching Rowan touch me and witnessing her confident little smirk because she could see how much her explorations affected me was unbelievably sexy.

Her thorough examination of the dips and grooves of my

biceps and triceps followed. In fact, Rowan seemed a little infatuated with my arms as she glided her fingertips from the bend in my elbow to the ball of my shoulder. Over and over. She murmured, "Your body is outstanding."

I'd received a multitude of comments on my physique over the years and never paid much attention to them. My body was a tool. A weapon. Since my injury I'd seen it as a broken piece of equipment. But the admiration and lust in Rowan's eyes, her words of praise filled me with pride that she saw it as an instrument of pleasure.

She ran the tips of her fingers across my collarbone. Up my neck. Over the curve of my jaw. Sweeping her thumb over my lips. "I like your face, Lund."

I laughed softly. "My face would like to say hello to your tits."

"Funny, my tits were just thinking the same thing." She rolled to her back and stretched her arms above her head.

I pounced on her, my hands cupping and squeezing the soft flesh as my mouth homed in on her nipples. I loved feeling the tips harden beneath my stroking tongue. I loved how Rowan bowed her back, trying to get me to take more of her into my mouth. Each nip, every hard suck, every scrape of my teeth made her squirm and buck and moan.

I wanted more—to hell with taking it slow. I had the burning need to turn her into a sweating, panting mess. To watch with pure male satisfaction as she lay boneless in the middle of my couch after I'd sated her desire to the point where she couldn't even move.

Hooking my fingers inside the band of her workout pants, I slid them down her legs, planting kisses on her quads, her knees, her shins. After I had undressed her completely, I pushed on the insides of her thighs as a signal for her to make room for me.

Her legs fell open and I lowered my weight onto her,

swallowing her gasp of surprise when she felt my erection jumping against her belly with eagerness.

Then I kissed a path from her chin to her belly button.

Rowan giggled and tried to squirm away. "It tickles."

"What? This?" I let the ends of my hair skim across the lower swells of her breasts. Then I trailed my hair down her belly, stopping to tease the smooth, sensitive section between her hip bones.

She twisted her upper torso, trying to get me to move. "Jensen. Stop," she said between giggles.

Locking my gaze to hers, I murmured, "Baby, you really don't want me to stop, do you?"

A long pause cooled the heat between us.

Her hand shook when she reached down to tuck my hair behind my ear. "It's just . . ."

I noticed that her face was flushed. I'd chalked it up to arousal, but now I suspected embarrassment. "Am I doing something wrong?"

"No. But I didn't shower."

"So that's why your scent is driving me wild." Beneath her belly button, I rubbed my lips from her left side to her right. And back. "Tell me what you want, Ro."

Her words tumbled out in a rush. "It's been a long time since I've had a guy go down on me and I forgot how exposed I am."

Okay. She needed more time. I could give her that. For her, I'd learned patience. Because I knew she was worth the wait.

I rolled onto my knees and then stood, trying to keep my balance on the wobbly cushions.

"Whoa." Rowan scrambled into a sitting position. "That didn't mean I wanted you to stop."

Sweet Jesus. She was killing me. I grinned at her. "I'm not stopping, sweetheart. Just leveling the playing field." Sliding my fingers inside the elastic band of my athletic shorts, I shoved them and my underwear to my ankles and kicked them away. "Now we're equally exposed."

Her wide-eyed gaze remained on my erection even when I dropped to my knees and snagged the box of condoms.

"Holy crap, Rocket. You *are* packing a rocket," she whispered.

I ripped the condom box open—literally tore into it with enough force that the strip of condoms went airborne and landed on Rowan's belly.

Yeah. I was one smooth motherfucker.

"Well, that's handy." Rowan tore a single package off the strip and used her teeth to open it. Then she shifted upright so we were facing each other. She curled her left hand around the back of my neck and reached between us, firmly grasping me as she rolled the condom on. "Not a level playing field, Lund. This is impressive."

I hissed out a breath and fastened my mouth to hers. Whatever momentum we'd lost, we regained in that explosive kiss, only pausing to rest our foreheads together and suck in a lungful of oxygen before our lips gravitated together again. Sliding, teasing, feeding the frenzy between us.

My hands started at her hips and traveled up, spanning her belly and resting on her rib cage. Her velvety smooth skin flowed like silk beneath my fingers and she trembled from my touch. I trailed openmouthed kisses from the corner of her lips, over her jaw and down her throat, tasting the saltiness and musk of her skin.

Every time I did something she liked, her fist tightened around me. When it became a constant squeeze and release, I had to break the connection of her hand on my dick.

"Too much," I panted against her throat.

She brushed her lips over my ear to whisper, "The way you touch me . . . It makes me want every part of you—your hands, your mouth, your cock—all over me, all at once."

Gooseflesh broke out across my entire body as she scraped her nails up my belly and across my chest to reiterate her desire for me.

"So touch me, Jensen. However you want. Just don't stop this time."

My dick went harder yet.

"Lie back," I growled.

As soon as she'd propped herself up with one arm behind her head, her hair a swath of red against the gray cushions, I rubbed my lips across her sternum, watching her eyes widen as I moved my mouth progressively southward.

I intended to tease her. Build her up and then pull back. Use every trick in my sexual arsenal to prove my oral mastery before I sent her soaring.

But a single whiff of the sweet cream between her thighs and I was done for.

Done.

For.

Raising her up to my mouth, I tasted the soft feminine flesh that glistened just for me. I demonstrated what it meant to devour. To feast.

Rowan gave herself over to my hunger without hesitation.

My every lick, every suck, every bite brought forth a sexy sound from her—need, pleasure, surprise. In time I'd learn what every shudder, sigh and gasp meant. Right now, I just knew she needed more.

It wasn't long until her fingers went from clutching the couch cushion to gripping my hair.

That bite of pain unleashed a primal need inside me. I was relentless in driving her to the tipping point.

As soon as her legs started to shake and she chanted that "oh god, oh god, oh god" mantra, she blindly reached for my hand as if she needed a solid piece of me to anchor her as she lost herself in the pleasure.

Rowan Michaels letting go might've been the hottest thing I'd ever seen.

Finally the tension in her hips and thighs and belly went slack.

I moved up her body, keeping as much of her skin in contact with mine as possible. Marveling in her softness and strength. Drawing her scent into my lungs. Swallowing down the tangy taste of her.

Feeling the change in her from languid to expectant, I slid our joined hands above her head and locked my gaze to hers.

I didn't need to guide myself inside her. Our bodies shifted into perfect alignment like we'd done this a thousand times before.

Her groan of satisfaction echoed mine when I filled her completely.

I eased out of that sublime tightness and thrust back in. Once. Twice. Three times.

As I kissed her, from her temple to her jaw, then dragged my lips down the cord straining in her neck, I picked up the pace, my heart pounding against hers, my skin slick with sweat, my blood pumping hot and hard enough to create a floating sensation in my head.

She arched up and whispered, "I can't breathe."

"Hold on." I rolled us to the side and grabbed the back of her thigh, draping her leg over my hip. In this position I wasn't crushing her, but I couldn't drive into her as hard. So with each upward thrust, I kept constant contact where she needed it most.

"God. That's so good."

"Rowan. Baby, look at me."

When she tilted her head back, I took her mouth in a no-holds-barred kiss. I needed a distraction to keep me from coming within the first two minutes of getting inside her.

Sweat dampened my hair. I rocked into her, feeling her tits bounce and slide against my chest. As hot as it was to feel her passion in the way she kissed me when we were joined like this, next time I'd bury my face in those luscious breasts as she rode me.

Rowan dug her fingernails into my lower back and tore her mouth away from mine on a gasp. "That's it. Like that. Just like that. Yes."

Good to know I wasn't the only one with a short fuse.

Her interior muscles tightened around me and she sank her teeth into the ball of my shoulder as she came undone for the second time.

With her clinging to me, biting me, her climax squeezing me, I couldn't hold back.

Fireworks, a nuclear explosion, a tsunami . . . nothing was as powerful as this.

The physical release unlocked something inside me. Something too overwhelming to give voice to. I pressed my mouth to the warm, sweet-smelling curve of her neck, grounding myself as the shudders racking my body slowly subsided.

In the aftermath, Rowan's hands caressed my back, clutched my ass, slipped between us to press her palm to my heart. She whispered, "Jensen Lund. I am so crazy for you I don't know what to do with it."

I mumbled, "You definitely should keep me around while you're figuring it out."

"That was a given." She nudged my face up and peered into my eyes. "Because you just moved up to spot one point five on my list of life priorities."

Twenty-one

ROWAN

From the night Jensen and I took that leap to being lovers, our day-to-day lives had changed dramatically.

Calder accepted us as a couple right away, even assigning Jensen his own place at our table. I attributed the ease of the transition to Jens being present in Calder's life from the start of our friendship. Now after we ate meals together, or watched TV at Jensen's apartment, or hung out at the pool or the playground, most nights Jensen went to bed with me. That seemed to be Calder's only complaint: jealousy that Mommy got to have more sleepovers than he did.

I still did most of Calder's care on my own: bathing him, driving him places and setting up the child-care co-op with our newfound friends in building two. But some nights he asked Jensen to read to him instead of me. Some afternoons I'd find them immersed in Harry Potter or destroying the kitchen when they played *Chopped*.

Calder was a rule-following kid, so discipline wasn't an issue. Jensen agreed to tell me if Calder acted in a way that might require "clarification." We got a huge kick out of that word—it'd become the safe word between Lucy and Jax at camp.

While Jensen and I were very much together, the only place we were completely open about it was at Snow Village. Jensen swore his clubbing days had ended with his injury. Hanging out in a bar on a rare child-free night didn't appeal to either of us. We weren't hiding our relationship. We just built it in a place it could flourish, among the people who mattered to us.

After we'd been a couple for a few weeks, we'd driven to my parents' farm. Between the football talk, the history talk and the sampling of the hard cider until the wee small hours, Jensen and my dad became fast friends. I sensed my parents' relief in Jensen's dealings with Calder and his open affection for both of us. I'd had to laugh—and blush—when after too many cups of apple wine my mother asked if Jensen's rocket rocked my world. But I'd known she'd worried about me acting too cynical about love and relationships because of my early responsibilities as a single parent. She wasn't impressed by Jensen's looks, charm, fame or money. Seeing me happy with him, and him happy with me—and Calder too . . . that impressed her.

Calder and I had met both of Jensen's brothers and their wives. Since Trinity taught at camp and Walker helped out building theater sets, Calder was comfortable with them. The fact that they had a swimming pool earned them bonus points. It'd taken him a couple of times to warm up to Brady and Lennox. Brady's love of Harry Potter had won him over, as had Lennox's new kitty, Chaos.

Jensen's sister, Annika, and her husband, Axl, were spending a month in Sweden, so they weren't around for the family gatherings. Neither were Jensen's parents, as they too were off traveling the world. I'd heard so much about Jensen's mother that the woman scared me. I had no idea how she'd take the news of her baby being shacked up with a single mother and her kid.

Friday afternoon I arrived at camp fifteen minutes before class ended. I hadn't seen Jensen's car outside, but I stopped into the office anyway.

Astrid was at her desk, conversing with a blond woman with her back to me.

Not wanting to interrupt, I started to back away.

But Astrid saw me and said, "Rowan. Wait."

I froze in the doorway when the blond woman turned around and I realized she was Jensen's mother.

Same blue eyes. Same blond hair. Same stunning bone structure.

"Mrs. Lund has been waiting for you," Astrid said.

Oh shit.

She unfolded from the chair, as graceful as a cat.

Her clothes whispered *money* as she started toward me. She wore a sleeveless silk shell the color of ripe peaches, the front embellished with beads and rhinestones. A sheer chiffon gold-toned blouse covered her arms and skimmed her hips, drawing attention to her trim waist. A band of satin hugged her hips, the shimmery mint-green fabric flowing into palazzo pants that ended above her ankles. Gold leather gladiator sandals completed the ensemble, making her look every inch the imperial Valkyrie—dressed like a goddess but the fancy wrapping didn't mask the warrior beneath.

Her smirk—identical to Jensen's—indicated her awareness of the imposing image she presented. Gold bangles rattled on her wrist as she offered me her hand. "I am Selka Lund. Jensen's mother."

I took her hand. "I'm Rowan Michaels. Pleased to meet you, Mrs. Lund."

"Come. Let's walk."

And I found myself being ushered out of the office, the Valkyrie still gripping my hand as she smoothly linked her arm through mine and bent me to her will.

Of course no one was in the hallway as she herded me out the side door to the playground.

Jensen had installed a picnic table so the staff could sit in the shade during lunch and keep an eye on the playground.

She sat on the bench and patted the spot next to her. "Sit. We shall chat."

"I'll stand, thanks."

She lifted one dark blond brow. "You are feisty? Or just contrary?"

"Both. It's harder for you to put me in a headlock if I'm standing across from you."

"Headlock." Her lip curled slightly. "I have no UPC moves."

UPC? What the hell? "You mean . . . UFC?"

"Yah. Whatever. I am harmless."

I laughed. "I doubt that."

"My niece Dallas tells good things of you."

"You came to judge me for yourself?"

She shrugged a slim shoulder. "I don't trust her aura voodoo stuff."

Did she mean *woo-woo stuff*? I'd corrected her once already, so I kept my mouth shut.

"What do you think of this camp Jensen created?"

"I'm thrilled my son gets to attend, and I'm grateful to LCCO for stepping in and making the camp even better than it was before."

"All Jensen's ideas. He is smart. Big brain in that big body."

I was not about to discuss Jensen's amazing body that I knew every inch of with his mother. "But LCCO implemented the ideas. As you know, Jensen is uncomfortable taking full credit."

"And you know my son so well? After how long? Two and one half months?"

There it was. "I'm guessing you're here to 'chat' about my relationship with him."

"You are friends, yes?"

"We were friends. Now we're more than friends."

She tilted her head. "My boy . . . first tells me months ago he only wants friends with you. You changed his mind?"

"No. He changed mine. But we wouldn't be where we are now if we hadn't been friends first." I exhaled a nervous breath. "The truth is, Mrs. Lund, I wasn't looking for a boyfriend or a relationship. For the past six years I've lived a two-dimensional life. There's my son and my work. At the end of the day, if I tuck my child in bed and he has a smile on his face, then it's been a good day. I haven't looked beyond having that because it's been enough." I paused. "Then I met Jensen. He showed me there's more to me, to the life I—we—could have with him, while respecting the life I already have. So my two-dimensional world is now 3D."

"He gives that to you. But what do you give to him?"

Wow. Mama Lund played hardball. "I ask myself the same thing. What does he see in me? He's sweet and thoughtful. He's funny. But he's also bossy and used to getting his way. He's so damn . . . tenacious. He had so much patience with me when I hesitated for us to become more than friends. He claims he knew it—I'd—be worth the wait. As a single mother, I'm overly cautious when it comes to bringing someone new into our lives. Because mine is not the only heart that gets broken if things end badly. My son's would too." I locked my gaze to hers. "Which is why Jensen is the first man I've welcomed into our family and our hearts."

She studied me but said nothing.

That kept me talking. "I don't blame you for questioning my motives. I'd do the same thing in your position. I don't know what the future holds for Jensen and me. But I do know that I'll fight to have a future with him because he's the most amazing man I've ever met. I only hope I'm doing as great a job raising my son as you've done raising yours."

She slowly stood.

It felt like an eternity before she spoke. "You give him that."

"What?"

"Acceptance. That he's more than athlete. More than rich, bored playboy. More than man of looks, charm and muscles. You show him his true worth. A man who can love without limits in ways that even he didn't know he was capable of."

Tears pooled in my eyes. "You really think so?"

"I'm his mother. I know so. You see inside to his heart and soul. Not just outer trippings."

I snickered. "You mean the outer trappings?"

"Yah, that."

"Thank you, Mrs. Lund."

"Thank you for putting happy sparkle in my son's eyes. Now we hug it out."

The woman gave good hugs. And she smelled great.

She patted my cheeks. "No more Mrs. Lund, yah? Call me Selka."

The door to the playground opened and kids rushed out. I stepped to the side and waved so Calder could see me.

He skipped over, happily singing to himself.

That familiar burst of love expanded in my chest. I crouched down to hug him.

"Astrid said you were out here, Mommy." Then he noticed Selka Lund standing next to me. He tipped his head back and studied her.

"Calder, this is—"

"Hey, you're Rocketman's mom. He showed me your picture in his kitchen."

"He did?"

"Yeah. Do you really got your very own pool?"

She laughed. "Yes. With a slide and everything. Come over to swim anytime."

Calder started to bounce. "Really?"

"Really and truly."

"And you'll make cookies? Jensen said you make the best Swedish cookies in the world."

I started to remind him of his manners, but Selka spoke first.

"Of course. All boys need cookies."

"That would be awesome!" He launched himself at Selka, giving her an impromptu hug. "I can't wait to tell Jensen!"

When he stepped back, I noticed he'd left black smears on her pants. In three places.

Selka noticed too. She tried brushing it off.

In five seconds Calder had ruined a pair of pants that probably cost more than I made in five weeks. "I'm so sorry. I'll pay for the dry cleaning, and if they're stained I'll pay to replace them—"

"Hush." Selka trapped my face between her hands. "Hugs from sweet boys are always worth more than fabric and thread."

My jaw would've dropped if she hadn't held my face.

"I miss messy little boys. This is happy reminder of those days." She kissed my forehead and released me. She crouched in front of Calder.

He blurted out, "I'm sorry!"

"It's okay. How about you ask your mama if I can push you on the swings?"

"Really?"

"Really and truly."

Calder looked at me. "Mommy, can I?"

"Sure. But we have to leave in ten minutes."

Selka held out her hand, and I'll be damned if Calder didn't take it and start chattering to her like he'd known her for years as he skipped away. I said, "Unreal," out loud.

"She has a way with little boys. Not surprising since we had three of them."

A shadow fell across me. I turned and came face-to-face with Jensen's father.

He smiled at me. "My wife wasn't too hard on you, I hope."

I smiled back. "She caught me off-guard, but it's all good. Unless you're here to play bad cop to her good cop?"

He laughed. He had a great laugh and now I knew where Jensen had gotten it. "I imagine Selka played both good and bad cop. I had no idea she planned to ambush you until my daughter-in-law called to tell me Mama Bear was on the prowl. So I'm here to bat cleanup."

"You Lunds and your sports analogies."

"Par for the course with all of us."

"Omigod. Jensen gets his love of puns from you!"

He laughed again. "Guilty." He offered his hand. "I'm Ward, by the way. It's great to finally meet you, Rowan. Jensen hasn't told me much about you, but his happiness the last two months tells me all I need to know."

And . . . there was the charm my man had inherited too. "Jens and I are twin beams of happiness, according to our neighbors on the second floor."

"So you and Jensen are out, loud and proud, as a couple?"

"Yes . . . and no. Jensen has lived at Snow Village longer than I have and he knows everyone. He claims they're trustworthy, so we hang out at the pool and the playground with Calder's friends' parents. As far as us going out together?

Either as a couple on a date or with Calder? Right now we're content to stay home. I work all day and Jensen is dealing with pretraining stuff. We're happy to flop on his ridiculously large couch and chill."

"And here at camp?"

"The staff knows we're . . . close. The kids don't pay attention. It's not like we're even here at the same time most days. My parents know we're involved, but they keep it to themselves." Guilt hit me. I shot him a look. "Shoot. I'm sure Jens meant to tell you sooner—"

"He did tell us. But that was weeks ago and we've been out of the country. So now we're back and Mama Lund tends to take matters into her own hands."

"I'll remember that."

"Now I'm going to sneak off before Selka gets back and chews me out for spying on her." He squeezed my shoulder. "Hope to see more of you, Rowan."

"You will. It was nice meeting you."

When he reached the side door, I said, "Ward? Can I ask you something?"

He turned. "Of course."

"What's Jensen's middle name?"

He laughed. "Ask his mother. It was her idea."

Twenty-two

ROWAN

The hot summer days and hotter summer nights with my man flew by.

Camp Step-Up was winding down even as Vikings training camp started in two days.

The more I worked with Astrid, the more she impressed me. I wished I had the budget to offer her a paid position scheduling practice and workout times at the campus training center, because we needed someone who could multitask.

Jensen returned home every night exhausted. I'd never overstepped my bounds and told him to train less or not push himself so hard, but I was sorely tempted after he'd nearly fallen asleep at the dinner table.

In addition to the physical demands of being a professional athlete, with the impending opening of the new stadium, it seemed the team PR machine had hit the overdrive stage. All of the players were in demand for interviews and appearances at community events. The only good thing about the accelerated promotion schedule was that no one questioned why the players and the cheerleaders were together so often. Jensen and I didn't avoid each other, but we also weren't making out in the locker room or walking hand in hand to events. I wasn't sure how things would change once we'd passed the preseason; I just knew things would change.

Whether that would be a good change for us . . . only time would tell.

I still hadn't heard from Martin about when he and Verily planned to return. Part of the deal with us subleasing from them? I was supposed to be looking at houses to buy. But besides occasionally browsing online, I'd pretty much blown off the house search. Did I have visions of moving into Jensen's apartment after Martin returned? I wasn't ready to answer that honestly. Since Calder was starting at a charter school, the school district we lived in was irrelevant.

The main issue for me was that I'd been an apartment dweller since I'd lived in the dorms my first year of college. It sounded weird to a lot of people—my folks included—but I liked living in an apartment complex. I'd heard the "throwing your money away on rent" argument more times than I could count. But the thought of being responsible for even more things in my life—yard work, shoveling snow, home repairs and maintenance—sent me into panic mode. I hadn't mentioned my aversion to becoming a homeowner to anyone except Martin. That was how I'd ended up subleasing his place: because he understood. He'd told me unless he moved out of the Cities completely, he planned to live at Snow Village indefinitely.

Since starting the child-care co-op, I felt we were part of a community. I liked that Calder had friends and a pool

and safe playground. I liked the location. I'd be content living there.

Thanks to Jensen, we now knew everyone in the complex
and there was a certain bond among athletes and former
athletes in Snow Village. The turnover among renters was
very low; the list to get vetted for consideration to rent a
place there was years long, according to everyone I'd talked
to. So the open apartments on the first floor bugged me.

Needing a break from the never-ending paperwork as a
new semester loomed, I'd ducked out of my office to grab a
soda for my caffeine fix. In the vending area I showed im-
mense willpower by not adding a package of M&Ms and
calling it lunch. Carrying my Diet Mountain Dew across
the mats, I stopped when I saw Bree talking with a big guy
in a ball cap—a very familiar big guy.

What was Jensen doing here?

I started toward them.

Immediately Jensen homed in on me and his lips kicked
into a half smile that meant he was thinking dirty thoughts.

He didn't wait for me to come to him; he half jogged
toward me.

Bree yelled, "Wait. You can't just—"

"It's all right. I was expecting him. We'll be in my office."
I motioned with my head for him to follow me down the
short hallway.

My office was on the small side, but I loved the coziness
of it. And it seemed particularly cozy with a six-foot-five,
two-hundred-fifty-pound football player crowding me
against the door the instant we were alone.

Jensen was all over me. Wrapping his hands around my
face and kissing me with a hunger that stole my breath.

He didn't stop kissing me until he was damn good and
ready. By that time, my thoughts were fuzzy, my skin sizzled
and my body had gone wet and achy with need.

Jensen buried his face in my neck and muttered "Fuck" on a soft sigh.

I slipped my hands under his shirt because I could. It still made me giddy that I had unfettered access to this amazing body, belonging to this amazing man.

He shuddered as I touched him. My fingertips tracing the grooves of his rock hard abdomen. My palms following the sides of his torso up and over his rib cage to the thick slabs of muscle that defined his chest. I swept my thumbs over his nipples and nudged his face with my shoulder so I could kiss the underside of his jaw.

"God. I needed this."

"What?"

"You." He groaned and pressed into me with more intent. "Is this a sturdy door?"

I tweaked his nipple before pushing on his chest. "It'll rattle like a freight train with as hard as you thrust. I don't need my students standing outside the door wondering what the hell is going on in here."

Jensen blew a raspberry against my throat and I squealed. "Dream killer." He stepped back. "No problem. I can adapt. I'll just bend you over the desk."

Framing his gorgeous face in my hands, I hated seeing the dark circles of worry and exhaustion beneath his usual sparkling eyes. "You okay? Not that I'm not happy to see you, but it's rare that you just drop by."

"I miss you." He closed his eyes. "That sounds stupid because I see you every day. But it's been hit-and-miss the past few days—"

"And you really want to hit this"—I thrust my pelvis into his—"doncha, big guy?"

"Am I that transparent?" He laughed softly. "But yeah. I want to lose myself in you for a little while, Ro." He rested his forehead to mine. "Can you play hooky for a couple of hours?"

"Aren't you supposed to be at practice?"

"I'm playing hooky too."

If Jensen had blown off practice to spend time with me, then there was more going on than him missing me. Calder wouldn't be done with camp for three hours, so we could have uninterrupted time alone. "Your place or mine?"

"Mine."

"I'll meet you there in fifteen."

After another toe-curling kiss, Jensen picked up his hat and took off.

Technically I could come and go as I pleased, especially this time of year when there were minimal students in the training center. So I changed the hands on the clock on my door, indicating I'd be back after three.

We didn't make it into his bedroom for the first round. I suspected Jensen had been pacing in his apartment while he waited for me. The instant I opened the door, he was on me. Kissing me as he stripped me. Impatiently tearing off his clothes when he'd gotten me naked. Dropping to his knees and using his mouth and his hands to send me soaring. Then bending me over the back of his couch and giving in to his need to take me hard and fast with a passion that rocked me to the core.

And after he'd found his release, he carried me into his bedroom, where he started all over again.

The room stayed dark, only a slight glow from the hallway through the crack in the door.

As much as I loved Jensen the impatient, intense lover, this tender, thorough side of him loving on me did me in. His hands gentled as they caressed every inch of my skin. His kisses were soft and sweet as he teased the hot spots that drove me crazy like the small of my back and the crease of my knee. His reverence with every sweeping caress . . . I didn't deserve it even when I was thrilled to have it.

His stunning masculine form deserved its own worship. So I mapped the dips and valleys of his musculature, but I also paid particular attention to gently stroking my fingertips across the wide expanse of his shoulders, down the middle of his back and lower to his firm ass. After the brutal training and physical impact he inflicted on his body every day, he deserved a soft touch from someone who understood that tactile pleasures of the flesh were just as important as that hard-driving rise to release.

We lost ourselves in the cocoon of darkness. Reveling in the luxury of indulging in this ultimate intimacy without the urgency. There wasn't a choreographed need to take turns tasting, touching, teasing. We wound each other up and then let go.

Afterward, Jensen kept me wrapped in his embrace, my back to his chest, our legs tangled, our bodies at rest, even when I knew his mind was back to racing a million miles an hour.

"Jens?"

"Yeah, baby?"

The only time he called me baby was when we were alone like this. "You owe me—"

"Hey, you wanted to blow me, sweetheart, I would've been fine—"

"Not that, dumbass. You ripped my yoga pants in the living room. Dude, that's the second pair in two weeks."

"Oh. Well, sorry, not sorry."

I elbowed him.

He laughed. "I'll buy you four new pairs. Two to replace the ones I ruined and two pairs that I can ruin at will, okay?"

"Okay."

"It's pretty obvious how much I missed you if I'm ripping your clothes off."

"Or you don't know your own strength."

"Or you're my weakness, baby."

I melted.

He nuzzled the back of my head. "I've never had this. I know you haven't either. That's why I love that it's this way between us."

"Were you worried it wouldn't be?"

He hesitated and I felt my stomach tighten. "I didn't know it could be like this, so my worries were more along the lines of . . . would this be a priority?"

For you went unsaid. *Don't take offense. He's being open and honest and that's what you asked of him.*

Jensen turned me to face him. "That's why I came to you today. I've not made you—or this—a priority the past week. I'm sorry."

"Four orgasms is a hell of an apology, Lund."

"I love you, Ro. I don't want to screw this up. I'm looking forward to training camp, but I don't want to be away from you and Calder."

I looped my arms around his neck. "I know. I love you too. I'll miss sneaking away for sexy times in the middle of the afternoon. It feels so naughty."

He grinned. "This is the best afternoon workout I've had all week."

"As much as I'd love to see if you can't get the day's orgasm tally into double digits for me, I do have to go back to work."

"I don't. I told Coach I was sick." He fake-coughed twice. "Want me to call in for you? Tell them that it's highly contagious and you need to be in bed the rest of the day."

"It's already going to be on the news that The Rocket

missed afternoon practice due to illness. You don't need speculation that you were playing hooky for some nookie on top of that."

"True." He rolled to his back with me plastered to his front. "Next go? You can be on top and do all of the work."

"Deal." I smooched his mouth. "Now I have to grab a pair of pants that aren't ripped before I head back to work."

Jensen followed me into the living room. He didn't bother putting his shirt back on, just his athletic shorts. I wasn't surprised when he followed me into my apartment too.

After changing my ripped yoga pants for a pair of khaki capris, I ducked into the bathroom to tame my sexed-up hair and check for love bites. My man loved seeing his marks on my skin. I checked. Dammit. I'd have to change my shirt too.

"What are your plans for the afternoon?" I asked Jens after I returned to the living room.

"I've gotta study plays, but I might do that by the pool." He snorted. "But that's guaranteed to bring Bob out."

It seemed every time we were out in the complex, Bob needed to talk to Jensen about something. I couldn't imagine what they'd have in common. "Has he said anything about why there are three empty units on the first floor?" It occurred to me that could be my housing solution. I could see if Bob would rent one of the units to me. That way I'd have my own space, close to Jensen and Martin, but not dependent on either of them, and Bob wouldn't have to comb through the waiting list for new, reliable renters. Would I have to argue my position that cheerleading was a sport, and therefore I qualified as an athlete?

Jensen's eyes narrowed on me. "Did you put on a different shirt?"

"Yes. I needed something to cover up the hickey."

"I didn't give you a hickey."

"Uh, yeah you did. Two of them."

"Let me see."

"No, I have to go."

"Let. Me. See." Then he grabbed me by the hips and lifted me over the back of the couch.

"Jensen!"

He laughed as I squirmed and tried to get away.

Then I heard the sound of fabric tearing as he tried to pin my shoulders down.

We both froze.

He said, "Shit."

"What?"

"Looks like I owe you a shirt too."

I glanced down. The shoulder seam of my blouse was ripped so far down my bra strap showed. "Dammit! You cannot keep ruining all my clothes, Lund."

He turned me so I sat on his lap—I assumed so he could apologize face-to-face. Instead, a wicked smile curled his lips.

"Might as well have some fun with this since it's not fixable." Then he grabbed hold of each side and yanked them apart. Buttons flew, fabric ripped like paper. Before I protested, Jensen's mouth slammed down on mine.

Now I'd really be late getting back to work.

I matched his hunger kiss for kiss. I even held my arms back as he wrenched my shirt off me and sent it sailing over the back of the couch.

I craved this greedy-lover side of him, the desperate man who couldn't wait to get his hands on me—even when he'd just had them all over me less than twenty minutes ago.

The greediest part of him was getting hard and ready for more. I snickered to myself that Jensen's stamina was unparalleled both in the bedroom and on the football field.

One quick twist and my bra was undone and sliding down my arms.

Jensen's rough-skinned hands covered my breasts, squeezing the soft flesh. He broke the kiss to growl, "Jesus, I love your tits," and latched onto one to prove it.

I arched back, gasping at the hot lash of his tongue on my nipple. Groaning when he opened his mouth over it fully and began to suck.

Work, torn clothing . . . not on my mind when Jensen's hair tickled my belly as he feasted on my breasts.

That's probably why neither of us heard the key in the lock.

But we definitely heard, "Cheezus! Sis, are you . . . topless?"

"Martin?"

"Put some clothes on!"

"Omigod! What are you doing here?"

"It's my apartment. And tell that dude to leave—"

"It's not *that dude*, it's Jensen," Jensen said sharply. "And it's not your apartment when she's subletting it from you."

"Dude, are you seriously lecturing me when you're naked with my sister?"

"We're not naked," he said. "Even if we were, how is it any of your business?"

I'd reached down and grabbed my bra. Better than nothing. I moved off Jensen's lap and stood to face my brother. "What are you—"

Martin used his forearm to block his eyes. "Seriously, Rowan, go put on a shirt!"

"Oh, knock it off. This covers more than my swimsuit top."

"Where is Calder? You'd better not be screwing around on the couch while he's taking a nap and he can just walk out and see this—"

"Hold on. Don't you *ever* question Rowan's parental judgment when it comes to her son," Jensen said hotly, vaulting the couch to get at my brother. "Calder isn't here. He's at camp."

"So the two of you can play grab-ass? Not cool." Martin glared at Jensen. "I let her move in here because she doesn't date athletes. I never thought you'd take advantage of her for a quick hookup—"

"Martin, shut up! Maybe he's *my* hookup, did you consider that?"

Silence.

"Jens, is that true?" Martin asked.

Jensen ran his hand through his hair. "No, Martin. It's not true. I'm in love with your sister. She knows that." He shot me a dark look. "Why are you trying to pass me off as a hookup?"

"I don't like him judging me, okay?" I said to Jensen. "Like I'm not woman enough to make a move on a hot guy because I want to bang the hell out of him."

The smart-ass Jensen smirked because of our history. Maybe I hadn't been confident enough to proposition him at first, but after embracing the sexual side of myself, I'd been making up for it—not something I needed to share with my brother.

Then Jensen crossed his arms over his chest, squaring off against Martin. "We gonna have a problem with this? You plan on taking a swing at me like you did Axl?"

"Different sitch, man." He shoved his hands in the front pockets of his cargo pants.

"What are you doing here? A warning you were on your way would've been nice."

"Three and a half months is too long to be gone, man. Verily and I had to hit Sweden to see her family. Made me miss my family, so I jetted home after a couple of days. She's staying there another month at least."

"Look, it didn't even cross my mind with everything

that's been going on to find another place to live. I thought I had time."

Martin's jaw dropped. "What have you been doin', Ro? You've had all summer!"

"I like it here. As a matter of fact, I decided to talk to Bob about renting one of the empty units on the first floor."

"No," Jensen said. "Those units are spoken for."

"How would you know that?" I pinned him with a look. "This isn't an attempt—"

"We'll talk about it later. The most pressing issue is, where is Martin staying? There's no room here for all three of you."

"I'll crash with you, Lund."

I burst out laughing. "He'd kill you, bro. Jens is a neat freak, and you are a slob."

"Guess that answers the question of whether you're moving in with him long-term," Martin retorted.

"You haven't lived with me for years," I reminded him. "I had to clean this place after we moved in, so I know—"

Jensen made the time-out sign when Martin and I continued to bicker. "Enough. I've got a sister, so I know that an argument can go on for hours. Martin, it makes the most sense that you crash at my place. But you absolutely cannot smoke in my apartment. Gotta have that promise."

"No problem, man. I cut way back when I was in Europe anyway."

Jensen and I exchanged a quick look; later we'd discuss what "cut way back" meant in Martin-speak.

"Oh no, heck no. You two are doin' the 'we're a couple and we have our own secret communication looks' and that is not cool. It feels like I stepped into the X-Men world where the time line is totally screwed up."

"That's not even the best way we communicate."

I was too far away to smack Jensen for that comment.

The timer went off on my watch and I was officially late getting back to work. "I have to go." I snatched up my ruined blouse on the way past to my bedroom.

Jensen cornered me. "Truth time, Coach. Are you really all right?"

"I wish there had been a better way for Martin to find out we're involved instead of seeing me bouncing on you half-naked."

"It could've been worse." He kissed me with sweet possession. Then he eased off. "Talia is bringing Calder home?"

"Yes, but they've been going straight to swimming lessons. Calder will be pumped to see his uncle, but that'll have to wait."

"Got it."

"I may have to work late to make up for—"

He placed his mouth on mine again. "I know. I'll take care of him. Don't worry."

And I wouldn't.

I'd never felt so confident in two little words when it came to my son.

JENSEN

Within ten minutes of Rowan's departure, Martin and I were at my place playing *GTA*.

"You look spooked, Martin."

"I am. It's just . . . weird. This doesn't even look like your apartment anymore, Jens. Calder's LEGOS are on the kitchen table. You've got throw pillows on this couch. And a candle on the end table." He pointed at the wall. "What is that?"

"It's a puzzle Calder and I put together and had framed."

"No, dude, what is the image supposed to be?"

"Dogs doing ballet. Hey, it's cute. It'll go perfectly with the dogs-baking-cupcakes puzzle we're currently working on."

He snickered. "I see my nephew has worked his magic on you."

"Yeah. He's a great kid."

"So you and Rowan . . ." He shook his head. "Never saw that one coming."

"It's not a casual thing with us."

"I picked up on that. And lucky for you that you're not dicking her around or else I might do something crazy like this." He blew up a Corvette on the screen and gave me an evil, non-Martin smile.

"Understood." I got sucked into the game for a bit before I said, "Why didn't you tell me about her? Or Calder?"

He shrugged. "They never came over here."

"That's the only reason?"

"Nope. The biggest reasons are yours, brosky."

"Meaning what?"

"Meaning . . . Ro violated all three of your rules."

"I told you about those rules?"

"Uh, Rocket, you told *everyone* about those rules."

Great.

"Fireball ain't your friend."

I hit pause on the game. "I need to talk to you about something serious."

"Yep, you can marry my sister." He nudged me with his shoulder. "Then we'll really be broskys."

"I don't need your permission to marry her. And the situation I'm in . . . sort of has to do with that."

Martin tossed the controller aside. "This gonna cheese me off?"

"Probably."

"Up front between us, true? I can take anything except you telling me you secretly don't like the little dude."

"No worries there. I freakin' love the kid."

"Good. Then what's what?"

"Remember last year when I had to postpone moving in and there was a bunch of red tape? Well, I had to buy in."

Martin frowned. "Little foggy about that."

"I had to buy in. As in . . . I had to buy the entire complex if I wanted to live here."

"Get out."

"True story."

"You find my secret stash, bro? Because that'd mean you've been lying to me for over a year."

"How is that lying?"

He shook his finger at me. "Lie by omission. Same thing."

"Wrong. If you'd said, 'Jens, you own this joint now?' and I lied and said no . . . that'd be different than you not asking." Or not knowing. For the first time since I'd bought this place, lock, stock and barrel, I felt guilty for keeping it a secret.

"Who all knows you're a Lund Land Lord?"

Martin cracked me up. I'd missed this guy. "My family. Bob. Sue in the business office."

"None of the residents know you're the resident evil who won't fork over the cash to fix up crap around here?"

I laughed. "No. But I have applied for permits for updates. It's a more complicated process than I imagined."

"Sorta sucks that I've been paying you rent and didn't know it." His eyes gleamed. "Hey, if my rent money paid for part of that Corvette, I should at least get to drive it sometimes."

"Nice try, buddy. But we've gotten off track. You gave Rowan grief today for not looking for a house. I haven't exactly encouraged her to look since we've been together."

"Because you're gonna build her a huge mansion?"

"If that's what she wants. But knowing her, if she really wanted to own a house, she would've already bought one."

WHEN I NEED YOU 305

"Too true."

"My tentative plan is to gut the three empty apartments on the main floor, plus the one where the lease is up next month, into a single-family residence. We'd end up with four bedrooms, a huge kitchen, a sweet master suite, a living room and a family room plus a private patio on the south end."

"So you'd live downstairs? You and Ro and little dude?"

"That's what I'm hoping for." But if Rowan decided she'd rather find a house, I'd be good with that too. The most important thing to me was us living together as a family. "Here's where you come in."

"Lay it on me."

"While I'm at training camp, I need you to convince her that you miss your old apartment and she and Calder should move in here."

"Why?"

"Because this couch won't fit over there. And my bed is bigger."

"TMI, Jens. She's my sister."

I poked him a little. "Is it TMI if I say the reason I'm so fond of this couch is because the first time your sister and I—"

"Stop talking, Lund. Seriously. First thing, what I saw . . . I can't ever unsee. And now I'm gonna be looking way too closely at this couch before I sit down."

"You're welcome. Glad you're back, Martin."

"That means you're ready to play?"

I laughed. "Yep."

"I ain't going easy on you because we're really brothers now."

Martin and Rowan both had that same sweet streak—and I appreciated it even more now. "I'd expect nothing less."

Twenty-three

JENSEN

'd survived the first two weeks of training camp in Mankato. Living in the dorms sucked, although this year a local mattress company had provided all the players with king-sized beds.

My body was strong, healed and ready to hit the field. Not practice. Not training. Real football. Part of me had always known that if I hadn't had such an amazing season the year I'd gotten injured, the team probably would've let me go. So while my teammates bitched about the lousy accommodations, I was just damn glad to be here at all.

Still, I missed Rowan. I missed Calder. I missed the life we'd started to build together. Getting through the season with all the traveling and training would test us as a family unit.

So there was no freakin' way I'd be late to Calder's camp

performance, because I knew I'd miss his other school events this fall.

When the new assistant coach—assistant to the assistant offensive line coach actually—demanded my presence to go over the days' training tapes immediately following practice, I said no.

Evidently he hadn't expected that.

Evidently he believed his power was greater than mine because he started to dress me down. On the field. In front of my teammates.

I walked off.

Evidently he hadn't expected that either.

Devonte had. I heard him warning Coach Wannabe to back the fuck off.

I managed to make it through a quick shower and was nearly dressed before the HR coordinator approached me in the locker room. Poor sucker did not know what he was in for this season.

"Rocket? I'm Trent from HR and I'm working on transitioning the new coaching staff with our veteran players. Coach Wallaby informed me that you've refused to attend the mandatory post-training meeting—"

"Yes, Trent, I did refuse. I'll watch the tapes next week, but it is not a possibility today."

"But—"

"And when I attempted to explain to this newbie coach why the meeting was not mandatory for me, he believed the best option was to yell at a veteran player. I opted to walk away at that point as I am under time constraints today."

Trent shuffled his feet. "Look, between us? This transitional-team stuff wasn't my idea. But I have to follow through and do my job."

"Great." I grinned at him. "Write up Coach Wannabe for

verbally abusive behavior. I've got witnesses. He knows I did nothing to incur that type of inappropriate response except exercise my right to say no to the meeting."

"Off the record? Why are you being a dick about this? It's two freakin' hours out of your day before you go home for the weekend. Is it really worth the hassle?"

"You want me to play that way? Fine." I slipped the belt through the first loop on my slacks. "On the record? If you don't believe I have full veto power of optional preseason meetings with nonessential coaching staff, please have management contact my agent, Peter Skaarn, about contract specifics. He will set them straight, trust me." No one fucked with my agent. "Off the record? My kid has a performance tonight and there's no way I'm missing it as it's already been set around my schedule."

Trent frowned. "Your kid? Since when do you have a kid, Lund?"

Shit. I screwed that up. "The boy is like a son to me. It's not something I talk about publicly, but I can trust someone from HR with that confidential information, right?" I had him pinned down and he knew it.

"Whatever. I'll have to put it in my report."

"You do what you have to, Trent. I'll put a call in to my agent so he'll be able to answer any questions that arise." I buckled my belt and reached for my duffel bag. "Have a good weekend."

I texted Astrid to let her know I was on my way. Then I called Rowan, but she didn't answer. I left a message—G-rated, so Calder could hear me tell him to break a leg. Traffic on 169N out of Mankato was heavy for a Friday as I headed back to the Cities.

Ten million things raced around inside my head and oddly enough, few of them had to do with the upcoming football season.

My entire family would be at the camp recital tonight.

Rowan's parents would be there as well as Martin. Would it be weird trying to balance it all out?

My phone rang. The ID on the dash display said: ASTRID. "Hey, what's up?"

"Jens, I forgot something major for tonight. And I'm here doing last-minute checks and run-through and close-outs and I can't possibly—"

"What do you need?"

"Individually wrapped roses for each one of the campers for when they finish the dance performance. And a bouquet of flowers for the teachers because we are introducing them at the end. Oh and flowers for the camp sponsors. God. I can't freakin' believe I forgot that! I'm so sorry."

"Astrid. Take a deep breath. There's three hours until showtime. I'll take care of it."

"You promise?"

"Yep. Is there anything else you need?"

"No. But I don't get why I'm so damn nervous."

"I feel ya. It's the culmination of everything you've worked on the past three months. It'll feel good to end it, as much as you don't want it to end."

"You really are so much more than just a 'playbook, end zone, taking one for the team' kind of bonehead jock, Lund."

"Hang on; let me grab a tissue, because that heartwarming sentiment might lead me to think you were crushing on me. Wait, has being around a real man like me caused you to rethink the whole lesbian thing?"

"And . . . you wrecked it. Get the flowers and don't be late." She hung up.

I laughed and some of my tension drained out. Dealing with the flowers? Right up my alley. As a former manwhore, I had several flower shops on speed dial.

———

I forced myself to stay away from the school until twenty minutes before the program started. While I'd gotten the ball rolling on Camp Step-Up, the credit for its success didn't belong to me at all. Astrid and Dallas were the real stars.

I parked by the back entrance and opened up the back of my Hummer. After I hauled the flowers backstage, I peeked through the curtain. The entire café-torium was packed. The front row had a RESERVED sign. I managed to snag Astrid's attention the fourth time she hustled past me. "The flowers are in the back corner."

She hugged me. "Thank you, thank you. Seriously."

"Who is handing them out?" *Please say me so I can stay back here.*

"Jaxson. During your speech and while you're introducing the staff after the program."

Panic slammed into me as hard as a hit from J. J. Watt. "You did not tell me I'd be speaking tonight, Astrid."

"Mr. Lund. Camp Step-Up is *your* LCCO project and your responsibility. During football season you do at least two national press conferences a week. Millions of people watch you on TV. Why is speaking in front of a hundred and fifty people—mostly children—putting that fear in your eyes?"

Because this time it matters. All the people who matter the most to me in the entire world are here tonight and I don't want to fuck up.

"You rock at on-the-fly adjustments, Rocket," she said with a smirk. "You'll be fine. Just follow your playbook."

"Hilarious." I pointed to the reserved seats in the front row. "Are you sitting out there?"

She shook her head. "I'm back here the whole performance. That's for you. Now shoo. I'm busy."

I killed another ten minutes moving my car. When I

reached the front entrance and heard the excited din, my hand automatically went up to adjust the ball cap . . . that wasn't there. Dammit. Maybe I should grab the extra one out of my workout bag.

Or maybe everyone already knows who you are and you should just take your seat so the program can get started.

A firm hand swept across my shoulders.

Two weeks I'd been without her touch.

Everything inside me settled and I could breathe again.

Rowan rested her head on my biceps. "You okay, big guy?"

"Antsy. Is Calder nervous? Does he get stage fright?"

She laughed softly. "Are you kidding? The boy is in his element. I'm more worried he'll deviate from the program and perform a dance solo."

"I'd be okay with that."

"The other parents wouldn't be." She squeezed my shoulder. "Calder was thrilled about the voice mail. Thanks for letting him know you were thinking about him. It was important to him."

"He's important to me." I angled my neck to kiss the top of her head. "You're both important to me. You've jumped to the top of my newly created list of life priorities."

"Jens—"

"I love you," I murmured into her hair. "Most days I don't know what the hell to do with it, but it's there. Every day. Without fail."

She slid her hand from my shoulder and lightly punched my kidney. "Don't you *dare* make me cry before this performance even starts, Jensen Bernard Lund."

I froze. "Where did you hear my middle name?"

"From your mother. But I don't believe her claim that she named you that because you weighed as much as a full-grown Saint Bernard when you were born." She nudged me. "Go take your seat. The show starts in five minutes."

I forced her to meet my gaze. "Aren't you sitting with me?"

"Nope. I'm in the back with my parents."

"No, you're in the front with me. You have the very best seat in the house to video every moment of Calder's performance."

Her eyes searched mine. "That's not fair to the other parents who were here earlier than me."

I got nose to nose with her. "They wouldn't even be sitting in the audience if not for you bringing the need for this camp to LCCO's attention. This time, baby, you get the perks because you deserve it. Now are you walking up there on your own steam? Or am I dragging you?"

When it appeared she intended to argue, I snagged her hand. "Suit yourself. We'll play it that way."

"Fine." Rowan tugged her hand free. "I'll sit with you. But I need to get the portable battery charger for my phone from my mom. Taking video wears the battery down."

"I have an extra one right here." I patted the pocket of my sport coat. "My phone is fully charged too if you need it."

"You're prepared. It's like you've done this kid's program thing before."

"I wanted to avoid a rookie mistake my first time, so I might've gone overboard in the pregame prep."

She stared at me. "This is why I love you."

"Because of my sports analogies?" I teased.

"No. Because you always think of someone besides yourself."

That was the first time in my life I'd ever heard that, but I'd be damn sure it wouldn't be the last. "Lead the way."

As soon as we were seated, the lights dimmed. Rowan already had her phone out.

Dallas had done an outstanding job putting the program together. The sets flowed seamlessly from a musical number to a dance number to a combination. In the theatrical production the students' talents even outshone the visually stunning backdrop that Walker and Trinity had created.

But when Calder was onstage, I didn't really see anyone else. At age six the boy seemed years ahead, talentwise, of all of the other students.

Or maybe every parent feels that way about their kid.

That thought didn't startle me. Rowan had raised an amazing little boy and I was so damn proud for both of them that I wanted to burst. I wanted to watch as Calder grew and changed from an amazing boy to an even more amazing young man. I wanted to play a role in making that happen.

The entire thing lasted an hour. As soon as the curtain went down, I snuck around to the side door and slipped backstage.

The blast of energy hit me with the same familiarity as when the team won a game. The arts and sports didn't seem all that different right then.

Astrid planted herself in front of me and thrust a clipboard at me. "Here's an alphabetical list of all the students' names. Read them off one at a time. Then introduce the staff members, do your speech thing and remind the audience all of the kids' art projects are displayed throughout the first two rooms and there is a reception with snacks in the library."

I frowned at her. "No offense, Astrid, but I didn't have a clue there'd be after-program activities. Who planned it?"

"I did. With help from Selka and Edie. And Talia helped out."

"Talia? As in Calder's nanny, Talia? Why would she . . . ?"

Astrid blushed.

Guess Astrid had crushed on a woman who crushed on her back.

"Anyway, you weren't here and I knew it was the type of 'fussy' stuff that you didn't give a damn about anyway—no offense—so I just handled it."

I grabbed her and hugged her hard. "Astrid, darlin', you are the bomb. Seriously. I'm writing you the most glowing letter of recommendation the world has ever seen. I swear if you weren't in college full-time, I'd hire you to be my personal assistant right freakin' now."

She started to tear up. Then she caught herself and rolled her eyes. "Dude. You *need* a PA. And you oughta know that I can get more stuff done in twenty hours a week than most people do in forty."

"True. We'll talk next week then. If you're seriously interested."

"Deal." She tried to shove me back. "Now, go do your speechifying and bring the house down because a few reporters set up in the back after the lights came up."

Great. But it wasn't anything new to my life. That thought allowed a sense of calm to steal over me.

You got this.

Clipboard in hand, I strode out onto the middle of the stage.

In addition to talking briefly about each kid—with a limited enrollment I had gotten to know them individually—and introducing the camp staff, I brought Aunt Priscilla, Aunt Edie and my mother onto the stage because they deserved recognition for all the good things LCCO did for the community. They even got a little teary eyed when they noticed I'd saved the biggest bouquets for them.

As soon as I finished closing remarks and encouraged everyone to wander the building, the reporters approached me. No matter how many times I tried to redirect, they were focused on getting the story about Camp Step-Up from The Rocket. I kept as much of the conversation away from football as I could.

So I didn't get to see my family until nearly half an hour later.

The hallway teemed with kids and parents, but I was looking for one kid in particular.

Calder spied me first. The instant he saw me, his face lit up. Then he was running toward me, dodging and weaving through people like I did on the football field—not that I'd make the comparison to his mother—when I had the goal line in my sights.

He threw himself at me and I caught him, crushing him to my chest as he wrapped his arms around my neck and squeezed me tight. I closed my eyes and let his excitement and his need to share it with me flow through me.

I'd missed this.

"Did you see me dance?" he demanded.

I propped him on my hip and smoothed his hair back from his face. "Of course I did. I was in the front row."

He chattered on and I listened with amusement to his analysis of every dance, which also led me to comparisons of how I rehashed a game, discussing the highlights and the mistakes. When he paused to breathe, I said, "You were outstanding, ninja-dance boy."

"What was your favorite part?"

I grinned at him and kissed his forehead. "Are you kidding me? When you took center stage and performed that move we saw on *Dancing with the Stars*! How long did it take you to learn it?"

He groaned. "All summer. I thought I'd *never* get it."

"Well, it looked like you've got it down, little dude, and you know the deal we made. You gotta teach it to me."

"'Kay."

Calder rested his head on my shoulder. "Seems like you were gone a loooong time. Are you done with football camp?"

"Almost."

"I'm glad you were surprised, Rocketman. Mommy was too."

"She didn't know you were working on that move?"

He shook his head. "I wanted to do it just for you."

I couldn't speak around the lump in my throat. I kissed the crown of his sweaty head. I glanced up to see everyone in my family—and Rowan's family—watching me.

Let them stare. This is you proving you give a damn about someone besides yourself and something beyond football.

Then I didn't see anything else as my beautiful Rowan walked toward me, a soft smile on her face. She pressed her palm against my chest and rubbed Calder's back. "You okay, sweet boy?"

"Uh-huh."

I said, "I'm good too."

When she said, "You sure? You want me to take him?" Calder burrowed deeper into me.

"Nope."

"You got waylaid for a while with the media. Is everything all right?"

"We'll see how it shakes out tomorrow."

"Come on, everyone is waiting to talk to the man of the hour." She gently nudged me toward our assorted family members.

"Hear that, Calder? Everyone is talking about that fancy-ass dance move you did."

He giggled. "No. They're talkin' about you, silly. And you're not s'posed to say the A-word, remember?"

"My bad."

For the next half an hour as I talked with the Lund Collective, as well as the Michaels family, Calder refused to let go of me. With all the noise around us, it surprised me to look down and see Calder's mouth slack and soft snores drifting out as he drooled on my shoulder. I grinned at Rowan. "Like mother, like son, huh?"

She whispered, "I drool on you for another reason entirely, Lund."

"But you conk out just like this after I wear you out," I murmured back.

She rested her head on my arm. "Can we go home now? I missed you."

I kissed her temple. "Let's say our good-byes."

Rowan's parents were staying in the Cities another day, so we made plans for a late dinner. And the Lund Collective insisted on changing the normal Sunday brunch time to an early-evening meal so I could come with Rowan and Calder.

We walked outside with my parents and Martin. The humidity had dissipated, leaving it a beautiful, balmy night.

Martin and Dad were laughing sort of hysterically about something that I didn't want to know about. Rowan was readjusting Calder's car seat. Leaving me with my mom.

She brushed my hair out of my face. I was twenty-eight years old and she still fussed at me. "Is this a bruise?" she demanded in Swedish when she noticed the spot on my cheekbone.

"Yeah. I got smacked kinda hard in practice today."

"I always hated that part of football."

"Getting pounded into the dirt isn't my favorite part either." Such a lie. I loved that.

"No, I meant the marks you've been getting since you were boy of ten." She ran the back of her finger over the spot. "Bumps, bruises, even broken bones. You loved the game so much that I had to hide my tears from you over every bump, bruise and broken bone. I had to pretend I didn't hurt to watch you training and playing when you were in pain. I had to suck it up and be proud, smiling mama on the outside when you caught the ball but took a hit hard enough to rattle your brain. I had to cheer when I watch you block and save a play but I see blood on your uniform and you limping off the field. I see you work harder and harder to become better, faster, stronger. I watch you become more football machine than man. I watch and I wait and I hope in silence for the day to come when there's no more bumps, no more bruises, no more blood, no more broken bones . . . no more hurting for you, even knowing, as your mama, that when that end day does come, it will hurt you more than any bone-rattling, jaw-cracking body slam you've ever felt."

I stared at her in utter shock. It was more than she had ever said about me playing football, not about my football career. It never occurred to me how much courage both she and my dad had to let me walk onto that field every time, knowing I'd be hurt every time.

"I will be good mama, supportive mama until that day comes, Jensen. I feel pride for all you have done. But know, in your heart, as I know in mine, that it is not all you *can* do."

"Why are you telling me this now?"

"Because I'm told . . . *hate the game, dude, not the player.*"

"Mom."

"Fine, I say nothing before because I get in trouble when being meddlesome botherer in your life. "

I snorted.

"But I'm telling you now mostly because I love you." She straightened my collar. "And maybe you're ready to hear it." She smiled softly at Calder. "He is sweet boy."

"Yeah. He is."

"Too bad you don't want more than *friends* with his mother, yah?"

"You're always going to rub that in, aren't you?"

She smiled cockily and for the first time I realized I'd

gotten that cocky damn smile from her. She patted my cheek. "Still my sweet, strong boy, Jensen Bernard Lund. You will make sweet, strong father. And you will make lots more sweet, strong boys for me to be meddlesome botherer with." She kissed my cheek and then Calder's before she turned and walked away, yelling at my father to *get the head out.*

I started to correct her: You mean . . . head out? Or get the lead out? But . . . nah.

Rowan moved in beside me. "Do I even want to know what your mother's flurry of Swedish was about?"

"Nope. But it's all good. I promise."

Martin wandered over and lifted Calder out of my arms.

I wasn't nearly as startled by that as Calder was. He blinked sleepily at his uncle and then at Rowan. "Mommy?"

"Hey, little dude," Martin said. "Guess what? You and me are havin' a sleepover in Jensen's apartment. I already spread your sleeping bag out on that big couch, I got *Lilo and Stitch* and *The Secret Life of Pets* cued up in the Blu-ray. I got us cheese popcorn, red licorice and grape soda. It's gonna be party in the USA, man."

"But . . . I wanted to read Harry Potter tonight," Calder said to me.

"Tomorrow night we'll read as many chapters as you want. I promise."

He turned his teary eyes to his mother. "But, Mommy, I thought I was gonna be with you . . ."

I expected her to give in.

But she didn't. "Uncle Martin has been planning this surprise for you for two days. I couldn't tell you because I didn't want to ruin it."

He looked at Martin skeptically.

"We've got some serious chillin' in front of the TV to do and . . ." Martin whispered something in his ear.

Calder grinned. *"Super Mario Brothers!"*

"Gotta learn the life of a gamer sometime, amirite? Tell your mommy and Jens good night."

After a round of hugs and kisses, we watched as Martin strapped him into the car seat and drove away.

"God, I love that kid."

Rowan stepped in front of me and twined her arms around my neck. "I can't tell you what it means to me to hear you say that." Then she pulled my head down and fastened her mouth to mine in a wet, dirty kiss. She murmured, "How fast you think you can get us home?"

Turned out when properly motivated, my Hummer could give my ZR1 a run for its money.

Twenty-four

ROWAN

With the first preseason game in the new stadium happening in two short days, I had purple, white and gold on the brain 24/7. Not only did I think about my part, I worried about Jensen because his part was much bigger than mine. Provided he was finally taken off the injured reserve list.

Since I'd never been involved with a pro football player, I wasn't sure if this was his standard preseason behavior— pulling back, pulling in. Turning quiet and contemplative. I didn't ask if this was the norm for him because I knew how he'd answer; there'd been no norm for him since his injury. So I let it go.

The only time he seemed like my Jensen was when he read Harry Potter to Calder.

Or after he crawled in bed with me.

My stomach did a little flip whenever I thought about

how thoroughly Jensen showed me he was mine and I was his when the bedroom door closed. We were insatiable. Neither of us had had this type of intimacy before, so we craved that connection all the time.

All. The. Time.

I hadn't understood how incredibly patient Jensen had been with me, letting the relationship build at my pace, masking his physical need—not just for sex but for affection—until I'd had a taste of his sexual appetite. The man wanted me morning, noon and night. Some days, he had me that often. I needed that body-to-body connection and release just as frequently. But I was glad I'd waited to share and explore that part of myself until Jensen because I trusted him with every aspect of my body—including my heart.

I'd gotten a message from Coach T to come in early before cheer practice. So as I paced in the spookily empty hallway outside of the conference room, I texted Daisy.

Me: Are you running late?

DO: Late for what?

Me: The meeting with Coach T.

DO: What meeting?

Me: The early one she called before tonight's practice?

DO: ??? There's no practice tonight. Didn't you see that on the group text message?

I scrolled to my message list. The last message I'd gotten from Coach T had been sent as a private message. I had nothing new from the group for over twenty-four hours.

DO: What's going on?

Me: I don't know. I think I'm the only one here.

Before I could add that I'd started to get a bad feeling, the door to the conference room opened and Angela, liaison between the team and the national sports organization, stepped out. I'd only had dealings with her one time, and my bad feeling transformed into dread.

"Miss Michaels? We're ready for you."

Who's we?

Don't ask; just move your feet forward.

When I cleared the doorway, I saw six people at the conference table. I knew three of them. Coach T; Izzy, the media director; and that Brian guy who'd given the "follow the rules" speech months ago.

Months ago when I'd gotten so infuriated with Jensen for acting like we were friends.

Oh, if they only knew how things had changed since that day.

Maybe they did.

"Please, Miss Michaels, have a seat."

They were spread out on one side of the table. I sat across from them like I was being cross-examined in court.

"I imagine you wonder why you've been called in today." This came from the woman I didn't know. No name tag, no indication of who she might be except efficient and annoyed.

"Sort of feels like I'm facing the Inquisition, and I'm woefully underdressed." I'd worn my warm-up suit because hey . . . I thought I'd be headed to cheer practice after the meeting.

"We brought you here to ask a few questions."

"Do I need an attorney present?" I said coolly, even when my stomach knotted.

"No. It pertains mostly to your contract." She smiled.

Okay. Maybe this wasn't what I'd feared.

"How well do you know Jensen Lund?"

And . . . yep. There it was.

Stick as close to the truth as possible. "I know him pretty well. He lives in my apartment building. LCCO, the charitable foundation that his family runs, sponsored my son's summer camp. And I've cheered for The Rocket for the past four seasons as well as cheering for him when I was on the cheer team at the University of Minnesota."

"Do you have a relationship with him?"

I have a beautiful relationship with him. He's a wonderful, loving man and I'm so lucky, blessed and excited to have him in my life.

But I couldn't say it. It killed me to say, "Yes. We're friends," instead.

None of them looked at each other, but they were all staring at me, as if I'd break in the silence.

Jensen always joked that the silent treatment was the best way to get me to talk.

Not this time.

"Do you have a personal relationship with Jensen Lund?" This from Brian, the blatherer.

"Are we personally friends?"

Brian imparted a condescending smile. "Come now. I think you know that's not what we're asking."

Should I force them to ask me if I was intimately and sexually involved with Jensen? But if I did that, I'd have to answer honestly. Or did I answer *this* question and see if it changed the entire direction of the questioning?

"Yes, I have a personal friendship with Jensen Lund. Why is this relevant?"

"It's relevant because we've been informed that you have a *very* personal relationship with Mr. Lund. The kind of personal relationship that is in direct violation of the contract you signed that expressly forbids any relationships between players and cheerleaders."

Ask if they have proof. Ask who informed them.

"There are pictures," Izzy from the PR center inserted. "We've managed to keep them out of the media."

Then I couldn't hold my tongue any longer. "Pictures of what? Of us coming and going from the same apartment building? Yes, that is a possibility because we both live there. Pictures of us talking at the LCCO children's day camp? Yes, that is a possibility because my son attended that camp for three months, so Mr. Lund and I did converse on occasion."

"But the situation, Miss Michaels, is those are not the pictures we're referring to. We were given access to the footage of you and your son at a party at the Lund family estate. Arriving together, the three of you, in Jensen Lund's vehicle."

I seriously doubted they had pictures of that, since Jensen told me the security surrounding the Lund estate was near NSA levels. And if someone working security for the Lund family had decided to leak footage or images, they would've gone directly to the media outlets for big money. Because The Rocket wasn't the only well-known member of that family. Footage would've included Jaxson "Stonewall" Lund, bad boy of the Chicago Blackhawks, and Axl "The Hammer" Hammerquist, of the Minnesota Wild and his wife, Annika Lund; they were still media darlings after Axl's very public proposal last year. Trinity Lund had become the new "it" girl on the local art scene, not to mention the rest of the Lund family members who sponsored charitable events nearly every month and ran businesses all over the state.

Yeah, that footage would be worth a shit ton.

So in my mind this had to be someone on the inside, who had just enough "proof" to cause a problem for me, but not for The Rocket because the organization needed him.

Raina.

Maybe she had seen Jensen, Calder and me going to the Lund barbecue. Or maybe she'd heard about the LCCO camp since it'd been on the news and she'd asked around. Even if she'd hung around the school, the only day she would've seen anything inappropriate was that first day of camp that Jensen and I kissed. But a picture like that would've been splashed all over the place, months ago. Greed didn't bide its time.

"Miss Michaels?"

I glanced at him. I remained outwardly calm even when inside I was seething. "Yes, I did attend Dallas Lund's bon voyage party at the Lund estate. I was Dallas Lund's cheerleading coach at the University of Minnesota for four years. Dallas also was the theater teacher at Camp Step-Up, and my son, Calder, was in her class. So Calder and I were invited to her party at her request. Since Jensen and I live in the same apartment complex and were going to the same place, we decided to carpool." I smiled coldly. "Saving natural resources and all."

"It appears you can explain away every example we present," he said brusquely.

"Because the examples you've given are exactly as they appear. Jensen Lund and I are friends."

Silence.

Breathe. This is a fishing expedition and they're pulling up short with a still-baited hook.

"I have to admit, what you're claiming doesn't ring true. As if your . . . *friendship* with Jensen Lund is just a coincidence. But you subleased an apartment in the same building, directly across from Mr. Lund's residence. A situation I'm sure you were fully aware of. Is it also a coincidence your son just happened to attend a camp sponsored by the Lund family? A camp run by Jensen Lund himself? And that Mr. Lund has been spotted on the University of Minnesota campus several times this summer, including in the training facility that houses your office?"

No excuses. No explanations. Do not even open your mouth.

"All of this together appears less coincidental and more along the lines of very shrewd planning on the part of someone who wanted to get much closer, much friendlier to a franchise football player than the distance she's required to keep from him on the field."

I knew what was coming next.

"So while we're mounting a full investigation into these 'coincidences' as per your contract, you are suspended from the spirit squad without compensation and banned from any practices, performances and games. Any violation of this will bring legal ramifications."

Other women might've had a *Norma Rae* speech going through their heads as they fumed and made plans to buck the system . . . not me. I just wanted to go home.

Jensen's challenge that night I'd told him he had the power to ruin my career came back to me. *I get that you are a list maker and a rule follower. What I don't get? That you're willing to blindly follow someone else's rule even if it causes you to lose out on something that could have a positive impact on your life.*

He'd been right. I loved that he'd been right because he *was* the best thing that had happened to me since the birth of my son.

But I'd also been right. My cheerleading career appeared to be over.

"Do you have any questions, Miss Michaels?"

"I trust that the media blackout on this investigation will continue as it is a confidential personnel matter."

"Why is that relevant?" the woman demanded. "Are you asking if Jensen Lund is being suspended also?"

People actually laughed at that.

"No, it's relevant because my livelihood is as an athletic trainer and a cheerleading coach with the University of Minnesota. Any unsubstantiated 'coincidences' that arise in the media may lead to questioning from my supervisors and my students, and even put my position with the school in jeopardy. None of what we've discussed today, or the time I spend as a part-time member of this organization, should be allowed to affect my actual career."

Coach T leaned forward and spoke for the first time. "I guarantee nothing from this meeting will be discussed outside this room except for with the most essential personnel, Rowan. You have my word on that."

"Thank you, Coach T."

"You're free to leave," Brian said. "We'll be in touch."

No, you won't.

As I left the building, I wondered if one of the assistant coaches had already cleaned out my locker.

"Rowan! Wait."

Dante caught me right before I got into my car. "What the hell happened in there?"

I said nothing.

"Coach T threw a fucking chair at the wall after you left."

"She did?"

"Yeah." He considered me. "I overheard something."

"Overheard?"

"Fine. I'm new enough as a full-time trainer that my job isn't secure and I listen in whenever I can to conversations I'm not supposed to know about."

"That's why you're always in the know. I figured you were sleeping with Izzy or something."

He snorted. "I wouldn't hit that for all the inside information in the organization."

"What'd you hear, Dante?"

"You're being suspended for violating the no-frat rule with Jensen Lund."

"You heard right."

"That's just fucking stupid. He didn't even know who the hell you were! And I know Lund, he's not a cheater. He wouldn't be stepping out with you, secretly or otherwise, when he's already involved with someone else."

I froze. "What are you talking about? Who is Jensen involved with?"

"This chick named Astrid. He told me about her months ago." His jaw tightened. "Do you want me to go in there and tell them they're absolutely wrong in suspending you? Because that sucks, Ro. Jens will come forward and tell them—"

"That they're right because we've been fraternizing in a big way for months."

Dante looked like he'd taken an actual physical hit. "What about Astrid?"

"Astrid is his assistant."

"But—"

"Jensen was protecting me because he's in love with me." I exhaled. "I'm in love with him too."

"Shit."

"I broke the rules, Dante. I knew what was at stake."

"It's a stupid rule."

"I won't argue with that."

His eyes searched mine. "Did you tell them that you and Jensen are . . . ?"

I shook my head. "I just reiterated that he and I are

friends. Because we are that. Their proof or whatever they want to call it is pretty thin."

"Did they indicate whether he'd face disciplinary action?"

"They kind of laughed and said, *Yeah right, like we're going to suspend a franchise player after a year and a half of being on IR.*" I groaned. "You know how I tend to blurt things out? I almost said, *Technically it's not fraternization when he's on the IR list*, but I stopped myself."

"Because you know that's total bullshit, right?"

"Yeah." After Jensen had tossed that in my face, I'd finally understood the lengths he'd go to, to convince me to take a chance on him . . . on us.

"Besides, he's off IR as of today."

I wanted to jump up and down and squeal with joy. "Omigod, does he know?"

"He found out at the end of practice." Dante grinned. "He'll want to celebrate that with you." His smile faded. "Or maybe not, because he will be pissed when he hears about you getting—"

"No." I got right in his face. "Don't you dare tell him about the suspension. I mean it. I've never asked you for anything, but I am begging you. Do whatever you can to keep this from him. He needs to focus on his game, on his career, on finally getting to do what he loves. I love him too much to let him put that in jeopardy because of me." I grabbed his arm. "Please. Promise me you won't tell him."

"Rowan—"

"Promise me, Dante."

"Fine. I promise. But how are you going to keep this from him?"

"I'll figure something out. He'll be so busy that it won't come up."

"Wrong. He'll notice when you aren't on that field. He might not have seen you before, but he'll be looking for you now."

"I haven't figured that part out yet." I blew out a long breath. "Or what excuse I'll tell Daisy. Because she isn't the type to believe what I tell her or to let it go."

Dante smiled. "Let me deal with Daisy, okay?" Then he hugged me. "I'm happy for you. Jensen is a good guy. Really. He deserves a woman like you."

"A woman like me?"

"With a heart as big as his. I should've known you two would be perfect for each other."

As much as I'd obsessed about how upset I'd be if I got fired from the team . . . when it actually happened? I was oddly calm.

Because you're in shock.

Maybe. But I wasn't going to dwell on it because I had major celebrating to do.

I unlocked the door to Jensen's apartment and found my guys snuggled up, reading. They didn't notice me at first, so I just leaned against the wall and watched them. Man and boy so comfortable with each other, so accepting of each other. It seemed so right, so natural, so normal a sight for me to come home to, and it always brought me joy and peace.

For a few moments, I stood and listened to Jensen's smooth, expressive voice. I'd told him if the whole football thing fell through he could become an audiobook narrator. But it sounded like he wouldn't have to worry about finding other employment.

Calder noticed me. "Mommy!" He popped up and held his arms out for a hug.

I squeezed him tight. "Hey, guys."

"Pile in," Jensen said reaching for me. "We're almost done with this chapter."

"You finish. I'm heading over to pour myself a glass of wine."

Jens pinned me with a look. "Practice was okay?"

"It was short." I looked around. "Where's Martin?"

"He stepped out for some fresh air. He'll be right back."

"Gotcha."

Calder slid down the cushion and nestled into Jensen. Then they were lost in the book again.

In my apartment, I poured wine and wandered through the space. A space that had gotten pretty cluttered. We hadn't decided which apartment to live in, so we sort of lived in both. And since Martin was still baching it, waiting for us to make a decision, his stuff was in both places too. Bob, the building complex manager, hadn't gotten back to me about the empty apartments on the first floor. I couldn't imagine that he wouldn't want to rent to me.

I peeled off my clothes and stepped into the shower.

I heard him before I felt him. The man might be fast and agile on the football field, but stealth wasn't his strong suit.

Then his callused hands were on my wet skin, the hands of a man who knew exactly how to touch me, the hands of the man who showed he loved me with every teasing, loving caress.

"Well, well, what do we have here? I thought we'd celebrate me getting cleared off the IR list with a glass of wine . . . but celebrating with a naked woman? I'll take that."

I spun around. "They cleared you?"

His grin was as wide as the Mississippi River. "Yep. I'm starting too. People who say preseason games are for scrubs can suck it."

I laughed. "I'm so happy for you."

He rested his forehead to mine. "I'm relieved, Ro. So fucking relieved I feel like I can breathe again."

"I'll bet." I started sliding my hands across his chest because I could. Anytime I wanted. "Did you already tell your family members the good news?"

"Right away." He leaned back to peer into my eyes. "Did I break a relationship rule?"

"What are you talking about?"

"Are you upset that I told them about it before I told you?"

"No, they've been waiting for this day. I'm sure they're all celebrating." I ran my hands down his spectacular arms. "Who else did you tell?"

"Calder. Who, by the way, is crashing at my place with Uncle Martin tonight."

"You told Martin before you told me?"

"Yeah. He was there when I told Calder."

"Anyone else?"

He gave me a sheepish smile. "I might've called my grandpa in Sweden."

Sweet, sweet man.

"And I might've called Michael."

"Michael," I repeated. "As in my dad?"

"He's a huge football fan, Coach. His daughter is banging The Rocket. He deserves the inside scoop."

I stood on my toes and nipped Jensen's chin. "You sure about the banging part? Because, dude, I'm like the twentieth person on the list."

"More like twenty-second tonight. I told Astrid and uh . . . Bob."

My hands stopped wandering. "Bob. As in . . . *Bob* the building manager?" I slapped my hands on his chest. "You told *Bob* before you told me? Seriously, Lund?"

"Hey, you said you weren't gonna be mad."

"I wasn't gonna be mad that you told your family first. But you told *Bob*?"

Jensen actually backed up at the look in my eyes. "Wait. He's a big fan—"

"I'm a big fan. I'm also seriously considering calling this

off for unsportsmanlike conduct for excessive celebrating in the end zone. *Premature* celebrating."

His eyes widened. "I'm sorry. Shit. So sorry. It won't happen again."

"See that it doesn't." I pushed him against the back wall in the shower. "Because next time I want to hear it from you first, not Dante."

"You knew?"

"Dante spilled the beans to me tonight before I left."

"That big mouth."

"Speaking of big mouth . . ." I kissed a path straight down his chest and dropped to my knees. "Anything else you want to talk about?"

"Not a damn thing."

The following afternoon when I was at work, trying to figure out a plan to explain why I wasn't at practice and why I probably wouldn't be cheering at the game, I received a text message from Coach T:

CT: You've been reinstated to the team. Practice at six tonight. DO NOT be late or you're running extra laps.

My thumbs hovered over the keys as I was tempted to text WHY? What changed?

But that might be pushing it and I'd take the end result since that's all that mattered.

Maybe I had convinced them that Jensen Lund and I really were only friends.

Twenty-five

JENSEN

After I'd finished practice, and before the press conference, Rowan's friend Daisy cornered me outside the
locker room. At first when she'd told me what had happened
to Rowan the night before, I hadn't believed her. Why would
Rowan keep something like that from me?

Because she knew how I'd react. I'd do exactly what I
did; hauled ass into the business office, demanded a meeting
with Brian, and the cheer coach, and the sports liaison, and
the highest-ranking management person in the building.
Then I delivered an ultimatum: Reinstate Rowan Michaels
and table the investigation, or I'd cause a PR nightmare the
likes of which they'd never seen. One day before the first
game of the preseason. In the billion-dollar stadium.

But it had worked.

Rowan would be on the sidelines today when we played.
Where she belonged.

Today was the day. A day of firsts, of new beginnings.

It was hard to process it all. So I didn't dissect it.

I fucking embraced it.

The sights—a sea of purple, gold and white in the stands.

The sounds—one of the best sound systems in the world combined with the noise of our fans? Twelfth man didn't have nothin' on us today.

The scents—nothing beat the scent of a brand-fucking-new stadium.

My team—pumped up like I'd never seen them.

The fans—giddy, crazy in the best way.

My family—loud and proud in the skybox.

The media—even it was on a "Twin Cities Proud" high.

Rowan's family—I'd scored them tickets in the section where Rowan cheered.

I was antsy in the tunnel, we all were. Waiting for that moment, after the sound of the Gjallarhorn, when we rushed the field, felt the electricity, the anticipation, the love for what we could do, for being part of a long-running history, for making history.

And then it was on.

We were on.

I didn't get close to Rowan as we rushed by en masse, but I noticed her.

All of the pomp and circumstance remained during the preseason. This exhibition game didn't "count" but for me, it was the most important game I'd play all year.

I drifted into that place where I heard the coaches, I heard the calls, I heard the crowd, but everything else faded when I hit that field.

The smash. The crunch. The trash-talking. The sweat in my helmet. The digging of my cleats into the turf. Hand on the ground. Ear to the call, brain on the play and eyes on the man standing opposite of me who gets paid a fuck ton of money to stop me.

Try and stop me, motherfucker. We own today.

When it got down to the wire, my fellow tight end Rudolph caught the first pass in the new stadium. That honor would stand until next month when the regular season started.

After the Chargers failed in their attempts to put any points on the scoreboard, the offense was back on the field. I blocked and kept blocking. I'd yet to even get my hand on the ball. Then the QB called the play I'd been hoping for.

I moved from the outside right to the outside left.

Followed the count, heard the snap and booked it around the far outside left and a sluggish middle linebacker. I turned just as the ball hit me right in the numbers.

Pickup of five yards.

I heard my name over the sound system, but I forced myself to tune out.

We marched down the field, a few yards here, a few yards there, taking it one down at a time. Finally I kicked in that burst of speed and ended up with a gain of twenty yards.

First and ten on the thirteen-yard line. This time I had double coverage so the running back took it all the way to the end zone.

We were up by fourteen at halftime and elated, visions of the Lombardi trophy taking a place of reverence in our new stadium spurring us on.

In the third quarter, the QB called the play that put me to the left outside again. But this time the double coverage would be on the running back. Leaving me in the clear if I could get to the spot . . . turn, watch, jump and pull it in.

Which I did. Textbook.

With nineteen yards to go, I watched for the signal the

QB had for a running play. But he gave the call for a three-man blitz. One of us on each side, one up the middle.

It seemed I was in the end zone before the outside line-backer knew I'd schooled him. I dodged an aggressive cornerback and watched as the QB looked to me and the two wide receivers.

Then back to me.

I ran to the right a few steps—my cornerback shadow followed. Then I pivoted to the left, shuffled backward and leapt into the air.

The ball was too high; it'd just graze my fingertips. At the moment I saw it slipping through my hand I threw my left shoulder higher and spread my fingers into the shape of a starfish. The ball smacked my palm; I brought it down one-handed, tucking it into my gut, protecting it all the way until I hit the turf.

The stadium erupted.

I heard the distinctive sound of a rocket blast off through the speakers, a sound that had been mine alone whenever I made a touchdown.

My teammates helped me up and clapped me on the back with enough force to knock the damn wind out of me. I skipped the celebratory dance in the end zone. Keeping the game ball was enough for me.

But I needed someone to keep it safe. And I saw her on the sideline. Red hair shining in the sun, leg straight up as part of the kick line.

I ran toward Rowan with the speed I was known for. So I made damn good time.

The other cheerleaders backed away and I could almost feel the puzzlement pulsing in the crowd.

I set the ball at Rowan's booted feet. I tore off my helmet. Then I grabbed her and kissed the hell out of her.

Murmurs in the crowd got louder and turned into a deafening roar.

When I broke the kiss I rested my forehead to hers.

"Jensen, what have you done?"

"Pretty sure I declared love and war at the same time."

She laughed.

I kissed her again, picked up my helmet and waved to the crowd as I took my place on the sidelines.

N othing that happened the last quarter compared to the third quarter, so even my time on the turf was a blur.

We won the game. Big thing to notch that *W* in our first game in our new stadium in front of a sold-out crowd of hometown football fans.

I thought my teammates would harass me endlessly about my game ball presentation to Rowan, but they all steered clear of me.

Coach gave his spiel, his shout-outs, his warning to the defense that they'd be watching the game tapes, and ended our postgame pep talk. Then he singled me out. "Rocket. Media room. Fifteen minutes."

Dante was waiting for me, after I got out of the shower.

"Please tell me you're aware of the can of worms you just opened."

"I want to know which worm outed Rowan as my girlfriend." I glared at him and reached for my clothes. "Did you have a part in that?"

"God no. I was there last night right after the meeting. She made me promise not to tell you what happened. She didn't want anything to screw up this game for you."

"That's the thing, D. Football is a game. She is my fucking life. I can walk away from this if I have to because I know she'll be waiting for me. I never had that before. I've always had my family. But she's . . . mine."

"I'm happy for you. I really am. You deserve it." He flipped me off. "That's for telling me you were with that Astrid chick. Maybe I won't tell you the rest, dick."

"What makes it even funnier is Astrid is a lesbian. But go on."

"Last night, Rowan forced me to promise not to tell *you* about the suspension. She didn't exact the same promise about Daisy. Daisy did exactly what I expected her to—she came to you."

"Thank you." I buttoned my shirt. "I need you to do me another favor, please."

"Name it."

"Make sure Rowan is at the press conference."

Dante shifted his stance, a nervous tic I recognized.

"What?"

"Is that a good idea? I mean, what if she doesn't want to be there?"

"Tell her I said tough shit and to get her ass into the media room." I grinned. "That ought to get her fired up and even more anxious to yell at me." I snapped out the cuffs of my shirt before I slipped on my suit jacket and shoes. Ties were required postgame, so I headed to the mirrors to tie the noose.

I glanced in the mirror behind me at my media escort, who'd finally shown her face. I said, "Let's go."

I stayed off to the side while the coach did his thing. Then the big franchise players had their moments. That took a while. Then the offensive line coach tipped his chin at me and it was go time.

We had our choice to sit or stand, and I opted to sit.

There had to be fifty reporters and at least twenty cameras set up. The lights were blinding and I wished I had grabbed a ball cap.

My media escort opened it up to questions. As an unwritten rule, the local TV stations got the first questions.

"Rocket, it's been twenty months since your injury. How did it feel getting back on the field today?"

"Like it's been a long time coming." Laughter. Then I did the PR spiel that had been drilled into me, with a few additions here and there that were more honest than I was supposed to share. I fielded question after question about any changes in physical abilities, my field time, the stress of blocking versus running on my Achilles. The press was very thorough, but I'd never been a two-word-answer player. Yet no one had asked the question that I'd been waiting for.

Misti Lane, local TV reporter who'd done the interview with Axl and Annika last year after Axl's on-ice proposal, signaled to me. I nodded at her; she'd be fair and yet not shy away from the tougher questions.

"Jensen, after your touchdown, you sought out Rowan Michaels, a member of the Vikings cheer team, and presented her with the game ball. What can you tell us about that?"

"The game ball is pretty self-explanatory, so I'm guessing you're really asking why I kissed the hell out of her."

Nervous laughter.

Misti smiled. "Yes, tell us about that kiss and why you chose to violate the no-fraternization rule during the middle of a prime-time game on national TV?"

"Well, first off, I kissed Rowan because she's my girlfriend. She was right there on the field and I wanted to share that special moment with her. Second, the no-frat rule is archaic and unfair."

"What makes you say that?"

"Look, I'm not a guy who uses my media time to stand on a soapbox. But this rule, issue, whatever, has been shoved under the radar for far too long." I pointed at the cameraman behind Misti. "If you started a relationship with him and your bosses found out, would either of you lose your job?"

Misti cocked her head. "No."

"Exactly. And I have a big problem with a rule that tells me who I can't be in a relationship with."

That started a buzz in the room.

A bunch of hands shot up. I nodded to another local reporter. He said, "What are the repercussions for violating the rule?"

"For me? Nothing probably. For Rowan? She's a professional athlete too, but she'll get released from the cheer team she's invested five years of her life in."

A few gasps, some louder grumbling about unfairness.

I didn't look to the media rep or the coaching staff. "So I ask . . . since when is falling in love a punishable offense? Football is just a game. It's fun, it's frustrating and I love it." I pointed to Rowan, still wearing her cheerleading uniform, leaning against the back wall, next to Annika and Axl. They'd struggled with their own relationship issues in the media last year and had come out on top with a romantic love story people couldn't get enough of. "But as much as I love football? I love that woman more. I figured if the rule stands and it's the first and last time she gets to cheer on the field, at least she deserved a game ball so she doesn't go home empty-handed."

All the cameras whirled around to get her reaction.

"I get to go home with you. And that's enough for me."

Boom. Microphone drop.

I slipped out when everyone's focus was on Rowan. I'd given Annika a heads-up about my postgame plans, and I knew she'd run with it. Having the media immediately associate Rowan and me as star-crossed lovers like she and Axl had been—PR gold.

It wasn't like I'd thrown Rowan to the wolves and abandoned her. Astrid was bringing my Hummer to a prearranged exit point. My agent was in the media room keeping an eye on things. I needed to make a couple of quick phone calls and grab my stuff. Then I could grab my woman and go.

Of course, we made sure the reporters witnessed everything. If I had to be in the public eye, I was going to have fun with it.

So they saw me poking my head in a side door of the media room and beckoning Rowan out. Camera flashes captured her huge smile as she ran toward me and then pictures of the big old kiss she laid on me. Then more snapshots of us hustling down the corridor hand in hand to our getaway vehicle.

I wasn't sure I even breathed until we were out of the maze of one-way streets surrounding the new stadium and out on the interstate with no signs of pursuit.

Rowan was quiet. Too quiet.

"Okay, Coach. Let me have it. How mad are you?"

"I'm . . . stunned. I have a million questions."

"Hit me with them."

"Are we going back for my stuff that's in the dressing room?" She gestured to her uniform. "Because I don't want to wear this any longer than I have to."

"I'll strip it off you, baby. As soon as possible. Don't you worry about that."

She whapped me on the leg. "Jensen. I'm serious."

"Your stuff is in the back. The ever-efficient Astrid got it all from Daisy."

"Oh."

"I know the next question is about Calder. Your parents are taking him to the big party at my parents' house."

"Party? I am not dressed for a party with your family, Lund."

I grinned at her. "Luckily, we're going home first. My mom and dad always have a big family deal for the first preseason game. You'll know everyone. I imagine Mom invited members of the cheer team too."

"I love your family, Jens. They're so . . ."

"Not what you expected?" I supplied. "I told you that at dinner the first night."

Rowan rolled her eyes. "I still don't know why you brought them up on basically our first date."

I grabbed her hand and kissed it. "Because part of me knew right away that you were it for me. You were everything I ever wanted in a woman."

"Liar."

I laughed. "If your next question is about what happened after the game . . . yes, some of it was planned."

"Like what?"

"Like even if I hadn't scored a touchdown, I planned to kiss you in full view of the cameras. I knew I'd have media time today no matter what, so I wanted to use it for a change. Annika handled getting all the right people lined up. She is a PR whiz. Enlisting the public's involvement in our 'fight to love' will hopefully help keep you on the cheer team."

"When you said you love football, but you love me more? Even if I'm off the squad, I don't feel like I'm losing anything because I found you." She leaned her cheek against my biceps. "Besides, it might be more fun to watch the game from the Lund skybox anyway."

I'd prepared myself for her anger, so this acceptance threw me.

We were each lost in our own thoughts, and we didn't speak again until after I'd parked in my spot at Snow Village.

"Thank god we're here," she said as I helped her out of

the Hummer. "Will I have time to shower after I fulfill your dirty sex fantasy of banging a cheerleader in uniform?"

"Yes. But I want to show you something first." Once we were in our building, I bypassed the stairs to the second floor and the elevator, leading her down the hallway on the first floor.

"Jens? Where are we going?"

"You'll see." I used my master key to open the door to the third apartment and ushered her inside.

"Did you rent this apartment for me?" she demanded. "Because that is breaking a relationship rule. We need to discuss things like this."

Pressed her against the door. "No, I didn't rent it for you since I own the whole damn building. The whole complex actually."

"What?"

"I bought the property over a year ago. I've kept it on the down-low for a number of reasons."

Her eyes turned sharp. "That's what you meant the time you told me you were dabbling in real estate?"

"Yeah. I thought that might be a career option if playing football wasn't an option."

"That's also why you were always talking to Bob?"

"I swear that man asks me more questions than you do."

She gave my chin a bump with her forehead. "Smart-ass."

"Anyway, let me finish. The other thing . . ." My hands shook when I curled them around her face. "I love you. I love you like crazy. I love Calder. I feel like we're becoming a family, but I want to make it official. So will you marry me, Rowan Michaels? I want to spend the rest of my life with you. I want to help you raise Calder. I want to have more kids with you when the time is right. I want to create a home for us here, in the place we met and fell in love."

"You're seriously asking me to marry you right now?"

Always with the damn questions. "Yes. I am. So what do you say?"

She smirked at me. "Would my answer be obvious if I started doing herkeys?"

I laughed. This crazy woman never reacted how I expected her to. I hoped that would never change about her. I stepped back. "Show me."

She did. She even tossed in a few high kicks. Then she launched herself at me and I caught her. She crossed her ankles behind my back and wreathed her arms around my neck. "I love you like crazy, Jensen Lund. But I have a few conditions to add to yours."

"Of course you do."

"In addition to us raising Calder, and you knocking me up at some point, I want a dog."

"Any kind but a Saint Bernard."

"Fine. And that ridiculously huge couch gets put in the TV room, man cave, whatever, but not in the damn living room in our new place."

"Done." I kissed her. "Anything else?"

"No more lists. No more rules. We can't seem to follow them for the long term anyway."

"Or we could start fresh. Call it the Lund family playbook."

She sighed. "I can't believe I'm marrying a jock. I'll be stuck with sports analogies for the rest of my life, won't I?"

I shrugged. "Probably. Is that gonna be a problem?"

"Nope." Rowan pressed her forehead to mine and smiled. "I can't wait."

DON'T MISS

All You Need

AVAILABLE NOW.

AXL

I watched as my "girlfriend" downed a dirty martini in two gulps and wiped her mouth with the back of her hand.

Classy.

"Let's conduct this portion of the conversation at the conference table," Peter said.

I returned to the chair at the head of the table I'd sat in earlier.

She muttered in English, assuming I didn't understand her.

Except I did understand her. In fact, I spoke nearly flawless English. It was hard not to react to some of the crazy stuff that came out of her mouth. Like now, hearing her mutter about finding a crowbar to forcibly remove my ass from the chair.

Go ahead, Princess. I'd like to see you try.

But having her here, skirting me, her sexy ass accentuated by her formfitting skirt, I felt the surreal situation sinking in. What had I gotten myself into? I'd screwed up Saturday night. I should've stayed in and gotten shit-faced with my buddies Martin and Boris, who lived in my apartment building, instead of heading to the same club I'd overheard Annika saying she planned to visit. After hearing so much about her PR superpowers, I couldn't resist the opportunity to see if she could keep me from getting lit up the one night of the year I pushed my limits of how high I'd blow.

"So here's the situation," Peter said. "Those videos are our golden ticket."

"How do you figure?"

"Because the lovers' spat caught on tape is a precursor for the two of you convincing the world you're a couple. And Axl falling for you means Axl is focused on two things: his hockey career with his new team and his new woman—in that order. It's the feel-good story of the year just waiting to happen."

Even I snorted at that pronouncement.

Annika demanded, "I get why Ax-hell would need to shore up his reputation, but what do I get out of it? Besides *my* reputation being questioned by my family, friends and everyone else I associate with? Because he is nothing like the men I usually date. Nothing."

I imagined the type of men she dated had soft hands and soft heads but a solid bank account.

"It's a three-prong plan, Annika. First, you agreed to do PR because your mother asked you to as a favor to me for taking your brother on as a client. She's on board with this new direction."

"Funny, she did not mention this new direction to me, the person it affects the most. She just assumed I'd go along with it like a dutiful daughter?"

I frowned. Her mother hadn't even asked her? That hardly seemed fair. Or professional for Peter to just expect her to comply with his plan.

"We'll get back to that," Peter assured her. "Second, if Axl's season goes the way we think it'll go, he'll be in high demand socially, and you'll look smart to be half of the 'it' couple in the Twin Cities."

"There's an incentive," she muttered in English.

I had to fight a smile. I sort of hated that she amused the hell out of me.

"Third, he will work tirelessly on any of your LCCO projects. Anytime, anyplace."

My head snapped up at that. "What?"

Peter's eyes flashed a warning at me. "I told you the Lund family is heavily involved in charitable causes. It goes without saying that you'd support Annika, since she will be supporting you."

"Just as long as it doesn't interfere with my hockey schedule. The only reason I considered doing any of this is to clear up some misperceptions about who I am off the ice."

Annika's eyes narrowed. "Misperceptions? The first time I met you 'off the ice,' you banged our waitress between the entrée and the dessert course."

Okay. She had me there. But the woman had smelled like cookies and my sweet tooth had started throbbing.

"You admitted tonight that you hooked up with the amateur videographer you 'met' at the club last week. I did my homework on you. According to what I read and saw online, you haven't been seen with the same woman twice. So, maybe the only person with the skewed perception about you . . . *is* you."

"You told me yourself everything could be spun, Miss PR. I did my homework on you too." From the moment I'd seen the beautiful blonde, I'd imagined her naked and in my arms while I swallowed her cries of pleasure. So I'd purposely presented myself as aloof because I couldn't act on my attraction to her. I'd known Peter planned to show up before the dessert course to ask for her PR help—I just hadn't been looped in on the particulars.

After we'd gotten ejected from the restaurant and Peter had torn into me about my self-destructive behavior, I decided to familiarize myself with the smart, sexy, sassy bombshell. As much as I hated doing an online search for personal information, it was the fastest means to gather data even if it wasn't the most accurate. After poring over pictures captioned by the media as the "Iron Princess" as she was seen with a parade of men over the years, I had proof she had no room to judge me. "Are you involved with every suit who escorts you to the excessive number of charity events you attend? What do you think is the public's perception when your picture is in the newspaper with a different guy week after week?"

That observation took her aback.

Good.

"Here's the difference between us. I don't give a damn how many of those dates you've slept with, because it doesn't matter; I wouldn't call you a slut. Yet you feel entitled to toss out the term 'manwhore' at me. If I'd slept with as many women as I've been accused of, I'd be too damn tired to hold a hockey stick, to say nothing of sustaining the stamina to practice every day and play over eighty games each season. So there *are* misperceptions about me I'd like to change. That's the whole reason I need your help."

A flush crept up her neck. She dipped her chin and her gaze fell to the table, immediately drawing my attention to the long sweep of her eyelashes resting above the razor-sharp edges of her cheekbones.

Contrite wasn't a look I'd expected to see on her, yet there it was.

But was it an act?

Peter cleared his throat. "We've gotten off track."

Annika slowly raised her head. She locked her gaze to mine. Her fiery gaze.

Shit. I'd awakened the beast.

"Actually Axl brought up some things I'd want to discuss with him if I was considering taking him on as a client. I'd still like to go through my questions before I make a final decision."

"Excellent idea," Peter said. "We'll just—"

"Alone," Annika said to him, maintaining eye contact with me.

I envisioned my entrails painting the walls the moment Peter left us alone.

"There's no need to worry about client privilege in this case, Annika, since Axl is my client."

"With all due respect, Peter, if Axl and I are going to convince the world we're in a relationship, we need to be able to speak freely to each other without you running interference."

She had some balls. I'd give her that. I said, "I agree."

"If you'd rather we had this conversation elsewhere . . ."

"No, that's fine. I'll leave you to it. I always have paperwork to catch up on." Peter glanced at his watch. "Axl and I have dinner plans with a sponsor. So no bloodshed." He stood and strode out, closing the door behind him.

Annika reached into her bag and pulled out several file folders before she looked at me. "Maybe this seems—"

I held up my hand. "Before I answer any questions, I want to explain about last weekend, because as Peter said, it is not normal behavior for me."

"Make it snappy. As you can see"—she gestured to the folders—"there's a lot of ground to cover."

"What, exactly, is all that?"

"Data."

I grinned at her. "Attila. I'm touched. You've been studying my hockey stats? How far back does that go? To my youth hockey days in Sweden when I broke all the national records? Impressive for a D-man, isn't it?"

"First of all, I don't give a puck about your impressive lats—I mean stats or whatever."

Lats? Freudian slip, Princess? Do you still have the picture of my bare torso? Because I saw more interest than annoyance in those baby blues after I'd sent it to you.

"Second," she continued, "I really don't need to know what specific bra cup size you prefer in your pack of puck bunnies—"

"Hold up." I refocused. "Where did bra cup size enter this conversation?"

"D-man ringing a bell, Ax-hell?"

"You know, Attila, do yourself a favor and buy *Hockey for Dummies* so you have the first clue about the sport your *boyfriend* plays . . . D-man is short for a defenseman, not a bra cup size." My gaze dropped to her chest. I preferred C's anyway.

She blushed. "It sounded sexual and you can't fault me for not knowing much about the sport."

"I can fault you, because your cousin is a hockey player. You've been to Jaxson's games. What position does he play?"

"You are purposely leading me astray so we don't have to discuss this." She waved the folder in the air. "Additional data Peter's assistant sent to me last week that she compiled from social media."

This should be fantastic. "What social media data?"

"Women who claimed they'd 'partied' with 'The Hammer' over the course of the last two seasons in Chicago. By partied, do they mean . . . ?"

"Come on, no euphemisms. Say it."

She rolled her eyes. "Women you pucked."

"The night didn't always end in pucking. And 'partied' is a broad term."

"Then it appears you've *partied* with a lot of broads," she muttered.

"What's the magic number I've supposedly 'partied' with?"

"One hundred and seventy-six."

I laughed.

"I'm serious. That's what it says."

"I was serious earlier about that being impossible."

Annika cocked her head. "No cracks about getting your stick bronzed for reaching that level of studliness—even if it's not true?"

I shook my head. "Never been my goal to be the player with the most notches on my stick. My only goal has been to be the best player I can be. I did what I had to do to get out of the cluster fuck that was Chicago"—*shut your mouth, man*—"so can I tell you why I got hammered last weekend?"

"By all means."

I paused to take a breath, glad she hadn't zeroed in on my Chicago slipup. "I'll summarize for you so I'm not wasting your time. Growing up, as far back as my memory goes, all I cared about was hockey. I lived it, breathed it and was consumed by it. I had that in common with my best friend, Roald. We played in every league in Sweden that would have us. We played internationally. Right after we turned twenty we were scouted by the NHL and invited to Detroit's training camp. A month before we left, Roald crashed his bike and ended up paralyzed from the waist down."

Annika reached over and squeezed my forearm. "That is awful, Axl. I'm so sorry."

"Long story short: I came to the U.S. and lived the dream he couldn't. It took four years of paying my dues in the AHL before I got called up to the Blackhawks. But Roald never knew. He died the summer before. So Saturday night was the sixth anniversary of his accident. Sounds sappy to admit that I feel lucky every day. But on the anniversary of his death, I can't escape the guilt that swamps me. I get drunk to try to forget and do stupid shit I don't remember." Given the last year I'd suffered through in Chicago, I tried harder for that state of oblivion and I found it sooner than I expected. In the morning I'd woken up facedown on the couch in the lobby of my apartment building with no recollection of how I'd gotten there.

"Total asshat behavior, but sadly it's behavior I'm familiar with. I have three brothers and three male cousins."

"I can promise you it won't happen again."

"Until next year."

"Then it won't be *your* problem, will it?"

"I guess not."

She studied me.

"What?"

"Two questions."

"Yes, that was a true story."

She bestowed an evil smirk on me. "Good. So I don't have to be callous and remind you of this awesome opportunity you've earned that your friend never got to experience. And ask if a night filled with booze, bunnies and blackouts is worth losing your life's dream and getting deported back to the land of lutefisk, ABBA and IKEA."

"Please tell me you plan on following up that comment with an evil witch's cackle before you fly away on your broom."

She drilled me in the biceps with her finger. "Consider me your reality check. I may not know a D-man from a goalie, but I did market research. You are twenty-six years old. If you screw this up? You're back to the AHL for good. No other NHL team will pick you up. You'll be too old to be a damn rookie."

"You think I don't know what's at stake here?" I exhaled.

"I'm sorry. It's not your fault I made a few bad decisions and I don't want to take my frustration out on you."

"But?" she said with more interest than sarcasm.

"But I'm not convinced a PR scam is in my best interest. That's what this 'girlfriend' angle feels like—as if we're trying to pull one over on the public. Wouldn't it be worse if they found out? Wouldn't it be better if I agreed to stay out of the media spotlight?"

Annika flipped the pen in her hand end over end as she scrutinized me. "For you? No. All your press in the past year has been bad press. The media loves a misbehaving bad-boy athlete. They're content to saddle you with that moniker your entire career. It happened with McEnroe. No one remembers he was a gifted athlete. So I agree with Peter. We need a positive spin for you. One where we can take you from Cassius Clay to Muhammad Ali. He was the same guy. The only thing that changed about him was the public's perception of him."

I looked at her with new admiration. "You're really good at your job, aren't you?"

The compliment startled her. Then she granted me a smile sexy enough to tighten my balls and sweet enough that I wanted to lick her lips to see if they tasted like sugar. "Yes, I am."

Not coy about her skills. I admired them too. "In your professional opinion . . . should we use the 'we're a couple' angle that Peter suggests?"

"It makes the most sense."

"Don't sound so enthused," I said dryly.

"Pulling it off won't be easy," she warned. "There are a lot of people in my life who won't believe that you and I are romantically involved."

Despite my desire not to react with antagonism, I said, "I'm not a troll or a serial killer, Annika. And I have a list of women who'd be happy to tell the world we're coupling."

She raised an eyebrow. "Dude. Think about it. That's *why* you have this problem."

Peter knocked twice and opened the door. He paused, his gaze winging between us. "What's the verdict?"

"Annika was just about to pucker up so I could kiss her to seal the deal."

"Puckered up, clenched up . . . same thing, right?"

I laughed. With her smart mouth and that hot body, she intrigued me as much as she annoyed me. Were her fingers as nimble as her brain?

Our gazes clashed and I could almost read her mind.

I'd take clever and cutting over vapid any day. These next few months with her would be a challenge. And I loved a challenge.

"Happy as I am to see that you two have found your own way to work together, there's one last thing we can all agree on: no one but the three of us needs to know the true nature of your relationship."

"The three of us plus my mother," Annika reminded him.

Why did she sound more resigned about her mother's interference than pissed off about it? That bothered me, but it wasn't a question I'd ask her in front of Peter.

Peter sighed. "So, to keep your personality clashes out of the spotlight, it'd be best if your first few strategy sessions take place somewhere private. Will I need to be there to referee?"

"No. We'll get it figured out," I said.

Ready to find
your next great read?

Let us help.

Visit prh.com/nextread

Penguin
Random
House